The Maiden: Revelations

By Kristine Plum

This is a work of fiction. Names, characters, businesses, places, events and incidents are either the products of the author's imagination or used in a fictitious manner. Any resemblance to actual persons, living or dead, or actual events is purely coincidental.

ISBN-13: 978-1514360088 (CreateSpace-Assigned)
ISBN-10: 151436008X
BISAC: Fiction / Romance / General

For all of those who wonder if the stories in their heads are worth sharing.

Prologue

Ariadne had spent all day in preparation for tonight's ceremony, and now it was almost time. She understood the significance of the ritual; she had learned about it since birth. She knew how important it was, but part of her couldn't get past her adolescent freak-out that she was about to publically have sex with her boyfriend. Well, "publically" might be misleading. No one was actually going to be watching. But the whole community would know what was hopefully happening. Ariadne herself had witnessed the last two Incarnation Rituals. If anyone knew that she and Ackley had already had sex this whole event would not be focusing on her. The elders would choose two other "pure-bodied" people.

Ariadne and Ackley had been chosen by the council of elders, the most powerful members of the coven, based on their current power, potential, and genes, and of course for their "purity". Ariadne was pretty sure that if the male counterpart wasn't her boyfriend and best friend since early childhood, she would have declined this honor.

She did truly believe that it was an honor. She had been chosen as the strongest young witch of the regional coven, not just of the twelve families that made up her local circle, but of the thirteen circles of the area. Her mother, Lady Aradia, the high priestess of the coven, was beyond proud that her daughter had been chosen as a potential vessel. But Ariadne also knew that as a mother, her mom wasn't fully relaxed about her sixteen year old daughter having sex, especially when the desired outcome was to be impregnated. This wasn't something that Ariadne was really looking forward to either, but if the Goddess blessed her by choosing her as the vessel, she would eventually give birth to the next Maiden of the Universal Coven, the governing body of all witches around the world.

Every five years, as part of the Beltane festival, an Incarnation ceremony had been performed by covens around the world, but not every ceremony yielded a baby. If this were to be the year, only one of the girls involved would be deemed worthy by the Goddess and become pregnant. If Ariadne would be blessed by the Goddess, she would give birth, and the baby would be given to the Triumvirate: the Maiden, Mother and Crone, who lead the

1

entire Universal Coven. The Triumvirate would then raise and train this child in the craft until the time when the current Crone passes on and the new Maiden is initiated.

It was definitely a lot to think about for a girl involved in the ritual, but Ariadne was trying not to think about all the dominoes that would be knocked over if she were the one to be blessed as the vessel. All day she had been going through Beltane rituals as well as the required ritual cleansings and anointings, but she was trying to think only of Ackley. They hadn't talked for over a week, not even today when they participated in the focal May Pole. They had been separated and "prepared" by the elders. Ariadne found herself struggling to keep her mouth shut several times in the past week, holding back giggles or outbursts of laughter. She was sixteen after all and had heard the "birds and bees" talk. She had already had sex for crying out loud. But she had tried to be respectful as the elders explained the ins and outs of the ritual and of course what to expect of the sex part. This was where she had to literally bite her tongue. She had thought briefly how scared a girl might be if she hadn't had sex, as it was supposed to be, and was as far as anyone was concerned. It would be even scarier if she didn't even know the guy. It could be anyone between thirteen and eighteen in the whole coven. Yes, Ariadne was lucky. And that is where she put her focus to keep her nerves in check.

The fires were lit. She could hear the singing as one of the elders started the chanting, letting everyone know that it was almost time. Ariadne imagined that now one of the priestesses would be casting the circle for the people who would be participating in the annual Beltane ritual. Another priestess would be preparing the circle around the tent where Ariadne and Ackley would spend their evening. Soundproofing spells would be in place so that the "spectators" couldn't actually hear anything inside. One of the male elders would be going to Ackley soon to lead him on his path from his preparation room to the tent, and Ariadne's mom would soon come for her. "I can do this," she told herself. She stood, willing her legs to move, afraid that when the door opened they would be locked in place. "I love Ackley, I love my coven, and I love the Goddess. I can do this." Ariadne closed her eyes and inhaled slowly. As she let the breath pass through her lips, the door opened. It wasn't as her mother that Lady Aradia stepped inside the room, but as the coven's high priestess, dressed in her light blue ceremonial dress with her diadem resting on her head. After taking in the ceremonial attire, Ariadne's somewhat nervous brown eyes met Lady Aradia's. Her mother's green and gold irises were alight with anticipation, pride and a hint of sadness. Lady Aradia's face softened as she looked at her daughter and said, "It's time."

Chapter 1

Cash

"Oye, Señor Italiano, ¿Estás saliendo para el aeropuerto?"

"Pronto." Cash Di Marco set his suitcase by a bar stool. He smirked at the nickname his partner and good friend, Rafa, had given him years ago when they met while Cash was still in boarding school. He had been living in Madrid for a couple of years, but Rafa still loved pointing out that he was Italian, not Spanish.

"¿A qué hora sale el avión?"

"In a couple of hours," Cash responded to Rafa's second question. Using the family's private jet had some perks. Right now the empty plane was on its way from Italy to Madrid to pick up Cash. Cash would still have to go through a few security checkpoints at the airport, but he would be escorted to the front of the line so he didn't have to worry about how busy the airport would be this afternoon.

Rafa sensed his lack of enthusiasm. "You know I've got this, right?"

"Yeah, I'm just worried you're going to steal my beautiful, delicious blood donors while I'm away. But I'll be back tomorrow, so don't get any ideas," Cash joked.

His hesitancy to leave had nothing to do with Rafa's competency. He had complete faith that Rafa could run both the bar and the nightclub for more than twenty-four hours, but a little bit did have to do with Cash not wanting to give up any of his control. He would eventually back off from this business to start another, but it was too soon to do so now. Before everything was thoroughly established, he ran the risk of decreasing the success beyond repair. That would no doubt please his mother.

His mother was the reason for the majority of his reluctance to leave Rafa on his own tonight. This was a complete power play on her part. She detested

4

his lifestyle: his well-earned playboy reputation, his night club businesses that provided an excellent dual-purpose vampire "bar" of willing "beverages", his lack of desire to be in Italy running the family estate with her and his siblings. She focused on the laidback qualities of his personality as a source of contention. Somehow she refused to see the aspects he had no doubt inherited from her, his need to control in his businesses for one.

To her dismay, Cash did love his nightclubs. La Noche Oscura was not his first or only club. His first was in Berlin. He had one in Rome and one in London. Each one started with special care by him, and was now run by a few select, trustworthy friends. His first business in Madrid was this tasca, or bar, he'd opened a couple years ago. It was still a popular spot for locals and tourists to get tapas and drinks in the late afternoon or evening. When the opportunity to snatch up some prime real estate right next door arose, perfect for a club, Cash jumped on it. La Noche Oscura had only been open a couple months, but she was doing well. Purposefully mixing vampires and humans was risky for secrecy and human safety, but Cash was very meticulous and strict. The humans didn't consciously know with whom or what they were mingling, and they were subconsciously very willing to provide a drink and maybe a bit more to the vampire club goers. The humans were treated with respect and left safe and happy, not remembering the exact details or faces from their evening. Vampires that broke any of the club rules were dealt with swiftly and in a manner that left a lasting impression for future would-be violators. So far, so good. No breaches in secrecy had roused any suspicion among the humans in any of Cash's clubs. Although he was in no way ready to hand over the reins of his newest club, tonight would be Rafa's first solo mission. Cash trusted him completely.

Instead of running his club tonight, Cash would be in Paris at a dull fundraiser for the art council to which his mother belonged. For whatever reason she could not attend and had informed Cash that it was his family duty to go in her place to deliver the family's contribution check. That, of course, was ridiculous. She could easily send her regrets and her check in the mail. No, this was her way of reminding him that she was the head of the family, and although she didn't agree with his current life choices, she was "allowing" him to make them. If she were to order him, he would ultimately have to obey. Cash loved his mom and he was sure she wouldn't really ever strip him of his free will, but she did occasionally like to remind him that she could.

Calandra Di Marco wasn't a scary woman, but she was powerful and intimidating. She was well over one hundred years old but didn't look a day over thirty-five. Such was the gift of a born vampire. One could stop or start the aging process whenever he or she liked. Cash had not yet decided to pause his aging, but he would soon be the same age his mom was when she first paused hers. She was in her thirties which was considered well past her prime at that time. Then, a few decades ago she fell in love and started aging so they could have a child. Sadly, but luckily for Cash, her husband died shortly after they had Cash's half-brother. She never talked about it, but there were rumors in the vampire world that her husband had gotten involved in some sort of questionable business dealings. The mystery of his demise and Calandra's reluctance to talk about it led Cash to believe that the rumors were true. Whatever the reason behind her first husband's death, it allowed for her to meet and fall in love with Cash's father, who was not a vampire but a witch.

Being half witch and half vampire, Cash and his twin sister Calla were able to choose which life they would lead. Both had chosen to be vampires. Cash's whole family, including his sister's human husband and their two children, lived at the family's centuries old estate outside of Florence where they currently ran a winery among other lucrative businesses. That was another of the excuses his mother had used for tonight's trip to Paris. Madrid was closer and it would be difficult for any of them to travel from Florence due to their schedules.

So here he was, preparing to fly to Paris, attend this fundraiser in a tuxedo, and hand-deliver his mother's precious check. It wasn't that he didn't think it was a worthy cause. He appreciated art a great deal, but he hated rubbing elbows with people who thought they were better than others just because they had huge sums of money. Add to the fact he would rather be running his club, and it was no wonder his mother's power play had left him bitter.

"Need a bite before you go?" Rafa asked with a sly smile and a little wink on the word bite. "That red head in the corner has been eyeing you."

Not a bad idea, Cash thought, "Take her a drink, on me."

As Rafa mixed up another fruity blend like the girl had ordered earlier, Cash searched her mind with his. Not surprising, she was definitely interested in him physically, with his black hair, a little shaggy on top, his Mediterranean bronzed complexion, his ice blue eyes that now were giving her the once over.

Cash had never met another born vampire that wasn't physically appealing, something in which evolution had no doubt played a part. In essence, vampires had to be attractive and alluring to their prey. That, along with their increased strength, speed, and the ability to manipulate human minds all helped the vampire race to secretly thrive amongst humans since the dawn of civilization. This girl's mind was no exception; it seemed very easily influenced.

He planted the idea in her head to come thank him personally for her drink. He could see how it would go, as he had suggested for her to be a little forward. Her memory would show that she had made the first move. As was the usual plan of attack, no pun intended, he would take her back to his office, a little kissing, a little biting, and he would make sure they both left with all other needs satisfied as well.

Even though he had influenced this scenario hundreds of times with minds easily susceptible to his charms, it still excited him, perhaps due to the power high, or the anticipation of the blood high, or the sexual activities, or a combination of all three. A sense of optimism began to creep in on his previous negativity about his upcoming evening.

Chapter 2

Ryen

Ryen was running through the woods behind her house. It wouldn't be dark for a few hours, but the trees were blocking the majority of the light, giving an eerie hue to the spaces not blocked out by the tree trunks and brush. She'd been running for a while, but she was afraid to stop yet, unsure if she'd gone far enough.

Mrs. Collins wouldn't be following her, if she had even woken up yet and realized Ryen was gone, but she may call for help or report Ryen missing. Her "parents" wouldn't be home until tomorrow night at the earliest, but more likely it would be the next day. They were usually gone for four to five days for their "retreats". So much had changed since she had found her mother's journals yesterday, blowing her world apart, but also dropping things into place that had confused her for years. She knew she would return home tonight, but she needed a place far away to think.

For nine years she had thought Joshua and Damaris were her parents. That was only partially true. Her mother's journals had revealed that Joshua was not her father, which explained why she had never really felt affection from him. That was shocking enough for a nine year old to discover on her own, but if that were the only thing she had learned, life might be able to continue with some normalcy.

Ryen had always had "unexplainable" things happen of which she was sure she had somehow been responsible: a flower blooming seemingly on command, candles lighting on their own, and it seemed to rain every time Ryen was really scared or sad. Her mother would tell her that Satan was tempting her, and she must never do those things again. Joshua usually looked at her as if Satan was already taking up residence within her. Although she had never felt anything evil inside of her, there was no other explanation. Or, there wasn't until yesterday. Now it made sense: what was happening, why her mother cautioned her to stop, and why Joshua felt such hostility towards her when these things would happen. Her mother's journals said that she was a witch, her mother used to be a witch, and her real father *had been one too. Although shocking, this was the part that actually made sense.*

What had caused Ryen to run today wasn't either of those revelations. Today she had read even more of those journals, discovering that the "retreats" her parents went on weren't the worship conventions they would tell her about when they returned. They weren't learning about Jesus, or helping establish new churches. They were hunting people, people that were supernatural, like other witches and vampires. The existence of vampires was also shocking, but reading that her God-loving and God-fearing parents were killing people because they were different, because they were like Ryen, was too much. Her mother had killed Ryen's real father and her whole family just before Ryen was born, because they were witches and because Joshua had wanted her to, to prove her new loyalty to his *Lord.*

The director of the Louvre knocked on the door, pulling Ryen out of the dream that she knew all too well, one of the strongest memories Ryen held onto from her childhood, the day she learned who she truly was. Ryen wasn't sure how she had dozed off. She had plenty to think about and to do right now.

"Mademoiselle Cardona, there are cars lining up outside. Would you like to open now? It's just a few minutes early."

"Well Didier, it wouldn't be profitable to keep the money waiting," she sighed. "I'll be out in a minute."

Ryen stared at the checklist in front of her. She was a little nervous. This was her first solo fundraiser. She had been working for the European Arts Council for almost five years. She loved traveling to all the museums in Europe to work with the employees. Mostly she dealt with the acquisitions, certification, and preservation departments, though her favorite place to be was on the museum floor, amongst the art, listening to visitors learning and talking about the artists and the pieces. Due to what the board of directors called her "fabulous human relations skills," she had been assisting in the public relations office as of late, and now she was on her own.

The food had arrived and was already organized by the staff. Ryen had just had the last conference with the doormen. They would open the doors momentarily. Each guest and an allotted plus one would present an authenticated invitation at the first checkpoint. After the doormen, the guests would stop at the entrance table to have their photo IDs scanned and sign the registry. After that the guests were free to wander about this wing of the museum, snack on hors d'oeuvres, sip exquisite champagne, admire the art, and of course make a very generous donation to the Council. Not only was this a huge responsibility to be collecting large amounts of money for the Council, but technically she was also responsible for the entire Louvre museum tonight. The curator, Didier, was there, but if anything went wrong Ryen would be left holding the bag.

It was Ryen's job to make sure the guests had a great time and dug deep into their wallets. Although it was technically Ryen's duty to work the room and accept the donations, there was no way she could get to everyone in a timely fashion; thankfully she had other workers dressed in their noticeable black shirts with yellow ties to help her collect. She also needed to make sure the servers kept the food and beverage trays full and circulating. On top of all that, she was there to answer questions about projects the Council was working on, questions about the artwork, and to protect the paintings. Normally when someone came to a museum during business hours, food and drink would be out of the question. There would also be several employees to make sure no flash photography was used or any touching of the pieces. Tonight all this was Ryen's responsibility. It was definitely a little stressful, but she thrived on the adrenaline.

Ryen glanced at her reflection in the mirrored wall. Her black and silver satin dress wound its way from the strapless chest to Ryen's ankles. Her brown hair, as always, looked as if it had gold laced through it and was down, with gentle waves cascading over her shoulders. Her hair would hide her tattoo, the telltale sign of who she really was. Most witches would recognize her on sight, but anyone else looking for her specifically would know by the tattoo on the back of her neck. That was the danger of this new PR position, it made it harder to keep her low profile out and about in the world. Hopefully she would be the perfect hostess tonight, ultimately sweet talking the donors into bigger numbers on their checks. She knew that in the Council's eyes that was what would determine her success tonight. Her green and gold eyes sparkled with excitement and a hint of nerves. As she turned to leave the room she whispered, "Goddess, let them be very generous."

Chapter 3

Museums, fundraisers, stuffy rooms, this was not Cash's type of party. He would much rather be at a club, bass vibrating in his chest, scantily dressed, inebriated girls wall to wall, whiskey in his hand. In spite of the numerous girls seen in paparazzi photos with him, he was solo tonight. The girls he usually took out to clubs, openings, and premiers were not the right sort to bring to the Louvre when he was representing his family. He made it a point not to be seen with one more than once, for various reasons. Most importantly there had never been one to whom he was willing to divulge his vampirism, and repeatedly altering someone's mind took its toll and became less effective over time.

Make an appearance, get a photo taken for publicity's sake, hand over the check and he'd be free to go. He handed the Di Marco family invitation to the doorman to be scanned for authenticity. They gave each other the once over. The doorman thought that his steroid infused muscles could easily take out Cash, as his proclaimed 6'4" frame was several inches taller than Cash, and he was about twice as wide. Oh, would he be surprised. Cash was stronger and faster than any human could ever hope to be. He also didn't feel physical pain as strongly as a human, and he healed much faster. Cash gave him a lopsided smirk as the doorman handed back the invitation and jerked his head to indicate for Cash to proceed to the next security check point.

Once he made it through the final security check, the first thing he did was look for an attendant to take the check in his pocket. The first one he came across was a petite girl with short black hair. She was attractive; perhaps they could find a little alcove somewhere to make this night worthwhile. As he was handing over the check, preparing to plant a suggestion in her mind, a hand clamped down on his shoulder.

"Mr. Di Marco, my boy, don't tell me your beautiful mother slipped through my fingers again tonight?"

Cash winked at the girl with the yellow tie, giving her a look that said he'd be looking for her later, and then turned to the boulder of a man that still had his hand on his shoulder. Full of charm, he let the man down easily.

"I'm afraid so, Lord Barton. She couldn't get away from Florence tonight." He couldn't help himself and added, "Nor could her husband."

Lord Barton nodded in understanding, but with a look that conveyed something as trivial as a husband would not stop his attempts. "Well, please send her my warmest regards."

He hadn't even been here long enough to grab a glass of champagne and already he was dealing with vampire politics. Lord Barton was not the first or only guy that tried to move up the power ladder by making connections with Cash's mom, nor would he be the last Cash would encounter. If he could help it though, Cash would avoid any more of them tonight. There weren't that many vampires in the room, but when you looked at the list of people around the world with deep pockets, many of those people were in fact vampires, and these were the ones Cash liked to avoid, that is unless he needed to sweet talk someone into financially investing in one of his businesses.

He'd make a few polite acknowledgements as he made a circle around the main room, and then out the door he would go. Forget the dark haired girl; if he left soon maybe he could make it back to Madrid with plenty of nighttime left at the club.

Cash hadn't made it to the door when a female voice spoke into a microphone, calling everyone's attention to her and the screen behind her. When he turned, he saw the most beautiful woman he'd ever seen in a black and silver dress.

...

The room was full; people seemed to be enjoying themselves, but Ryen couldn't quite get her heart rate to slow to a normal pace. She knew there were vampires here tonight, not just because she recognized some names from the guest list, but she could sense their power buzzing about the room. There were no more than twenty in attendance, but that was nineteen more than was necessary to put Ryen on edge in a normal situation where she wasn't the focus of attention. Here at this gala, it was a completely unreasonable fear, but still a fear Ryen continued struggling to shake. She couldn't let her fear and loathing of vampires distract her tonight. *Focus on the task at hand*, she told herself. *Focus on being nervous because you are inexperienced and could ruin this evening within minutes. Yes, that was a much more reasonable fear to focus on,* she chided herself sarcastically. She rolled her shoulders back and took a deep breath as she spoke into the microphone to get everyone's attention.

"On behalf of the European Arts Council, thank you all for attending this evening and thank you in advance for the generous contributions you all are making. We encourage you to take time tonight to enjoy the art and the hors d'oeuvres. I'll only take a few more minutes of your attention. We have a video highlighting some of the things your money has helped to fund this year. One thing we are feeling very positive about is the youth involvement program. I'll be around after the conclusion of the video if anyone has any questions about any of our projects or if I can help you calculate the appropriate donation." Ryen added that last part with a little wink. Some sophisticated playful flirting couldn't hurt. The lights dimmed a little for the video, and then Ryen mingled the rest of the evening. Surprisingly and without consciously noticing, she found her flow.

...

To someone watching it would appear that the woman in the black and silver dress was completely in her element. Smiling, flirting, handling the logistical side, talking art, and answering questions about the museum, the Council, the programs the video mentioned. Cash watched this intriguing woman the entire night, staying much longer than he had been planning. He was trying to put himself in her path, but no matter how he maneuvered, she was always just out of his reach. He hadn't even been able to hear her name. He was very frustrated, not only with seeming to be one step behind, but no matter how hard he tried to get in her head, it too, seemed just out of his reach. Maybe it was due to all of the other minds mingling around hers, or maybe he needed something a little thicker to drink, but this had never been a problem for him before. In fact, by the time the crowd was drifting to the door, Cash was so frustrated he didn't even bother planting a suggestion in the black haired attendant's mind. He just told her she was coming with him. Maybe she'd be just the distraction he needed for his ride to the airport.

Chapter 4

She had made it. The gala was over, and Ryen could relax. She still had to go over the totals for the night, make records of the donations and then deposit the money in the bank before she could fully relax, but the most stressful part was complete. She breathed a sigh of relief as she joined the curator, Didier, in his office along with Ryen's assistant Sophie and the head of security.

"All staff and guests have left. The infrared scan confirmed there are no more bodies in the museum," reported the head of security. "I'll wait in my office to escort you all out and to escort you, Mademoiselle Cardona, to the bank."

"Merci Patrick. I'll let you know when we're ready to go." Ryen turned to the others, "Status report?"

Didier responded first, "I'm almost finished with the second calculation, and then they will be ready for you to run the numbers. I must say, with the check amounts tonight, you may have secured a permanent role raising money."

Ryen smiled warily. The fact that the totals were good pleased her, but this was not what she wanted to do. She had been granted freedom to pursue this other part of her life and work for the Arts Council under the assumption that she would remain in Florence. The Council, however, had decided that her talents could be better utilized if she traveled to various museums. Right now the majority of her time was being spent in Madrid, but she still considered Florence her home office. If this job became too demanding, she would have to resign, a thought that saddened her more than she could ever admit to anyone. "What about you, Sophie?"

"I'm almost finished scanning the checks so we can put the donors and amounts in the records."

"I guess I'll just wait for my turn then." Ryen was a little relieved to have a couple minutes just to sit and let the stress leave her body. She picked up her cell phone from the desk where she had left it earlier. Hmm, three missed calls; one from Kora, then one from Chesna, and one from Kora again. There were also several texts. Kora's last text read: "Nothing to worry about here. Just checking in to see how your night is going. Call us later."

Ryen sent a quick text back: "Just finishing up here. I'll call after I've made the deposit."

Ryen wondered what could have those two all fired up. If it had been an emergency they would have said, so she didn't feel the need to call them right away. Earlier today she had thought of calling them. That strange feeling she had of something shifting like a gear within the universe merited a conversation, but she didn't think it necessary to get into before tonight's gala. As she sat, her mind drifted back to the dream she was having before the gala began. That day was the reason she was sitting here today. Who knew what she would be doing now if she had never discovered her mother's journals, or if she'd even be alive.

Once she had stopped running she was so tired. She sat down to rest in the small clearing, surrounded by the tall trees. The trees had always made her feel safe. After she would have one of those unexplainable experiences she would often find solace in the forest. If the moon was out, it had an even more calming effect on her. Now it was as if the trees were hiding and protecting her. She had always felt at home amongst them. She had never been afraid of the creatures in the woods that other kids worried about. She closed her eyes for a few moments, and then she noticed the light shining through the trees. At first she feared that Mrs. Collins had already reported her missing, but as the light came closer it felt warm and seemed to grow instead of getting smaller and refined, like a flashlight.

When the light reached the clearing three women materialized behind it. They were all different; one appeared maybe ten years older than Ryen, but not much bigger, with straight red hair that hung down to her waist and bright green eyes that reflected a light from within. Ryen thought of Irish fairy tales when she looked at her. The one in the middle was older, but not as old as Mrs. Collins, with dark brown hair pulled up into a curly pile on top of her head. Her eyes were chocolate brown as was her skin, contrasting with her hair like dark and milk chocolate candy. The oldest had a grandma-like quality, grey hair in a long braid down her back, quite a few wrinkles, and grey eyes oozing with wisdom and love. All three were smiling and had tears running down their faces. She had never seen any of them before, but somehow she felt like she had known them her whole life.

The oldest one spoke, holding her arms outward as if to embrace Ryen, "My child, we have been searching for you for a long time! It seemed that you had been lost to us forever, but we never gave up hope that we would find you. And here you are."

Ryen should have been feeling stranger-danger, especially out here in the middle of nowhere, where no one knew where she was or could hear her if she screamed for help. She was sure, however, that those worries did not apply here. She was not in danger, and the fact that they were so secluded seemed to be the best setting for this encounter. More as a statement than a question Ryen said, "You are witches, too."

All three smiled again and said in unison, "We are." Then one added, "What do you know of witches?"

"I've always been taught that witches and other non-human creatures were real and evil, an abhorrence to God. But I discovered yesterday that I am a witch." Ryen told them what she had learned in her mother's journals, about what her mother had done to her entire family, and what she was currently doing, and then, noting that the three exchanged knowing glances she asked, "Who are you? How did you find me here?"

The oldest one spoke again, "The Goddess guided us here. I am the Crone." Ryen had never heard mention of the Goddess before, but in that moment she felt more real to her than the God her parents believed in ever had.

The middle one, who looked older than her mom, but not too old said, "I am the Mother. Blessed be, my dear."

The youngest one said, "I am the Maiden. Blessed be."

"Those are funny names," Ryen said with her face scrunched in thought.

The three women gently laughed. Again it was the oldest who replied, "Those titles are who we are, not our names. The three of us, Maiden, Mother, and Crone, lead the witches around the world. We were appointed by the Goddess at conception to be who we are. As one soul passes, we move up in roles and a new Maiden fills in the open spot. Most address me as Lady Alethea, but you may call me Maggie. This is Lady Celeste, and that is Lady Luna," she said motioning first to the middle aged woman and then to the younger one.

Lady Celeste said, "You may call me Chesna, I knew your grandmother well."

Lady Luna said, "You may call me Kora. Did your mother's journals tell you who you are?" Ryen shook her head in confusion, so Kora continued, "Sweetheart, you are very important to us, to the world. You are the future Maiden." They all bowed their heads in respect towards Ryen.

This story sounded like something from a fairytale, but things started clicking inside Ryen. She understood what they were telling her and in her heart she believed it to be true, more than any story she had ever heard in Sunday school. The middle one, the Mother, or Chesna she had called herself, misinterpreted the feelings running across Ryen's face. She said, "We don't mean to scare you. This must sound crazy to you, especially on top of all you've recently learned."

"Not really." Ryen responded. Although she was a little confused, she wasn't afraid. She thought she knew why they were here. "Are you here to take me away, to save me?"

The three women exchanged concerned looks. The older one, Lady Alethea, or Maggie, said, "My dear, we aren't physically with you. We are merely communicating with you. Somehow the Goddess connected us when we've never been able to reach you before. We don't even know where you are. We are in Italy."

"Italy? I'm in Virginia." Italy was so far away. Hope sunk within Ryen that she hadn't realized had built up so much. Panic started creeping in. If they

weren't really here maybe they weren't really real, and if they weren't real then no one was coming to help her. Her parents would kill her. As she started to cry, it began to rain.

"Your turn," Didier's voice brought Ryen out of her memories. Some of the panic that nine year old Ryen had been feeling in her memory had crept into Ryen's heart as she relived that day. How scared that little girl had been at that moment. But somehow she had pushed through that fear and come up with her own plan. The fight inside her that had surfaced that day had gotten Ryen through so much in the past two decades.

Ryen shook her head to clear out the past and turned a weary smile towards the others. Sophie gave her a slight frown as she looked between Ryen and Ryen's cell phone.

"They called you too, didn't they?" Ryen asked Sophie with annoyance in her voice, glaring at the blonde-haired, blue-eyed girl, who looked a few years younger than Ryen.

Sheepishly Sophie confessed, "Just once, just before you came in. They wanted to know how you were doing tonight."

Did they not think she was capable of running this gala, or was something else going on? Ryen tried not to be annoyed with Sophie. She wasn't just Ryen's assistant; she was also a witch, the only one in Ryen's museum work that knew who she really was. Sophie had grown up going to school in Florence with Ryen, but they hadn't really been friends. When Ryen took the job with the Arts Council Chesna and Kora had insisted that Ryen have someone with her in case of an emergency, especially when the Council relocated her away from Florence. Sophie was now Ryen's friend, or the closest thing Ryen had to one.

Oh well. Ryen would deal with her irritation with Sophie talking to Kora and Chesna behind her back later. She had checks to count, money to deposit, and mysterious messages to return.

20

Chapter 5

With all of the Council business concluded, Ryen was on her way back to her hotel for what remained of the night. She would have thought the bank manager would be grumpier, getting called out of his bed at this hour to open the bank so she could make the Council's deposit. The large sum of money now locked safely in his vault must have cheered him up. At this hour there was not too much traffic on the streets, and the car would arrive at the hotel shortly. Ryen was looking forward to a hot shower and to collapsing in her bed, so now would be the best time to place her call.

After only one ring she heard Kora's voice, "Hello, dear. Everything go well tonight?"

"You're going to see me tomorrow or later today actually, so what's with the monsoon of messages and missed calls?" Ryen was one of the only people who would dare talk to Kora this way. She wielded nearly as much power as Ryen, and being a highly respected Universal Coven leader, people revered her. Ryen had the utmost respect for her as well, but Kora had always been like an older sister and mother figure to her. Their relationship was much more informal than the relationships they had with others.

"Chesna sensed things changing around you, and she thought we should check in." As an afterthought, because she knew that Ryen would think the worst, she added, "but not in a negative way. She actually sensed a lot of positive energy, but it wasn't clear."

"And it couldn't wait twenty-four hours to tell me something so vague?" Ryen already sounded less irritated than she had been initially. Chesna and Kora were very protective of her, especially since she had been lost to them for so many years in the beginning. It was actually amazing that they ever let her leave Florence without them. She should be thankful that they didn't physically hover over her twenty four-seven. In fact, Ryen was sure so much of the leniency she was granted to pursue things outside of her witch duties was because they still felt bad for her for how her life began. The three of them were a family, and Ryen was certainly spoiled as the youngest.

"I'm sorry for sounding bitchy. I know you worry about me. Everything went well. We collected a lot of great donations. Nothing out of the ordinary happened that I'm aware of." Ryen paused a moment and then added, "Actually there was something I wanted to tell you guys about, but it didn't have anything to do with the gala. It was this strange sensation I had earlier. I'll tell you more in person. I don't think it's anything to worry about, just a shift of some sort, possibly what Chesna sensed."

"Hmm, that sounds intriguing. I'm sure she will want to talk to you more as well when you get here. What time does your plane arrive?"

"4:30, if there are no delays. Anything on the schedule that I need to know about tonight?" Ryen asked, trying to gage how busy she'd be when she returned to Florence. Wednesday was Beltane, so there would be preparations for a big ceremony in the days leading up to it, plus the daily duties, meetings, and spells that would be required of her being back at their witch headquarters. It was also the year of the Incarnation Ceremony, so there would be extra preparations, and if this was *the* year, they would be taking a trip to meet the girl who would give birth to the next Maiden on Thursday. In the past they wouldn't have made that trip until the baby was born, but since things did not go as planned with Ryen, they weren't taking any chances with future generations.

For the nine years Ryen had been missing and presumed dead to the Universal Coven, they held Incarnation ceremonies every year instead of every five, in hopes of providing a new Maiden. The fact that none of the ceremonies had worked gave the Triumvirate the hope that Ryen was still alive somewhere. No matter the power they combined, they couldn't locate her until she had realized she was a witch. Somehow that knowledge had unlocked the power inside Ryen that allowed her to mentally connect with them and communicate.

"Nothing tonight that requires your attention. We have a few spells to do tomorrow that will need the three of us, and there are some dedication ceremonies that were scheduled before Wednesday so you could be in attendance. Sophie should have your schedule for anything else."

"I'm pulling up to the hotel now. I'll text you when I board the plane. I'll see you soon."

"Sleep well, sweetie. We love you," Kora said.

"Love you, too," Ryen answered as she hung up the phone.

It was dark, but Ryen could still see the four guys in the room with her. No matter what spell she tried to come up with in her head, nothing was happening. She couldn't break her hands free. In fact, she couldn't even move her fingers; she couldn't move anything but her eyes. It was as if she was paralyzed, but she could still feel everything. She was bleeding from several impacts of fists and hard objects, and from several bite marks as well. Tears had dried on her cheeks leaving itchy streaks and made her hair wet where they had landed. As one of the guys approached with his pants undone, Ryen tried to scream, but her vocal chords were also paralyzed and no sound came out, though her cries surely would have been drowned out by the storm raging outside.

Ryen sat up suddenly. The sheets were soaked with sweat. It took her a minute or two to calm her breathing as she reminded herself that she was alone and safe in her Paris hotel room. She still couldn't escape those memories of so many years ago. She attributed her nightmare to the close proximity to vampires at the gala. This was usually the effect she experienced. That was one reason she tried to avoid vampires, but also because she still held a powerful grudge against an entire species for something four idiots had done to her. She had relived this memory so many times that although it still shook her to her core, she could push it aside now and focus on the day ahead of her: another shower apparently, some room service and off to the airport to fly home to Florence.

Chapter 6

Cash was still grouchy. He had sent the girl from the gala home when he arrived at the airport and made sure she would take the iron supplements he gave her and eat a couple of steaks in the next twenty-four hours, always covering his tracks. Then he had collected three other girls before boarding his plane: two American college girls on their way to Madrid anyway and a flight attendant who had the next day off. When he arrived in Madrid, he sent those three off in the same manner as the girl in Paris. None of this was new or unusual behavior for him, but he was not feeling the way he usually felt. Sure, he was full of blood and all four girls had great memories of their activities last night, but he was not satisfied. He felt as if he was mildly hung over from excess blood consumption, and sex had not calmed him or made him any less frustrated than when he left that damned gala. What was his problem? He knew it had something to do with that "bella donna" that had eluded him all night. Perhaps if he figured out whom she was and arranged a meeting with her, maybe he could shake this feeling that had him all out of sorts.

He called the Louvre, but the head of security in the main office, who claimed to know everything that went on there, also claimed he had no idea who she was, just that she worked for the Arts Council, not the Louvre itself. The curator of the Louvre, who surely knew who she was, was on vacation starting today. Next he checked in with the Arts Council. They directed him to their PR department, but whomever he talked to there, said they were not permitted to give out employee information. This person suggested checking their website. A quick scan of the profile pictures of the female employees came up empty. Despite the lack of success, he certainly wasn't deterred that easily. He'd keep digging. Hopefully being back at the bar and club would help lighten his mood.

His evening did not fare any better, nor did the next few. Cash could sense his vampire employees were picking up on his mood, Rafa especially. Cash had noticed his friend's keen dark eyes assessing him more than usual, and at this point even the human employees were at least sensing to stay out of his way. He tried dancing, doing paper work, bartending, and some pleasure indulgence in his office with more than one eager girl. Nothing was working to get him out of his funk. What was worse was that he didn't even care about having sex with any of the girls that were throwing themselves at him. Rafa most definitely noticed that. Cash had confided a bit about Paris to his partner and friend, not everything, but enough to get Rafa to assist him in this search of his. So, when girls started leaving the back office only drained of a little blood, Rafa started to push the subject with Cash.

"Is there anything I can do or get for you, hermano?"

"Gracias, but no. I don't know what my problem is! If I could erase those few hours from my life, then nothing would have changed, life would be great. Do you think it's some silly feeling that I think something slipped through my fingers?"

Rafa didn't respond right away. Cash knew that Rafa loved him like a brother, and he could tell that Rafa wanted to help him, but he wasn't sure how. "Maybe, like those English clichés: the grass is always greener, or you always want what you can't have?"

Cash scowled at Rafa, and Rafa gave him an "I'm sorry" shrug. But maybe what Rafa had said actually made sense. Up until now Cash had always thought of his grass as the greenest, and he had never encountered something he wanted that he didn't get. That meant Cash had two choices: get over it or keep digging until he could get what he wanted. Cash was anything but a quitter, so it only took him seconds to solidify his decision. He would find that mystery woman, and once he did everything would be back to normal. He had never met a woman who could resist his charms, and he knew this one would be no different. Now, with his realization and his new determination, he just needed to adjust his attitude a little.

Chapter 7

Ryen loved being home. Florence was her most favorite place on earth. She loved wandering around the city, mingling with the tourists, sitting at a café as the sights, smells and sounds enveloped her in feelings of peace and happiness. She had decided to use some of the free time on her schedule today, otherwise known as personal reflection time, to come into town and enjoy what she had been missing in the months she had been traveling from Madrid to Paris to Milan to London to Florence to Rome, back to Madrid, on and on. She had been back to do Coven business during that time, but she never had extra time to spend in Florence itself.

She tried to avoid the Uffizi so she didn't get pulled into museum work. She was on official museum vacation for the next two weeks. But she did lurk nearby to listen to the tourists talk about the historical landmarks they were visiting. She sat on a bench near the museum for a while looking at the Arno River and the Ponte Vecchio. These were among the sites of Florence she missed so much when she was away. This was the same view she had from her office above in the museum.

The Universal Coven's headquarters was just outside of the city. The building Ryen called home was quite the piece of architecture, though it was cloaked from non-witches for privacy and safety. It was modeled after the Doge's Palace in Venice, stone and marble inside and out, wide walkways forming a rectangle around the central courtyard with sculpted fountains. The outside of the walkways held doors leading to private residences, classrooms and offices depending on which of the three levels you were on. From there, on her balcony, Ryen could easily see the Duomo of the Cathedral Santa Maria del Fiore. It had been the view she had awoken to this morning, calling her into the city.

There really wasn't a season with a lull in tourism anymore, and May was the gateway to the busy summer. Even though temperatures could get quite warm, tourists still flocked to Florence, and elsewhere throughout Europe, during the summer months. Florence always seemed full with the addition of the university students as well. Ryen listened to a few of them behind her as they discussed what they had just seen in the museum. Their conversation brought another smile to her face. Ryen inhaled deeply, letting the chatter of the tourists all around calm her. No one at Coven headquarters would understand, but this was a peaceful retreat for Ryen.

Ryen looked at her phone and sadly accepted that her time in the city was done for today. She needed to get back home and prepare for the dedication ceremony planned under the full moon tonight. Her cohorts might not agree with her, but she counted her time in the city as some of her meditation time. She definitely felt more centered and clear minded.

As Ryen stepped out of her ritual bath, she found her ceremonial dress hanging in the closet off of the bathing room. She picked off some rose petals that were stubbornly stuck to her arm and dried off with the towel Sophie had left by the bath. During ceremonial preparations, most things were done for Ryen, getting her towel, bringing in her clothes and jewelry, so that she could focus on cleansing her body, mind and soul for the upcoming events. Tonight's ceremony was to dedicate new initiates to the Goddess and to their path of knowledge over the next year and a day. It was a little less intense than if Ryen were going to be using her powers for spell work, so the preparations were less intense as well; just a cleansing bath after meditation.

Ryen's dress was white and would be until she took on the role of the Mother; then her dress would be red. The sheath of fabric was sleeveless with a V-neck and came in slightly at the waist. A slit ran up the front of the right leg for freedom of movement. Ryen was always amazed at the fabric. It was silky soft and light, with a natural shimmer to it, but it breathed like cotton. After combing through her hair, which she left hanging freely, she placed on her head her diadem with the waxing crescent moon that fell towards the middle of her forehead. The silver diadem was embedded with crystals, mostly various types of quartz, to help channel and focus power. It had been worn by every Maiden before her including Kora, Chesna, and their dear Maggie. On most days Ryen looked like any normal average person, but looking in the mirror at herself in her traditional attire made her smile. There was no hiding the power that radiated from her as she was dressed in her witchy best, nor did she attempt to conceal it. She was home. She was powerful, and there was no need to hide it here amongst her people.

Ryen walked from her dressing chamber through the private hallway that led to the ceremonial room. Her hallway met those of Kora and Chesna at the door where the three of them would enter together as one. She was the last to arrive and gave the other two women a nod in quiet greeting. As the youngest of the trio, Ryen was to enter first. With a surge of mental focus she sent power into the main room causing the lights to dim down and go out while at the same time candles all around the large room came to light. This not only prepared the room for the ceremony, but it let the people in the other room know it was time to start and that the Triumvirate would soon enter. After a minute or so, Ryen opened the door and stepped through, followed by Kora in a dress similar to Ryen's except it was a deep red, and she had a diadem with a full moon at her forehead, and then Chesna in a black version of the other dresses and a waning crescent on her diadem.

The room resembled a round theatrical auditorium. In the center where Ryen and the others stood there was a circular stage of sorts, slightly elevated from the rest of the floor. There were no chairs, but the floor itself gently inclined from the stage to allow for visual access for those in the back as well as the front. The ceiling was covered in skylights to let in the moonlight, but there were no other windows in the room for the privacy of the participants. The Triumvirate used this room for a majority of the rituals and spells they performed. Only the monthly esbats, or full moon rituals, and the eight sabbats, or annual holidays, were celebrated elsewhere, either in the central courtyard or outside of the compound in the field nearby. Tomorrow night's Beltane ritual would be held in the field.

Tonight the room held about a hundred people. There were twenty initiates being dedicated, of various ages and origins. The others were their families or coven members that were there to witness, support and celebrate. All were silent and slightly bowed in respect as representatives of the Goddess stood before them. Ryen, Kora and Chesna joined hands and said in unison, "Blessed be, brothers and sisters."

A varied chorus of "Blessed be, my Ladies," answered them.

Kora spoke to the crowd, "We will cast the circle and call forth the elements for protection and blessing. Then we will invite the initiates to enter the circle. The sponsors may come forward to stand outside of the circle at that time."

The stage on which they stood had a circle formed deep within the stone floor where the physical representations of the elements would be called forth. Inside the circle the ritual props had already been placed by one of the assistants. Ryen picked up the athame. The double sided blade of the ritual knife reflected the flickering candles. She walked along the edge of the circle, symbolically creating the sacred space. She then joined Kora and Chesna as they closed their eyes and raised their hands in power as they called forth the elements.

They turned towards the east, "Powers of air, we ask you to join us this evening and to protect this circle." As they spoke a breeze rose from the crack in the stage. To an outside observer it may have looked like a mechanical trick, but all present could feel the power emanating from the three women at the center of the circle and knew that it was a product of that power, not a trick.

Next they turned to the south, "Powers of fire, we ask you to join us this evening and to protect this circle." This time it was flames that rose around the circle.

They turned to the west, "Powers of water, we ask you to join us this evening and to protect this circle." A circle of water joined the air and fire that were still circling the three women.

Lastly they turned to the north, "Powers of earth, we ask you to join us this evening and to protect this circle." Sand rose up from the stage.

The three women then turned back towards the crowd, but raised their heads to the skylights above, "Lord and Lady, we ask for your presence and protection of this circle tonight and in the education and guidance of these initiates."

As the women dropped their arms, the physical presence of the elements dropped back into the floor, but the charged energy remained, invisible to the eye but tingling on the skin of everyone in the room. Again Ryen picked up the athame, but this time she did not walk the circumference of the circle, but went towards the people in front of her. With a slash of the athame, she symbolically cut a door to the circle. Chesna spoke as Ryen stepped to the side of the "door" she had created.

"Those who wish to be dedicated to the Goddess and commit to a year and day of training, please enter the circle of your own free will and desire."

The people who were acting as sponsors for each of the initiates moved to the outside of the circle. The initiates formed a line. As each one approached the invisible door, Ryen held the athame with the tip of the blade touching the initiates' chest. To each one she said, "If there is no fear or hesitation in your heart, I yield to you." As each initiate stepped into the circle, Ryen allowed the athame to move away without harm. After all twenty had entered the circle Ryen symbolically closed the circle in the same manner in which she opened it and joined Kora and Chesna again.

This time Kora spoke directly to the people inside the circle, explaining that tonight begins their year and a day of training and study, but that did not mean that their learning would abruptly end; it was a lifelong journey. Those who completed their training would become official members of their own covens as well as the Universal Coven. Upon that accomplishment they would also receive their tattoo that claimed them as a child of the Goddess, a symbol of the three moons on the Triumvirate's diadems. The very one Ryen had on the back of her neck. The location of the tattoo was completely up to the witch, though most were visible in some way. Everything about Ryen's life as a witch had to be cloaked in secrecy, so the neck, where she could cover it with her hair, had seemed like a good compromise. Kora and Chesna both wore theirs on their wrists. The Triumvirate's tattoos were slightly different from other witches. As each stage of their leadership was entered, a moon on the tattoo was filled in, specifically identifying them as Maiden, Mother, and Crone, not just a witch.

Ryen recalled her own dedication. It had been the very day she had arrived in Florence when she was nine. The witch that flew with her across the Atlantic had explained many things about being a witch. Ryen never really felt it was a decision; it was something she wanted and was supposed to do. So, upon meeting Kora, Chesna and Maggie in person, she told them she wanted to be dedicated. It had been done in this very room with just the four of them present.

Kora spoke of the responsibility that was before them. Their guiding principle was "harm none." Those who chose to use their gifts to purposefully or continuously violate that principle would be excused from the Universal Coven and its protection. She also reminded them of the rule of three, or what some called karma; whatever magic you do, good or bad, comes back threefold. That was something with which Ryen was all too familiar. Her scars served as a daily reminder and so did the occasional revisiting of her torture in her nightmares. It didn't matter the reason, everything had consequences, and not for the first time, she wondered what her mother's had been or would continue to be. There was no timeline for these things, and her mother hadn't stopped violating the "harm none" principle.

Ryen focused her attention back to the ceremony at hand just as Kora was finishing. "If you accept the journey in front of you, come forth, and offer your sacrifice."

Again the initiates formed a line. As they approached the small table in front of the Triumvirate, Ryen offered them the athame once more. By their own power they pricked their finger and placed a drop of their blood in the small cauldron on the table. The contents would later be buried by Ryen, Kora and Chesna, outside in a special spot after the ritual had concluded. When all twenty had finished, Kora lifted the cauldron, presenting it for a moment in each direction to the elements and then to the sky, "Earth, Air, Fire, Water, Lord and Lady: witness the vow of our brothers and sisters and accept their sacrifice."

She placed the cauldron back on the table and motioned for the initiates to face the crowd, as she spoke to those outside the circle, "You all have also witnessed." To those inside the circle she said, "Go forth and seek knowledge. Be compassionate and responsible. Honor your coven and yourself."

All three women joined hands again, closed their eyes and said, "So mote it be." The others in the room echoed.

Kora addressed those in the circle and asked them to join the Triumvirate in thanking the powers. Together they all addressed the Lord and Lady, and then turned to each of the directions in the opposite order from the casting of the circle, thanking each for their presence. When they finished with the Power of Air, Ryen took the athame and walked counter clockwise around the circle, dismissing it. As the initiates left the stage to join their friends and families, each was hugged warmly by Ryen, Kora and Chesna.

A little party followed in celebration. Ryen, as well as Kora and Chesna, stayed awhile, but they all felt the others would be able to celebrate more freely without the anxiety of the Triumvirate lurking around. Some of the initiates would be going home to their covens to complete their training. Others had opted to stay here at the compound. A woman, a mother of an initiate that Ryen guessed to be about the same age she had been as an initiate, approached her, "Lady Reina," the woman said, bowing her head, "We are honored that Mia will be staying here to learn from you, among others."

"We are happy to have her," Ryen said to the woman. To the girl she said, "Welcome, my child. You have an exciting and wonderful journey ahead of you."

The little girl smiled shyly and nodded her head as she hugged her mother's side. Ryen could tell the little girl was hesitant about leaving her home and family for a whole year, so Ryen added with a warm smile, "You know your family can come visit you whenever they want?" To her mother Ryen said, "We know that it is hard to leave your only child. You and your husband are more than welcome to stay here with her or have extended visits if you wish."

"Thank you, my Lady. We were planning to stay in town for at least a couple of weeks while she settles in."

Ryen shook her head in disagreement, "Nonsense, you will stay here! We have more than enough room. Now, I must take my leave and let you all celebrate. We shall see you tomorrow at the Beltane celebration." They said good-byes, and Ryen made her way to the door from which she had entered before.

Chapter 8

The compound was buzzing with energy and extra people. Ryen had been happy to see many of the faces from last night's ceremony at the sunrise yoga class. It was a good thing that the weather was beautiful so the class could be held on the roof instead of the smaller space inside. The good weather was also a blessing for the Beltane celebration that had activities going on all day, leading up to the official ritual under the moonlight. This loving, happy excitement was one of the things Ryen loved about being a witch. This is what every day was like here, which was why Ryen loved coming home, and why she understood that so many others loved to be here too.

The compound was more than just the home of the Triumvirate, training facility in all things witchy, and a boarding school of sorts for witch-children that wanted a regular education mixed with learning or strengthening their powers in the craft. Ryen likened it to the Catholic community with the Vatican and the Pope. But to Ryen it was where she had met her true family, where she had learned everything she knew about being a witch, and it had been her school until she went to the university in town. It, and the people within, had helped her get through some pretty harrowing events, one being coming to terms with what her mother had done, and continued to do, and what one day could be Ryen's responsibility to stop. Today was a celebration though, so she needed to stop thinking about the past or what someday may be, and focus on the present.

Ryen was aware that Chesna had been watching her as she was observing the activities around her, but also as her thoughts turned inward, and the emotions she was feeling shadowed across her face.

"Lady Reina," Chesna addressed her formally since they were among other witches. In private they always used their real names. Their formal names were given when they took their oath upon becoming the Maiden. Ryen smiled as she remembered how she had wanted to pick a new name as soon as she had arrived at the compound, back when she was nine. She wanted to pick her own name to go with her new, true self, and no one argued because it was necessary to help hide her from anyone who might be looking for a little American girl who had disappeared. Maggie had suggested that Ryen sleep on it for one night. When she had awoken the next morning, she eagerly told the others that in a dream she had seen the name Ryen written all over books and walls, and she knew that was her name. "Reina" had come to her in quite a similar way the night before she took her Maiden oath.

"Lady Celeste," Ryen greeted her, and patted the space on the bench next to her, inviting Chesna to sit.

"You are always thinking, my child. Your past is never far from your thoughts, is it?"

Ryen gave Chesna a lopsided smile and a little shrug, affirming Chesna's assumptions. She looked at Chesna, that chocolate skin and dark hair had changed with the age and wisdom Chesna had acquired since Ryen had first met her. Her hair was laced with more grey than brown now, and her skin showed the wrinkles of years and the stress of being the Crone. But those brown eyes were still warm and bright. "Our past makes us who we are," she answered aloud though it was something she knew the other woman knew all too well.

"Yes, it does. But do you truly know what that means to you? It's not just the past you've accumulated in this lifetime. You are an old soul. You would not have been deemed worthy of your role if you weren't. *All* of that past provides us with a well of wisdom. Have you explored any of your past lives? Reached out to those strong women who also played a part in molding who you are?"

"No," she said quietly. Ryen knew that this was not her soul's first experience in this world, but she had never actively done anything to learn about *that* past. She had always thought the knowledge would come to her when it was relevant.

"You know that Beltane is not just about fertility. Now, like Samhain in the fall, the veil between worlds is thin. Perhaps you should take this opportunity to explore those memories during this month. Knowing yourself makes you a better leader, as you are aware."

"Perhaps I will do my own ritual this evening. Thank you, Lady Celeste." Ryen leaned over and hugged Chesna, who returned her hug with equal love and affection. Chesna had always acted as a mother to Ryen, looking out for her in a way only a mother would do, or at least in a way that Ryen imagined mothers who really loved their children unconditionally would do. Sadness filled Ryen as she thought about the Incarnation Ceremony that would be taking place among Coven members all over the world tonight. If a baby were to be conceived, it would mean that Chesna's time in this life would start its official descent from this cycle. She still held so much wisdom that needed sharing. It had been hard when Maggie passed on, but Ryen had only known her for a few years. Chesna's passing would have a much greater effect on her.

The last couple of Incarnation Ceremonies had been unsettling, but she felt even more anxious today. Coven members the world over celebrated this event with hope and excitement. To Ryen it suddenly felt morbid, like hoping for the end of their lives. She shook that selfish thought from her mind as quickly as it came.

Chapter 9

After the annual Beltane ritual had concluded, Ryen had come to the ceremonial chamber to do her own private ritual, to open her consciousness to what was buried in her soul, to connect with her past lives. Now that she had finished, she was a little disappointed that nothing had come to her while she was in the circle. She shouldn't have expected something so powerful and significant to happen so easily. She didn't really struggle with impatience, but usually she could see something at least beginning to manifest without having to wait long. She felt the ritual had been successful, so now she just needed to be patient. Apparently those women, whom Chesna had suggested she get to know, had to come to her in their own time.

Ryen could still hear the post-ritual celebration going on outside: music, singing, dancing, eating, and drinking. She should probably go back and join the party, but all of the rituals in the past few days had left her a bit exhausted. Plus, in the morning she'd be back at it with Kora and Chesna, checking to see if the Incarnation Ceremonies had fulfilled their purpose. If they had, they would be traveling within the next twenty-four hours. With that thought Ryen decided to pass on the party and get some much needed rest before the sun rose.

Ryen was not sure where she was. She felt awake, but this was not her bedroom where she had fallen asleep, and she had never been prone to sleepwalking. As she looked around the room, nothing looked familiar. She heard people talking and moving in the hallway, so she made her way to the door. She opened it carefully, in case somehow she was in danger. As she opened the door though, it was as if she was invisible. The people in the hall walked right by her without even glancing in her direction. Then it dawned on her; she was dreaming. Apparently she was merely an observer in this dream. She would be careful though, in case something changed and her actions altered the outcome of what was happening around her. Dream magic could be dangerous if not respected.

She followed the group of people that had passed her door. As she took in her surroundings and what the people were wearing, beautiful white shifts, and golden jewelry on their arms, waists, and heads, skin bronzed, black straight hair, she concluded she was in ancient Egypt. She had to admit she didn't know a lot about ancient Egypt, mostly what she had learned in history class and her classes on different gods and goddesses.

The group she was following led her into another chamber. This one was different from the room she woke up in; it was a fairly large, open space. There was a pond, or maybe a stream moving under the floor. The people in front of her were crossing what seemed to be a walkway over the water that led to the large form in the middle of the room. It was some sort of couch/bed combination, and lying on top of it was a woman in great contrast to the others around her. Her hair was black but cropped short at her shoulders. Instead of wearing white like the others, she had a deep blue gown that was held together by the ornate golden belt around her waist. She had gold jewelry hanging from her neck, ears and arms. Her eyes were outlined in charcoal, the stereotypical ancient Egyptian way. The golden crown that sat on her head like a headband led Ryen to believe that she was some sort of royalty. Well, the crown, and the fact that she had people fanning her, holding trays of fruit at her finger tips, as well as a tray with a pitcher and cup, and it seemed that everyone else in the room revolved around her.

Around her "bed" several bare-chested young men lounged on big, fluffy pillows, all watching her as if awaiting her command. They were all very attractive. The group that Ryen had followed in joined others dressed exactly the same, who were doing various tasks around the room. Along with their attire, they looked very similar to each other: black hair braided down their backs, and identical gold bands Ryen had previously noticed on their arms. She could now make out the symbol of the goddess Isis; a hieroglyph of a throne and a goddess, meaning queen. Ryen did not think the woman in the center was actually Isis, but perhaps she had been right with her previous thought of royalty.

It still seemed as if no one noticed Ryen's presence. She had not followed the group as they walked across the room, so now Ryen was standing alone, in plain sight. A few more moments passed as Ryen observed her surroundings. The woman in the center motioned for one of the young men to join her. Ryen was taken aback by what transpired between the two, with all of the other people still in the room. In fact, the guys on the floor were still watching, waiting. Ryen wondered if it were not out of the ordinary for this woman to ask more than one to join her. Growing more and more uncomfortable with the situation, Ryen redirected her attention to the other women in the room. They were still going about their business, even the ones holding the trays around the "bed" area. For the most part, they seemed happy, even though they appeared to be this woman's slaves. As her eyes kept moving from figure to figure, she froze. Although Ryen had thought she was invisible to these people, one of the young women was looking right at her. As their eyes locked, Ryen noticed the girl had green eyes filled with gold at the center just like hers. The other girl bowed her head slightly as if greeting Ryen.

Realization hit her. Her spell had come to fruition; one of her past lives had made contact. This young woman, one of the Egyptian queen's hand maidens, shared her soul with Ryen. A name popped into Ryen's head, Zeta. Ryen felt like windows had been opened, and fresh air was filling her lungs, but there were no windows here. The feeling must be from the door to Ryen's history opening up before her. Would Zeta come speak to her, or would Ryen continue to watch only as an observer?

Since Zeta made no attempt to come towards her, Ryen concluded that the latter was her answer. Ryen strained through her history lessons locked deep in her long term memory vault. She recalled that often Pharaohs and queens were treated like gods themselves. It would have been a great honor to be chosen as a personal attendant to one of them. That must be why the young women seemed happy to be here. It was also known that Pharaohs and queens had as many sexual conquests at their fingertips as they desired, even if they were married. This was expected, not frowned upon.

Ryen felt she understood her surroundings now, but not what was significant about what was happening here. Surely she was being shown this part of Zeta's life for a reason, something that would connect with Ryen or that Ryen needed to know or learn to better understand herself.

Ryen had been so lost in thought, that she hadn't seen the new group of young women enter, but now she saw that the group Zeta was with was leaving. Zeta made eye contact with her once again, inviting her to follow. Ryen had no desire to stay and watch the woman in the middle of the room philander with even more guys, so she gladly followed Zeta and the others out.

It was dark outside with the sun having just recently set. Ryen could still feel warmth radiating up from the sand as she followed Zeta away from the palace they had been in, down streets, into narrow passageways between buildings. At last Zeta stopped in a little garden area that was secluded from the streets through which they had just passed. Although it was dark, those streets were still filled with people, and Ryen could hear the bartering and chatter even though this garden seemed to be removed from most of the noise.

Zeta looked around cautiously, and then Ryen could see her body relax. As a very handsome young man walked out from behind one of the bushes, Zeta's face broke out in a huge smile, and she ran forward and threw her arms around the young man. He was gorgeous: bare-chested, like the others Ryen had seen today, shoulder length black hair, strong lean muscles covering his body, and beautiful ice blue eyes. Those eyes are what piqued Ryen's interest. Not because of their beauty, but because although the man's face smiled and appeared happy to see Zeta, his eyes held a sadness that didn't match the rest of his body language.

Zeta took another hesitant look around, and then kissed the young man with reckless abandon. The young man kissed her back with a great deal more passion than the young man that had been with the queen earlier, and Ryen had to look away as she blushed. Earlier she had been uncomfortable with the situation, with the fact that all those people were present for the queen's exploitations, but here Ryen felt she was intruding on something so deeply personal that it was meant only for the two people in front of her.

"Oh Zeta," the young man sighed, "I love you." Again Ryen sensed more sadness that didn't match his words or his body.

"And I love you, Tarik," Zeta responded. "Come with me behind this bush, and I'll show you how much," Zeta added in a mischievous tone and a wink of her eye.

"Not here, Zeta. If the queen finds out you are no longer a virgin you'll be dismissed from her service and very likely punished for betraying the kindness she has bestowed upon you. We have to be careful, especially now."

As Tarik began talking, Zeta seemed to ignore his words of warning, running her hands along his arms, tempting him to follow her, but as he said his last sentence she stopped trying to seduce him, and a worried frown took the place of her flirtatious grin. "Why 'especially now'? What has happened that you aren't telling me?" She seemed to pick up on the emotion that Ryen had recognized earlier in his eyes.

Tarik's shoulders fell, and he let out a sigh before he answered her. "Because I too, have been chosen for the queen's 'service'," he said with bitterness emphasizing the last word.

Zeta's face looked horrified, and tears formed in her eyes as the word "No" escaped her lips as a plea.

Oh, thought Ryen. It had taken her a second to figure out what was going on. By "service" it seemed Tarik was implying he was to be one of those lounging young men around the queen's bed.

Zeta and Tarik held each other. He tried to comfort her as she cried. When she had regained some of her composure Zeta asked, "Maybe you can talk to Pharaoh. He likes you. You've been a great and loyal warrior for him."

Tarik shook his head in defeat. "He loves his sister more than me. He won't deny her what she has requested. Zeta, you are my life. What are we going to do?" He rested his chin on Zeta's head.

After a few minutes of contemplation Zeta took Tarik's face in her hands and tilted it down so he was looking in her eyes. "You are my life. I will not give you up. This just means we need to be more careful."

"It won't bother you to know that I have been with her? Oh, god, what if you are in the room when she calls on me? I don't think I could do that."

Zeta interrupted him, placing her finger on his lips, "Shhh. We both have duties to fulfill. If one or both of us should fail in those duties, as you said before, there will be punishment. So we won't fail. I love you too much. And if, by some force I do fail, I will not betray you."

"Nor I, you," Tarik said as his lips met hers with an even greater passion than he had shown before.

Ryen turned away, shut her eyes, and focused on the noises from the streets. Zeta and Tarik were showing each other the depths of their love, and she didn't need to watch that. She felt a great sadness in her heart. The longer she spent here with Zeta, the more connected they became. Ryen had read too many stories, fiction and non-fiction alike, to know that the odds were not in the lovers' favor.

She didn't know how long she stood there, but when she opened her eyes it was no longer dark, and she was no longer in that garden. She was inside the palace again but in a different place. This room was larger than the queen's chamber. There were many people crowded into different corners. At the front of the room, Ryen saw a throne with a powerful looking man she guessed to be the Pharaoh. Next to him in a lower throne sat the queen, looking as she did the last time Ryen had seen her but with more alertness in her eyes. Actually, she seemed pissed. Maybe Tarik had gone to the Pharaoh, and he had granted his request.

But as Ryen scanned the rest of the room, she knew that had not happened. Standing a short distance from the thrones was a little stage, and on the stage stood Zeta. Ryen didn't have to ask to know what she was feeling. Their connection was even greater, and Ryen could feel her emotions, and almost hear her thoughts, as if they were her own.

Zeta was scared, but not for herself. She had accepted her fate, but as she had sworn, she refused to betray Tarik. Zeta thought that her punishment would be death. She only hoped to spare Tarik from the same.

The Pharaoh spoke in a loud voice, silencing the crowd in an instant. "Hand maiden Zeta, you stand accused and found guilty of defiling the honor the queen bestowed upon you in her service. As a result of your crime, you have been sentenced to public raping."

Zeta's and Ryen's eyes flew open in shock. Zeta had been sure it would be death by whipping, but now she understood. Through a public rape the Pharaoh, or more likely the queen, hoped to smoke out her co-conspirator; either she would give up the name to stop her punishment, or her cohort would speak out on her behalf. Ryen saw Zeta's gaze meet Tarik's for just a second. Her head gave a very subtle shake, and her eyes pleaded with him to keep his mouth shut. There was no need for both of them to be punished.

The pain Ryen saw in Tarik's eyes brought tears to her own. However briefly, she had witnessed their love for each other, and she could feel what Zeta felt, but Ryen was helpless to do anything here. She felt the resolve come over Zeta as she prepared herself for what was to come. Ryen wasn't sure she could stay here and watch this. She knew all too well what Zeta was physically about to endure. Ryen's feelings of panic began to increase. Zeta looked at Ryen, and Ryen wondered if Zeta could feel her emotions as well. If she could, Ryen was only making things worse. She focused on blocking out her own memories and tried to remember that she was here for a reason. Maybe focusing on the significance of these events would help her hold herself together.

Zeta was led to a stone slab that was between her and the thrones. With a motion from the Pharaoh, several men from his guard stepped forward towards Zeta as she was being restrained. Ryen's stomach turned. Multiple men were going to rape her? This was testing a strength Ryen hadn't had to use in years. Ryen was a little surprised that the crowd remained silent. Either they agreed with Zeta's punishment, or they were afraid to say anything against it. Ryen could tell Tarik was having a hard time keeping himself under control. She knew she had no influence here, but she said a quick prayer to the Goddess that this would not get any worse.

As Zeta's punishment took place, Ryen could feel her pain and humiliation. Zeta's heart was also breaking, knowing that Tarik was being made to watch. The slightest move could incriminate him as well. Ryen was impressed that Zeta did not cry out in pain or fear or concession. Zeta stared at the ceiling. Ryen saw a tear escape down the side of her face. She could hear Zeta's inner prayers to the Goddess Hathor, who was responsible for women, love and justice.

As the third man prepared to do his part in Zeta's punishment, Ryen noticed movement from the corner of her eye. She turned her head in time to see Tarik step forward, as he spoke, "Stop! I am responsible. She is innocent. I take responsibility."

Zeta's head shot in his direction as she cried out, "NO!" Ryen could hear Zeta's thoughts cursing Tarik for implicating himself, more worried for him than her own self.

Tarik looked at her and mouthed "I love you" before turning back to the thrones. The queen had a satisfied smile on her face. It appeared that she had known who else was involved all along. Ryen sensed that she was more jealous that Tarik would rather be with someone else over her than the fact Zeta was no longer a virgin in her service. Ryen sensed malice emanating from her.

The queen spoke to Tarik, "Thank you for your honesty. May Anubis and Osiris take mercy on your soul. My mercy will be to grant you a quick death."

Zeta's sobs could easily be heard throughout the silent room. Tarik glanced at the Pharaoh with a pleading look. The look the Pharaoh gave Tarik conveyed regret that he could not save him, even if Tarik had been one of his most trusted warriors. Tarik did not fight as two guards grabbed his arms. A third

44

guard brought a long blade and stood in front of Tarik. Tarik and Zeta looked at each other.

Out loud, for all to hear, Tarik said, "You are my life. I will always love you."

Zeta stopped her sobs and said in return, "I will always love you. I will see you in the next life."

As tears fell from Tarik's blue eyes, the guard slid the blade across his throat. Moments after Tarik's body hit the ground, the queen turned her attention back to Zeta, "You will be joining your lover sooner than you think." She nodded to one of the guards that had been stationed near Zeta. He pulled out a blade similar to the one that had killed her lover. As it slid across Zeta's throat, everything went dark.

Chapter 10

Ryen knew she was in her own room. She could smell the incense she had burned before falling asleep, and she could feel her familiar quilt under her fingers. But she didn't want to open her eyes for fear that she'd be back in Egypt if she did. She felt completely exhausted, as if she had really just experienced all of the feelings and events. Some of those feelings she had never felt before, or at least never that strongly: the desperation to save someone, the willingness to sacrifice herself, but above all else, that incredibly intense love shared between Zeta and Tarik. She understood now that Zeta was part of her, and all of those feelings and memories were now part of her too.

After several moments pondering what she had seen and coming to some degree of acceptance, she opened her eyes. Her curtains were drawn, so the room was dark, but Ryen could sense the sunrise was coming soon. As her eyes moved around the room she sucked in a startled breath. Standing at the end of her bed was Zeta.

"I apologize for startling you. I thought you might be expecting me," Zeta said.

Ryen was speechless. She felt the need to let Zeta know how sorry she was that all of those things happened to her. She thought of Tarik's attempts to save her from her torture. Thinking of that torture stirred up Ryen's own memories again, and she shuddered.

Zeta continued speaking when Ryen didn't respond, as if knowing what Ryen was thinking, "I hope that your pain was not the fault of my transgressions."

Ryen was confused, "I'm not sure I understand."

"You are aware that souls are connected through lifetimes, but I fear that events follow us as well. You know, karmic retribution so strong that it isn't content to be confined to one lifespan."

"I don't blame you for what happened to me. I blame four scumbags and my own naiveté. As a result I made my own bad choices, so the pain I still feel from it is from my own doing."

Zeta gave Ryen a half smile as she said, "Yeah, karma's a bitch."

"But what happened to you was because of the queen's jealousy. She humiliated and killed both of you out of spite."

Zeta appeared to take a deep breath before she spoke, even though it was not a necessity. "She was jealous and spiteful, but I broke my oath to her and to my position, first by having sex with Tarik, then by concealing it, and thirdly by continuing my relationship with him after she had claimed him. You may not understand my culture, but I made several selfish choices knowing the consequences."

"And you reaped those consequences," Ryen added. "If you could, would you change any of your decisions?"

"No. To ask to be released from the queen's service would still have been a slight to her, and even if it had been granted, she may still have selected Tarik. The queen thought that killing me was the climax to my punishment, but she didn't understand that if she hadn't done it, I would have done it myself. I could never live in a world without Tarik. He is, was, and forever will be my soulmate. As I am part of you, he is part of me."

The depth of Zeta's love and commitment to Tarik baffled Ryen. She could feel Zeta's feelings, but that didn't mean she understood them.

Zeta looked towards the window where light was trickling in through the cracks around the drapes, "It's good to be known by you, Ryen Cardona, Lady Reina, Maiden of the Universal Coven."

Ryen was a little puzzled, "You know all that about me?"

"I am you; you are me; we are one soul. Just because you have never seen me before or didn't know anything about me, doesn't mean I haven't been with you your entire life. It's time for me to go, but I'm always within you."

"Thank you," was all Ryen could say before Zeta vanished before her eyes. She wondered if she should tell Chesna and Kora about this, or at least Chesna. She would contemplate these events more before sharing. Today was not the time to be concerned with herself. They had some spell casting to do to see if a new Maiden had been conceived overnight.

Chapter 11

Cash's laptop sat on the bar, and he leaned on his elbow while he listened to the phone trilling in his ear. This certainly wasn't the first call he had made to the Louvre, but he was hoping for it to be the last.

"Thank you for calling the Louvre. How may I direct your call?"

Cash appreciated the cheerful female, *human* voice on the other end. He was easily irritated by automated phone menus. "I'm calling for the curator, Didier Pichon."

She was apologetic, and Cash wondered if she recognized his voice. He was sure this was the same woman who had been the recipient of most of his calls. "Mes excuses, monsieur. I'm sorry. He's out of the office."

"Yes. He doesn't seem to take his job very seriously. Do you know when he will be back in the office?" Cash didn't try to hide his annoyance. All he wanted was for someone to answer his questions about who this woman was for whom he was searching. This Didier person was the only connection he currently had.

"Any day, monsieur. Would you care to leave a message?"

Cash had left more messages than he cared to count. He tapped his pen on his forehead as he debated his next step. He had asked once before and been shot down, but he decided to give it another try. He added a little seduction to his voice. "I don't suppose you could give me a number where I could reach him in the meantime?"

He didn't have the same pull over the phone as he would in person, but Cash could tell that the woman on the other end was struggling with not being able to complete the desired task satisfactorily. "Again, monsieur, I apologize. It is not permitted for me to give out personal information or numbers, but I can let him know you called if you'd like to leave your name."

"Fine. Cash Di Marco, again. You should already have my number." Cash's sigh and frustration were clearly audible.

"Yes, Monsieur Di Marco. I have it. I will make sure he gets your messages as soon as he returns."

"Merci, mademoiselle." Cash sat his phone down next to his computer and stared blankly at the screen. He hadn't been successful in reaching anyone who could help him with the identity of his mystery woman, but he had gotten his hands on security footage from the Arts Council event at the Louvre. He didn't know her name, but her face taunted him from the safety of a photograph.

Cash could feel Rafa's eyes on him from the far end of the bar. He knew that it wouldn't have taken much effort for his friend to have heard both sides of the phone conversation that just ended. He was very much aware that his change in mood and behavior was starting to wear, not only on his best friend, but on most of his other employees as well.

There was no one else in the bar at this early afternoon hour, and Cash knew that Rafa would hear him without overtly calling out, "If you have something to say just say it."

Rafa slowly walked towards his friend. He didn't speak with judgment, just observation. Cash was impressed. "It seems you've exhausted your resources. Have you considered asking for assistance?"

Cash raised a skeptical eyebrow. "Do you have some hidden detective skills that I'm unaware of?"

A mischievous grin spread across Rafa's face. "Oh, I have many skills. But I was referring to some of the more cyber-inclined friends or employees of ours. I know you have a picture of her on your computer that you don't want anyone to see, but maybe one of our associates could hack their way to the information that you are looking for."

"Hmm." Rafa's suggestion was decent, and Cash was a little irritated with himself for not thinking outside of the tiny box within which he had been maneuvering so far. "That's not a bad idea. Thanks, hermano."

Of course there was always his last resort, asking his mother for help. He really didn't want to have a conversation with her to explain what he was after, but he knew with one phone call to the Arts Council his mother would be able to get her hands on the name he so desperately sought. That maternal favor would cost him dearly, and he wasn't there yet. He would save that option until he was sure there was no other hope.

Chapter 12

After she had showered and gotten dressed, Ryen bundled her hair gently on top of her head. That was one of the great things about being home; she didn't have to worry about hiding her tattoo with her hair or clothing. Today's work did not need formal ceremonies, so no ritual bathing or ceremonial dress was necessary. Ryen put on a comfy cotton, strapless sundress that ended at mid-calf. It was orange with small yellow, white, and lime stripes running in an inverted V-pattern. The colors made her feel cheerful after the night she'd experienced. Before leaving her room, she grabbed her smoky quartz pendent and fastened it around her neck. She would be using it for her part of the spells today.

As she walked down the spacious, open corridor that looked out over the central courtyard and down the steps to find Chesna and Kora, she replied to the various greetings of "Lady Reina" with "blessed be" or "good morning". Everyone knew what she was going to do, but they also knew that if there was any news of importance, they would be told as soon as it was verified and deemed safe. People, though anxious, were going about their business; some leaving for jobs outside of the compound, some heading off to their classes within, and others off to do something with their free time.

The door to the room that she shared as a private study with Chesna and Kora was closed, so she knocked before she opened it and entered. Each of them had their own office where they met and consulted with members of the Coven, and there was a nice sized library on the grounds as well, but this was the room where they kept all of their shared items and where they did smaller spells that didn't require the ritual chamber. This room had windows, as did their offices, but all of them were on the second level so that didn't present a problem with privacy.

Both women were already there, seated in plush chairs in front of the massive fireplace. Florence didn't get too terribly cold, but during the winter when the temperatures wavered right around freezing and the sun was blocked out by overcast skies, everyone was happy that this old, stone building had numerous fireplaces.

Ryen sat in the open seat next to them. A feeling of anticipation hung in the air and all three women, even wise Chesna, were full of nervous excitement. Kora broke the silence, "Shall we get started? We know there are only two outcomes; either this is the year, or like we have for over a quarter of a century we say, 'There's always the next one in five years'."

Chesna and Ryen both nodded in agreement. All three rose and joined hands, forming a tiny circle. Together they invoked the Goddess to guide them, "Blessed Lady, we come together today, seeking if you have again joined us in this world, in a soul that will someday merge with us as the Maiden. We ask you to guide our work this morning and open our eyes to the truth we seek. Blessed be."

After a few moments of silence, they parted and went to separate areas around the room. Chesna's specialty was visions, so she made herself comfortable on a large pillow on the floor by a window and shut her eyes in meditation as the sun shone in on her face.

Kora's talent in seeing the future was not as strong as Chesna's, but she preferred divining through water. She sat at a small table where she had already prepared her shallow bowl of sacred liquid.

None of Ryen's powers helped her to see the future; they never had. She was able to use her power to pinpoint locations, as long as they weren't cloaked by powerful magic, by using her scrying crystal and a map. Since the location of a possible conception could have happened in several countries the world over, she started with continental maps, most populated to least. Chesna or Kora would probably be successful before Ryen could narrow down a location, but in case their visions didn't produce a location, Ryen would have a head start in that department. She laid out a map of Asia first on her table.

The spell could be performed by just one, but having all three of them work on it allowed the information to be confirmed by different sources. The girl, if there was one, who had become pregnant last night, would have been visited by the Goddess in her dreams to be told of the gift for which she would be responsible for the next forty weeks. She would most likely contact the Triumvirate as soon as possible, but nothing was being left up to chance, and it would have to be confirmed by the Triumvirate before any announcements were made or actions were taken anyway.

In the past, the pregnant girl had the choice of remaining with her coven and family or coming to Florence for the duration of her pregnancy. After the tragedy surrounding Ryen's birth and her being lost to the Coven for nine years, this option was no longer on the table. Once they confirmed a conception and located the girl, the Triumvirate would travel to her today to escort her back to Florence. After the baby was born, the girl would be welcome to continue her stay at the compound, but the Triumvirate would take responsibility for the upbringing and education of the child.

After spending a good thirty minutes on Asia, Ryen concluded there was nothing there and moved on to a map of Africa. Not long after, Chesna let out a relaxed breath and said, "Blessed be!" She did not elaborate, but Kora and Ryen exchanged knowing looks that she had just seen some sort of confirmation. Kora seemed to double down on her efforts of concentration on her bowl of water, and Ryen and her crystal returned their attention to Africa.

As Ryen was exchanging her map of Africa for one of North America, Kora let out a thankful, "Blessed be!"

Ryen didn't want to disrupt the concentration of either of the other two, but her excitement and impatience got the better of her, "I'd be obliged if I could get a clue as to on which continent I should be looking," she asked aloud.

Kora replied, still staring into the water, "I'm thinking North America, but it could also be Europe".

Without opening her eyes Chesna added, "It's most definitely the States."

A tiny shudder went through Ryen. The United States did not hold good memories for her, and going there could present some interesting safety challenges, but she got out a new map, just of the U.S., and got to work.

Less than ten minutes later Ryen had a location. It wasn't her state of origin, and who knew if that was even where her mother still lived, but its location would still present some travel concerns. "I've got the location, but you two aren't going to like it."

After Ryen had relayed her information to Chesna and Kora she asked, "Does that correspond with any of the geographical markers you may have seen?"

Both women had a worried crease across their foreheads and their mouths were turned slightly downward. "Yes," they both answered.

"Well, who wants to do some research on our destination, and who wants to get started on travel details? I can have Sophie work on booking flights if you want," Ryen talked quickly, hoping the other two would get involved in the details and stop focusing on what was causing their worry.

Kora spoke, "I'll research the destination, but Ryen, you can't go with us." Chesna stepped over to join Kora, forming a little alliance between the two of them.

"That's ridiculous," Ryen said flatly. "We are stronger as three, and in physical powers I am the strongest. If something should go wrong, I should be there."

"That may be true," Chesna said, "but we run the risk of someone discovering you. They have to know what last night was. They are probably watching international flights for the next few days, knowing that we won't wait long. As far as we know, we've kept your existence from them, but for you to go back, I fear we are inviting trouble."

"And what if they are watching for us and something happens to this girl or one of you two, or all of you, and I'm not there? My presence could mean the difference between success and traumatic failure." Ryen was not taking no for an answer. She knew returning to the United States could blow her cover. Her mother and "father" believed she was dead, or at least they had when she faked her death when she was nine. If somehow her real identity was revealed to the wrong people, it could lead to a global war. Right now her mother's fanatical group of murderers was working within the confines of the U.S., but if her mother knew that the Coven had gotten their hands on her daughter, whom she believed dead, they may bring their genocide across the ocean. If that were to happen, the Triumvirate would have no choice but to retaliate.

Chesna and Kora knew how stubborn Ryen could be, and they also couldn't deny Ryen's argument for the safety of the whole. Retrieving this pregnant girl was priority number one. Chesna conceded first, "We will take as many precautions as we can. Perhaps take a private plane to Madrid or Paris so we aren't as easily connected to Italy for starters. We'll also have a good cover story for anyone with whom we come in contact."

Ryen smiled in victory. She had already sent Sophie a text to come to their study at once, so it was perfect timing that she knocked on the door as Chesna finished speaking.

Ryen said loud enough to be heard through the thick wooden door, "Come in."

Sophie poked her head in cautiously, not knowing what to expect from within. "Did you need something Lady Reina?" Sophie was being respectful, but it had been quite a while since she had been addressed as such from Sophie.

"Sophie, we need you to work on immediate travel plans and accommodations to Mt. Vernon, Iowa," Ryen instructed her.

"For five people," Kora added. Ryen gave her a questioning look. Kora continued, "Sophie will come with us, and we will also take someone of the appropriate age for a college visit. I saw a college there.

Chapter 13

While preparations were being made and bags packed, they received the final piece of their confirmation: a phone call came from Mt. Vernon, Iowa. Before they left the compound to head to the airport, the Triumvirate called the occupants of the compound together to inform them of the news that the rituals had produced the future Maiden, but did not share with them the information of where they were going. They were instructed to keep the news private until everyone returned with their precious cargo. Secretaries could confirm the conception with covens making official inquiries, but no information would be given over the phone to anyone without the official codes for this sensitive situation.

Sophie recruited seventeen year old Elise to be their potential college student. Elise was actually from the U.S. Both of her parents were army officers, so she had lived in several countries before coming to Florence to study for her secondary education. Her auburn hair often hung loose at her shoulders. Her brown eyes were always full of curiosity, complementing intelligence. She was eager to help, and her background made her a believable recruit for the small liberal arts college she would be visiting. Maybe she would actually end up going there. That scared Ryen a little. She constantly worried about witches in the United States. Although there were many open minded people there, it still seemed that if you didn't fit into the mainstream Christian mold you were persecuted, not to mention the fact that her mother's group was literally persecuting, torturing and killing witches that they hunted down. If someone were to ask Ryen if she thought they should visit or move to the U.S. she would tell them no. If she could get all American witches to relocate, the whole Triumvirate would rest easier. Although Ryen wondered how long the U.S. borders would contain her mother and her hunters.

As Chesna had suggested, the five women took a private plane from Florence to Paris. From Paris they took a commercial flight to Chicago, but they opted for first class seating to allow for more privacy. Ryen was very glad for their first class arrangements. She hadn't flown such a long distance since she was nine. Even though she was fairly slender, she didn't like the idea of being crammed into the coach seats, literally rubbing elbows and everything else with the people around her.

Due to the mixed company, or more likely the mission, a nervous anxiety hung in the air. For the first half of the flight she watched a movie with Sophie and took some time to get to know Elise better. Ryen knew her from some classes she had taught when she was home off and on that Elise attended, but she didn't know very much personal information. Ryen blamed this on the fact that she was often away from Florence working for the Arts Council. Elise loved art and was very interested in Ryen's work for the Council, so they had an easy and lengthy conversation.

Neither Chesna nor Kora were very chatty, listening to music with their headphones. Though they hid it well, Ryen could tell they were justifiably on edge. They wouldn't relax until everyone had returned safely to Florence, so Ryen left them be. With about four hours of the flight remaining, Ryen suggested that everyone try to get some sleep. When they arrived in Chicago there would be a visit to customs, and then they would get on another plane that would fly them the much shorter distance from Chicago to Cedar Rapids, Iowa. Apparently the Cedar Rapids airport was not large enough to handle international flights. They opted for a private plane for this short flight as well to further confuse anyone who might be trying to track them. From Cedar Rapids, they would travel about thirty minutes by car to the small town of Mt. Vernon. After spending the night, they would do the whole trip in reverse tomorrow, barring any complications.

Ryen put in her ear buds and selected a calming playlist on her iPhone. Although she was also anxious about the next twenty four hours, it didn't take long for her body to relax, her eyes to shut, and her consciousness to drift away.

An increasingly familiar feeling came over Ryen as she opened her eyes. This was not a regular dream. Ryen didn't recognize anything she was seeing, so she knew she wasn't reliving one of her memories, but this felt different from her observance of Zeta's life that she had experienced the previous night. She was not invisible here. She was sitting in a car and there was a man sitting next to her. They were being driven somewhere in the dark, and she couldn't get a good glimpse of the guy to her right. She felt nervous but she had no idea why. When the guy spoke, she thought his voice was familiar, but she couldn't place it.

"Are you prepared?" he asked, still looking straight ahead.

"Yes," came out of Ryen's mouth, but she didn't say it. She tried to lift her hand to her face, but her hand wouldn't move. Whoever she was, Ryen had no control here. It appeared she was merely observing again, but this time through the eyes of her host. Something about this made her very uneasy.

"How far away do you want me to drop you off?" the driver asked.

The guy next to her answered, "Take us as close as you can get. If she's been completely honest, they won't be expecting anything."

From where did she know this voice? It was driving Ryen crazy, that and the fact that she was completely helpless here. Her body took a deep breath, and she had a feeling of dread that was not her own. Was this guy making this person do something against her will? Ryen tried to further dissect the unfamiliar feelings. No, she didn't think this person was being forced into anything, but she was feeling hesitant nonetheless.

Before long the car approached some sort of neighborhood. They had been driving through a wooded area, not a city, so this was a little unusual. When the car stopped, she got out. As she stood, the woman's hands ran over her stomach, and Ryen realized she was pregnant.

Oh no, were they going to tell someone that they had accidentally gotten knocked up? Ryen was still having a difficult time getting a read on the situation, and no matter how hard she focused, her head would not turn toward her companion.

The man instructed the driver, "After we go in, wait about five minutes, and then have the others fan out around the perimeter."

As Ryen and her mysterious companion walked farther into the neighborhood, Ryen could see several houses lining a few streets, forming the square mileage of maybe three city blocks. All of the streets seemed to lead towards the center.   They hadn't gone too far when a teenage boy approached them. He wasn't a gangly, scrawny boy. He was tall and muscular, and attractive. His hair was shaggy and brownish gold, with gentle waves. He seemed like he was going to come forward and embrace her, but he stopped short as he locked eyes with Ryen's companion. When his eyes met hers they were dark in the moonlight, but they were filled with worry, and a little relief.   His voice was deep with emotion as he glanced at her companion again and asked, "Where have you been? Everyone has been really worried. Why weren't you answering your pages?"

Pages? Ryen knew what they were, but nobody used pagers anymore. They were from a time before cell phones were prevalent. This couldn't be a past life; they would be too close together.

Her host avoided the boy's questions, and the hurt in his eyes. As she spoke it felt as though a hand had squeezed her heart, just enough to cause her to flinch slightly. "Ackley, tell my mother that we need to talk to everyone. We'll wait by the fire."

More emotion appeared in the boy's eyes, and a deep scowl covered his face. He nodded and turned to walk away. Ryen assumed he was doing what he was asked.   She and her nameless companion walked down the street to where a large bonfire was burning. There were a few people already gathered near it. Some looked up as they approached and waved or nodded in greeting, though others had confused looks on their faces.   The eyes Ryen was sharing looked around and scanned the area outside the nearby houses, the woods. As her head continued to circle around, her eyes finally got a look at the guy next to her.

If Ryen could have screamed, she would have, and then focused all of her powers on getting the hell out of there as soon as possible. He was younger and his facial hair was different, but standing next to her was Joseph, the man she had known as her father.

Understanding hit Ryen like a ton of bricks. In fact, it felt like that "ton of bricks" had slammed into her stomach. She couldn't do anything, and she couldn't wake herself up. She didn't want to be here; she didn't want to see this. This had to be the night her mother killed everyone in her coven. Ryen wanted to cry, scream, yell for help, or hit something, but she was helplessly bound within another's body.

From her host, she felt a nervousness, but she couldn't sense any remorse over what was about to happen. More and more people were joining them near the fire. Soon, too soon Ryen thought, an authoritative woman approached her with Ackley. The woman was as tall as the boy she walked beside. She was wearing a long light blue dress, similar to the one Ryen wore for rituals, but this one had long sleeves, and the body was looser fitting so there was no need of a slit up the leg. Her hair was in a relaxed French braid that hung past her shoulders. She did not acknowledge Joseph. Her green-gold eyes were sharp and bore into Ryen's as she spoke, "Ariadne, you wanted to speak with us?"

"Yes, mother, but my name is Damaris now." As the words came out of Ryen's mouth, her heart broke. There was no denying that she was reliving an event from her mother's life, and she was looking at her grandmother for the first time. Under other circumstances Ryen would have loved to absorb her grandmother's appearance and mere presence, but those desires were overshadowed by the severity of the present situation. Her grandmother was suspicious, but she clearly had no idea what was about to happen. Ryen couldn't warn her or anyone else here. She felt like vomiting, and although her host was pregnant, she knew that was her reaction alone.

Ryen's eyes gave another scan of the area, and Ryen felt she was checking to see if everyone had gathered, or maybe she was trying to see those "others" that would be fanning out around the perimeter as Joseph had instructed. Ryen was screaming "RUN!!" at everyone her eyes ran across, but of course they couldn't hear her.

Ryen's eyes fell on the boy, Ackley, and she felt that grab at her heart again, and then they settled on her grandmother. She alone heard the words being uttered under her breath, "Flames and fire heed my command. Rid this abomination from this land."

As the hands of Ryen's host rose so did the flames, obeying her will. All of a sudden, the fire erupted with the sound of multiple cannons going off. Hundreds of balls of flame shot out of the fire and struck the people gathered there, as screams came from their mouths. Ryen could also hear yells from the woods as people with guns and other weapons came running to join her and Joseph.

Ryen shot up from her reclined position, and were it not for her seatbelt, she would have slammed into the seat in front of her. Hands were on her arms as well. As she worked to steady her breathing, she looked around at the faces watching her. A few strangers were looking concerned and eying her suspiciously. They were probably wondering if she was mentally stable enough to be sitting near them on this trans-Atlantic flight. The others were the very concerned faces of her traveling companions. Poor Elise, who was sitting next to her, looked terrified even though she was strongly grasping Ryen's arm. Past her, Kora and Chesna were staring at Ryen from across the aisle.

"What was that?" Sophie asked from her other side.

Ryen turned toward her and tried to sound nonchalant, though she was sweating and her hands were shaking. "I had a bad dream."

The flight attendant had approached, and Kora assured her that Ryen was fine now and apologized for the disturbance.

"Disturbance?" Ryen asked.

The grips on Ryen's arms lessened their strength but did not let go. "You were screaming and crying," Sophie explained.

Ryen realized her cheeks were damp and her throat felt a little raw. "What was I screaming?" she asked concerned that she had relayed her entire dream to the first class section of the airplane.

"Nothing coherent," Kora assured her. "What was that?"

Ryen's mind was rushing to understand why she had dreamt what she did. It was not her memory, nor was it one of her past lives. What if her mother sent that to her and was actually using the connection to find them? Did her mother know she was alive? That was the last thing Kora and Chesna would want to hear, but if it were true, Ryen had to tell them.

Ryen assured Sophie and Elise that she was fine now, and they could let go of her arms. Then she settled in to tell the others what she had experienced. She was careful to keep her voice quiet enough that the inconspicuous eavesdroppers couldn't follow her story. Hopefully if they did overhear anything they would chalk it up to a crazy girl's nightmares.

As she finished she said, "At least we know how it happened now. We knew my mother was responsible from what I read in her journals, but she didn't write down the details." Ryen also shared her fears about why she had the dream. Kora seemed concerned, but Chesna's interpretation surprised her.

"Perhaps it *was* one of your memories." Reading the confusion on Ryen's face she continued, "You *were* there. You saw that your mother was pregnant. It wasn't long after that that you were born. Maybe on some level you were aware of the events and the spell you cast to reach out to your past brought this memory to your consciousness."

"Maybe," Ryen said, "but we'd be stupid not to consider the other possibility." Ryen wasn't sure that she had much faith in Chesna's attempts to make the situation less grave.

Chesna asked her another question with what appeared like tears forming in her eyes, "Did you see your grandmother?"

Ryen remembered when she had met Chesna that Chesna had told her that she had known her grandma. Now she realized they must have been good friends to elicit such emotion from her. "Yes. She seemed suspicious of my mom, but it was clear they all were caught off guard by the attack."

Ryen was surprised to see a tear roll down Chesna's wrinkled cheek. "It would have been a close fight even if she had expected it. Alone, she could have beaten your mother, but with you inside her, your mother could tap into your strength even though she was probably unaware that it was happening. I'm guessing that's where her power for such an attack came from. There wasn't anything extraordinary about her abilities."

A new guilt caused a lump in Ryen's chest. Had she played a role in that mass murder, her mother's first kill, which resulted in the death of her family? She knew she didn't have any control over it, but she now felt a sense of responsibility.

She didn't want to think any more about that. So she pushed those feelings down deep and focused her attention on Chesna. "I forgot that you knew her. Were you close?"

"Yes," Chesna answered, wiping away another uncharacteristic tear. "She attended school in Florence during my early years as Mother. We had a lot of things in common, so we were fast friends. I mentored her. I was very proud of her when she was appointed High Priestess. It gives me a little peace to at least know how her life came to an end."

"What was my father's name?" Ryen asked. There was something about her dream that made her curious.

"Ackley," Kora answered. "You didn't know that?"

"No. My mother's journals mentioned that she had killed him, but she never wrote his name. I never thought to ask you guys, and if you ever mentioned it in my presence I must not have been paying attention."

Kora spoke softly, as if she were reading a story to Ryen, "They were in love before the Incarnation Ceremony, or at least that is what we were told at the time."

64

Chesna nodded, "Yes, they were. That was something that comforted your grandmother. Both of your parents were excited about your conception. Not just that you would become the Maiden, but because you were a result of their love. I don't know what happened during those later months of your mother's pregnancy, but everyone was happy in the beginning."

Ryen was thoughtful for a moment before she added, "I think she still loved him, even when she killed him. Both times she looked into his eyes I felt a pain in my heart, or her heart rather. Too bad it wasn't enough to change her mind."

They didn't have time to discuss it any further. The captain came on to tell the passengers that they were starting their descent into Chicago. All of their thoughts focused on what was ahead. They all had to be vigilant with their security.

Chapter 14

The black cloud that hung over Ryen didn't disappear as they boarded their private plane to Cedar Rapids, nor when the nice man, Drew, from the coven they were visiting picked them up with a limo, but nothing bad happened. All of them were a little surprised by the limo being their mode of transportation. Kora even questioned Drew about it, assuring him that although appreciated it may draw too much attention.

Drew nodded his head in respect, causing his straight red hair to fall into his eyes. He was middle aged and dressed casually in jeans and a sweatshirt, but he was clean-shaven and the sides of his hair were trimmed close to his head.

His dark green eyes twinkled as he raised his head and spoke to Kora in a matter of fact tone, "Normally I would agree with you, Lady Luna, but for one thing. This car will provide us the space and privacy to travel together. And lucky for us it is prom season, so the limo is actually less conspicuous than you may think."

Sophie was confused by the word "prom", so as they drove Drew and Elise explained the concept to her. Ryen felt relaxed in the car and was amused watching the exchange between Kora and Drew. They were alike in their looks, though he was much taller. They appeared to be about the same age, Ryen guessed, although Kora was older than she looked, as were all Triumvirate members. But what held Ryen's attention was how they kept stealing glances at each other, occasionally meeting eyes. Maybe it had been the way he had challenged Kora in regards to the limo, Ryen wasn't sure, but there was definitely a little fire burning between the two now. Ryen glanced at Drew's left hand and smiled when she saw the lack of a ring on a significant finger.

They were headed to the house of a coven member, Teresa, where Gelina, the newly pregnant teen, would be meeting them. Teresa lived at the edge of town, so it had more privacy than other members' homes.

Ryen knew that witches in the U.S. had moved away from the idea of living secluded from non-witches, mostly as a way to blend in. Ryen imagined it made locating an entire coven more difficult if someone was on a mission to exterminate witches as well. There were also a number of solitary practitioners in the U.S. Unfortunately, without having a coven to check in with and watch their backs, those solitary practitioners were all too often the victim of Ryen's mother's group of witch hunters.

As they approached Teresa's house, Ryen took in her surroundings. Most of the houses were barely more than ten feet apart from each other, with garages sticking out as the first thing she noticed. All of the houses were also close in color: tan, white, pale yellow. Ryen concluded that it must be a fairly new neighborhood, because the few trees that lined the streets were very young, and there were a couple of empty lots on the street with only dirt and some signs advertising contractors, and specialized construction materials.

Teresa's house was no exception to what Ryen had seen, but it was at the end of the development area, so it wasn't smashed between other homes, and there was a small wooded area that butted up to her backyard. Teresa, herself, was a very bubbly, energetic person. She was out on her front step before they had even finished pulling in the driveway. She was also dressed comfortably in yoga pants and a long sleeved shirt. She had short brown hair that needed no accessories to keep it out of her face. Ryen noticed an array of crystals adorning her fingers, neck, wrists and ears. They all worked harmoniously though, adding to the woman's vibrant personality.

It was well past midnight, but Teresa ushered them inside and down into her basement. As they passed rooms upstairs and entered the basement, Ryen noticed as many different wall colors as the crystals Teresa wore. In the basement the windows were at ground level and looked out to the backyard. A grey cat lounged on the sofa under one of the windows. It looked up, annoyed with the commotion, as the six new guests invaded its space.

Once everyone was downstairs, Teresa welcomed her guests, "Lady Celeste, Lady Luna, Lady Reina, blessed be! Please make yourselves at home while you are here, and don't hesitate to let me know if there is anything I can do for you. The others should be here shortly. Drew called us when your plane landed. Would anyone like any coffee, or if you need, the bathroom is right over there," she said pointing down the hall to her left. She politely acknowledged Sophie and Elise although she didn't seem concerned about whom they were, or maybe she was waiting for them to be introduced instead of being forward and asking.

Coffee, Ryen thought, was maybe the key to this woman's energy. Chesna introduced Sophie and Elise, and as expected, Teresa was very warm towards them after that. Then Drew and Teresa excused themselves to bring down everyone's luggage. Each person had only brought one carry-on bag, but they were still in the limo.

Sophie wandered through the basement and reported back that there were two rooms with beds, one without any windows. Hopefully Teresa had more rooms upstairs if there were at least seven guests spending the night, or it might be wise to pair up for safety. Although nothing unexpected had happened, Ryen still hung on to the uneasy feeling she'd had since her dream about her mother.

Drew and Teresa returned not only with the bags they went to retrieve, but with the rest of the expected guests, and then some. A woman in her late thirties, with shoulder length blonde hair and a wary look on her face, came down the stairs, followed by the girl that had to be Gelina. She looked like a cheerleader ready for practice: blonde hair in a ponytail, yoga pants, a fitted t-shirt, and flip flop sandals even though it was a chilly evening. She smiled with enough sincerity that it showed in her brown eyes, but she looked tired. Behind her followed a young man Ryen assumed was her partner from the Incarnation Ceremony. He had some Latino qualities to him, with shaggy black hair that hung in his eyes. He smiled too, as his eyes nervously took in every face in the room. Another young man, with hair so short Ryen immediately thought military, followed behind the shaggy haired boy. Military boy had concern written all over his face, and he looked over everyone in the room with scrutiny.

Teresa began the introductions with the overseas guests, "You will all recognize Lady Celeste, Lady Luna, and Lady Reina."

68

She paused so the appropriate "my ladies" and numerous offerings of "blessed be" could be exchanged, and then she continued, "This is Sophie and this is Elise. They will be visiting Cornell in the morning as part of their cover story for being here." Turning to the newest arrivals, in the order they had come down the stairs, "My Ladies, may I present to you, Mary, Gelina's mother."

Mary nodded her head respectfully, and she reached out for her daughter's hand. Teresa continued, "As I'm sure you've figured out, this is Gelina," she said beaming. Gelina smiled again and nodded her head. Ryen noticed she gave her mother's hand a squeeze.

Before Teresa could continue, Ryen addressed the blonde girl, "Gelina? As in Angelina?"

The blonde answered her politely in a soft but strong voice, "It's short for Evangelina actually. It was my great grandmother's name."

She and Ryen smiled at each other, and Ryen could sense some tension leaving the girl's body.

Turning to the shaggy haired boy, Teresa said, "This is Nate. He is, was, Gelina's ritual partner, the father." Teresa seemed to stumble over her words as she described Nate. Nate nodded nervously, eyes darting about. His hair remained in his face and he seemed to shrink backwards a bit, away from the rest of the group.

Teresa paused, unsure of how to proceed, so the last member of the group spoke up for himself, "I'm Holt," he said very confidently. "I'm Gelina's fiancé. If she's going with you, I'd like to escort her," and then he quickly added, "if that would be all right."

Ryen admired Holt's respectful forwardness and she could clearly see now that Nate was intimidated by the self confidence of this older boy. The fact that he was Gelina's fiancé, well, that undoubtedly added to the tension between the two. Ryen wasn't going to answer first. This was unorthodox. Not only that Gelina was engaged, nor that he wanted to come with them, but because he was not a witch.

Chesna took the lead, "Tell us about yourself, Holt, and why you'd like to come with us?"

Holt looked at Gelina and she gave him her warm smile with a nod of encouragement. "I know I'm not a witch, so you probably don't want me to know your secrets. But Gelina and I are engaged, and we'll be married before I join the Marines next summer. I already know everything about who Gelina is, and what she's doing." He paused for a moment. Ryen could tell he was struggling with something internally. She guessed it had something to do with what his fiancé had done with Nate last night. He collected himself quickly and continued, "I know this is a huge deal for you guys, but this is a big deal for Gelina too, and I want to make sure she's safe and that she's ok emotionally. I can't imagine her doing this without me or me doing this without her."

"Do you have a desire to join the Coven?" Chesna asked.

"No ma'am," he responded in a respectful tone. "I'm well aware of Gelina's beliefs and I have no problems with them. I just don't know if they are my beliefs. I would do anything for her, but I can't be something that I'm not. That would be deceitful to her and to myself."

Ryen's respect for Holt grew and Chesna was noticeably impressed as well, "Well done. You seem very self-aware. However, the safety of many is at stake here. We don't normally allow average humans to be privy to our headquarters. How do you suppose we solve that problem?"

Holt looked at Gelina again, as if confirming something they had previously discussed, "You may put a spell on me so I don't remember where we are, if that will help."

Kora spoke next, "You are not opposed to us using magic on you?"

"I'm not afraid of magic; I'm just not sure I want to be a witch. I don't know if I believe in any higher power enough to make that sort of commitment. But like I said, I'll do anything for Gelina. I know some crazy stuff happened with you all in the past with outsiders, but that's not me." His last sentence made

Ryen shudder. She had just witnessed what those "outsiders" had accomplished. Nobody wanted a repeat of that history.

Chesna replied, "You may stay with us tonight, but we will have to discuss this. We'll have an answer for you before we leave tomorrow." To Nate she asked, "Is it your wish to come with us?"

Nate reminded Ryen of a cornered mouse. She wondered if he would be different under other circumstances. When he answered his voice sounded just as nervous as his face looked, and his voice cracked a couple of times during his response, "Yes, I think I should. My parents think I should, but if you don't think I should, I understand."

"Relax, my child, you are welcome if that is what *you* want." To Mary she said, "I assume you will be joining us, especially in the midst of all this excitement," she gestured towards the two boys.

Mary replied with a simple "Yes," and then added, "My husband will be joining us closer to the birth."

Chesna nodded in agreement and then to Teresa she asked, "It is already late, and we have a long day ahead of us tomorrow. Would you be so kind as to show us where we will be sleeping?"

Teresa snapped to attention after being caught up in the little drama playing out in her basement. "Well, I assumed you would want to determine the 'who', but as for the 'where', there are two rooms down here, both with queen-sized beds, and both of these couches pull out into beds. Upstairs I have two guest rooms available as well."

Chesna wasted no time in her decision on sleeping arrangements, "I think Elise and Gelina should get to know each other, so they can share the room down here without windows, for safety. Lady Reina, would you like to be on guard in their room?"

Ryen felt Chesna was thinking the same thing as she, not just as a safety precaution, but maybe Ryen could get some insight into the situation and these two boys that might be joining their group from Gelina. Of the three in the Triumvirate, if this girl was going to open up to anyone it would probably be her. The whole thing was bizarre, but then again this was Ryen's first experience with it all too. She wanted to be someone that Gelina could trust. "Of course," she said to Chesna.

Drew, who had been quiet during this whole exchange, added, "I'll stay up stairs in case anyone needs anything." As he finished, his gaze lingered on Kora, and she gave him an almost unnoticeable smile. Ryen wondered if it had been noticed by anyone other than her.

Kora motioned for Chesna and Ryen to join her in the back bedroom, as everyone else started moving to get pillows and toothbrushes.

Once the door to the bedroom was closed Kora asked, "Well, what do we think of these boys?" Both she and Chesna turned to Ryen first.

"Well," Ryen began, "it's an interesting situation. This Holt character seems on the up and up. I didn't get any negative vibes from him. He seems like he genuinely wants to be with Gelina, regardless." She knew that her admiration and curiosity were both apparent in her tone. "The other boy, he's another story. He's very nervous and doesn't seem sure what to think about any of this, but that could also just be the adolescent in him. I think he's no older than 16, and I'd guess Gelina and Holt are 18."

Kora concurred, "Yes, I think we should keep an eye on Nate. He may be more in need of our guidance and support than the others. Holt is willing for us to use magic on him, so I think we can trust him."

"I agree about the shifty one. We'll keep an eye on him. Ryen, do you think you can find out what Gelina thinks of him?" Chesna asked.

"I'll do my best before she falls asleep, but she may not be excited about sharing personal information with people she's just met."

"I think the time for privacy has passed," Chesna said. "There will be no such thing as privacy for the next months of her life. She may as well get used to it now."

Ryen felt a pang of empathy for Gelina. She knew what it was like, showing up in Florence where everyone already had opinions formed of you and plans laid out for you. Everyone would want to get to know her and be a part of her time at the compound, and unintentionally they would be intrusive and annoying. Gelina had accepted her role for the Incarnation Ceremony, but Ryen wondered if she had thought about the duty that comes next. At least Gelina didn't have a whole life of duty ahead of her. She'd be welcome to stay with her daughter forever if she wanted, but that would be her choice.

There were few doors that were forever closed to Ryen; love, marriage, and children were about the only ones. Before she knew her role in life she had been too young to think too much about those things anyway, but as she got older, every once in a while the lack of possibility would try to claim power over her. It never lasted more than a few minutes, but it gave her just enough time to think about what her life might be like if she weren't the Maiden. She didn't really mind. Ryen loved the certainty and purpose of her life; there was a feeling of safety in it.

"I'll be alert for any signs of danger," Ryen said as she got ready to leave the bedroom Chesna and Kora would share. She brushed her selfish thoughts behind a door in her mind and closed it.

"You should try to get some rest too," Kora told her.

"After the last two times I've fallen asleep, I could use a break from that sort of 'rest'," Ryen said, thinking again of the dream she had on the plane and the visit she received from Zeta.

"Your spell worked didn't it?" Chesna asked. "I thought that was the case, that is why I said that on the plane, but did someone visit you?"

"Yes," Ryen confessed. "I can tell you all about it on our flight tomorrow. It will sound like recounting a book I've read to any nosey travelers. Although neither experience had a happy ending. So, should I tell Sophie that we will have a total of nine in our group?"

After a moment of thought, Kora nodded and Chesna said, "Yes, nine. I'm sure everyone back home could use a little excitement. This will definitely shake things up at the compound."

Kora added, "Let's hope this doesn't cause too much excitement."

Chesna proceeded to crawl into the bed, "I'll take the side by the window, Kora."

Kora hesitated slightly before responding, "Don't wait for me. After being scrunched on plane all day I'm in need of a little walk to stretch my legs and calm my mind before bed."

Ryen smirked knowingly at her. *Yeah, and I bet there's a gentleman upstairs who is planning to escort you on this walk*, Ryen thought. Aloud she said to Chesna, "I wouldn't wait up if I were you." A little grin appeared on Chesna's face as well, and Kora narrowed a glare at both of them, then shrugged and winked as she walked out of the room. Chesna shook her head in amusement and said to Ryen, "I guess turn the light off on your way out."

"Good night," Ryen said as she flipped the switch. She could see Chesna getting comfortable with the light from the moon outside shining through the window.

She thought of Kora, and the "walk" she was going to take. Marriage and children might not be in the cards for any of them, but that didn't mean they had to live a life of celibacy. Celibate, Kora was not. She shook her head and laughed a little too as she crossed the hall to the room she would share with the two teenagers. She could hear voices on the other side of wall, so first she went to give Sophie her instructions for their flight plans tomorrow.

Teresa was still bustling about, trying to make sure everyone had enough blankets and pillows for the night. Again Ryen was drawn to all of the different crystals the energetic woman was wearing. Ryen, herself, was wearing peridot earrings that had been a gift to her shortly after she arrived in Florence. When the sun hit them, they were a similar color to the green in her eyes. If she wasn't dressed up for some event, these were the earrings she chose to wear. She had her smoky quartz pendant, that she was never without, around her neck and an amber ring she had purchased on a personal trip to Venice a few years ago.

An idea popped into her head. "Teresa, do you have an extra moonstone I could borrow for the night?"

"Of course, my Lady. Are you having trouble sleeping?"

Not wanting to divulge too much information, Ryen answered as truthfully as she felt necessary, "Just a few energy draining dreams. I could use a night off."

All too eager to help out, Teresa responded, "I know just what you need." She hurried off, up the stairs.

At about the same time Ryen was becoming uncomfortable standing awkwardly around while the others were preparing to sleep, Teresa reappeared with a little cloth satchel in her hand. "I made you a dream bag: a moonstone, a little lavender, and some chamomile oil. That should help you sleep, dream, or no dream, whichever is your goal. If you recharge it with energy each night it should last you about a week."

Ryen was overcome with gratitude. She knew if she asked for something just about every witch in existence would bend over backwards to do as she wished, but she had merely asked to borrow a stone for the night. Teresa went well above and beyond. "Thank you. You didn't have to do all of that. I really appreciate it!" She squeezed Teresa's hands as she handed her the satchel.

"No trouble at all. I'm glad I could do something to help, hopefully. I wish you a peaceful rest." With that, she went back upstairs. Ryen said good night to the already sleepy foursome in the main room and headed to the windowless bedroom.

There were still voices coming from the room, but Ryen knocked softly and entered. Both girls were seated on the bed, and appeared to have already formed a friendship.

"Lady Reina, we figured that you would like the bed tonight, so just let us know when you want us to get out of your way," Elise said full of respect.

"Nonsense," Ryen said. "You are doing us a favor by being here, and," turning to Gelina with a little wink, "you are pregnant, get used to special treatment. You two may share the bed." As she looked around the room she happily added, "I'll take this comfy looking recliner!" That was a pleasant surprise. She wouldn't push either of the girls from the bed, but she was glad the room had a chair. Sleep or no sleep, the chair would be much better than the floor. She also added, "And while we are in the privacy of this room, feel free to call me Ryen. There's no need for formalities here." Maybe that would help Gelina open up more around her too.

Ryen put her sleep satchel in the pocket on the front of her dress and settled into the chair in the corner of the room. The girls stopped talking and looked at her, clearly wondering if they were disturbing her. She assured them that they were fine. "You guys can talk as long as you want. You won't bother me."

Through their conversation Ryen learned that Gelina had also visited Cornell, but she had planned to attend a community college in the fall and then transfer somewhere else when Holt found out where he'd be stationed after basic training. She and Holt had gotten engaged just before Winter Solstice. Ryen noticed she seemed sad the more in depth she spoke of her relationship with Holt. Ryen couldn't help herself, "How does he really feel about this? I know he said he supported you, but this has got to be a lot for a boyfriend/fiancé to handle."

Gelina was very hesitant to answer. Ryen figured it was more due to whom she was speaking than the topic. After a few moments of thought she slowly began her answer, "I told him right away that I had been nominated for the Incarnation Ceremony. I explained what it was about, and how much of an honor it was, and that if I was selected, I would accept. He grew up in the church, so I compared it to Mary being chosen to have Jesus. As expected, at first he was upset. He didn't want me to do it for obvious reasons. But after he saw what it meant to me, he said he would support me no matter what happened. I don't think he really thought I would be the one the Goddess chose for this honor. I'm not sure that I really thought it would be me either. He was waiting for me this morning, and I knew he could tell from my face that our lives would no longer be what we had planned. For a moment I saw something in his eyes that made me want to cry, but then he hugged me and told me he loved me. That was all I needed to hear."

Ryen could sense her inner turmoil. Gelina truly felt honored, but with resignation, like being the chosen sacrifice to the gods in some ancient civilization. "I can only imagine how hard this will be on your relationship, but it shows great courage, in both of you, that you are both willing to do this together. I think you've found a very respectable guy."

"I know. Thank you for saying so," Gelina replied.

Ryen decided to push a little further, "So where does Nate fit into all of this?"

Gelina let out a big sigh, "I don't know. I think he expected this even less than I did. I'm not sure that it has really sunk in for him yet, but his parents insisted that he at least come along. I don't know how long he'll stay. Holt makes him nervous for obvious reasons, so his presence won't make it any easier on him."

Ryen withdrew herself from the conversation and closed her eyes. She was still listening, but only partially. She was thinking of her sleep satchel, still afraid to fall asleep but so wanting a few hours of rest. She thought about tomorrow, hoping their return trip would go as smoothly as the first half. She thought about Gelina, Holt and Nate, and about how their lives had been turned upside down. She thought about the little girl that had started growing inside Gelina this morning, and how someday she would join Ryen and Kora in leading the Coven. Somewhere amidst all those thoughts Ryen drifted off into a peaceful, dreamless sleep.

Chapter 15

"If you don't wake up, we're contemplating leaving you here. And I'm pretty sure Teresa would be overjoyed to have you as a house guest indefinitely." Sophie shook Ryen's shoulders trying to stir her to wakefulness through violence.

Ryen slowly opened her eyes. She was still in the windowless bedroom, so regardless of the time it was dark. Somehow, some time during the night she had moved from the chair in the corner to the bed. A little confused and a little irritated with Sophie she asked, "Don't you have a college visit to chaperone?"

"Yeah, that already happened. I bought you a t-shirt," she said cheerfully.

Ryen sat up so quickly she got a little light headed. "What do you mean 'that already happened'? What time is it?"

"It's 11:30, so if you want to shower or anything, you need to get up now."

"11:30?!? How did I sleep that long? Why didn't anyone wake me? Gelina's coven members were coming this morning." Ryen rattled off her questions while climbing out of bed. With the minimal light coming in from the hallway, Ryen stumbled to locate her bag.

"We tried to wake you before we left for Cornell, but you wouldn't wake up. Lady Celeste said you needed rest, so Drew and Holt moved you to the bed. Gelina's coven members came, and were received by Lady Celeste and Lady Luna. A lot of them are still here actually, upstairs. We leave for the airport in less than thirty minutes now."

None of this made sense. Ryen had never been that heavy of a sleeper. Was it just the peace the sleep satchel provided, or did someone put a spell on her? A little panicked she asked, "Nothing out of the ordinary has happened has it? Anything we should be on our guard about?"

"Not to my knowledge, but I don't know that I'd be told all pertinent information. Everyone seems fairly relaxed though, no more on edge than to be expected." Ryen knew Sophie wasn't lying, so maybe things were still ok.

"Fine, I'm going to take a super quick shower. Can you tell the others I'll be upstairs in a few minutes?"

"Yep, sure thing," Sophie said with a smile as she turned the light on for Ryen on her way out of the room.

No one was very talkative in the car. Ryen spent her thirty minutes watching out the windows for vehicles that might be suspicious or following them, but nothing seemed amiss. Nor was there anything out of the ordinary at the small airport. Ryen tried not to focus on the emotional exchanges taking place between those leaving and those staying.

Once again Ryen was reminded of her past. The last time she was in the United States boarding a plane to leave the country she was nine. No one was seeing her off. Only the woman posing as her mother knew their trip was not a vacation, but an escape. Ryen had been terrified the whole time that her real mother would know what she had done and be scouring the country looking for her, most likely to kill her now that Ryen was no longer ignorant to the world in which she belonged. Kora, Chesna, and Maggie had come to her rescue after all. They had arranged for a witch from Pennsylvania to meet Ryen with fake passports and plane tickets in less than twenty-four hours of their telepathic encounter. It had been Ryen who had come up with the plan to fake her death in the river near her house. The fact that it had worked was proof to Ryen that the Goddess was on her side.

When her mother and Joshua returned from their "retreat" to find her missing, search crews discovered her sandals and towel at the edge of the river as if she had been going swimming. The recent rains had made the river dangerous, so it was quite believable that a nine year old girl would have gotten swept up in the current. To Ryen's credit, search dogs were unable to track her scent anywhere else but the river's edge. Pieces of Ryen's t-shirt and swimsuit washed up miles downstream, and after several days it was presumed that her body had been washed out to the ocean.

Luckily for Ryen, no one thought about looking upstream for her. Thanks to a movie she had watched, and the help of the witch the Triumvirate sent, without her parents' knowledge she used a series of ropes tied a ways up river that had allowed her to walk and swim against the current to the shallow crossing. She had been on a plane to Europe before anyone even knew she was gone.

Ryen gave her head a little shake to bring herself back to the present. Their private plane was waiting for them. Their party had already started walking towards it from the terminal door located at ground level. Being one of the last to leave, Ryen observed the exchange that went unnoticed by everyone else. Drew had just kissed Kora's hand as they smiled at each other, sharing a secret. Ryen looked away before she was discovered, but as Kora joined her to walk to the plane, she couldn't help herself from saying, "Looks like Gelina's dad may not be the only visitor from Iowa we could expect to see in the future."

Kora's green eyes twinkled with mischief, but she just smiled and gave a little shrug. "I'm not usually one for strings, but we'll see."

Chapter 16

Cash reached over and hit snooze on his alarm. He wasn't motivated to get out of bed yet, so he lay staring at the ceiling, replaying the events of the past evening.

It had been a lucrative night at La Noche Oscura. The club had been packed; a hot, new DJ had drawn in a big crowd. Every cell in his body had been pulsing with the beat of the music, but the frustration of not getting what he wanted and the pressure of Rafa watching his every move had clouded his judgment. No, not clouded, more like blocked out all together.

The useless prick from the Louvre had finally returned Cash's stack of messages, but had nothing helpful to offer. Cash could tell through his voice that he knew exactly of whom Cash was asking, but he insisted that the Arts Council did its own thing and he was merely a liaison; he had no knowledge of the woman from the gala. Cash had refrained from calling him out on his bullshit only because he didn't think it would do any good. Had he been within physical proximity it would have been a different story. The weak human mind of the incompetent curator would have melted under Cash's powers. And had that failed, at this point Cash wasn't opposed to using physical pressures to get answers.

Still staring at the ceiling, Cash ran his hands through his hair. He should have gotten on a plane right then and flown to Paris to talk to Monsieur Pichon. Had he done that instead of staying, brooding at the club, he couldn't help but believe that the night would have gone much differently. He imagined that perhaps he would be lying next to his mystery woman right now, not reliving a mistake that could have cost him everything he had built.

He prided himself on keeping and enforcing the rules of his establishments. No humans were to have anything done to them against their will, nor would they be mortally harmed by his vampire patrons. Cash himself had even doled out punishment to people who merely brushed that line. His clubs were safe and prosperous because of his diligence. But last night, when the fog in his head had cleared, it was his hands that had been holding a girl whose pulse was so faint it was hard to pick up even with vampire hearing in the silence of his soundproof office.

When he closed his eyes he saw her seemingly lifeless body still draped in his arms, her long black hair cascading towards the floor, and two puncture wounds from his teeth dotting the pale smooth skin of her neck. Cash clenched his jaw, knowing that if Rafa hadn't heard his panicked mental cries and come in with a cool head, then the poor girl might actually be dead this morning instead of recovering nicely at the hospital. Not only had Rafa been calm, but he had the necessary mental clarity, as Cash had been frozen in the shock of his actions, to come up with a plausible cover story when the ambulance arrived: having too much to drink and falling on and breaking her glass. It wasn't completely rock solid, but the paramedics had believed them, and no police showed up afterwards. The girl's mind would know nothing different, also thanks to Rafa. Although her health was stable now, it did little to improve his mood.

Cash was normally cool and collected. He couldn't remember the last time he had fallen victim to impatience, and he hadn't lost control like last night since he was a child. It had also been a very long time since Cash had struggled with an outcome not being what he wanted.

So far his two employees who claimed to be master hackers had yet to turn up anything useful within the Arts Council's databases, though he knew that they had only been working on it for a couple of days. He was aware that his need to find and conquer was the real issue. He had been back and forth with his remaining options, and he hated to admit that it might be time for his last resort. He had always been an independent spirit, much to his mother's chagrin, but it wasn't until he was an official adult that he realized he didn't have to obey her every wish and whim. Although she had the ability, with her status and power, to strip him of his free will, Cash gambled every day that it would be more embarrassing to do that than to allow him to keep refusing her subtle and sometimes not so subtle demands. However, he did not doubt that she would use a slip-up like last night to her advantage. Cash took a deep breath. He needed to clear his head of last night and of the things that had gotten him there in the first place.

This was a dire situation. He couldn't afford any more lapses in judgment or control. Cash reached for his cell and dialed a number. Hating himself for what he had almost done, and hating what he was about to sacrifice for the chance to get what he was after, he cringed at the voice that cheerfully greeted him on the other end of the line. "To what do I owe the pleasure of such an early morning call from my youngest and most rebellious son?"

"Good morning, mother. I didn't realize this was considered early for you."

"It's not. I was referring to *your* business hours. But then I guess you must be just getting to bed." Cash chided himself. He had left the door wide open for that snide comment. Normally he avoided the topic of business with his mother, though she usually found some way to bring up the fact that she didn't consider his work legitimate, or worthwhile.

He knew he had to lay the groundwork just right or Callandra Di Marco would sniff out his ulterior motives. "Actually, quite the opposite. I've been doing some thinking since I traveled to Paris. I have decided to stop fighting you, at least somewhat."

"I am intrigued. Continue." Her tone was suspicious, and rightfully so. He would need to be careful how he played his hand. Cash mentally kicked himself for calling before even getting out of bed. He was far from the top of his game. He knew he couldn't just come right out and ask her for a favor. This was the necessary foundation he needed to put down. On one hand it might be easier just to ask for what he wanted and let his mother make a counter offer, but this way he might be able to develop his own useful connections and cut out the middle man, or woman in this case.

"Your plotting to get me involved in something seems to have finally been successful. My trip to Paris piqued my interest with the Arts Council."

He could hear the calculation in her voice through the phone. "It is true that I hoped the gala would be a good experience for you. And it does please me to hear you've finally decided to take on some of the family responsibility. Although I am curious to what has all of a sudden changed your tune."

Cash took his time to give an appropriately thoughtful response. The latter part of his answer grating against his instincts, with aversion to the upper echelon of vampire society, he replied, "I've always thought it's a worthy cause. Frankly, there are many important people involved, and it would be valuable for me to become better acquainted with them."

"So this is a selfish move." It wasn't a question and Cash refrained from responding. His mother continued, "I suppose I'd be surprised if it wasn't. Someday, my wayward son, you will realize where your place is and abandon these childish ventures of yours. Perhaps your involvement in the family's humanitarian activities will further that along more so than my pushing has done. The Arts Council is a decent place to start."

Cash took slow, deep breaths through his nose. He had expected this to be painful, but listening to his mother speak so pretentiously, having no clue what his life was really like and belittling his successes, he was struggling to hold his tongue. He felt the walls closing in around him as he often had in college while taking the classes she chose for him, making the choices she wanted, to groom him for the family business. Although hesitant, he had started this call with confidence and optimism, but as his old feelings of being trapped by someone else's life were resurfacing, he wasn't sure he could pay the price she would undoubtedly demand.

He let her go on for several minutes even after he knew he had lost his nerve. He wanted to find the mysterious beauty that consumed his thoughts, but he wasn't ready to be shackled the way his mother would have it. When she eventually realized that he would not follow through, she would chalk it up to yet another disappointment, one of many on her list from the son for whom she still had such ridiculously high expectations. Once again the image of the black-haired girl pushed its way to Cash's mind. If his mother got a whiff of that near-disaster she would claim her power and demand he come home. His failures would be all that she would see. Cash hoped that one day she would be able to see what he had done with his life as success. He wanted her to be proud of who he was, not whom she wanted him to be. Maybe someday she would see him as a man in his own right and not a little boy in need of her guidance.

They ended the conversation with plans to sit down to further discuss Cash's new role. It wasn't entirely his mother's fault, but Cash hung up the phone feeling a combination of deflated, desperate, and even more frustrated than he had been when he woke up this morning. So much for solving all of his problems before breakfast.

"Tell me I did not just overhear what I think I heard." Cash had been so distracted by the muddy water of the various women currently residing in his head that he had not noticed Rafa enter his apartment.

"It's not what you think. I was finally attempting to use my mother's connections to find that girl from the gala. It didn't go quite as I had planned."

"So, what now? Are you leaving for Florence to be your mom's bitch?" Although Rafa said it jokingly, they both knew there was truth in his words, and Cash knew in his friend's eyes he looked defeated.

"No. I realized about halfway through our conversation that it was a bad plan."

"Good." Rafa threw the shirt that had been hanging over the chair at Cash. "Now go take a shower. I have somewhere to take you."

Cash gave him a questioning scowl. "I'm not really in the mood for a fieldtrip."

"And therein lays the reason. I was thinking that maybe I wasn't very sensitive last night." Cash winced at his friend's words. "It was a big deal; it still is. But I need to make up for being an ass and you need to blow off some steam over all the women in your life."

Cash chuckled at Rafa's last comment. Cash's reputation with the ladies was legendary. He was usually the master of control. The last few hours would certainly contradict that. Letting off steam sounded like a great idea. "What were you thinking?"

A devilish smile broke out across Rafa's face. "I called in some favors at the racetrack. There are two new-model Aston Martins waiting for us."

Cash let his friend's excitement infect him. This sounded like the perfect remedy for his mood today. "Rafa, you are a good friend. Give me five minutes."

Chapter 17

Ryen sat down with her tea at a table outside her favorite café down the street from the Prado. Being back in Madrid was bittersweet. She was excited to get back to work. She had missed her coworkers and her second favorite museum, but she would miss being in Florence. She felt guilty, partly for not fully doing justice to her role as Maiden, but there wasn't a whole lot going on now that Gelina was safe at the compound. If she were being completely honest, she needed a break from the craziness of the past couple of weeks. Having four new residents had thrown the compound into slight chaos. To Gelina's chagrin, everyone was fawning all over her. She was trying her best to take it as humbly and graciously as possible, although she did beg Ryen to take her with her to Spain, claiming her four years of high school Spanish could be useful. Ryen felt sorry for her, so she promised to take her in nine to twelve months.

People were uneasy about Holt's presence, but Ryen still stood by her first impression of him. Nate, on the other hand, had opened up a bit. He was really enjoying taking classes, and he was emerging from the shadows of his parents, the Incarnation Ceremony, small town life, and the struggles that so many adolescents experience. Ryen was glad that he was proving her first impression of him wrong.

Ryen looked at her phone; she had at least forty-five minutes before she needed to be in her office, the perfect amount of time to get her museum mindset together. Thanks to Teresa's strong sleep satchel and Ryen's power, she was well rested, but it had probably run its course. Tonight she'd go back to sleeping without its aid. It was going to be a busy day at work since she'd been out of her Madrid office for almost a month and completely away from the Council for a good two weeks. With everything she had to catch up on, Ryen doubted that she'd have difficulty sleeping when she finally settled down. Sophie had wanted to go get a drink and some tapas after work at some bar for months, but Ryen had at least convinced her that they could wait a few more days.

She pulled up her schedule for the day from the email Sophie had sent her last night after they arrived in Madrid. She would have some time to herself once she arrived at her office, but then she had to check in with the restoration department, and she had some follow up phone calls to make regarding some pieces the museum was attempting to acquire. Some of them were through private owners which meant she'd need to have the provenance of each checked out, but there were a couple that were going up for auction. She'd need to be on top of those if the Council was going to win the bidding. Inevitably there would be some Arts Council patrons interested in bidding for their personal collections, and Ryen would have to do her best to convince them otherwise.

Taking a moment to savor some more of her tea Ryen noticed a young man sitting at the table next to her. A majority of people had already made their way to work, leaving the café nearly deserted. The boy had a Spanish-English pocket dictionary on the table before him, as well as a map of Madrid, and a booklet about Madrid's "must see" attractions. She always felt the need to encourage others to appreciate art, so she interrupted his research and asked, "Are you planning on visiting the Prado?"

At first the boy was startled, but he also seemed relieved to find someone who spoke English, "Um, yes, I am. I'm in town for only a couple days so I want to make the most of my time."

"It's good to have a plan. If you like modern art you'll want to make sure to go to the Reina Sofía museum." Ryen reached into her bag and pulled out a couple of entrance vouchers for both museums. She always carried a few with her to generously share her love of art.

"Thanks," the boy said looking Ryen in the eye. There was something familiar in his dark brown eyes. She took a deeper look at him trying not to come off as creepy.

"You won't need to wait in line with those, so that should save you some time to enjoy more of Madrid. You're only here for a couple of days? Are you on a school trip or visiting family?" Ryen wasn't sure why this boy made her so curious.

"Neither. This is actually my first stop in Europe. I was going to have a layover here, so I decided to take advantage and make it a few days instead of a few hours. Rome is my final destination."

"What's in Rome?" Ryen asked, still wondering why she kept pushing.

"I'm going to be doing an internship at the Vatican," he answered, sounding excited and apprehensive at the same time.

"Business, artistic or religious?"

"Mainly business related. I'm not Catholic, but I'm looking forward to the religious connections as well."

For some reason this was unsettling to Ryen. This boy didn't appear to be a fanatic or even someone who believed in the supernatural, but that didn't mean he couldn't be. What was it about this kid? "I'm sure your parents are proud of you for scoring such a prestigious internship. The Vatican is very private, so you must be something special," she said with sincerity.

"Yes, they are. They would love for me to still be at home, but they couldn't deny the importance of such an opportunity."

"Well, I hope you enjoy your time here, and good luck in Rome," Ryen said as she gathered her things to head to work. "I'm going to the Prado later; maybe I'll see you there. What's your name?" She didn't want to tell him she worked there, and she was uncomfortable giving him her name, but she wanted to know more about him.

"Elijah Turner, but my friends call me Eli. Thanks again for the tickets." He was genuinely gracious and unsettlingly flirtatious.

"No problem," Ryen said as she turned and walked away. After she had turned the corner she hit one of the direct contacts on her phone. When the person on the other end answered, Ryen didn't even take the time to say hello, "I need you to run a confidential search as soon as possible."

"Did you somehow find a secret acquisition on your way to the office?" Sophie asked, not reading the concern in Ryen's voice.

"No, this is Coven business, not for the museum. I'm not even sure what has me on edge, but I figure it's better to be safe than sorry. I don't want anyone to know about this unless it's something worth knowing." No need to have everyone think she was paranoid.

"Are you at least going to tell me what's going on?"

"If it turns out to be something, then yes. Sorry Soph."

"You know my imagination will take its own liberties, but ok, who I am looking into?"

"An American by the name of Elijah, or Eli Turner. He recently arrived in Madrid and is headed to the Vatican for an internship. Not sure where he's from, but I'm guessing he's around twenty."

"I'll get on it today," Sophie assured her.

"Thank you. I'll see you in about five minutes," she said as she pressed the "end" button. Hopefully this was nothing. But if Ryen's inklings were even close, this could be a matter of security.

Chapter 18

Ryen's first week back at work was busy but uneventful. Paranoia caused her to check the security footage of the entrance each day, and Sophie was waiting to hear back from her government friend. She hadn't seen the café boy at the museum all week, so she was certain he was no longer in town.

Ryen hadn't made as much progress with her acquisitions as she had hoped either, but there was at least some progress to note. Being gone for so long filled her schedule. She usually worked through lunch and the days flew by with little time to take a breath until she left for the day. She was glad today was Friday, and she didn't have to come in to the office tomorrow unless she wanted to. To be honest, she probably would at some point, but no need to set an alarm for it.

In spite of her original reluctance to go out to a bar, by the time she and Sophie were ready to leave the museum, Ryen couldn't wait to get some tapas. Her stomach growled as she thought about some ham and olives.

"How far is this place?" Ryen asked as they made a train switch on the metro.

"We'll get off in a couple of stops and then it's just around the corner."

"Not that my stomach would care right now, but it's supposed to be good, right?"

"Yes. It's not new. It's been open for over a year, but it really got popular last summer when a usually harsh critic gave it a really great review. Now it's being mentioned in travel magazines and books. I appreciate you finally agreeing to come with me."

Ryen heard the insecurity behind Sophie's words. Ryen really did consider her to be one of her only friends, and because of her duty to Ryen, Sophie didn't have many other friends either, especially when she moved around to different cities following Ryen. But Ryen walked a fine line of what she was able to share with people outside of the Triumvirate, so Sophie often felt more like an employee than a friend.

"Well, I'm starving. Let's hope it's not too packed with tourists. What's it called again?"

"Fortuna," Sophie said.

Ryen could feel Sophie's enthusiasm increase as they exited the metro and walked down the street. The metro and the streets were filled with people, locals and tourists alike, but this stop wasn't that close to any tourist sites, so maybe Sophie was right about this place. It was only seven, and the restaurants they passed wouldn't be opening until eight at the earliest. The tourists were scouring the streets for places to eat, not being used to the late dinner hour here in Spain, and the locals were heading for a drink on their way home from work. With it being the start of the weekend, the streets would only get more crowded as the evening approached. With only a couple other bars in the area, this "Fortuna" bar had certainly picked a prime area for successful supply and demand.

"Oooh, look! That new nightclub is right next door. Maybe we can hang out for a while and go there afterwards," Sophie was about to explode with elation.

Nightclubs were definitely not Ryen's thing, they never had been, and now she felt she was too old for that scene. For Sophie she might consider it, but tonight was out of the question. "How about we spread out the fun, Soph? It's only our first week back in town. Maybe in a week or two?"

Although Ryen could tell she was disappointed, Sophie was also encouraged by Ryen's willingness to try it out. "That's probably a good idea. I heard the place has a dance floor on the roof too. I'll look into any guest DJs that may be coming soon, but I hear their regular DJ is pretty good."

Ryen smiled as Sophie babbled like a teenager. She made a mental note to let Sophie out more often to have fun. As they approached the door to Fortuna, Ryen stopped short.

"What's wrong?" Sophie asked, "I thought you were starving?"

"Sophie, this place is crawling with vampires. I can feel them without even going in."

Sophie's face showed how Ryen had just burst her bubble, but she wasn't giving up that easily. She practically pleaded, "No, Ryen. Remember, food critic, tourists, even if there are vampires, this is a popular place. It's never been mentioned in the news for anything bad."

"And you know that not everything bad gets reported in the news." Sophie scowled and pouted a bit and Ryen continued, "Fine, but anything remotely dangerous, and we're out of there." They had come this far; she may as well humor Sophie a little more. She made sure her mental shields were operating at full force and reminded Sophie to do the same.

As they entered, Ryen noted that it was well lit. There were a number of humans, out numbering the vampires she had sensed. The two guys behind the bar were definitely vampires, but as she scanned the room, there were maybe only three or four more she could see, and they were sharing food and drinks with human companions. While she was here, Ryen vowed to keep an eye on those ones in case they tried to take advantage. She thought she had felt more from outside, but maybe she was wrong.

There were a couple of available tables, but Sophie wanted to sit at the bar. Vampire bartender number one came over to take their order and attempted to dazzle them. He was physically good looking, like all vampires, but his tall lanky form was not attractive to Ryen, on top of being a vampire. His dark brown hair had unnatural highlights and was spiked in various directions. He had eyeliner accenting his dark eyes, and Ryen thought his shirt could be a size or two bigger as well. He spoke to Sophie first, "Hola, Soy Rico. Gin and tonic, on the rocks, dirty, right?"

Sophie beamed, clearly impressed, and nodded in agreement. As he turned to Ryen he frowned. Ryen smiled at him and sent a mental message, *"Can't read my mind?"*

Attempting to ignore the stumble her mental voice caused, he recovered quickly, "And for you?"

Ryen answered without adding any sweetness to her voice, "We'll share a bottle of the house Rioja, but bring the bottle here and open it in front of us." She gave him a tight-lipped smile that didn't change the glare in her eyes. When he walked away she chided Sophie, "God Sophie, close your mind! He totally pulled your drink order right out of your head! Please be smart."

Sophie made a pouty face, but nodded in understanding. Ryen watched vamp bartender number one as he appeared to be filling vampire bartender number two in on what had just transpired. Bartender number two was more natural. His thick blonde hair hung in waves just past his chin. Although shorter than number one, he was thicker, and his tight shirt accented his muscles instead of looking like it belonged to a toddler. He seemed more authoritative than vamp bartender number one, maybe a manager or something of that sort. He glanced over at Sophie and Ryen. Ryen could feel tingling around the edges of her brain as he tried to get inside her head. He frowned slightly as he realized it wasn't working, and number one continued to talk. He was probably complaining that they were demanding and a pain in his ass, but Ryen could care less as long as he followed her instructions.

Outside of the compound or one of her apartments Ryen didn't accept a drink she hadn't opened herself, or seen opened in front of her. She'd learned that lesson the hard way. Bars were usually the most resistant to her request. If she really wanted to piss them off she'd order a top shelf shot and demand a brand new bottle be opened. Food was usually safe, but if she weren't so hungry she would think twice about ordering food here.

Chapter 19

Cash was working in his office that was connected to both his bar and the club. The increase in tourism as summer edged closer had increased business at the bar. Tapas time was coming to an end, and most tourists would be heading back to sightseeing or their hotels. It worked well to keep the bar open for longer hours when the club was open. People leaving the club wanting food, or people wanting a break from the noise of the club could easily find what they were looking for right next door. It also provided a more low key location for any vampire clients and the human delicacies they found at the club. He hoped the club would be as busy tonight as it had been every weekend since it opened. Cash was loving the business success. On a personal front, there still hadn't been any breakthroughs in his own search for the elusive woman from Paris, nor through the hacker search. Even with the several setbacks, including the failed attempt to enlist his mother's help without her knowledge, he was far from being ready to give up.

Despite the recent protocol scare Rafa was still encouraging him to drown his temporary detective failures in the indulgence of beautiful club goers, but he still had no desire for them. Along with a new fear he would deny, they bored him. At this point he attributed it to having a variety of cheap alcohol in front of him, but what he really wanted was the expensive, premium, limited release bottle that was difficult to acquire, the glass that would be slowly savored and worth every penny.

The door opened and Rafa's blonde head appeared. Cash asked, "Were your ears burning?" Rafa gave him a confused look that Cash waved away adding, "Something wrong?"

"We have an interesting situation out front. Rico is freaking out. There's a couple of high maintenance chicas out there getting on his nerves, but that's not the weird part. Neither of us can get a read on one of them. Rico swears that she spoke to him telepathically though. She's not a vampire. Thought you'd want to know in case she causes any trouble."

"I'll come check it out as soon as I finish the beverage order for next week." Rafa closed the door behind him, leaving Cash to his paperwork. He wasn't too concerned about the girl at the bar. Rico was easily rattled, so he probably just imagined that she had communicated with him. He'd look into it though, just in case. He could use a little distraction, but he didn't need any new trouble just hours before the club opened.

It took him less than ten minutes to finish the beverage order, and he polished off the glass of whiskey on his desk before he headed out front. He opened the door near the bar and made eye contact with Rafa who nodded his head in the direction of the girls in question. As Cash's gaze moved towards them, he froze, dumbfounded.

SON OF A BITCH! He recovered quickly, but a glance at Rafa let him know he had projected his thoughts farther than he had realized. *That's her,* he sent back to Rafa. This was unbelievable. After weeks of searching, using his connections and powers of persuasion, and employing seemingly useless computer hackers, he hadn't been able to find the woman who had been occupying his every thought. He had thought he would go mad from his failure, and now here she was. *She* had wandered into *his* bar.

She was still as beautiful as when he'd first seen her, but now she was dressed in a black linen business suit that covered most of her skin instead of the elegant dress she had worn in Paris. She and her friend were enjoying a plate of ham, olives, and cheeses, along with a bottle of wine. Also, causing him to smile, they were biting into his new bacon wrapped dates. The mystery woman's body seemed tense, more so than when she was speaking in front of a room full of people. Her hair was up, although the style's hold had weakened from a day at work, and several stray pieces were falling towards her shoulders. He reached out with his mind to get a deeper glimpse at what made this woman tick and was met with a solid wall. He kept trying, growing more adamant as the seconds ticked by and he couldn't get through. After his third attempt she turned her head and her green eyes, laced with golden fire, bore into his with a fierce hostility.

Back off, vampire, he heard from her mind.

Holy shit! Rico was right; she had spoken to him telepathically. She wasn't a vampire; he knew that much from seeing her at the gala. He'd known humans who could successfully block out mental intrusions, but most weren't strong enough to last for a prolonged amount of time, and he'd never encountered one who could effectively communicate with their mind. She continued to intrigue him. She also knew he was a vampire. It took a moment for it to click, but she had to be a witch.

She looked at him again and raised her eyebrows as if challenging him with a "so what?" expression. Had he projected that again? He glanced at Rafa, who was still watching him, but he didn't seem to be hearing Cash's thoughts. Was this maddening woman inside *his* head without him knowing it? He threw up his own shields to be fair. She smirked and turned back to her friend.

He couldn't approach her and be successful after that mental encounter, but he still wanted more information about her. Rafa hadn't said anything about her little blonde friend, so he'd start there.

Cash appeared to be doing some work behind the bar so as not to be completely obvious to this devil woman. He was pleased to find Sophie's mind wasn't nearly as impossible to penetrate as her friend's. She had some defenses up, but either she wasn't aware enough or strong enough to notice when Cash made his way past them.

Her mind was what he had expected, what he usually found in girls' minds: a constant string of errands, desires, irritations, questions. It seemed her boss sitting next to her kept her on a rather tight leash. Although his ultimate target clearly harbored ill feelings towards vampires, this one did not. He'd be naughty and plant a suggestion for her that would inflict revenge on Rafa for his pressures and interference in Cash's sex life. He was fairly certain that his friend would end up happily satisfied, and Rafa could definitely help this one break free of her cage. Of course it would be sure to ruffle her friend's feathers in the process.

Trivial things aside, he did get some information that would have made the past weeks' search much easier. Her name was Ryen. It had not occurred to him that she would have a nontraditional name. He was guessing if he went back to those online profiles, he would find her name next to one of the picture-less descriptions he had passed off as a guy. That was frustrating. Currently she and Sophie were working here in Madrid at the Prado. Those were things he could work with.

Suggestion planted successfully, he heard Sophie ask her aloud, "Can't we stay and go to the club tonight? We're already here."

Ryen shot him a look again suspecting that he had gotten into her friend's head. A smile tugged at his lips as he tried not to laugh. He didn't play fair; it would serve her well to figure that out now. He was in no way finished with her.

She let her anger at him seep into her voice as she answered Sophie, "They're in your head Sophie! I think it's time we get out of here and get you some fresh air." She didn't bother motioning for either bartender to come over, she just spoke in their direction knowing that they would hear her, "Can we get our check, please?"

Cash sent a quick message to Rico that their visit tonight was on the house. He had to stifle another laugh watching her try to decide what to do as Rico told her there was no charge. He could tell she didn't want to accept his gift and wanted to leave money to cover it, but that would mean her money would be given as a tip to the bartenders, and he'd bet she hadn't planned to tip them at all. Generally at a restaurant the tip was included in the total of the bill, but at a bar it was at the customer's discretion. She was riled up enough not to be generous tonight regardless of the quality of service.

Finally she closed her wallet, looked at him again, and said "Gracias," but the sarcasm in her voice expressed that she didn't mean a bit of it. Cash chanced her control exploding and gave her a wink before she turned and walked towards the door, pulling poor little Sophie behind her. *Yes*, Cash thought, *this was only the beginning.* She might be a tough one to crack, but Cash was due for a challenge, and he'd enjoy the ride...

"I think the dark haired one liked you," Sophie said as they walked back to the metro stop. Concern consumed Ryen. She had only suspected that those vampires had gotten into Sophie's head, but her silly chatter confirmed it. Just how much had they planted in there, and what information had Sophie unknowingly provided them? Hopefully they were content to get a rise out of their customers and leave it at that. But just in case, she'd see what she could find out about this bar and its employees and owner.

"Sophie, they are vampires. They are ruthless and blood driven. They were just messing with us. Unless you can improve your mental defenses, it would serve you well to stay as far away from that place as possible." Ryen didn't care that Sophie was stung by her reprimand on her skills or that Ryen had basically forbade Sophie from returning. Sophie was too trusting, and apparently too weak, to protect herself with vampires.

"I apologize for being so frank, my Lady, but that's bullshit! And you know it. Maybe that dream you had on the plane connected you to your mother's blind prejudices more than we thought." Ryen could tell Sophie was sorry she said it as soon as it came out of her mouth, but she couldn't stop herself. Her hand flew up and smacked Sophie across the face. The horrified look in Sophie's eyes matched the feeling inside Ryen.

"I'm sorry, Soph. I didn't mean to hit you. I couldn't stop myself." Tears were running down both of their faces.

"No, I deserved that. I don't know what made me speak to you that way. I was way out of line."

"I think it was our encounter at the bar. It took all of my control not to do something to that smug jerk back there, and I know they were in your head," Ryen said taking a closer look at Sophie's cheek.

"I'm sorry, Ryen. You're nothing like your mother, but you have this hatred towards an entire race. You are always so open-minded, but it's like you can't see that they are just like everyone else. Ok, sure, they have powers that put them above humans, but so do we. Just like humans and us, there are good ones and bad ones, and some that walk that fine line."

Ryen knew that ultimately Sophie was right, and she was being a hypocrite, but Sophie didn't know what she had experienced at the hand of vampires;

no one really did. She had never told anyone the whole story, not even Kora and Chesna. "Sophie, my mother takes the lives of people she and her fanatic church group think are evil just by existing. My aversion to vampires is based on experience, not ignorance for something I don't understand. I don't trust them, and think we should be cautious. I've never set out to kill someone." Guilt hit her that Sophie couldn't see. She may not have set out to do it, but that didn't mean she wasn't directly responsible for someone's death.

"Let's just get back to our apartments and forget this night happened," Sophie said. Ryen gave her shoulder a squeeze and agreed. This night couldn't be over fast enough.

Chapter 20

The sun was warm on Ryen's skin. It had been a hot summer day, but the sun was going down now. The past week had been a tornado of emotions: the pain of Maggie's passing mixed with the excitement of taking her oath as Maiden, and to top it off, she was on a date with the guy she had been crushing on for months. She had basically stalked him and his friends every night as they hung out around Florence. He hadn't noticed she even existed until the other day. Maybe she looked older and more beautiful now that she had the power of being the Maiden coursing in her blood.

She had been sitting next to the fountain in the Piazza de la Signoria watching him. Suddenly he had come over and started talking to her, asking her if she wanted to get some gelato with him sometime. She had almost passed out. He was way too old for her, but he was so gorgeous: short sandy brown hair, hooded blue eyes, and lean athletic body. Watching him and his friends play soccer was one of her favorite pastimes. Being a vampire only made him more alluring.

It had taken Ryen awhile to convince Kora and Chesna to let her go on a date. In the end they had consented because it was only for a couple of hours, before dark, and they ultimately felt Ryen could take care of herself. She was one of the most powerful witches in recent history, even though she hadn't touched on the depth of her true powers yet. Ryen thought their decision also had something to do with letting her experience some joy after the sadness of mourning had been hanging over the compound.

Now she was walking along the Arno with Cai. Every once in a while he would reach over and link his pinky finger with hers, causing her heart to skip a beat and her cheeks to turn bright red. That probably amused him.

"Hey, I'm meeting some friends for soccer practice. Would you like to come watch?" he asked. Maybe he had noticed more about her than she had thought; then again, she hadn't been too subtle in her stalking.

Ryen struggled with her answer. She really wanted to go, but she had told Kora and Chesna that she wouldn't be gone for more than a couple of hours. "Um, yeah, but could I borrow your phone? I forgot mine."

"Of course," he smiled, showing his beautifully straight, white teeth, as he took his phone out of his pocket.

Ryen avoided talking directly to either Kora or Chesna, and dialed the main line to the compound, getting the switchboard secretary. She left a message to tell them that she was going with some friends to watch a soccer practice and would be home later. She smiled shyly at Cai as she handed him back his phone. He sent a text before putting it back in his pocket.

As they walked north, they stopped to get a couple of waters. Ryen waited outside the store for Cai to bring out the drinks. She was really thirsty and drank hers within a couple of minutes. After a while Ryen's head started to feel hazy, and her legs were becoming lethargic. When she mentioned it to Cai, he assured her they were almost there. She assumed he knew where he was going, but as they were nearing the train station and some industrial buildings she was confused. She'd never seen any good places to play soccer around here.

"Cai, are we almost there? I think I need to sit down. I'm feeling a little lightheaded."

"It's just over here," he assured her. She blacked out before they reached their destination.

Ryen awoke in a sweat. She knew when she went to bed she would be visited by some version of this dream. Such was her fate whenever she had an encounter with a vampire. Another reason to despise that jerk from the bar. Tonight's dream didn't seem too terrifying, maybe even pleasant. Except Ryen knew what happened next: waking up in that dark warehouse, not being able to move, or scream, or use her powers, and the guy of her dreams turning out to be a monster.

It was still dark outside, but Ryen didn't think she could go back to sleep. She got up, took a hot shower, and made herself some tea. Maybe she'd feel better if she went on the offensive, just in case. She pulled out her laptop and sat down in her big fluffy chair. She wondered if she should dwell on this, but typed "Fortuna Madrid" into the search box.

One of the first things on the list of results was a recent article from a local paper. Ryen clicked on it and began skimming. It was mostly complimentary, similar to what Sophie had said: good critic reviews, tourist destination. It mentioned the bar's proprietor, an Italian named Cash Di Marco. Ryen looked over the comments on the article, seeing nothing negative. There were a lot of comments from women talking about "hot employees", others about good service, good prices, and there were some mentioning the club next door, La Noche Oscura. Ryen wondered if the reason there were only positive comments was because the employees made sure everyone at least thought they'd had a good experience when they left.

Ryen typed the club's name into her search box next, and found an article from a couple of months ago when the club first opened. She wasn't that surprised when she read that this Cash Di Marco was also the owner of the club, and apparently he had other clubs in different cities throughout Europe as well. Neither of the articles she read had any pictures, but she had a hunch. She went to her search box one more time and typed in Cash Di Marco.

Sure enough, the picture that popped up was none other than the irritating jerk from the bar. She was definitely not letting Sophie go to this club now. If there were vampires at one establishment, there were sure to be vampires at the other. Ryen glared at his pictures for a few moments before reading the information that was beneath it. Successful entrepreneur... late twenties... eligible bachelor...paparazzi favorite, yeah, that was not a surprise either. Ryen was sure he probably flocked to the spotlight at every chance. The next part was a little surprising: born in Florence...Swiss boarding school, college in the United States...Harvard Business School dropout...left the family business. Maybe that's why his name seemed familiar to Ryen. She was aware of the Di Marco Estate and Winery outside Florence. Ryen felt sorry for his family. He seemed like quite the pain in the ass all around.

Ryen couldn't help herself from clicking on the link for photos. What she found disgusted her. There were dozens of pictures with model type girls, never the same one more than once. Not that she wanted to stereotype models, but these poor girls were probably easy targets for mind manipulation. Ryen didn't want to think about what he did with them before he dumped them for the next one. They were no doubt victimized without any recollection.

Ryen's internet search had not helped her calm down from her dream; it had only left a bad taste in her mouth. She still didn't think she could go back to sleep, so she decided to go for a jog. The sun was starting to rise, and maybe a run would help clear her head and calm her down.

Chapter 21

"Good morning, Sophie," Ryen said as she walked across the common space towards her office. "I can't take any calls this morning. I only have fifteen minutes before I have to go down to restoration. I'll forward you the emails you can handle for me."

"No problem," Sophie said. Things were getting back to normal. For days after the incident outside of Fortuna, both Sophie and Ryen had tried to overcompensate for the guilt they both felt for their parts, and then there was simple avoidance. Work had been the easiest. There hadn't been any downtime at the Prado for a good two weeks. Outside of work, Ryen was trying to give Sophie some space but was still keeping an eye on her. To her credit she hadn't tried to go back to that bar, or to the club. Ryen was glad for that.

"Did you do anything exciting yesterday?" Ryen asked, already knowing the answer due to her watchful eye.

"No. I did laundry, caught up on some TV, cleaned, you know." Sophie said it as a figure of speech, but Ryen did know. She felt guilty for spying on her friend, but she didn't trust her judgment. It didn't help that every day of the last two weeks Sophie had delivered a message that Cash Di Marco had called and had some business to discuss with her in regards to the Arts Council. Ryen thought it was nonsense of course and did not return any of his messages, but it meant that he was talking to Sophie each day, and Ryen wasn't sure if he could influence her over the phone or not.

Ryen sat down at her desk and pulled out her planner. She had her meeting with the restoration department at 8:30, then a walk through with the curator and the head of restoration to decide which pieces to take off display next, then she had to head across town to an auction house where there was a Goya painting going on the block. The auction would take at least a couple of hours from her day. At four she had a conference call with the Arts Council board. Ryen pulled up her email, skimming its contents and forwarding ones that didn't need her personal attention to Sophie. The others she would work on when she was on the metro today or during anytime she may have here at the office.

Ryen jumped at the buzz from her desk phone, "Sophie, I said I didn't have time this morning."

"Sorry, but I think you should take this."

Ryen pushed on the blinking button for line one. "Ryen Cardona," she said into the receiver.

A silky baritone voice answered her, "Ah, Señorita Cardona, I've reached you at last." Her irritation with Sophie nearly shot her through the ceiling. Ryen knew who it was before he continued, "My name is Cash Di Marco, and I've got something you may be interested in."

Ryen knew she had no interest in anything he had. She was fuming at Sophie. It was clear that he had gotten her name and where she worked out of Sophie at the bar, and now he'd convinced her to ignore Ryen's instructions. This was definitely dangerous, and she wanted nothing to do with him. "Not interested," she said more calmly than she felt and hung up before he could say anything else. As she exited her office to go to her meeting, she looked at Sophie and said, "We'll discuss this later." If it were anyone but Sophie who was the recipient of that tone, they would be worried about their job. Sophie, however, wasn't really "employed". Her duty was to the Coven, but her recent lapse in judgment may be putting even that in danger...

Cash had been truly excited when his little secretary pet had put him on hold instead of taking his name and number for the eleventh time. He knew this woman was going to be hard to crack, but he didn't think she would ignore messages at work that were intended to be about business. He had been wrong, and now she had hung up on him without even hearing why he was contacting her. Perhaps it was time for a face to face, but the plan he was hatching would involve going over her head. No doubt that would piss her off, but at least she wouldn't be able to ignore him, and of course he'd keep working on her assistant. Little Sophie was more stubborn than he had first

106

thought, but he was close to breaking her from a distance. If he had a face to face with her as well, then he might be able to move along that part of the plan too. He realized Rafa had stopped his cleaning behind the bar and was watching him with an amused expression.

"She hung up on you?" Rafa asked, trying to conceal the smile that was forcing its way across his mouth.

"It would appear so," Cash responded. "She is maddening, but I'm just getting started."

"Yeah, leaving messages is quite the master plan," Rafa teased.

"Is that a request for time off, without pay?" Cash threw back at him, but Rafa knew he was only joking. "For your information, I've decided to change my approach."

"Probably a good idea since you can't get into her head, and your name and looks aren't getting you anywhere this time."

Cash hated to admit that Rafa was right. He was out of practice. He had never had this much trouble acquiring a woman he wanted, but he could step up his game.

Chapter 22

After speaking, even briefly, with Cash on the phone this morning Ryen was expecting some part of her nightmare to visit her. She had not expected a visit from a past life, but similar to her experience with Zeta, she was now wandering around a castle or a more modern version of one, with that feeling that this was a memory.

The chilly stone reminded her of the compound in Florence, but here the walls were covered with tapestries and there were no modern conveniences like electricity. She had been going from room to room looking for someone, anyone, from whom she could gather some information, but she hadn't found anything but conservatively furnished bedrooms. The hallway was dark except for where natural light peaked out through doorways.

She went into one room to look out a window and could see green and golden fields and trees for miles in each direction. There was noise coming from a building she guessed to be a stable, but she still didn't see any people. Finally she found a staircase and headed down the stairs, eventually finding the kitchen. There were several people here, and just like before, they were oblivious to her presence. Ryen listened to their conversations, trying to figure out where she was.

Some of the women were putting together a platter of meats, fruits, and cheeses that were to be served soon, for breakfast. The others were busying themselves with preparations for tonight's dinner. It seemed the master of the house was expecting an old friend. Ryen turned as another girl spoke from the doorway to the hall where Ryen had just entered, "Lady Marlow is on her way down."

This caused several of the women to gather up platters of the breakfast food and hurry out a door on the wall to Ryen's left. She followed. The hallway they walked down was small and dark, but the women in front of her did not falter in their steps. Before too long they entered a large room with windows stretching up two levels. There were multiple fireplaces with openings large enough for a group of people to walk into, again reminding Ryen of her home in Florence. Down the center of the room was a long, wide wooden table with huge wooden chairs. The women were setting their platters down at the far end of the table. Just as they sat the last platter down, the door a few feet behind the chair at the head of the table opened.

At first Ryen only saw the man holding the door, dressed in male clothing that resembled the natural colors and fabrics worn by the women she had followed from the kitchen. But then a woman dressed in such contrast to the others in the room entered. As she did, the women from the kitchen gave a bow and greeted her with, "Good day, Lady Marlow."

Ryen watched her enter with grace. She nodded her head and said, "Good day. Thank you for breakfast. You may take your leave." With that the women turned and went back through the hall from whence they came. Lady Marlow was wearing a dark red satin dress that split at the empire waist revealing cream colored fabric down the front. The dress had long sleeves with slits at the elbows and armpits to allow freedom of movement. Lady Marlow's brown hair was braided down her back, and a silver medallion hung past her chest from a long string of pearls. She wore no modern makeup, but her natural beauty was more than sufficient.

The man that had been holding the door came over and pulled the chair out for her. "Thank you, Charles," she told him and then lightly waved her hand, dismissing him as well.

Ryen wasn't sure if she should have followed one of the servants out of the room, but she couldn't take her eyes off of the elegant woman in front of her. After a few moments of watching Lady Marlow pick a few items off the platters, she spoke out loud without looking up, presumably to Ryen, "Would you like to sit down?"

Ryen quickly walked over to a chair near Lady Marlow and sat. Lady Marlow looked up at her, and Ryen recognized her own green and gold eyes. "Welcome to my home, Ryen."

"Thank you," Ryen said, feeling awkward and not knowing if she should be quiet or ask the questions that were burning in her head.

"My name is Afton. This will be our only time to speak. As you know, this is my memory that you are seeing, but aside from this conversation I have no control to change anything. You will see the events as they played out in my time."

"Thank you for allowing me to know your story," Ryen told her, not knowing what else to say.

"My history is your history," Afton said and then began eating her breakfast. Ryen took that as her cue to go back to being invisible.

Afton hadn't quite finished her breakfast when both she and Ryen noticed a commotion coming from what Ryen assumed was the front of the castle. Soon the door burst open and a tall muscular man with dark brown, shoulder length hair, and a closely trimmed beard came bustling through. Afton rose quickly from the table and turned to greet him. Ryen felt warmth inside her as the man took Afton in his arms and kissed her quite thoroughly on her lips. When he pulled away he placed her face between large, strong hands and smiled down at her. The look he gave her made Ryen blush.

"Lady Marlow," the man said in a husky voice.

"Lord Marlow," Afton replied smiling back at him. "I have missed you."

"Likewise, my love. I would take you upstairs and spend the day reacquainting myself with your beauty, but I have brought my dear friend with me, and I fear that would be rude."

Ryen was impressed; Afton hadn't blushed at all, but Ryen's cheeks were on fire. "Then I shall look forward to this evening," Afton said, running her hands over his broad shoulders and winking.

"Temptress," Lord Marlow said with a growl. Then he took her hands in his and started to lead her from the room. Ryen followed closely behind.

As they reached what Ryen could only describe as a foyer, if a castle could actually have one, her eyes were captured by a strong man who was looking around at the décor. His hair was a dark auburn, appearing brown, but was deep red when the light from the massive open front door hit it. He was tall like Lord Marlow, but where Lord Marlow's muscles were large and bulging, his were long and lean. Ryen guessed he was skilled with the sword that hung at his waist. Both men were wearing leather boots that came to their knees, over tight riding pants that looked as soft as suede. Lord Marlow's coat was properly buttoned up the front, but the other man's jacket was completely undone, as was the top of his white shirt, revealing a V of tanned skin on his chest. He looked over at the couple approaching and Ryen noticed gorgeous blue eyes.

When those eyes took in the woman walking his way, he was mesmerized. "Bradford, I thought surely your descriptions of your wife's beauty were an exaggeration. I see now that your descriptions did not come close to her exquisiteness."

"My dear, this is my childhood friend, Shaw, Shaw Cooper. Shaw, this is my wife, Lady Afton Marlow."

Afton held out her hand, which Shaw took and raised to his lips. "Pleasure to meet you Mr. Cooper," Afton said as she curtsied.

"Believe me, the pleasure is mine." To Bradford he said, "It's a good thing you didn't introduce us during your engagement, or I would have stolen her away from you." He was obviously joking with his lifelong friend, but something in his tone was very serious as he looked into Afton's eyes. Ryen felt something coming from Afton, but she didn't quite understand it. She was flattered, and Ryen could tell she thought this Shaw was good looking. But Ryen had felt before how much she loved her husband, so the stirring in her center that Ryen felt didn't make sense.

Like her previous experience with past lives, Ryen closed her eyes for a moment to think, and when she opened them her surroundings had changed. It was nighttime now. The fireplaces and candles provided the light for the large room with the table. There were plates of partially eaten food, with more than enough to feed twenty more still on the platters. A couple of musicians were in the corner with guitar or fiddle type instruments. Afton and her husband were dancing nearby to a lively tune, while Shaw lounged in a chair by the fire, watching the couple with a keen eye. Ryen felt a pang of protectiveness for Afton, but knew she was being silly.

Afton and Bradford were laughing as they danced. This Afton was almost a complete opposite to the woman Ryen had watched enter this very room earlier today. Now she was having fun, relaxing, freely being herself. A hint of jealousy flared in Ryen. She could relate more to the Afton from earlier than to this one; though she could hesitantly admit she wouldn't mind relating to the latter at least once in a while.

Ryen pulled her attention from the happy couple to look at the man by the fire. He was smiling, enjoying watching his friend's fun, but Ryen still saw something serious in his eyes. Ryen noticed as the song slowed and Bradford pulled Afton close to nuzzle her neck, her eyes focused on Shaw. The two of them looked at each other from across the room, and Ryen felt that stirring inside Afton again. It made Ryen uncomfortable, and she was glad when Bradford announced he was taking his wife to bed.

"Charles will be at your service tonight, Shaw. We shall see you for breakfast, unless we are otherwise engaged." He elbowed his friend in the ribs and Shaw gave him a knowing smile, but something else lingered in his eyes. This time both Afton and Ryen blushed.

Ryen closed her eyes in hopes that she could fast forward through the night's activities and was relieved that when she opened them it was daylight. She was with Afton, Bradford and Shaw again by the front door. Afton was sad and pleading with her husband, "Do you have to go? You just returned."

"I don't want to leave you again, especially so soon, but this is urgent. I'm needed in the village as soon as possible before the discord gets out of hand. Hopefully it will only take a day or two at the most."

Afton pouted, eliciting a hug and deep kiss from Bradford.

"My friend, I shall accompany you to assist in any way I can," Shaw offered to Bradford.

"My dear friend, you could assist me most by looking after my wife while I'm away. She has been left alone too much of late."

"Of course," Shaw said. Ryen saw the glimmer in his blue eyes. It was as if he had offered to go knowing what his friend would say, prompting his friend to practically beg him to stay and care for Afton. Afton's eyes showed a bit of worry, more for whom was staying than who was going. He's clever Ryen thought, and Afton looked at her as if she had heard her and was agreeing.

Ryen watched throughout the day as Shaw shadowed Afton through her daily activities. He often asked her questions, sometimes things he already knew the answers to, just to get her to speak.

"I'm going to take advantage of the sunlight and read in the library now," Afton announced. "Feel free to get some fresh air if you'd like. Charles can have someone saddle a horse if you wish to go for a ride."

"I'd rather have company for a ride, especially when I'm unfamiliar with the area. But I don't mind reading a bit."

Ryen could sense that Afton was trying to distance herself from Shaw, but not because she found him undesirable company. No, it was because she was drawn to him. That was the feeling Ryen had been getting since yesterday that she was just beginning to understand. But if Shaw was feeling this pull, and Ryen was sure that was the case, he was doing nothing to stop it. His disregard for his friend angered Ryen, and she wanted to tell Afton to kick him out.

"Wouldn't you rather sew or paint or play an instrument to pass your time?" Shaw was insinuating that reading was not a desirable activity for a woman, at least by society's standards, not necessarily his. His motives seemed to be getting a rise out of his companion.

"I do all of those things, but I prefer reading to those other indoor activities."

"Is reading your favorite indoor activity?" He asked with a little bit deeper voice.

Afton understood his implication and answered, "Of the activities I do without my husband, yes."

Good girl Ryen thought. This exchange and Afton being here alone with Shaw were making Ryen anxious, but at least no one was being killed in this memory. At least not yet.

Ryen spent the early afternoon watching Afton read and pretend that she didn't notice Shaw staring more at her than the book he had on his lap. Once in a while Afton would look up at Shaw, and Ryen could feel the secret messages being sent between the two. She could feel the battle taking place within Afton. When Shaw asked if she'd accompany him on a ride around the grounds, Ryen could hear her argue with herself.

Afton weighted being rude and sending him out alone or being alone with him when there weren't servants around every corner. She could use the fresh air, she liked riding, and it would pass the time. Afton knew he wouldn't betray his friend and she wouldn't betray her husband. She stared at him, imagining the softness of his hair, the strength in his hands. Ryen knew Afton's resolve was fading, and she wasn't surprised when she eventually agreed to go.

They dismounted their horses in a wooded area to walk along a stream. As they walked, Ryen saw Shaw's hand brush Afton's. Ryen felt an electric jolt in her arm. A few minutes later he wrapped Afton's hand in his as they continued to walk. This time the jolt was a continuous current of thrumming electricity. Ryen could feel Afton focusing on staring straight ahead and concentrating on putting one foot in front of the other. Shaw pulled her to a stop and turned her to face him. Afton shut her eyes and lowered her head. Shaw put the hand that wasn't holding hers under her chin, guiding her face to look up at him, but she kept her eyes squeezed shut.

"Shutting your eyes won't stop what you're feeling," Shaw said.

"How do you know what I'm feeling?" she asked still squeezing her eyes tight.

"Because, I feel it too. I felt it as soon as I laid eyes on you yesterday, and I know you did, too."

Slowly Afton's eyes opened, "He's a good man. I love him."

"As do I," he said with his face so close that Ryen knew Afton could feel his breath on her face. It was warm and had an earthy smell, like a summer day.

Both of them were breathing slowly, but Ryen felt Afton's heart rate increase as Shaw brought his lips down to hers. At first Afton resisted by trying not to respond, but that electricity that the contact with his hand had created was now tingling on her lips. He persisted gently, and she let go of that last bit of resolve she had been holding onto. As her lips parted, the electric current set her whole body on fire.

Shaw's arms pressed her to his hard lean body and she molded hers to his. She raised her hands to run them through this thick hair that was as soft as she had been expecting.

Shaw broke the connection of their lips to blaze a trail of kisses down her neck, and Ryen thought Afton was going to pass out. Afton's hands pulled Shaw's shirt from the waist of his pants and she ran her hands across his warm, hard chest. While he continued to kiss her neck, and ears, and her mouth, Shaw worked at unfastening the buttons at the back of Afton's dress. When he had completed his task, he swept Afton up in his arms and laid her down on his jacket.

Ryen turned away, embarrassed that she had kept watching for so long. She closed her eyes to be taken somewhere else, but instead she continued to feel what Afton was feeling. She had experienced something similar when Zeta and Tarik were together in the garden, but that had been an intense, deep love of a couple whose love had grown stronger and stronger over time, hadn't it? What she was feeling now was a passion she had never known, physically nor emotionally. Right then she forgave both of them for betraying Bradford. She knew they couldn't help it. Something was pulling them together that they had no control over, and it was supplying that current that

115

Ryen knew was running over every inch of Afton's body, because she could feel it too. Ryen wanted to cry for the feeling of happiness that Afton was experiencing. As she heard Afton cry out, a tear rolled down Ryen's cheek.

Ryen was relieved when she opened her eyes and was back in the castle. She was aware that a few days had passed since the event she had witnessed, and she knew that in that time Shaw and Afton had been together more than once. But now they were whispering in the dark of Afton's room.

Afton was crying, "I know this is how it has to be."

"If we were to tell him, it would destroy him, and I know neither of us wants to hurt him."

Afton was nodding, "I love you, and I always will."

"I love you, too. But we can never see each other again. I left him a letter in my room saying I had to leave suddenly to tend to my ailing father, which isn't even a lie. I will not accept an invitation to visit again, although it will take all of my strength. You were happy before, you will be happy again."

"You have to go now?" Afton asked with pained surprise.

"I wouldn't be able to control myself to see you in his arms, and I fear that if he saw us in each other's presence we would betray our secret without a word."

After several moments of silently starring at their entwined fingers Afton sighed with resignation, tears streaming down her cheeks. "I know you're right. I just don't want to let you go."

"And that's why I have to go." Shaw wiped the tears from her cheeks with his thumbs as he held her face, and then he kissed her with the same passion Ryen had felt at the stream. The electricity was still there, but this time, when he pulled away, Ryen felt Afton's heart being pulled from her chest. Both Afton and Ryen watched Shaw walk reluctantly from the room and close the door. Ryen knew if she followed, she would see him continue to the stable to get his horse and ride away. When the door shut, Afton fell to the bed in

116

convulsive sobs. Ryen's heart literally hurt. She felt her time coming to an end. She closed her eyes and waited for her escape. Before she opened her eyes to see her own room, she saw a brief glimpse of another scene.

Bradford and Afton were walking along the path by their home with a little boy. When the sun hit his hair it was a deep red, and Ryen saw his blue eyes.

Chapter 23

When Ryen awoke in her room she was crying, crying from the intense feelings Afton had for Shaw, crying for the pain Afton felt when Shaw left her forever, and crying at seeing the little boy with his father's hair and eyes. Ryen wondered if Bradford had ever figured it out. He would have had to have been blind not to see his friend's characteristics in the boy, but in the last scene Ryen saw a happy father and mother, a family. If Bradford knew what happened, it appeared he kept that knowledge to himself.

Ryen was at a loss. She had cast the spell to learn about her past lives to help her understand herself, to help her grow and be more wise for decisions she would have to make. As she analyzed these two parts of her history she wasn't sure what lessons she was supposed to have learned. She could argue that both women had felt guilty for doing things they shouldn't have, even if they didn't regret them. Both had had intense relationships that Ryen knew nothing of herself. Both had been stripped of those relationships. Although it wasn't something she thought of often, maybe the purpose was to help her come to terms with how that kind of love was not meant to be part of her life, now or in her past. Maybe her predetermined life-path was actually saving her from that sort of pain.

As a member of the Triumvirate, her duty and focus were to the Coven. A personal relationship, or at least a serious or committed one, would conflict with her purpose. That was precisely why she had ended her last relationship over a year ago. That guy had wanted things to be more serious than to what Ryen could commit. Kora had plenty of personal relationships, and though Chesna was more discreet, Ryen was aware of her ongoing relationship with someone inside the compound. But to her knowledge neither of them had even had relationships the likes of Zeta nor Afton. And yet the compound was filled with love. It was an assumption proven by history that the Triumvirate members were physically incapable of having children, but they were a family unto themselves. They raised the future Maiden as if she was their own child, and they took care of children who came to the compound for education, so in that aspect they weren't denied the love of being a parent.

Despite how Ryen had had her virginity ripped away from her, she had learned that sex could be enjoyable, though it had taken her quite some time to be willing to take the risk of being intimate in that way. It wasn't easy for her to find someone with whom she was willing to make that connection. Witches were out of the question because they knew who she was and it was awkward. Were they really attracted to *her* or her power and position, or did they think they had to serve her out of duty?

This seemed to be Ryen's problem alone. Kora and Chesna stuck with witches. For Ryen, that left random strangers or a co-worker when lack of better judgment won out. Being human, they couldn't know anything about the supernatural, so multiple encounters with one person were difficult. Sometimes it felt like more work than it was worth. Even then, she had never felt the same physical or emotional intensity as Zeta or Afton. It seemed a little cruel now, but she knew because of whom she was, she never could nor would.

While Ryen was laying there pondering the meaning of sex and love, her alarm went off. Since she was already awake she didn't hit snooze like she usually did, but pulled up her email to check her schedule for the day. There was an emergency message that a last minute meeting had been scheduled at nine this morning with the chairman of the Arts Council and the curator of the Prado. She wasn't supposed to meet with the chairman until next week. Something must have come up, causing him to change his travel plans. Ryen was a little frustrated. She had planned to have all of her acquisitions in order for the meeting, but since it had been moved up by several days she was out of time. She had a feeling the chairman was going to be less than impressed with what she would have for him today. Oh well, she could at least show him what she was working on, and that she had been able to get the Goya at the auction yesterday. She sent Sophie a quick email to organize the files she'd need for her meeting before heading to the shower.

119

Chapter 24

Ryen smoothed the front of her dark blue dress as she walked into the front room of her office area to Sophie's desk. The light weight cotton and knee length were good for the outdoor temperature, but the three quarter sleeves helped in the cool, temperature-controlled museum environment. Unfortunately, the cotton was prone to wrinkles if Ryen was seated for too long.

"Sophie, do you have those files for me? I need to get down stairs. I'm already running behind."

"Here they are. But Ryen, there's something I should tell you."

Ryen held up her hand to stop Sophie, "It will have to wait until after my meeting, Sophie. I have to go. I can't be late this time."

"I know, but I think you'll..."

"After my meeting! I don't have anything else to rush to afterwards, so I'll come straight back here," Ryen cut her off as she walked out of the office. She didn't know what had Sophie so worked up this morning. It wasn't like Sophie was the one who had a surprise meeting with her boss and wasn't as prepared as she would like.

Ryen walked down the stairs to the floor below where the curator's office was located. He had a small conference room attached to his office where they would be meeting. She just needed to relax. Demitri had never been displeased with any of her work, so he would understand that she hadn't had time to thoroughly accomplish what she had hoped to present to him. He was always professional at work, even after she had broken off their very short relationship, but sometimes his Eastern European personality came off harsher than he meant, especially to people who didn't know him well.

Ryen was so wrapped up in what she was planning to present that she wasn't paying attention to her senses that usually guided her. If she had been paying more attention she may not have been as stunned when she walked into the conference room.

120

She knew she was a couple of minutes late due to having to go upstairs first, and Demitri was never late, so she began apologizing for her tardiness as soon as she opened the door. "Demitri, Pablo, I'm so sorry I'm late, but I had to..."

She didn't finish her sentence as her eyes fell on the third person in the room. All three men had stood when she entered, but the dark haired man in the expensive grey pinstriped suit, with the lavender shirt that brought out the blue of his eyes, was who had caused Ryen to temporarily lose her ability to speak.

Her eyes narrowed as she looked at him. *What the hell is* he *doing here?* She thought.

"Come in. Have a seat Miss Cardona."

Miss Cardona? Demitri hadn't called her "Miss Cardona" in over two years, and he hadn't used that tone with her since the conversation that ended their relationship over a year ago. Ryen didn't like whatever was going on. "Of course, Mr. Petrov," Ryen said pointedly as she took a seat at the round table.

Ryen decided to hold her tongue until someone explained what this meeting was about. She scolded herself for not taking five more seconds to listen to Sophie. She had no doubt been trying to warn Ryen about what she was going to find in the conference room. Now she kept her eyes on Demitri, still questioning his behavior, as she avoided looking at the man to his left. Demitri's pale green eyes were serious, and he had recently cut his light brown hair. His normally pale skin was even paler around his hairline. The longer hair he had on top was slicked back, accentuating his striking cheekbones.

Demitri did not shy away from her stare but ended the silence before it became too uncomfortable. "Miss Cardona, this is Mr. Di Marco."

Ryen let her eyes move towards Cash but she did not speak or give any other acknowledgement of his introduction. He seemed to be enjoying how she had been caught off guard, and she was sure he was getting more information than Ryen would like out of Demitri's head. *Damn this vampire* she thought only to herself. *What is his agenda?*

"Now, Miss Cardona," Demitri continued. If he called her "Miss Cardona" one more time she just might spear him in the eye with her pen. "Mr. Di Marco called me because he was concerned that you weren't giving him the appropriate courtesies."

What? Ryen thought. *This jerk complained to my boss because I wouldn't take his calls?*

"Now, as I know you must be aware, Mr. Di Marco's family is a very generous member of the Arts Council family. However, I assured him that you have been very busy, leading you to have difficulty returning his calls." Cash cleared his throat as if prompting Demitri's next comment, "And he was disappointed that the two of you were disconnected yesterday."

Disconnected? So he hadn't tattled that I hung up on him? Was he so pissed that he couldn't control my mind that he's going to try to get me fired? Ryen continued to focus on Demitri although she could feel Cash watching her, and she knew if she looked, he would have that annoying smirk on his face.

Since no one else was joining the conversation Demitri continued, "Mr. Di Marco was attempting to contact you regarding a painting his family is considering parting with, and he is hoping the Arts Council will be interested."

Oh, he is devious. Painting, my ass! Ryen thought, her anger building with each passing second.

"I offered to work with Mr. Di Marco personally, but he said he would like to continue working with you, here in Madrid." His voice was very steady so Ryen couldn't get a read on how Demitri felt about that. She didn't really believe Cash's family was getting rid of a painting that would interest the Council, but now Demitri would be watching over her shoulder to make sure the Di Marco family was being treated appropriately. *Damn this vampire bastard!*

Oops, she hadn't meant to project that past her barriers. Cash put his hand to his chest and faked a pained look, then his face smoothed over and that annoying smile returned as he winked at her. This all went unnoticed by the other two men in the room.

Looking back to Demitri, in her most dutiful employee voice, Ryen said, "I, of course, will do whatever the Council needs of me, Mr. Petrov."

Demitri nodded to Ryen, sensing her subtle sarcasm, and then turned to Cash, "Mr. Di Marco, is there anything else you need to discuss?"

For the first time Cash spoke, "I think that does it for today. Thank you for your prompt attention, Mr. Petrov," reaching out to shake his hand after both of them had stood. Ryen had never heard his voice in person and she cringed at the sound, a confident baritone, seeping with patronization. It attempted to caress her auditory senses, but she would not allow his vampire powers to work on her.

She stood to take her leave, but Demitri stopped her. "Miss Cardona, could you stay a moment? I'd like to have a word with you in private."

Cash looked at Ryen. Keeping the humor in his eyes out of his voice he tried to provoke her, "I'll be in touch, Señorita Cardona. I'm sure your secretary and I can arrange a meeting for us to discuss this possible transaction as soon as possible." Ryen's temper flared as he turned and walked out the door. He was probably headed upstairs now to talk to Sophie while she was forced to stay here and listen to whatever it was Demitri needed to speak with her about. Had this been part of Cash's plan too?

Pablo had returned to his office through the adjoining door, no doubt confused by what had just transpired in his museum, and anxious to flee from the tension in the room. Demitri relaxed his posture, but his tone was anything but, "Ryen, what the hell is wrong with you? Blatantly ignoring one of our biggest donors?"

Here was the familiar Demitri she knew, "I had reason to believe he was just being annoying. It never occurred to me that he had serious business to discuss."

Demitri's gaze scrutinized Ryen for a moment as he debated what he wanted to say next. He clenched his jaw before he spoke, "I thought I sensed something between you two. Are you losing your touch? Another relationship gone sour?"

Disgusted by his implication, but also saddened by the hurt she could still hear through his sarcasm after more than a year, Ryen wasn't exactly sure what to say. She pushed her anger aside and went with mostly the truth, "I ran into him a couple of weeks ago at his bar. I didn't even really talk to him, but I guess I offended him somehow. I honestly thought he was just messing with me," *I still do.* She added to herself.

"Sometimes I think you are completely oblivious to your coldness. I know you don't mean for guys to fall all over themselves for you, but sometimes you can be a bitch."

She wasn't prepared for his bluntness, but she guessed she deserved that. She had allowed her relationship with Demitri, a relationship that should never have happened in the first place since they worked together, to go on far longer than she knew was wise. He had been completely blindsided when she ended it. She couldn't tell him the real reason why she had broken it off, nor could she tell him the real reason she had ignored Cash or why she thought Cash was playing this little game. She had to keep his human innocence intact even if her feelings had never been as deep as his.

Demitri continued when she didn't argue with him, "I'm sorry, this is still a business meeting. I shouldn't have brought personal issues into it, nor should you bring personal issues into business here." Although his apology had started off almost sweet, his message was clear in the end. Basically, get over yourself and make sure you do your job.

"Understood," Ryen said. Anxious to change the subject Ryen motioned to the files she had laid on the table earlier, "Do you want to go over the acquisitions I've been working on, or are we still meeting next week?"

"We can meet later. I'll even push it back another week. Maybe you'll have the Di Marco acquisition to present by then."

"I'll do my best to wrap that up as quickly as possible. You know I'd never do anything to intentionally damage the Council's credibility or reputation."

"Of course you wouldn't. Ryen, I've never doubted your ability to do your job. Frankly I was quite surprised when Mr. Di Marco called me yesterday with his concerns. That's why I insisted on meeting with both of you immediately."

"Thank you, Demitri," Ryen said, hoping he knew she meant it for multiple things. "I'll try not to let you down again." With that she picked up her files and rushed back upstairs. If she was lucky she could interrupt Cash and save Sophie from his influence and blatant mind control.

Chapter 25

As it would turn out, she was not fast enough. Cash was long gone by the time Ryen returned to her office. Sophie was profusely apologetic for not warning Ryen before the meeting. She was also very nervous to tell Ryen about her conversation with Cash minutes ago. Ryen assured her that she was not upset. It had been Ryen who didn't want to listen before, and her meeting with Demitri had kept her occupied just long enough for Cash to complete whatever he was up to.

Almost afraid, Sophie showed Ryen when she was now scheduled to meet with Cash. He would be back tomorrow afternoon. Ryen would make sure she had errands for Sophie to run so that her head could be safe from Cash. She was still waiting to see how much damage had already been done...

Cash was very pleased with himself as he left the museum. He had been caught off guard and completely surprised when Ryen had appeared in his bar. Today he took great pleasure in returning the favor. Her face had been priceless when she had seen him. His plan was working out much better than he had expected, and thanks to the mind of Mr. Petrov, he had a whole new insight into Ryen Cardona. The Council Chairman had some very entertaining memories. He was amused that her ex thought something was going on between her and Cash, but Cash wasn't sure why he was so irritated that the man still harbored feelings for her. He chalked it up to her being his conquest at the moment, and even though he wasn't afraid of a little competition, he had a sense of possessiveness.

Her boss had done a great job calling her out on her unprofessional behavior in regards to Cash's phone calls, although his mind betrayed the fact that he would apologize as soon as they were alone. Cash smiled at how that had worked in his favor. He had plenty of time to visit his little secretarial pet before Ryen could interfere.

Cash had informed Sophie that his good friend Rafa had taken an interest in her and was quite upset that she'd had to leave so abruptly. He had already run this part of the plan by Rafa, and he was always up for a little fun. Sophie was to subtly work on Ryen this week to get her to accompany Sophie to his club this weekend. Cash also hoped his time alone with Ryen tomorrow would help to soften her up a bit to the idea as well. He'd be optimistic in his powers of persuasion, but he was also being realistic. This was no ordinary woman, he'd known that from the beginning, and she was proving immune to all of his charms.

Now for the trickiest part of his plan: calling his mother again. He would need to convince her that he was serious and couldn't wait to sit down with her. His explanation for missing their scheduled meeting would be a half-truth; the opportunity to meet with the Arts Council on his own had presented itself, and overcome with generosity he had told them the family had a painting available. He hoped she would consider his "initiative" as a positive step, even though he hadn't consulted her first. However, she would not be pleased that he had offered them one of her paintings. The most difficult part would actually be convincing her to give him a painting without divulging his ulterior motives, especially after their previous conversation. He may have chickened out then, asking for her help, but he would follow through now, even if it cost him. He was prepared for the strings to be attached this time.

Chapter 26

When consciousness returned, Ryen knew she was alone. She could no longer hear, see or sense anyone else. It was very dark inside the building, and from the Plexiglas sections on the ceiling she could tell it was dark outside as well. Not expecting any success, she tried to move her hand. Tears welled in her eyes when she could move not only her fingers, but her entire arm. The tears were both from the relief of being able to move, and from the pain that she felt over her entire body threatening to keep her immobile. Although they were serving no purpose at the time, her captors had restrained her with ropes on her wrists. She didn't know when it had happened or if they had done it before they left, she only knew that neither her physical strength nor her failed powers were responsible, but one of her restraints had been ripped free.

She had no idea how long it had taken her to get herself up and make her way out of the abandoned building. The crisp, cool evening air was such a welcome feeling; her eyes filled with fresh tears. It had to have been shear will to survive that gave her the strength to fight through the continued pain she felt and stumble down the street that was empty due to the hour. She tripped over her own feet, not being able to completely lift them, and fell to the ground. The physical strength that had helped her get this far was gone, and she still didn't have enough mental strength to access her powers. The ground was cold, a welcome contrast to the heat of the burning wounds on her naked skin. As her eyes closed, she said a prayer to the Goddess that someone would find her soon.

When Ryen awoke in her own bed she cursed Cash Di Marco out loud, although she knew in her heart that reliving her worst memories was her burden to bear, along with her guilt, for what she had done as a result of her attack. At first, when she had these nightmares, she had thought it was due to post-traumatic stress. But as she came to terms with what happened to her and chose to be a survivor and not a victim, the dreams had continued. Further observation revealed that she only had them after an encounter with a vampire. Some mental health professionals might say it was still PTSD, but Ryen knew better. She had crossed the line when she made the split second decision for revenge, and this was one of the things she had to live with in return.

Ryen lay in bed staring at the ceiling. She still had a few hours before she would need to get up. Since she had an appointment with Cash today she expected another dream when she went to bed tonight, and if she couldn't wrap up this supposed acquisition from his family quickly, she'd be revisiting her nightmares frequently. No doubt if Cash knew what resulted in his presence, he would string this along indefinitely just to torture Ryen. She didn't think being direct and asking why he was doing this would result in the truth, but she would at least try when she met with him today.

She continued to stare at the ceiling thinking about her choice to do harm. After she had passed out on the street someone had found her and called an ambulance. Ryen had regained consciousness when she was being wheeled into the hospital. One of the nurses was a witch and somehow through all of the cuts and blood and swelling, she had recognized Ryen. Her recognition and the quick spell that started some healing had saved Ryen's life. Her spell helped Ryen hang on long enough for Kora and Chesna to arrive and do a more powerful spell that should have healed her completely. Except Ryen had already thrown events into motion, and some of her wounds remained, leaving scars as a visible reminder of what she had suffered and what she had done. The nurse's spell gave Ryen a small burst of mental clarity; it was just enough for her to access her power and send out a spell of revenge; even though it was merely a thought she hadn't meant to act on.

When they watched Ryen's reaction to the news that three vampires had died, she knew that Kora and Chesna suspected something. The closest they came to outright asking was after the news of the third death. Chesna had looked at her with fear in her eyes and asked, "Is there anything you'd like to tell us?"

Ryen kept her scars hidden well, still today, even with an occasional glamour spell to make them temporarily invisible. She had answered Chesna, telling her no, with the most innocent look she could muster at the time, but she didn't think she had fooled her. For the average witch, her behavior would have resulted in "excommunication" from the Coven, and most likely a trial

129

by vampires, for justice in their eyes as well. But to Ryen's knowledge, no Triumvirate member had ever been in that situation. She wasn't sure what her Coven punishment would have been. It would have been up to Kora and Chesna, or to the Goddess herself. Ryen wouldn't have fought it. She knew what she had done was wrong. Not her karmic punishment, her guilt, nor any amount of good she would do could erase the blood on her hands.

Knowing she needed more sleep if she was going to be useful to anyone today, and if she was going to be prepared for her dreaded meeting this afternoon, Ryen took the moonstone Teresa had given her out of the drawer in her nightstand. She hadn't recharged the dream satchel, but with Ryen's power the moonstone should be sufficient in helping her get a few more hours of sleep. As she held the moonstone in her hand and closed her eyes, she started making a mental list of the errands Sophie would be doing away from the Prado today: dry cleaning, groceries, post office.

Ryen was hoping the day would drag so she could have as much time as possible before meeting with Cash, but that was not the case. The morning had flown by. Sophie was not pleased as Ryen handed her a long list of errands, both business related and personal.

"You don't have to send me away. You should have someone here with you," Sophie said.

"No offense Soph, but you've sort of been a liability where these vampires are concerned. I'll be better equipped to deal with him if I don't have to worry about you." Sophie had looked hurt at first, but acceptance worked its way across her face as she admitted to herself that Ryen was right.

"Fine," Sophie said as she put some things in her purse. "I'll tell security to be ready in case you need them, but Ryen, I don't think you will. Keep your mind closed to him, but at least listen and try to give him the benefit of the doubt. I really don't think he's dangerous."

Ryen took a deep breath to keep control of her emotions. Not dangerous? He had already infiltrated Sophie's mind, filling it with delusions of his goodness. Unable to keep her sarcasm at bay she looked pointedly at her friend, "Sure Sophie. I'm sure he's never used his power to manipulate anyone."

Sophie frowned and turn towards the door, "Good luck. I'll see you tomorrow."

Five minutes before their scheduled appointment, Cash arrived. Ryen didn't need Sophie to let her know he was there. Ryen could sense his presence when he got off the elevator. She had left her door open, and as she heard him enter Sophie's domain Ryen made sure her mental barriers were secure before calling out, "Come in, Señor Di Marco."

Chapter 27

Cash was feeling a mixture of anxiousness and excitement. He had been looking forward to this meeting since he had engineered its making yesterday, but he had been looking forward to time alone with this woman since he had seen her in Paris. This was his chance to lay on the charm and win her over. His anxiousness was from his apprehension that his charm may not be enough. It infuriated him that she made him question his abilities as no one else ever had.

Cash thought that he usually did well dressing himself. To be honest, it was difficult for him not to look good, but today he wanted all of the advantages he could get. He decided to enlist Fortuna's fashion diva, Rico, to help, which brought great amusement to Rafa. His snickering had earned him a supple leather loafer to the head before Cash banished him from his apartment entirely. When they were finished Rico promised girls and guys would be following him around Madrid, needing bibs for their drool. Cash was dressed in white linen pants and an azure blue linen dress shirt, to be casual and playful. Then Rico had added a striped tie and tan vest to keep him looking professional. Cash had no idea if Ryen would have anything good to say or not. He knew next to nothing about her: what made her tick, what she liked.

During the course of the past couple weeks of being blatantly ignored, he had tried to find out as much as possible about Ryen Cardona, but there was little to find, no pictures, and barely any information: she worked for the European Arts Council, and she had attended the University of Florence for Art History. That was it, nothing else. He had gotten more information out of her ex's head yesterday, but that was tainted with Demitri's feelings and Cash hadn't found anything he could use to his advantage today.

He knew Ryen would have her mental shields up to keep him out, so before he entered her office he put his up as well. He opened the door expecting to see his little secretary pet, but her desk was empty. He frowned and then smiled. Ryen must have sent her away to keep her away from him. Too bad he had already given her number to Rafa, who was planning to ask her to dinner tonight. Before he could fully revel in his amusement, he heard her speak, "Come in, Señor Di Marco."

How had she known he was here? Probably the same witchy powers that had let her know he was a vampire. *Game on,* he thought to himself as he walked confidently into her office.

Ryen barely glanced up from the papers in front of her when Cash walked in. So much for Rico's guarantee, but Cash couldn't take his eyes off of her. He stifled a laugh. She hadn't appeared to be fashion-challenged, but what she was wearing today would cause poor Rico to faint with fashion frustration. Cash assumed that she had done it on purpose, trying to make herself the least attractive as possible while still appearing professional. The boxy tan pantsuit with the pale yellow shirt did nothing to enhance her complexion, and completely hid any reference to a figure, but regardless, she was still gorgeous. She had her hair up in a tight bun, and Cash's imagination started concocting hot, naughty librarian fantasies. He couldn't hide the smile that spread across his face, but Ryen still hadn't pulled her attention away from her papers, so she didn't notice.

Cash got a hold of himself. "Is this a bad time?" he asked, feigning annoyance.

Ryen finally looked up and met Cash's gaze, but there was nothing warm in her eyes. "What would you say if I said yes?" she responded in all seriousness.

Cash didn't like having to threaten her, but it wasn't beneath him, "Well, I'm sure your boss wouldn't be pleased." Fire flared in her green eyes, highlighting the gold in their center, and something stirred inside Cash. He was sure there was a tiger inside her that no man, least of all Demitri Petrov, knew anything about. That fire shifted his ultimate goal. It was no longer enough to merely get her to want him, he would make it his mission to unleash that tiger, and enjoy every minute of it.

Ryen showed no sign of concession as she replied, "That will not be necessary. Please have a seat." Cash sat in the chair across from her and leaned back comfortably, never taking his eyes from hers. He could tell thoughts were racing through her mind although he couldn't hear a one. He continued to smile at her, unsettling her more and more.

When he could tell she couldn't stand the silence anymore she spoke, "Shall we get down to business? Where is this painting your family wants to part with?" Cash could hear the challenge in her voice. She didn't think he had anything to offer. He was impressed that she had figured out his ruse so quickly.

An "I knew it" expression lit up her eyes when he said, "It's not actually a painting." But her excitement at being right vanished as he continued, "It's actually a sketch, an early Picasso."

He could tell she was still skeptical, but very interested. "Do you have its provenance?"

There was no need hiding its origin, she already knew he was a vampire, "Not exactly. My mother knew him personally and it was a gift."

Her surprised expression questioned his credibility, so he added, "My mother and my family have been patrons of the arts long before your Council existed. A Picasso is barely scratching the surface."

She seemed annoyed by his last comment, but intrigue radiated from her eyes, "Did you bring it with you?"

"No, I thought we should work out the details first." He frowned because she was clearly disappointed. Cash hoped her disappointment was due to the fact that he didn't have it with him, and not that she would have to meet with him again, though sadly he knew it was probably a mix of both leaning towards the latter.

"How much does your family want in exchange? I'll be upfront and let you know that with other acquisitions we have in the works, I don't have a huge budget to work with."

"I'm not asking for any money in return." Cash watched the emotions play on her face again, wanting so badly to hear what she was thinking. He could tell she didn't think this was going to be a free gift, but it would be interesting to hear what her assumptions were. Even though he knew he wouldn't be able to get through her shields, it didn't stop him from trying. Every time his failed efforts were rewarded with a flare in those green and golden eyes.

Cautiously she asked, "So what are the terms of exchange you had in mind?"

A slow smile spread across his lips and he took his time answering letting the full force of his persuasive powers reach across the desk towards her. "Dinner with me," he said.

Fire exploded in the gold of her eyes, "That's out of the question" Her nostrils flared at what she clearly thought was an unreasonable request. "Seriously, let's figure out the appropriate monetary amount that will make both parties happy."

Cash knew it wasn't going to be that easy, but again he was hurt by the revulsion that laced her voice when she rejected him. In a calm and serious tone he said, "Those are my terms. I believe your boss is expecting an amicable exchange, so I'm sure you will make the right decision." He gave her another of his usually irresistible smiles to no effect.

Her next question surprised him, "Why are you trying to get me fired? What is it you want from me?"

Cash wondered what her reaction would be if he told her the truth. She wasn't ready for that yet; she would flat out reject him again in disgust. He decided not to give her a straight answer and to push her a little farther, "Why do you ignore me and refuse to join me for an innocent business dinner?"

She scoffed at his use of "innocent", and her frustration was apparent, but she was unwavering in her control. "What reason would you like first?" she asked with total calm.

"There's more than one?" Cash asked playfully, but he was concerned with the negative effect she was having on his confidence and his feelings.

Ryen's eyes narrowed as she tried to decide whether or not to continue this banter with him. She pushed back from her desk and crossed her legs, an action Cash would have enjoyed more if she were wearing a skirt instead of pants. When she didn't answer right away Cash continued to bait her, "I'm assuming with the way you mentally sling the word 'vampire' at me like an insult that my race is one of those reasons?"

Ryen gave a little shrug of her shoulders confirming his assumption. "Well, technically I'm only half vampire. My father is a witch." He used the word "witch" in the same way she had been using "vampire" though he had no prejudice towards witches. *There, let her ponder that information.* "If you're worried about me biting you, you needn't be. I'm not deprived of nourishment."

Her judgmental tone was laughable, "Oh, I have no doubt in your abilities to secure your 'nourishment', nor do I have any desire to be added to your collection of paparazzi arm candy."

Cash held back the smile of satisfaction he felt that she, too, had obviously been doing her research. That was a very good sign. Instead he gave his most convincing "hurt" expression and said solemnly, "You don't know me. The internet doesn't always hold the truth, and tabloids fabricate stories for the sole purpose of making money." Again he had to keep his amusement locked unseen as she looked like she had been caught with her hand in the cookie jar. She hadn't meant for Cash to realize that she had been looking into him. He also hoped she was rethinking her prejudgment, but without being able to get inside her head he couldn't be sure.

He decided not to push it anymore today for fear of erasing what little progress he had made, "Why don't you consider my offer? I'll be in touch." When she didn't move as he stood he added, "I'll see myself out."

As Cash walked to his car he replayed the events of the meeting. He had thought that maybe he had made some progress with breaking Ryen, but as he analyzed her words and actions he was slowly losing his confidence. Heading back to Fortuna, he became more frustrated with himself. Why did nothing work on this woman? He wasn't sure that she'd agree to ever go to dinner with him even with him subtly threatening her job. To be honest, in order for that to really happen he'd have to convince his mother to help, and that would not happen without threats and promises he would have to fulfill. He, alone, didn't really have the pull to get Ryen fired, and that wasn't what he wanted anyway. If she called his bluff on that he'd lose the only leverage he currently had. He needed a drink, one that was thicker than whiskey. It was late enough in the afternoon that hopefully there would be someone at Fortuna to quench his thirst, and his ego could use a boost too.

The look Cash gave Rafa silenced him before he could ask how the meeting went. Cash scanned the customers in the bar. There was no sign of any vampire clientele yet, so he had his pick of the available *beverages*. A girl with golden brown hair sitting alone caught his eye. He wasted no time by sending her suggestions. He walked right up to her, flashed his smile, and asked if she'd like to join him for a drink. His ego felt a little better when she instantly agreed and followed him anxiously to his office.

He glared at Rafa as he sent Cash a warning to go easy. Cash knew he was bordering the line between frustration and anger, and Rafa's concern didn't help. He usually didn't drink from anyone when he was so emotional. It was too risky, especially after the recent incident, but he didn't care today. He didn't acknowledge the other part of Rafa's comment either, because he had already had the same thought; her eyes were the wrong color green.

Chapter 28

Ryen waited until she could no longer sense Cash's presence before she allowed herself to relax. Elbows on her desk, she let her head fall into her hands. This was some sick game to that bastard. Could it be possible that the only reason he was doing all of this was because he wanted to go out with her? No, she didn't think a date was all he had in mind. He was trying to break her because he was threatened by her, because he couldn't control her. She would expect nothing less from a devious vampire manipulator like him.

The fact that he had to stoop to attempting to threaten her job was proof that she was stronger than him. She wouldn't put it past him to see his threat through to the end, but Ryen wasn't sure that Demitri had the balls to fire her, even with the wrath of the Di Marco name threatening him. But she could be wrong. Even so, that wouldn't break her. The Arts Council was not her life. She could walk away at any time, and she knew that someday she would have to anyway. But to have it be due to this prick's games, she didn't know if she could handle that.

He had been so smug the whole time. His seductive smile maddened her to the point she had wanted to slap it off of his face. First with Sophie and now with him, other than his extreme arrogance what was it that incited Ryen to such anger? The ability to charge her with assault would probably thrill him to no end. There was no way she was going to have dinner with him, and Ryen was pretty sure Demitri would back her up on that at least. She wouldn't like doing it, but she would play to his lingering feelings for her if necessary.

Hopefully it wouldn't come to that. Ryen opened up her laptop and decided to figure out what an early Picasso sketch was worth, so she could at least show Demitri she was trying to work with Cash rationally.

After a good hour, Ryen felt she had some reasonably sound numbers to work with that would fit with the Council's budget and not be insulting to the Di Marco's. She printed out her findings and sent an email of them to Demitri, letting him know that Mr. Di Marco did not come with a monetary number in mind. There, she was being proactive and showing him that she was doing her best to work with Cash in a professional manner. Next she sent Sophie a text about joining her for a drink. Sophie replied that she had other plans. To Ryen's knowledge she didn't really have any friends in Madrid aside from a couple of witch acquaintances. Then again, maybe Sophie was still irritated and avoiding Ryen for not trusting her around Cash, or any vampire.

After her last bar experience, Ryen did not want to go get a drink alone, but she didn't feel like going home yet either. She changed from her heals to a pair of flats for easier walking, grabbed a wine glass and a blanket from her closet, and headed down the street to the little wine shop she passed every day on her way to and from work. Its main clientele were tourists visiting the Prado, but Ryen wasn't a wine snob by any means so she was sure she could find something suitable.

When she had a decent bottle of Rioja in her bag, she headed back towards the Prado. The back side of Retiro Park was located just behind the museum. This side of the park was usually free from large amounts of tourists since the main attractions were closer to the front entrance on the opposite side, but it was perfect for the peaceful atmosphere Ryen needed. Her head was throbbing. She had never had to focus so much power on keeping her mind shut off to intrusions. There were only two other witches with powers even close to hers, so keeping witches out of her head had never required much energy, and she was not in a habit of socializing with vampires, so the brief encounters she usually had didn't really stretch her muscles either. This was different. Cash was relentless. He didn't accept that he couldn't get past her barriers, and he kept trying. Ryen couldn't relax for a second.

Ryen found a nice tree to lay her blanket under, poured a glass of wine, and tried to relax. She felt the energy from the tree at her back and from the earth beneath her, but her mind kept returning to the disastrous meeting from earlier. When she closed her eyes she saw Cash sitting across from her with his "I'm so sexy" smile, and his "don't you want me?" stare. Ryen gave her head a shake at an attempt to remove his image. She'd be lying to herself if she said he wasn't attractive, but all vampires were. Still, if he wasn't a vampire and if she didn't find everything about him annoying, she might not trust herself to be alone with him. That was a lot of "ifs", and there was something unnerving about his eyes that she couldn't quite put her finger on. He was clearly dangerous in more ways than one.

And now he's half witch? She thought. What was she supposed to do with that? Was telling her that hinting that he knew who she was? Did that have something to do with his obsession? Was his goal to discredit the Triumvirate? That didn't seem likely. What would vampires stand to gain? Aside from her personal hatred, witches and vampires got along quite well. He was from Florence, but Ryen didn't know any witches by the name Di Marco there, or anywhere for that matter, but clearly she didn't know the name of every witch. She was pretty sure she knew all of the ones in Florence though. Maybe his witch parent was no longer part of his life, or maybe he was lying.

All of this speculation was not helping Ryen to relax. She poured herself another glass and pulled her headphones out of her bag. Maybe some music would help clear her mind or at least change the focus of her thoughts. She was prepared for a nightmare tonight, but would Cash return tomorrow demanding her to accept his offer, badgering her until she caved? Ryen hoped he would at least give her a couple of days to think about it, although in her mind there was nothing to think about. She would not succumb to his pressure, even if it meant quitting her job at the museum...

"Fine, you were right," Cash said to Rafa after he had helped put the girl into a cab.

"Always good to hear, but for what exactly?"

"That was stupid. I came dangerously close to draining her like the other one. I was just pissed. I should have listened to you. I don't know what's wrong with me." That wasn't entirely true. Cash knew the problem was this situation with Ryen; he just didn't understand why she was having such a strong effect on him. Sure, she was taking his ego down a few notches with every encounter, but she was just one girl, one of hundreds, thousands. Why did he care so much?

"Did you at least have fun this time?" Cash knew Rafa was referring to his lack of sexual desire lately with his blood encounters. Though he doubted it, he hoped his answer would end the conversation. Rafa knew him better than anyone.

"I had sex with her if that's what you're asking." At least she had enjoyed it. The whole thing continued to anger him. Cash had gotten a little rougher than usual with her, but it turned out she was into it, so everything worked out in the end.

"Good! That's not exactly what I meant, but at least it's a step in the right direction. I would expect a different type of answer if you'd actually enjoyed yourself."

"Don't you have somewhere to be?" Cash asked, wanting this conversation to be over. It was hard enough for him to face his issues, let alone share them with Rafa.

"Indeed I do. Thanks again for her number. She seemed quite eager." Cash could tell by the look in Rafa's eyes that Sophie was in for a night to remember.

"Just remember, she has to be able to go to work tomorrow so she can tell her boss all about it." To himself he added, *Oh I wish I could see her face when Sophie tells her. It will be priceless.*

"No worries, she'll have plenty of stories to tell," Rafa said with a wink as he grabbed his jacket and headed for the door. "You know I'll do whatever I can to get this Ryen chick into your bed so you can get back to being you." Rafa ducked out the door just in time for the bottle of beer to hit the door instead of his head. Cash could hear him laughing from outside.

Jackass! Cash sent to Rafa's mind, but only half-heartedly. As much as Cash hated to admit it, Rafa was right. He hadn't been himself lately, and now he had to sit back and wait. If the next part of the plan was successful, she would come to him. He needed their next meeting to be on his turf.

Chapter 29

Part of her was grateful that she kept losing consciousness. It made for brief escapes from the pain and the fear of what else was going to happen. She felt new pain in her neck and thighs. She couldn't move her head to see the wounds, but she knew they were deep bite marks, and her blood was still trickling out of them. From the ache in her abdomen and between her legs, she guessed someone had just taken his turn with her. Her eyes were the only things she could move, and she could see Cai lounging on a chair on the far side of the room.

"Oh look, she's awake again. My turn! It's more fun when she knows what's going on," one of the other guys said as he approached her. If she would have been able, Ryen would have screamed for help, but she knew that part of her body was immobile as well. Tears fell from her eyes, running into her hair and ears.

"Don't cry little witch," the same guy said. Ryen looked him in the eye and tried to force as much hatred as she could through her eyes alone, as she thought a torrent of insults at him. She was so focused she didn't see it coming. His arm flew up and back handed her so hard blood spurted across the room from her mouth. Ryen wondered how much force it would take for her neck to break.

"You only make it harder on yourself," he said as he took a knife and started making cuts across her stomach, licking the blood that flowed. If she was capable of moving or using her powers, she would fight as hard as she could to get away, but she had nothing with which to fight. Her thoughts were her only weapon and they only caused her more pain.

She was staring at the ceiling trying not to see what he was doing to her. A sharp pain between her legs let her know he had moved his attention away from her stomach. Maybe he'd get careless with that knife and make a fatal mistake. He smiled, knowing what she was thinking as he forced himself inside her. More tears fell from her eyes as she accepted that death was her only escape.

Every time Ryen awoke from one of her nightmares she felt ashamed that she had wished for death. At the time she had seen no other way out, but instead of being a brave and powerful witch, she had allowed those guys to break her. Obviously she had been broken physically, but it was the mental destruction that had wounded the deepest. It had taken her months to trust herself again, not to jump at every sound, to be able to leave the safety of the compound. It had taken years before the idea of physical intimacy didn't send her sprinting in the opposite direction. If she hadn't lived it, she wouldn't recognize that poor little fifteen year old girl as the same person she was today. Once that girl felt safe, Ryen had vowed never to feel like a victim again.

She would use that determination to maneuver through this ridiculous situation with Cash, but today she'd try to not think of him at all, unless he showed up to irritate her again. The sun was shining as she walked from her metro stop to the museum. It would be warm today, but there was a gentle breeze. Ryen absorbed as much vitamin D and fresh air as she could before heading inside for the day.

"Good morning Sophie. That's a pretty scarf, I don't think I've ever seen you wear it before." It seemed that Ryen had startled Sophie with her greeting, and Sophie was acting a little nervous.

"Hi, thanks, it's new," Sophie stumbled over her words. Ryen tried to remember Sophie ever wearing any scarf. Except for winter, she couldn't.

"So," Ryen said, "Did you make new friends or were you still upset and avoiding me last night?"

Sophie looked down and fiddled with her bracelet, "Actually, I did make a new friend."

Uneasiness edged over Ryen. She had a bad feeling about whatever Sophie was about to say, "Sophie? Did your new friend give you that scarf?" Ryen hoped her answer was no, but she feared that was not the case.

"Maybe. Why?" Sophie's hand self-consciously went to her neck.

"Let me see your neck, Sophie."

"NO! Why? It's not what you think, Ryen."

"And what do I think? That you allowed a vampire to take advantage of you? That he convinced you he wouldn't hurt you if he bit you? And you wonder why I don't trust your judgment. Where'd you meet this 'new friend'?" Ryen wanted to shake her. What was Sophie thinking? With everything going on with Cash maybe it was time to send Sophie back to Florence for a while.

"It's not like that at all. It wasn't some random vampire," Sophie was speaking softly and looking around, making sure no one was coming into their office area as she spoke of supernatural beings. "I already sort of knew him. He asked me to dinner. I said yes of my own accord, and I had a great time, a *really* great time actually."

Ryen's stomach turned at the understanding of what Sophie implied, and then she stopped short, "What do you mean you sort of knew him? Oh god, Sophie, it wasn't Cash, was it?" That thought caused a mixture of feelings in her. She wouldn't be surprised; it fit with what she knew of him, but what was that other feeling? She wasn't sure what it was, but the fact that it was there made her uncomfortable.

"No, of course it wasn't Cash. He's not interested in me. It was his friend, Rafa, one of the bartenders we met at Fortuna." Ryen was relieved that it wasn't Cash, but his friend was just as bad. Any connection to Cash created complications with whatever was going on. Ryen was sure that Cash was behind Sophie's date, but she decided not to push Sophie. She had been pretty harsh with her lately, and Ryen feared she was close to doing irreparable damage if she didn't back off a bit.

"Look Sophie, I know I can't tell you what to do with your personal life, but please be careful. I hope you'll see the wisdom in keeping your distance from these guys." Ryen was ready to leave it at that and turn her focus to work, but Sophie had one more surprise for her.

"Thank you for recognizing that I'm not a little girl. I'm a grown woman and if I want to see him again I will. In fact, I am seeing him again, but I'll be careful, Ryen."

"When are you seeing him again?" Ryen couldn't help asking.

"I'm going to Cash's club with him on Saturday," Sophie said defiantly. As a challenge she added, "If you're so worried about me, maybe you should come along."

There it is. Now she knew Cash was behind this. He was trying to lure her to him, and he was using Sophie to accomplish it. She probably had no idea how she was being manipulated. Since she was technically responsible for Sophie's wellbeing, Ryen really didn't have a choice. If Sophie was going to be reckless, Ryen would have to go with her. She had to hand it to Cash. She knew he was devious and cunning, but she really had underestimated him. He had thoroughly thought out his elaborate plan. Now she could only hope he'd give her some peace until the weekend. Maybe it was time she recharge that dream satchel so she would be functioning at full power when she saw him again.

Sophie's voice pulled her out of her thoughts. It was filled with sadness and longing, "Do you know what I wish? I wish we really were friends." Ryen started to interrupt her and tell her that they were, but Sophie held up her hand to silence her, "If we really were friends, I could have come to work today, or even called you last night and told you all about the incredible time I had. And even if you didn't like the guy I chose, you'd still listen and be happy that I was happy."

There was a moment of silence where Ryen wanted to hug her and tell her that she *was* her best friend, or the closest thing she had ever had to one. But part of Ryen also knew Sophie was right. Ryen would always see herself as the adult and Sophie as the child, needing her guidance and protection. And in this situation Ryen couldn't even fake her way through hearing Sophie talk about her date with a vampire. Instead of responding, she gave Sophie a look of remorse.

A sad smile pulled down the edges of Sophie's mouth as she nodded in acknowledgement of the truth of the situation, "I have a meeting with a private investigator about that background check you wanted. I won't be back until after lunch. Your schedule is in your inbox, but it's pretty open today." Ryen watched her leave and took a deep breath. Such was the life of a leader, she thought with bitterness, a leader who was tainted by her own past.

Ryen spent the whole morning thinking about what Sophie had said. There was no way she could stomach listening to the details of Sophie's night with a vampire, especially the part where he bit her, but she tried to remove her prejudice. If Rafa was just a guy, and Ryen took away the "vampire" label, she probably would be happy for Sophie. Ryen squared her shoulders with resolve. She might not be able to be the friend that Sophie wanted and deserved, but she'd try to keep her mouth shut. That didn't mean she still wouldn't do everything in her power to protect Sophie, but she'd keep her opinions to herself while doing it, and the sooner she closed her business dealings with Cash Di Marco the better off everyone would be.

The dread of going to this retched club had haunted Ryen all week and put a strain on her relationship with Sophie. Ryen had kept to her promise to let Sophie make her own mistakes. Although she had subtly tried to get out of going to the club tonight, her efforts had not been successful in getting Sophie to change her mind. Cash had not tried to contact her since their meeting, solidifying Ryen's theory that tonight was part of his scheme. Thankfully the dream satchel had still been useful, and Ryen had been able to get several nights of dream-free sleep. There were a couple of times she had caught a glimpse of Zeta and Afton as if they were watching her. Had they wanted to communicate further they must have had trouble getting through the magic. Ryen hadn't spent much time thinking about her history because she was focused on getting through tonight.

In a couple of hours she would be accompanying Sophie to La Noche Oscura. Thanks to some much needed rest and the help of tonight's full moon, Ryen felt ready to deal with whatever Cash had up his sleeve. She had allowed

Sophie to help pick out her outfit, but Ryen had implemented some veto power. They had compromised on a loose-fitting, sparkly, black and silver camisole-style top with white leggings. Sophie had wanted Ryen to wear a ridiculously high pair of heals, but again they compromised and Ryen was wearing black boots that came up to her knees and had more conservative heals. Knowing it would be hot in the club, but still wanting to keep her tattoo covered, Ryen put her hair in a loose braid. Sophie, on the other hand, was planning to wear a tube top and a super short skirt that Ryen thought would be impossible to sit down in if any of the fabric was supposed to be a barrier between the chair and her butt.

As she waited for Sophie, Ryen ate a snack and tried to meditate to keep her head clear. When Sophie knocked at the door, Ryen realized she'd never feel completely prepared, but she couldn't postpone this any longer. Ready or not, it was time to go.

Chapter 30

There was already a line formed outside of the club when Ryen and Sophie arrived. In terms of club punctuality they were a little early; it was only eleven o'clock, but this place was clearly popular. Ryen could hear the bass from the street, and it accentuated her heart beat as it threatened to jump out of her chest. She was sure the bass, even louder inside, wouldn't camouflage her heart from vampires, so she needed to get a grip on her nerves before they entered. Much to Ryen's chagrin, and to that of many of the scantily dressed girls waiting in line, Sophie walked them right up to the door. The doorman let them in without delay when Sophie gave him their names. Ryen tested out her powers among the chaos and found her assumptions were correct. The doorman was relaying their arrival to his boss even before she and Sophie could make it through the door.

Even though clubs weren't her thing, Ryen had been to a few in the past, and in comparison La Noche Oscura was impressive. There was a huge bar to one side of the main floor with several small tables of varying heights mingled around it. The DJ stage was on the wall opposite the bar and there was a large, packed dance floor in the middle. The flashing lights highlighted people everywhere dancing, singing, drinking, and gave the dark room an aura of excitement that put Ryen a little at ease. If she could remove the dozen plus vampires she could feel, she might be convinced that she could have a good time here. Up some stairs there was a V.I.P. section that was roped off, and there appeared to be another dance area another level up from there. Sophie had mentioned there was a rooftop dance floor as well. This place was pretty big. If she wanted to keep an eye on Sophie she was going to have to stay close to her. Ryen shuddered at the thought of being an audience to whatever Sophie planned to allow Rafa to do to her in public.

Realizing that she was being watched from across the room, Ryen reeled in the awe she was feeling as she observed her surroundings. She refused to look towards the bar to where she knew she would find Cash, but Sophie directed her attention there anyway, "There's Rafa. Let's go get a drink. Maybe that will help you relax a little."

Before they walked towards the bar though, Sophie turned and grabbed Ryen's arms. Looking into her eyes, she pleaded, "Please try to have fun tonight, Ryen. Not for me, but for you." Then she turned back towards the bar and led Ryen by the hand.

"Hey beautiful," Rafa said to Sophie. He nodded to Ryen and the look she saw in his eyes confused her. She could have sworn she saw protectiveness in them, but a quick feel of his emotions told her that he was just having fun with Sophie, so his protective feelings weren't for her. "I'm just helping out behind the bar until the other bartender shows up. He's running a little late tonight. What would you like?"

Ryen let Sophie order on her own this time, sticking to her promise. "I'll start with a martini, with extra olives." As she reached into her purse she asked, "Can we start a tab?"

"Your money's not good here tonight, ladies," Rafa said looking at both of them.

That didn't surprise Ryen, but it did finally make her look towards the face that had been staring at her since she arrived. As expected, he wore that cocky smirk that irritated her to no end.

Bienvenida floated seductively across her mind. She narrowed her gaze and turned away. She'd see how welcome she'd be here after she took full advantage of him covering their drinks. She had no plan on drinking too much to affect her abilities, but she knew where that line was, and she could rack up a hefty bill without crossing it. She looked at her choices of top shelf beverages, paying special attention to the really expensive bottles that were probably reserved for his rich vampire friends. "I'll start with a double shot of Gran Patrón, and shots for my friends here as well," she said motioning to the group of four girls sitting to her left at the bar. That would be at least 100 euros retail.

Ryen smiled when she saw a muscle twitch in Rafa's jaw and his eyes flashed to Cash before he reluctantly reached for the glasses. Feeling more satisfaction at seeing the bottle on the shelf was almost full she asked, "Oh, and could you please open a new bottle where I can see it?" Her question produced another twitch from that jaw muscle, but he did as she asked. Apparently he was told to comply with Ryen's requests.

Unfortunately the other bartender showed up before Ryen could order another drink from Rafa. The latecomer was the one she had pissed off a few weeks ago, so she thought it would bring the same enjoyment. Rafa led Sophie to the dance floor, but they were still in view so Ryen stayed at the bar. It took her a minute to come up with his name, and he looked irritated when she addressed him, "Rico, is it? I'm ready for another drink."

He reached for the tequila bottle that Rafa had opened. "No, I'm done with tequila for the night." Turning to the new group of girls that had joined the bar she asked, "Do you girls like whiskey?" They seemed a little confused but they weren't picky about their alcohol. That only made this more fun, wasting such good liquor on people who weren't able to tell the difference between it and the ten euro bottle from the supermarket, and downing it as a shot instead of savoring the quality.

"We'd like the Macallan please," she said. "And remember to open a new bottle," she said with a smile. The mental onslaught of curses she received from poor Rico made her smile grow wider. Ryen chanced a glance in Cash's direction to see if her behavior was having the same effect on him as it was on his bartenders. He was still watching her, but she couldn't tell what he was thinking about the situation. Another bartender, who had just poured from the bottle of Macallan she had ordered, handed him a glass. Ryen couldn't get a read on him and he still wore his signature smirk, but he lifted his glass to her with a slight tilt of his head.

Damn, she thought. It wasn't working, or at least he wasn't going to let her know he was pissed. His confidence was so unnerving. As Ryen looked at him, trying to decide what her next step would be, she took in the scene around Cash. It was clear that he belonged here. He fit into this world perfectly, not because he was a womanizer or a vampire, but the confidence coming from him tonight wasn't the same as she had observed before. It was as if the atmosphere, the darkness, the colored flashes of light, the music,

151

everything was feeding him, supplying him with energy he was projecting out towards her now.

For the first time Ryen allowed herself to really look at him as she had tried to think about Rafa before, without the vampire label. She could definitely understand why he had girls gathered around him and wasn't "deprived of nourishment" as he had put it. His black wavy hair blended into the darkness around him. His icy blue eyes were a bright contrast to his hair and the lightly tanned smooth skin of his face. He wasn't a body builder, but his lean strong body was apparent through the fitted black button up shirt he wore with the sleeves rolled up and the top few buttons undone.

Ryen caught herself staring far too long and physically shook her head to rid her mind of his image. He was still watching her, but now he had an eyebrow raised, questioning what she was thinking. Thankfully, her mental shields still held strong. What the hell was she doing? Maybe it was the alcohol or the bass that was pounding out a primal rhythm in her chest, but she needed to focus her attention elsewhere. She reminded herself of the events that had brought her here, re-firing her anger and irritation, and she searched for Sophie. She was still dancing. If Ryen was going to join her she needed one more drink.

She ordered another glass of the whiskey, not bothering to continue her plot of destruction through the waste of high priced liquor, and took more time drinking this one. As she drank and kept an eye on Sophie, she listened to the music. She knew that pop music tended to be themed with sex, but she wondered if the songs she heard now were meant as messages: sex, slave, wanting, obsession. Maybe she was a little paranoid, but she wouldn't put anything past Cash at this point. She finished her drink and joined Sophie on the dance floor. She told herself she could at least attempt to make Sophie believe she was having a good time. The warmth she felt from her alcohol consumption relaxed a bit of her tension from earlier, but she remained focused.

After a couple of songs Ryen was not surprised by the presence she felt approaching. She turned around to face him before he got too close. He was at least an arm's length away, but to prevent him from coming closer Ryen sent him a mental message to make sure it was heard over the noise of the music, *"Don't touch me!"*

Appearing to accept her physical boundaries, he didn't come any closer, but he didn't move away either, and in his eyes she saw challenge. For two songs Cash behaved himself, and Ryen tried to ignore him dancing nearby. She was careful not to get too close in case other dancers bumped either of them in the wrong direction. She made sure to smile at Sophie every once in a while to keep up the act that she was enjoying herself. Sophie, on the other hand, was definitely having fun. Ryen didn't think there was air between her and Rafa at any point in the evening so far. There was plenty of touching and kissing. Ryen looked the other way during those moments to keep from interfering. She made sure to keep her eyes away from Cash's as well. She still felt in control, but just in case she had underestimated her ability to handle her booze, she didn't want to take any chances with her mind being in a vulnerable position if her control failed.

The music started to slow and people were drawing even closer than before, if that were possible. Ryen turned to leave the dance floor, when a hand grabbed her forearm. Her gut reaction was to turn and slap the face she knew she would see, but the feelings radiating from where his hand was in contact with her bare skin had her frozen in shock. Ryen felt as though an electric current was running up her arm from where their skin touched. The only other times she had felt something similar had been through the memories of other pieces of her soul.

Mere seconds had passed before she was able to get a hold of herself and turn around. She was going to tell him to let go of her, but before the words reached her lips Cash had closed the distance and lowered his mouth to cover hers. The electricity she was feeling in her arm exploded throughout her entire body. For a second she lost all control. Ryen was too stunned to resist, as his icy blue eyes warmed with passion and determination. Images of those blue eyes flashed before Ryen, Cash's looking at her, as Shaw's looking at Afton, and Tarik's eyes looking at Zeta.

Chapter 31

No, Ryen thought as understanding sunk in. It was barely a whisper in her head, but she clung to it as if it was keeping her from falling off a cliff. Realizing she had lost momentary control she slammed her mental barriers back into place. She gathered her strength and this time she projected as she pushed away from Cash, *NO!*

Ryen's breath was coming in gasps from the kiss, from the feelings, from what she had just learned. She looked at Cash. He didn't seem to have had quite the same realization that she had, but he was clearly confused. Ryen wasn't sure what, if anything, he had been able to get from her mind in those seconds, and that was almost as terrifying as what she had just discovered. Completing the action she had previously planned, she slapped him hard across the face. She backed away slowly shaking her head, and then turned and ran for the door. She paused when she reached the sidewalk, bending over to put her hands on her knees and catch her breath. Her mind was reeling.

She jumped when Sophie touched her shoulder, "Ryen, are you ok? Oh my god, I can't believe he kissed you. I'm so sorry."

Ryen stood up slowly, "It's not your fault Sophie. Look, I have to leave, but promise me you'll watch yourself tonight."

Sophie was stunned that Ryen was willing to leave her alone, but right now Ryen had more to think about than stupid choices Sophie might make. Sophie was rambling on, "Nobody wants you to leave, Ryen. Please come back inside. I know he's a vampire, but he's not bad. I know he shouldn't have kissed you, but..."

Ryen cut her off, "This is so far beyond that, Sophie. I can't explain. I need to go. I'm sorry," and with that she hurried towards the metro, leaving Sophie standing in disbelief outside the club.

Ryen could feel her phone vibrating in her small clutch. The caller ID read "Chesna". The metro train was fairly deserted, so she wasn't worried about somebody eavesdropping on her conversation. If anyone had answers it would be the Crone. Before Ryen could say hello Chesna started talking, "Are you ok?"

"Did you know this was going to happen?" Ryen demanded.

"You know I can't see your future; I've never been able to. I would have saved you so much turmoil over the years if that was possible. I only see what's around you now."

Ryen trusted she was telling the truth, "But you knew something was going on?"

"Things have been shifting around you for weeks. You even said you felt it before you came home. I didn't know where it was headed, nor do I know where it's going now. So much of that depends on your choices."

"That's why you told me to do the Beltane spell, isn't it? You thought communing with my history would help me with whatever was coming."

"I thought it might. Has it?"

Ryen wasn't sure how to answer that. She'd been trying to analyze what she had seen of Zeta and Afton's lives but, she hadn't comprehended most of what they had experienced. "Right now all I can think is that they were trying to prepare me or to help me recognize... but maybe there's more to it. I don't know, I can't think right now. I need to be alone."

"Use the moon tonight to help you. Go somewhere safe and spend some time in meditation. Call us tomorrow to let us know you are ok. We love you."

Ryen could hear the concern in Chesna's voice mixed with the confidence she always had in Ryen to figure out what she should do. "I will, I love you, too."

Ryen needed a direct sight to the moon, so when she reached her apartment she escaped to the roof and made sure the door locked behind her. She often used this space for her own personal rituals, so she didn't need to stress about privacy or what was up here. She quickly focused her energy to mark a protective circle around herself. With respectful haste she called the elements to protect and conceal her from anybody to whom she might be in view. Ryen felt earth, air, fire and water all surrounding her as she fell to her knees and cried.

Fate is a cruel bitch, she thought. She had accepted her role in life gratefully when she had been able to escape her mother and Joseph. Only a handful of times had she ever really thought about the things she would miss out on, and now fate was dangling them in front of her, and no doubt laughing. She had no choice, even if she really wanted something different. She couldn't just quit being the Maiden, and these two lives could not mesh together. Maybe that's why Zeta and Afton had shared those parts of their lives with her, to show her what sacrifice looked like, to prepare her for the only choice she had.

The fact that Cash was a vampire, that he irritated her beyond reason, and though she hated to admit it, that she was afraid of him, had all been overruled in one instant. It didn't change the things Ryen had felt before, but it added a layer of complication, uncovering the feelings Ryen would have refused to acknowledge even if she had been aware of them. The irony was too much for her to wrap her mind around.

Looking up at the full moon she questioned the logic of the situation out loud, "Goddess, what wisdom am I to gain from this? I don't understand." After several minutes staring at the moon in silence, she pushed aside her selfish feelings, "Grant me the vision to see the purpose, and the strength to do as I must."

Ryen knew what she had to do now. Maybe one of the reasons this happened was to set her priorities straight. Out of respect for the Council she would finish the projects she was currently working on. She would turn her back on this new unwanted temptation, and then she would head back to Florence for good, to where she was meant to be.

Chapter 32

Cash didn't care that an audience of at least a ten person radius had just witnessed his encounter with Ryen. He wasn't exactly sure what had happened, or what it meant, but it was the most intense thing he had ever felt. He had known from the first time he had seen her that there was something about her. It drew him to her, and caused him to become obsessed with her. He had been enjoying the little game they were playing tonight. Ryen thought she was being clever and trying to unnerve him. Little did she know she'd been doing that very thing for weeks. Tonight was nothing new.

Cash had respected her request for space on the dance floor, but he couldn't let her leave when he'd gotten so close. He had expected fireworks in response to him grabbing her, but he was thinking more along the lines of anger and violence. What he had experienced was so far in the opposite direction. When he touched her arm it set him on fire. Something had been pulling them together. That same force, beyond his control, led him to kiss her, though he wouldn't have fought it if he could. He had kissed hundreds, maybe even thousands of girls, and never came close to what he felt tonight.

He hadn't even realized her mind was open to him until the strength of his feelings was cut in half when she shielded her thoughts from him again, although even half of what he had been feeling was more than he knew how to explain. He had been overcome with an unknown fire and physical passion, but there was this feeling that some piece of him had fallen into place even though he'd had no idea it was even missing. Even now, with her gone from his presence, there was a hole in him he hadn't noticed before. He might even think he had imagined it except for the sting he felt on his cheek.

What does this mean? Cash didn't have the answer to that, but one thing was clearer to him than anything, he'd move heaven and hell for this woman, whether she wanted him or not.

Cash had wanted to go after Ryen when she ran from him, but he let Sophie go, and now he couldn't reach Sophie's mind through all the people in the club in order to hear what was happening outside. He walked over to the bar and Rico handed him a glass of whiskey without having to ask.

Rafa joined him moments later, "Luckily, as far as I could gather, no one from the V.I.P. section noticed that exchange on the dance floor."

Cash continued to stare toward the door, not acknowledging Rafa's comment though he had heard him. "Cash? Did you hear me?"

Without taking his eyes from the door, he spoke in a distant tone, "Yes. Thank you."

"Look, hermano, I don't know what happened out there. You allowed her to strike you. It could definitely be seen as a sign of weakness, not being able to control a human..."

"She's not human," Cash said quietly, cutting off wherever Rafa's thoughts were headed. He pulled his eyes from the entrance to look Rafa in the eyes, "I'm aware of what it could have looked like, but that's not what happened."

"Then what the hell did happen? It looked as though this game of yours would be ending soon, and now?"

"I have no idea," Cash said shaking his head. Then very seriously he added, "But whatever it was I'm afraid it's far from over, and it's no longer a game."

Sensing the magnitude of Cash's emotions Rafa let out a heavy sigh, "I never thought I'd see the day."

Cash gave him a skeptical look, "What?"

Now it was Rafa shaking his head, in disbelief, "The day that Cash Di Marco would fall in love."

Cash didn't know how to respond. He'd never thought he'd see this day either. Was that what this was? Luckily Sophie returned at that moment so he didn't have to continue his conversation with Rafa. "Were you able to catch her? What did she say?"

Sophie was taken aback by the urgency in Cash's voice, but she answered reluctantly, "She said she was fine. She just needs to be alone." Then she rounded on Cash, her voice filling with anger, "Why did you have to go and kiss her? It's your fault she's so upset! What were you thinking?"

Cash laughed softly, "Apparently I wasn't. My intention wasn't to upset her." An idea occurred to him "Perhaps if I could explain to her? You could give me her address?"

"She would kill me," Sophie said.

"You're probably right," Cash replied with mock disappointment. He hadn't expected Sophie to give up Ryen's address, but he was hoping to pluck it from her mind. Maybe she had been expecting that too, because for once she successfully closed her mind to him, but not before he had at least gotten a phone number.

Chapter 33

The sun warmed Ryen's skin and roused her from her sleep. Hoping last night had been a nightmare, she looked around. She was still on the roof, wearing the outfit she had worn to the club. Nope, not a nightmare. Come to think of it, she hadn't had a recurrence of her familiar nightmares either. Ryen wondered at that. Maybe fate had decided last night was enough to take the place of karma's punishment for once.

Sadly, the white leggings she had borrowed from Sophie were covered in dirt from the roof. They looked the way that Ryen felt. She didn't think any type of cleaning would help them. It seemed she owed Sophie a new pair of pants. She was still inside the protection of the circle she had made, so she stood and raised her head to the sky. Letting the sunlight soak in the skin on her face and arms, she thought of the words to one of her favorite Kellianna songs, "From the darkness, day is dawning. In my darkest hour I seek the light. All my pain and all my sorrow, may it ease with this new day…may my strength and may my power lift me up and light my way. I seek faith and I seek wisdom at the dawning of this new day."

She thanked the elements and dismissed her circle. On her way to unlock the door, she knew a shower was definitely on the to-do list, not only for physical cleansing, but she hoped the hot water would soften her tense muscles. She wondered how much of that tension was from sleeping outside on the roof and how much was brought on by the stress of her present situation. Regardless, after a shower she had some work to do. If she was going to get the Council projects wrapped up sooner rather than later she'd need to put in some extra hours. Maybe that would keep her mind from drifting to places she wanted to avoid as well.

At some point her phone had died, so she plugged it in when she finished with her shower. There were several texts and missed calls from Sophie. She didn't want to talk about last night with anyone, and she couldn't explain to her what had really happened. A slave to her emotions, Sophie would be the opposite of helpful with what Ryen knew she had to do.

Ryen sent a quick text: I'm fine. Still don't want to talk about it. I'll see you Monday at work.

She figured Sophie wouldn't give up, but hopefully, at least she'd reserve her concern for texts and not show up at Ryen's door. She also sent a quick text to Kora and Chesna to let them know she was safe. There were several missed calls from another number she didn't recognize. No texts or voicemails, but Ryen thought she knew to whom the number belonged. She tried to ignore the pang that gripped her chest.

She wondered if the person who had started all of this would have some answers. Ryen wasn't sure that it would work, but she closed the curtains and lit a candle on the coffee table. She closed her eyes and took a deep breath before speaking to the empty room, "Zeta, if you can hear me, please join me here."

Ryen focused all of her energy and power on the image she knew of Zeta in her mind. She didn't know how long she had been sitting there, but after some time she felt a shift in the energy of the room. Slowly, she opened her eyes to find Zeta, in her Egyptian beauty, seated on the opposite side of the table. A sheepish smile on her face, Zeta nodded her head in greeting, "What can I do for you, Ryen?"

What indeed? Ryen thought. "I just figured since this was your doing, maybe you had some answers for me."

"What is my doing? I have no control over what happens to you."

"Maybe not, but this started with you didn't it? With you and Tarik?"

At the mention of Tarik's name a pained look crossed Zeta's face, "You know how this works. You've read and heard enough to know the basics. Tarik was the other half of my soul, the same soul I share with you. The universe strives to put pieces of the puzzle of life together. Sometimes it succeeds, and sometimes it doesn't. It succeeded in my time and in Afton's time, and now in your time."

161

"Succeeded? You and Tarik were killed, your love ripped apart! And Afton, her heart was never truly complete. You call that success?"

The wise smile Zeta gave Ryen inflamed more anger, "Those were the results of the choices we made. The universe's success was in guiding us to our soulmate."

Soulmate. That word made Ryen flinch. She wasn't ready to admit that to herself yet. "What's that supposed to mean?"

Zeta took her time answering. Ryen knew she was trying not to interfere, thus being as ambiguous as possible, "Souls form connections. The bond between soulmates is the strongest of those connections, but as souls are reborn they aren't necessarily in the same time and place as the others to whom they are connected. That is the universe's goal, to provide pathways for those souls to reconnect. However, the choices one makes can alter the course, causing someone to miss the connection. Your soul, our soul, has lived more than three lifetimes, but that doesn't mean we found our soulmate in each one or that it ended in disaster if we did." After a pause she quickly added, "Nor does it mean it didn't."

Ryen eyed her with irritation. She understood Zeta wanting her to come to her own conclusions, but Ryen needed answers, not riddles. "So you're saying that fate wanted you to be together?"

Zeta nodded her head, "But there's always freewill and consequences."

"What if freewill doesn't exist because there is no choice? What of the consequences of choosing the side of fate?"

Zeta spoke softly but her gaze was filled with implication, "There's always a choice. The universe, the Goddess, fate, they're all rooting for you, but it's you who determines your future."

Was Zeta trying to tell her something? Was Ryen missing what she was saying between the lines? She thought the answer to both of those questions was yes. Ryen looked at the ceiling and ran her hands through her hair in frustration.

162

"Ryen, it's time for me to go before I say too much. We have a strong soul, *you* are strong, strong enough to make the decisions that you know *in your heart* are right. Good luck. We're rooting for you," Zeta said with a sincere smile as she faded away, leaving the chair across from Ryen empty.

Chapter 34

Ryen's no nonsense mood was clear as she arrived at the museum Monday morning. She had successfully avoided any conversations with Sophie over the remainder of the weekend, but she was dreading the face-to-face encounter upon entering her office. She would stick to her schedule. She was very busy and didn't have time for small talk or personal matters.

"Good morning, Sophie."

Sophie's head snapped up to look at Ryen. The giddiness that she was exuding did not match the concern in her voice as she addressed her friend/boss, "Good morning Ryen! I've been dying to talk to you. How are…"

Ryen cut her off, not wanting to open the door to a conversation she was not willing to have, "I made some additions to my calendar as I'm sure you saw. I'll need the files this morning for my meetings this week. Also, could you get Demitri on the phone for me? It needs to be before lunch. Thanks, Soph."

Ryen walked away before Sophie could verbally formulate any questions. When she walked into her office she saw what she assumed had been the cause of Sophie's giddiness. On the corner of her desk was a huge bouquet of sunflowers, reminding her of the sunflower fields of Italy. They were beautiful. Had Sophie felt guilty for bugging her? Was she trying to cheer her up?

Ryen opened the card and felt that pain grip her chest again. They weren't an apology from Sophie. They were an apology from Cash. Ryen closed her eyes and took multiple deep breaths, trying to calm that little voice in her head that was trying to contradict everything she had felt for so many years. She realized that there would need to be closure with this before she could go home. Not wanting to face Sophie after discovering the flowers she surely had a hand in getting to her office, she picked up her phone and buzzed Sophie's desk.

"Marguerite said Demitri is in a meeting right now, but she'll have him call you as soon as it's over."

"Thanks, Sophie. Um, could you please forward the documents that I am emailing you now, and contact Señor Di Marco to set up a meeting about his sketch? I have some time on Thursday afternoon."

Sophie's voice was filled with hope, "Absolutely. Is there anything else you'd like me to tell him?"

Ryen knew she was referring to the flowers. She wouldn't be surprised if Sophie thanked him of her own accord. Ryen debated the damage that thanking him might cause. Did he send the flowers with the expectation that Ryen would thank him or to continue to unnerve her, or was he sincerely apologizing? Would thanking him lead him on? Would not saying anything make her the bitch that Demitri accused her of being?

Either way it didn't really matter. She had started the arrangements to be back in Florence by next week. "Do not read anything into this, Sophie, but you can tell him 'apology accepted', and that's it!"

Demitri was not pleased with Ryen. He had not been expecting her to give her resignation when he returned her call. He didn't understand, and he didn't accept her reason of "personal matters". Ryen promised to have the open acquisitions closed by the end of the week, including the Di Marco piece. She had also agreed to advise her replacement via phone for the next month to help smooth over the abrupt transition.

Making the decision to quit was the right thing to do, but actually taking the steps to do it hurt Ryen's heart. She had always said she could walk away at any time, but she hadn't realized the extent to which she loved her work with the Council. Logically she knew she never should have had a job outside of being the Maiden, and now she was facing the depth to which she had taken her opportunities for granted.

The similarity of the situation hit her, and Ryen let out a laugh mixed with despair. All that talk with Zeta had her subconscious weighing options she didn't have. If there really was a choice and she chose fate, someday she'd be making the same decision with love as she was now making with her job.

Kora, Chesna, and Maggie had all spoiled her, letting her believe there was nothing that was out of her reach. Now she was experiencing just how untrue that was. The safety and security she had always felt with the certainty of her future now felt like a chain, holding her down.

Chapter 35

The week had gone faster than Ryen had thought it would. Aside from the Picasso sketch, she had successfully acquired all of the other pieces she had been after. Her meeting with Cash was in a few minutes, and hopefully they could agree on a monetary price. Tomorrow Demitri would be introducing her to her replacement; she would finish cleaning out her office and say good-bye.

The information Sophie's private detective had been able to dig up about the mysterious boy she'd met at the coffee shop had been delivered yesterday. Ryen forwarded it to Florence this morning. Her suspicions had been warranted. As it turned out Elijah *Turner* was the only son of a Damaris and Joseph *Turner*. He was homeschooled and had finished his secondary education at age seventeen. He then attended a small Christian college and had been interning at his family's church. His current residence was listed as Tennessee, and he and his family were members of some small reform church. The detective had found a family photo in his research as well. That photo was all the confirmation necessary. They had changed their last name, and although more than twenty years had passed, it was impossible for Ryen not to recognize her mother and "father".

So, she had a little brother who was doing an internship in Vatican City, less than three hours from the Coven's headquarters. All the more reason she needed to be in Florence, the sooner the better.

The knock on her door proved how lost in thought she had been. She looked up to see Cash standing in her doorway. He was wearing an expensive suit just like the first time he had come to her office. It was black with a pretentious vest, matching his hair, and a cobalt blue shirt contrasting with the blue of his eyes; those eyes, which really were the doorway to the soul.

His signature smile played across his face, still filled with seductiveness, but it was missing the antagonism that Ryen usually saw. She wondered if that was his doing or her softening towards him.

Ryen stood and motioned to the chair in front of her desk, "Thanks for coming. Please have a seat." Suddenly she was very self-conscious about the flowers she still had sitting on her desk. Truthfully she liked the flowers even if the reason and the person behind their existence made her uncomfortable, but what would Cash read into their presence?

Cash watched her carefully, and she could tell he was trying to get a read on her. She didn't blame him when she felt that familiar tingling around her mind. She wondered if he had any idea what fate had imposed on them.

"I'm assuming you've had a chance to look over the information Sophie sent you on Monday. Is our offer acceptable to you?"

"Ryen," he began.

"This is a business meeting, Señor Di Marco."

"Indeed it is, *Señorita* Cardona," he retorted.

"Do you have a problem with acting in a professional manner?"

Cash laughed, "Certainly not."

"Is something humorous?"

"I just find it funny that you are questioning my professionalism as if you were the poster child for it." His tone was light, but laced with accusations of hypocrisy.

"Excuse me?"

"You're right, I'm sure there was no one more qualified to be your assistant than your best friend," his voice full of sarcasm. "And let's not discuss your relationship with your boss."

There was that aggravating man she knew. Let him think what he wanted about Sophie's qualifications. He had no idea the real reason she had been given the job, so if he wanted to think it was nepotism, so be it. She would probably kick herself later for letting him bait her, but how dare he suggest she and Demitri had an inappropriate relationship, "That relationship was over long before he became my boss, so your assumptions are incorrect."

Cash's eyes sparkled. Ryen wondered if it was due to the fact that he had successfully roused her anger. "Whatever you say. Look, I'm not really sure what's going on here," he motioned between the two of them, "but I think we're past the pretense, don't you?"

"Very well, *Cash*. Do you think we can come to an agreement on the Picasso?"

Disappointment that she didn't take the opening to discuss what happened at the club showed on his face but he didn't let it faze him. His smile returned with a challenge, "I already told you my terms. Have dinner with me and the sketch is yours. No dinner, no sketch," he shrugged and his lips turned downwards in a playful frown.

Ryen almost broke her pen in half. Her frustration was clear in her body language and her voice, but she didn't care, "And I told you that wasn't an option. Now look, I'd like to have this wrapped up before the weekend, but if that's not going to happen I'll have Demitri be in contact with you regarding further negotiations."

"Are you refusing to work with me?"

"No, but after tomorrow I will no longer be working here."

Genuinely curious he asked, "Why?" and then playfully, "Did you get fired?"

"No, I quit." Despite the calm conversation the room was full of electrified energy. Ryen could feel it brushing along her skin and filling the air.

"Why? It's not because of me, is it? I mean, because of me giving you a hard time with the sketch?"

That was a loaded question. Technically quitting did have to do with him, but it was also about Ryen focusing on her priorities. "No, it's not because of you. I'm moving back to Florence to deal with family issues." Well, that was mostly true.

This news stunned him and he didn't try to hide it, "You're leaving? When?"

To avoid his intense scrutiny, Ryen took some papers to her filing cabinet and pretended to put them in the empty drawer, "My plane leaves tomorrow night."

She had her eyes closed, focusing on keeping her breathing and her heart rate steady. She hadn't heard him get up or approach, but as soon as his hand fell over hers that sensual electric current went shooting up her arm. Ryen tried to pull her hand out from under his, but Cash tightened his grip.

"Cash, please," she pleaded, barely a whisper.

He grabbed her shoulders, turning her to face him. His hands were no longer touching her skin, but she could still feel a buzzing sensation through her shirt. "I know you feel that," he said accusingly.

She gave him a pained look, "Cash, it doesn't matter. Please let go of me." Her voice was calm, not betraying the turmoil boiling inside.

He let go, and turned away in frustration. "What is this? Did you put a spell on me? I've been having these crazy dreams about us all week. I can't get you out of my head. It's like you're in my veins, without a drop of blood exchanged. When I touch you, god, when we kissed, I'm not even sure I can explain it."

Cash's comment about exchanging blood slapped her out of the trance she had felt she was in, allowing her to regain control. "Did you say you've been having dreams?"

Cash nodded, frustrated further that the dreams were the part of his confession she had decided to acknowledge. For clarification she asked, "Dreams about us? What kind of dreams?"

"I don't know, weird historical fiction dreams I guess."

"But it was you and I in them?"

"Yes, you and me," he spoke slowly, clearly confused by her lack of understanding.

"Where were we?" Ryen realized she sounded crazed.

"All over, Egypt, mountains, castles, houses."

"So you had more than just a couple different dreams?"

"Yes. Why? Have you been having them, too?"

Ryen avoided his question, "How did the dreams end? Generally, like happy or not?"

"Some were happy, some were definitely not. Are you going to answer me? Do you know what this means?"

"No," and that was at least partly true. Zeta had alluded to the fact that Ryen had had other lives. Was Cash seeing the ones that Ryen hadn't? How was he seeing them? She was pretty sure he hadn't done a spell like she had. When she looked at Cash he looked defeated. He really had no idea what was going on. He had hoped that Ryen knew and could explain it to him. If he didn't know, she couldn't tell him. That would make her leaving even harder than it was already turning out to be.

"I'm sorry," she added after several moments of pained silence, and she truly meant it. This wasn't his fault, and it was apparent that he had no clue what was going on. He looked at her a few times questioning if she was being honest with him.

"Have dinner with me tomorrow before you leave." It was a plea filled with desperation; all of the confidence that had irritated her for weeks was gone. Seeing him like that caused that pain in her chest again.

"Fine. But it's just dinner. It doesn't mean anything and won't change anything," the last part she added for her own benefit as well, already fearing the consequences of her decision.

171

As if flipping a switch, Cash's whole demeanor changed. The acridity in his voice was like a slap in the face, "Fine, you come to dinner, you get your sketch. You can leave knowing you've wrapped everything up here in Madrid."

They gave each other a long hard look, both trying to reach into the other's mind, but hitting barriers. Then Cash strode out of her office.

Chapter 36

Cash silently fumed the whole car ride back to Fortuna. He ignored Rafa when he tried to ask how things had gone. Cash went straight to his office, finally letting the detonation of his anger go behind closed doors. He was sure Ryen knew more than she was saying. He knew she felt the connection between them; he could tell by the way her mental shields could not contain her emotions when he touched her. He had stupidly thought after they had kissed that it would be easier to get close to her.

And now she's leaving. With no job to come back to, would she ever return? How was he supposed to react to that? There was no way he was going to let her go. What was wrong with him? What had happened? If she asked he would literally rip open his chest and hand over his heart.

His mind slowed, and he fell onto the white suede sofa in exhaustion. Rafa knocked on the door before opening it, "Is it safe to come in now?"

Cash opened his eyes and started to ask what Rafa was talking about. The question never came out as he looked at the destruction around his office. With the exception of the sofa, most of the other pieces of furniture were damaged, some beyond repair. Frames were torn off the wall and thrown across the room. Papers were scattered everywhere.

My god, did I do this? Cash thought. His hold on his control was being constantly tested these days.

Rafa broke Cash's silent inventory of damage assessment, "I gave some free drinks to the customers to keep them from being too interested in what was going on back here. I'm guessing your meeting didn't go well?"

Cash let out a snort of air as he shook his head, "Well, on the one hand she agreed to have dinner with me tomorrow, but on the other hand she's moving back to Florence afterwards."

Rafa had helped to clean up the office, and new furniture would be delivered tomorrow. Since Cash had destroyed his desk, he was using the bar at Fortuna to do some work before the club got busy. He had only one more chance to win Ryen over, so he was making elaborate plans for dinner. He had debated the opulence of *La Terraza Casino* with its rooftop terrace or the more secluded *Sergi Arola Gastro* with a private dining room. He concluded that the fewer distractions the better and had made reservations at *Sergi Arola* for ten o'clock. With it being the day before and the restaurant having occupancy of only thirty diners, it took some negotiating to procure the private dining area with its view of the kitchen.

Sophie had done him the favor of coordinating with the private plane Ryen was flying in back to Florence. It was now scheduled to leave at one instead of nine. Two hours was not a lot of time, but it was more than he had in the past. Cash wasn't making any strategic plans past dinner, either out of the confidence that he wouldn't need any, or because if dinner was a failure he wasn't sure what the next step would be. Sadly, he feared the latter was more likely. Could he let her go? If the past weeks were any indication of what his mood would be like without her, he would need to give raises to all of his employees, especially Rafa, and perhaps invest in a furniture company.

Rafa interrupted his thoughts, indicating the models at the opposite end of the bar, "You've got some admirers. They stopped in to get some drinks while they wait for the club to open, and they are also hoping to get their names on the list so they don't have to wait in line."

Cash barely glanced their way, "Go ahead and put their names on the list."

"Is that it? Maybe a drink would do you good, or you could redirect that energy that torpedoed your office earlier."

"Not interested," was all Cash said. He could feel Rafa's concern and frustration without looking up.

"Well, they're more interested in you, but I'm certainly not going to let them go to waste. Think Rico can handle the bar by himself for a bit?"

Without looking up from the papers in front of him, Cash said casually, "I can help him if need be." Then he smirked and looked up to wink at his friend, "Good thing the sofa was left intact."

"If you change your mind, feel free to join me," Rafa said as he walked back over to the girls to invite them to see the "wine selection" room, aka the office that currently only held one sofa. Cash's thoughts drifted back to how much he had changed since he saw Ryen in Paris, shaking his head at what he had allowed himself to be reduced to...

Ryen had already shipped a few boxes of personal things to Florence during the week, and the remaining boxes would be shipped by Sophie in the next few days since she was staying in Madrid for a few weeks to help both her and Ryen's replacements at the museum. Ryen had one suitcase of clothes and essentials that she was taking with her tonight, and Sophie was going to handle finding a buyer for the apartment.

The car Cash was sending for her would arrive soon, and Ryen looked around thinking of things she was going to miss, not only about her apartment, but about all of Madrid. Was Cash one of those things? Ryen shook her head, reminding herself of the impossibility of the direction her thoughts were heading.

Cash had texted her the information about dinner. Ryen had never been to the restaurant they were going to, but she knew it was upscale. She hoped the dress she had on would be dressy enough for dinner and comfortable enough for the flight so she didn't have to think about changing. She looked in the mirror that would be sold with the rest of furniture to whomever bought the apartment. Her hair was up in a loose ponytail. She had fallen asleep earlier after a shower with her hair in a twist so the ponytail had little waves. Her black dress was one of those wrap style dresses that tied on the side. Assessing the amount of skin it revealed, Ryen felt comfortable. It had three-quarter sleeves and came down to just above her knees although the characteristic wrap left a deep V in the front. The dangling turquoise earrings and matching artistic looking necklace added a fancier element to her look.

The buzz that jolted her out of her self-assessment let her know that the car was downstairs. Ryen slipped on her strappy heels, put her bag over her shoulder and looked around her apartment for the last time before grabbing her suitcase handle and closing the door behind her.

Chapter 37

Ryen was a jumble of feelings as the car approached the restaurant. There was the sadness of leaving mixed with the apprehension of the dinner ahead of her. The car was going to wait for her and take her to the airport so she was leaving her suitcase and bag inside. As the car came to a stop Ryen grabbed a little clutch out of her bag to take in with her. The driver came around and opened the door for her and also walked her up to the restaurant and opened that door as well. She took a deep breath and squared her shoulders. Her focus was interrupted by a vibration in her clutch. She stopped to read a text from Sophie: Good luck, and try to enjoy yourself ☺

Shaking her head at Sophie's message distracted Ryen from the figure walking towards her. As she felt a familiar tingle around her mind, she looked up and sucked in a shocked breath. She wasn't sure what it was, admittedly he always looked good, but tonight in his black dress pants and cream colored cashmere sweater she was sure he could win over any enemy. She dug her nails into her palm to get a hold of herself. He smiled as if he could read her mind. Ryen quickly checked her mental defenses. They were securely intact, but she reminded herself that tonight would need focus and control. As if she hadn't been second guessing this dinner since yesterday, she made a mental list of all of the reasons it couldn't work between them, and all of the reasons for which she had disliked Cash from the beginning.

Cash directed her towards their table. He seemed as hyper-aware of her as she did of him, and he refrained from touching her as they walked. The restaurant was dark, with modern interior architecture and design, and it was small. Slight panic ran through Ryen as she realized they were headed away from the other diners to a private area. She relaxed a bit when she saw their table had a view of the kitchen. Although secluded, they were not completely alone, and the activity would provide a distraction if things started to get out of hand.

Ryen allowed Cash to help with her chair. That chivalrous act did not escape her, but she kept her focus on the list she had made. She had been expecting the hostile Cash that had left her office yesterday, or at least the aggravatingly arrogant Cash she usually encountered, but the Cash with her tonight was completely new. It was as if he had dropped all of his defenses, though his mind was still sealed off, and there was something else. Ryen was having trouble putting her finger on it. He was being genuine without the aura of the player he was. As Cash took his seat across from her, he handed her the wine list. "I'm assuming we'll get a bottle, with your desire to have your beverages freshly opened, so why don't you choose."

Not surprised that he remembered since she had shoved it in his face at the club, Ryen was slightly impressed that he was indulging her paranoid behaviors, pleasantly perpetuating this new version of himself. She took a moment to peruse the extensive list. When the waiter asked if she'd found something to her liking Ryen indicated an Italian wine, a montepulciano, she missed from home. Her choice caused Cash to laugh to himself silently in amusement, "Sorry, would you like something different?"

Without looking up from his menu, still smiling he said, "No, it's just funny that with over five hundred choices you chose the one my family produces."

"Oh. I hadn't realized that was from your family's estate." Her favorite wine would forever hold a different meaning. Fate was going to make this as hard on her as possible it seemed.

Still looking amused, Cash took the lead with the food, "I thought we could order the chef's special eight course "one bite" offer and share? Unless you'd prefer something different."

Ryen wasn't sure that she was going to be calm enough to eat, "That sounds fine." This was going to be a long dinner. Both she and Cash seemed to be avoiding eye contact, and the relative "small talk" put Ryen on edge. She thought maybe she should ask about the sketch before anything happened that might result in an early exit. Before she could ask though, Cash stole the words from her mouth.

"You are probably wondering, but no, I don't have the Picasso with me. It's still in my mother's possession. You are welcome to get it when you get to Florence, otherwise I'll have it shipped to Demitri on Monday."

Ryen was tempted to get it herself. She really wanted to see it in person, but she felt a clean cut of those ties was best. "You can have it shipped. I don't work for the Council anymore, so legally it wouldn't be safe in my possession."

"You're going to miss it aren't you, working at the museum?" Either Cash was very perceptive or Ryen was being more transparent than she realized. He must have sensed her concern because he continued before she could answer, "It just seemed like you really enjoyed your job. When I heard you speak about art in Paris you were full of this energy that engaged people who were normally bored to death by art."

Ryen couldn't keep the confusion and shock from her face, "You were in Paris?"

"Yes, I was at the gala at the Louvre representing my family. That's the first time I saw you."

Ryen's thoughts were racing. She hadn't seen him there; she was fairly certain she would have remembered him. That was the day she had sensed a shifting in the universe, and also when Kora and Chesna had tried to call her wondering how the gala had gone. Had Chesna seen him there? Chesna had told her after the incident at the club that she didn't see it coming, but had she known since Paris? Surely she wouldn't have lied to her?

The waiter brought the wine, and Ryen held back from downing the whole glass at once to calm her nerves. Bread arrived also and not sure how to respond to Cash's confession, she grabbed some to keep her mouth busy.

Adamant to keep the conversation going in spite of Ryen's reluctance, Cash pushed a little further, "If you don't mind my asking, why do you insist on opening new bottles?"

Ryen didn't want to share, but sadly, her reason was commonplace enough, "It's a safety precaution. I was drugged once."

Cash was stunned. Ryen watched a myriad of emotions play across his face, but Ryen's tone was clear. She wasn't willing to elaborate. Instead he marveled her with another perceptive observation, "I've never heard you speak Italian, but you speak French and Spanish very well, and your English sounds American. You're from Florence?"

"Not exactly, I moved there when I was a child." Ryen didn't feel comfortable sharing too many personal details, especially where her past was concerned, but she couldn't ignore him and she didn't want to lie. She'd have no problem omitting things, but if he asked a direct question she felt she would have to answer honestly, unless she could avoid answering at all.

In an attempt to shift the conversation away from her, Ryen grabbed at the first thing she could think of in her mentally frantic state, "So why did you drop out of Harvard?"

Cash tilted his head and narrowed his eyes, contemplating something, "It was a twofold opportunity, a business dream and a way to defy my mother."

"You don't get along with your mom?"

"I do, but let's just say we've never seen eye to eye on my future. She thinks I'm wasting my potential."

Ryen wasn't sure if she really wanted to get to know Cash. It pushed her dangerously close to a line from which she wanted to be far, far away. He was willing to open up to her and that scared her. She had to keep reminding herself of the list she made when she got to the restaurant because with each minute that passed, she felt drawn in further. She couldn't help herself, "So how did you get into the club business?"

"That was actually the business opportunity that arose. I was on vacation in Spain from boarding school when I met Rafa at a club. We bonded over being the only vampires there and came up with this idea to open our own club someday that could benefit vampires. When I was at Harvard, Rafa called me to inform me he'd come across a rich vampire that was looking to invest in potentially lucrative endeavors, and he was interested in our idea. He offered to back us as a silent partner, so I left school. After the success of our first club in Berlin, Rafa and I had enough money to branch out on our own. It drives my mother crazy," he said smiling.

Ryen found his story very intriguing. She had originally thought that being a dropout made him a failure, but it wasn't that at all. She admired his rebellion against what was expected of him, but the vampire friendly concept of his clubs made her apprehensive. She wanted to ask what that meant, but maybe she didn't want to know those details. Something must have shown on her face to prompt Cash's question to her, "You don't like clubs?"

"It's not that," she paused, deciding whether or not to continue, but if his lucrative business was harming innocent people she couldn't just stand by, "so how are your clubs beneficial to vampires?"

Their food started arriving, but Cash didn't let that stop the conversation, "Sorry, you've been so pleasant I'd forgotten that you hate vampires."

Ryen couldn't tell if there was sarcasm hidden in his tone or not, but he sounded normal, albeit a little cautious as he continued, "There are rules. Rules create safety, and safety creates a stable environment. Basically when a vampire comes to one of our establishments they agree to be respectful with the humans and careful to uphold our secrecy. We provide a safe opportunity to acquire blood and whatever else the human is willing to do, and a safe place to do it. The humans involved are looked out for afterwards."

Ryen knew the horror showed in her face, "They have no idea what they're doing? They are manipulated into being playthings?"

"No, they know. It's much harder to manipulate an unwilling mind. No one is forced to do anything they don't want to. They just might not state their desire vocally." Cash was being defensive, but he was also trying to convince Ryen that there was nothing wrong with the service he provided. She just wasn't sure if she was buying it.

"Look, if everything wasn't above board it would draw unnecessary attention, hence the rules. The rules still apply if someone leaves the club to do their *business* elsewhere. If negative attention is drawn to us or the club, it would risk our secrecy, and as I'm sure it's similar with witches, our secrecy from humans is of the utmost importance."

"I think it's more so with vampires. Witches, or at least pagans, are accepted more and more into the main stream. But as for witches with manifest-able powers, you're right." *Just know that I may start keeping an eye on your businesses to make sure things stay on the up and up,* she added in her head. Cash gave her a very inquisitive look, wondering if she was really as accepting as she sounded.

"We're actually thinking of broadening our locations. Rafa and I might go check out New Orleans. It seems like a great place and we don't have any locations in the States."

"You can't go to America! It's too dangerous," Ryen almost shouted in panic. That definitely piqued his interest.

"There are already vampires in the U.S., so we wouldn't be adding any new danger to the humans." Cash sounded like he had misunderstood Ryen's concern, but the look in his eye told her he did indeed understand, and he was curious for her to explain.

Crap! She had to give some sort of explanation. Regardless of whether or not this was the last time she was going to see him, the thought of Cash going to the States and running into her mother's hunting party scared her beyond reason. "I'm not concerned about the humans. The U.S. isn't safe for supernatural people."

"How so?" He gently prodded for more information, or maybe hoping Ryen would make some confessions of her own.

Ryen couldn't tell for sure if Cash was only interested in the information she had, or if he was pushing for her to explain her personal concern in the matter of him traveling there. Right now she didn't care, "There are fanatical religious groups that make it their mission to hunt down supernatural people and kill them."

"How do you know about this?"

182

Ryen hesitated to share those very personal details. They could result in her true identity being discovered not only by Cash but by others, leading to danger for her. After a moment of internal struggle she decided to go with honesty. "Because my mother and her husband lead one of those fanatical hunting groups."

Cash was shocked again and momentarily unblocked his mind. In a flash Ryen heard the rush of more questions all directed towards her. He must have realized what had happened because his mind went silent again. He gave Ryen a look that conveyed he knew she had just heard his thoughts, so she decided to answer his unspoken questions.

"My mother is a witch, but somehow she got mixed up with a religious group via her current husband and for some reason decided to betray her heritage and her family. Before I was born she destroyed her own coven including her family and everyone she had once loved. I found out about it when I was nine and the Universal Coven offered me sanctuary."

"What happened to her?"

Not understanding what Cash had meant Ryen reiterated what she had told him before, "She's part of, or leads a fanatical group of murderers."

More food arrived and both Cash and Ryen ate, but the food did not stop the conversation, "No, I mean, wasn't she punished?" Ryen's confused looked led him to explain his question further, "With vampires the most important things are secrecy, loyalty, family and power. Those priorities may be in different orders depending on the vampire, but all vampires hold those as core values. Even if the vampire's family did not punish him, the Council of Elders would step in, especially for serious matters like death and power."

"Oh," Ryen knew that to some extent. When she had been attacked she could have reported her attackers to the police or found vampires to listen. The vampires' families would have made the public charges disappear, but they would have dealt with the crimes themselves. Thinking back to her mother, no one knew what had really happened or where she was until Ryen had somehow contacted the Triumvirate, and then the number one priority had been Ryen. "No one knew where to find her for years, and even now she keeps her identity and location secret. The Universal Coven has vowed to take action if her group brings their killings across the ocean."

"Can't your witch leaders do anything, strip her powers or something? Is there retribution from the 'universe' or your Goddess or someone?"

"I'm sure karma will eventually find her, but no. Powers can be bound, and the Coven would do that except the person in question has to be physically in their presence. It's not the place of the Triumvirate to punish. I'm assuming she is still using her powers to some extent to help with the group's murders, or at least in helping to locate the victims. I think that's why they have been successful," to herself she added, *and because no one powerful enough has challenged them.*

"I'm sorry that happened to you. I can't imagine what that would be like, to find out something so horrible about someone you love, who is supposed to protect you," he said very sincerely. "I appreciate the warning and we'll be alert to the danger, but there's a large market in the U.S., and if we don't capitalize on it, someone will."

She wasn't sure if he was just being honest, or trying to get more of a reaction out of her, but she couldn't help what came out of her mouth, "Cash, please don't go there. It's dangerous, and if something happened…" realizing what she was about to say she let the end of her sentence drop off.

A fire flared in his eyes, and he reached for her hand. She saw it coming and tried to move away, but she wasn't quite fast enough. That electricity shot up her arm, and she fought for control. In a corner of her mind her imagination got the best of her. She saw the people in the kitchen fade away. Cash pulled her from her chair and kissed her with the same crushing urgency she felt, and then he laid her on the table.

Luckily for Ryen, the waiter chose that moment to bring the last of the dessert courses, pulling her back to reality and causing Cash to let go of her hand. Judging by the lethal look Cash gave the waiter, he was not as grateful.

The electricity from a moment ago still charged the air, making it heavy, difficult to breathe. Dinner was practically over, and if she didn't leave soon she might not be emotionally capable. She looked at her glass of wine. How many had she had? She knew the waiter had brought a second bottle at some point. She started thinking of ways to politely excuse herself. It was still a bit early for the excuse of needing to get to the airport, but at least she had it as a last resort.

Once again her thoughts were interrupted, "Thank you for coming to dinner with me tonight. I know that you didn't want to." Ryen knew she'd regret it, but she looked up at Cash's eyes, filled with sincerity and a longing she was feeling too, "I've enjoyed talking to you openly without the usual hostility and walls between us."

Ryen could tell that it was taking great effort for Cash to be so honest, but she couldn't bring herself to tell him what she was really feeling. Instead, she took the opening she'd been looking for to exit, "Yes, well, me too. Look Cash, thank you for dinner. This place is incredible. I hate to eat and run, but I really should be getting to the airport. I still have to go through security points even though it's a private flight. On behalf of the Council, thank you for the Picasso."

She had stood somewhere amidst her ramblings. Cash had stood as well and was inching nearer to say good-bye. The irrational part of Ryen was anticipating a kiss, much like the one she had imagined earlier. The rational part was screaming at her to run now! She saw the pain in his eyes as she mumbled more good-byes and thank-yous. She practically ran to the car as the gripping pain in her heart was nearly incapacitating.

Chapter 38

Cash's encounters with Ryen never turned out the way he planned, the way he'd come to expect things to work out, especially in regards to women. Tonight was no exception. What was he supposed to do now? He could desperately run after her, but that wasn't him. He wouldn't allow this stupid crush to reduce him to a groveling weakling. Crush! He knew it wasn't a crush, but to admit that he loved her beyond reason was a punishment in and of itself since she didn't feel the same. But didn't she? He'd felt her emotions seep through her shields more than once, and he heard the concern in her voice when he'd spoken of going to America. Short of kidnapping her or actually coming out and saying he loved her, he'd done all he could. She, on the other hand, had not openly admitted to anything, so maybe she didn't feel the same.

The hopelessness had reached every part of him by the time his car pulled up to the club. The models from last night were back, and they were eyeing him as he got out of the car. *What the hell,* he said to himself as he flashed them a dangerously seductive smile. They giggled to one another, and he motioned for them to follow him.

Maybe the best way to get over her was to throw himself back into his old life, no matter how much it felt like he had outgrown it. Back in his office he allowed the models to remove his sweater. Their hands were *all* over him and they were kissing his chest, neck, ears…he closed his eyes trying to go with it, but all he could see was her face. Those golden green eyes staring accusingly at him, filled with hurt. He growled in anger that she was still interfering with his life even after turning her back on whatever was going on between them. Still staring at those eyes in his head, he grabbed the closest girl, intending to drink deeply from her soft neck. Those golden green eyes widened in horror and tears fell.

Even fake Ryen in his head had too much power over him. He pushed the girl aside before piercing her skin. He brushed off the touches of the others as well and sent the appropriate suggestions to their minds: they had a great time dancing all night at the club; they didn't meet anyone interesting; they just drank and danced. He escorted them through the staff entrance to La

Noche Oscura. As he went upstairs to his apartment, he was full of frustration and anger at himself, and at Ryen, at the whole pathetic situation...

As Cash's car drove her to the airport, Ryen couldn't help but think of what a disaster dinner had been. She had only agreed to go for the Picasso, or so she tried to convince herself. She felt she had at least made that clear to Cash, but somehow his aggravating charm had unraveled her strength. She still had all of her guards up, but the other side he showed tonight made her feel so damn comfortable. She had shared more personal information than she would have liked. If he were a witch or if he relayed her story, her true identity would be evident. Every tiny piece of information seemed to encourage his pursuit of her. Hopefully distance was what she needed. If she didn't have to worry about running into him everywhere she went maybe she would feel safer. Then why was there some little part of her thinking about staying?

Ryen felt relieved when her phone rang, something to distract her from the confusing thoughts she was having. She had already responded to Sophie's incessant texts, letting her know dinner was fine and she was headed to the airport. Kora's name appeared on the caller id. She was probably calling to see if Ryen was boarding the plane yet. She and Chesna would have had plenty of time to go through the information from Sophie's private detective as well. Ryen reminded herself there were pressing matters awaiting her in Florence.

"Hey, Kora," she said as she put the phone to her ear.

"So, should we no longer be expecting to see you in the morning?" Kora's tone was inquisitive, but also held the hint of amusement.

Ryen let out a sigh. "If Chesna keeps having visions of my decisions it would be more helpful if she could let me know each morning so I don't waste time working through things myself." She sounded more annoyed than she actually was. Chesna couldn't control when or what she saw. It just added more frustration to the situation that she was now having visions that involved Ryen and Cash. It worried Ryen more than she was willing to admit and if Chesna had seen things about Paris and not told Ryen...

Kora seemed to ignore Ryen's tone, "You know better than anyone not to let fear influence your choices. Don't be afraid to make decisions you may see as selfish."

"You know, just as I do, that being selfish is not a luxury our lives allow." The sadness in Ryen's voice caught her a little off guard. She had never before felt such a desire to be selfish, at least not when it wasn't related to safety, and she hadn't realized that maybe she wanted to be now.

Kora's voice seemed soaked in wisdom as she responded, "Good leaders are balanced leaders. Your life and all aspects of your life need to be in balance for you to be the leader you want to be. Trial and error, learning from all of our experiences, good and bad, that is what provides us with the wisdom we need to help others. You know what regret feels like, but it's better to regret something you've done than something you were afraid to face. And, it's better to receive permission for something after you've made up your mind rather than before. That way you know how you really feel and what you really want."

Ryen's silence on the other end left an opening for Kora to continue. "The choice is still yours. We love you no matter what. And as for the matter of what the investigator found, it doesn't appear urgent. We will look into it and we'll let you know if we discover anything that needs immediate attention."

Ryen's voice was filled with resignation, "I love you, too. Thanks. I'll talk to you later." As she pushed the "end" button her head fell back on the headrest. She could see from the front window that they were approaching the airport. She also knew that Cash's driver had overheard both sides of the phone conversation and was drawing his own conclusions, but she didn't care about that, "I no longer wish to go to the airport. Take me to your final destination for the night."

Chapter 39

Ryen could still turn back. Rafa was the only person who had seen her arrive, other than the driver, but that didn't really concern her now. The question was, could she take the next step? Rafa had let her in through the side door as he was escorting a wobbly girl from the club. She could sense his feelers trying to probe her mind, but he wasn't having any luck.

"Is Cash here? I just need to speak with him for a minute." Yes, she needed to speak with him, but she had no idea what she was going to say. Maybe he wasn't even here, or maybe he'd refuse to see her.

"He's upstairs in his apartment. Would you like me to call him down for you?"

"No!" Ryen almost shouted. She needed a couple minutes to work up more courage. "Sorry, I didn't mean to sound so, I mean, would it be ok if I went up? But please, could you not tell him I'm coming?" To herself she added, *in case I chicken out.*

Rafa was very intrigued. He appeared to be weighing the dangers to his friend if he allowed Ryen to go upstairs. "I'll unlock the door for you," he said even as he was pulling out his keys and reaching out for the doorknob. He pointed to the carpeted stairs in front of them that led up a dimly lit hallway. There was a light at the top of the stairs where Ryen could see the door to Cash's apartment. "This door will lock behind you, but you will be able to get out."

"Um, I was, am, on my way to the airport. Can I leave my suitcase here by the door?" The last thing she needed was to show up on Cash's doorstep with luggage, like she was planning to move in.

"Yes, I'll set it just inside the door," he had a little smile on his face, and Ryen swore he winked at her as he turned around and closed the door behind him.

Ryen stood frozen at the bottom of the steps. Did Cash hear the door to the stairwell? Could he hear her heart pounding right now? Everything in her, which had been conditioned for years to dislike and distrust vampires, was screaming at her to go, but there was no other logical reason she could think of in this moment. There was nothing pressing, needing her to fly to Italy tonight. Cash had never given her any reason to be afraid of him, aside from merely existing, and the Cash she had dinner with was so kind and inviting. Plus, she had resolved in the car that she owed something to the women who shared her soul, that's what had finally convinced her that she wasn't being completely selfish. Now that the connection had been opened between her present and her various pasts, she would be aware of them for the rest of her life. She had a feeling that this was what Zeta had wanted from her all along, for her to connect with Cash so the others could reconnect. Still, none of them had experienced what she had; she was walking into the enemy camp.

Subconsciously she had been having this battle within herself for weeks, only realizing it on a conscious level tonight. Would she even be here if the stupid soulmate pull didn't exist?

Enough! Somehow, while Ryen had been running through her excuses again, she had made her way up the stairs. This was it. Run away, or face it head on? Ryen took a deep breath, raised her hand, noticing the slight tremor from her nervousness, and knocked on the door.

Faintly Ryen heard Cash's voice say, "It's open."

If it were even possible, her heart beat a little faster as she opened the door and stepped inside. As she shut the door behind her she was able to shakily let out the breath she had been holding since she had knocked. She wiped a sheen of apprehensive sweat from her forehead.

Ryen turned back around and took in Cash's apartment. It was open, more like a loft than what she had pictured. To be expected, it was very masculine: dark wood floors, dark leather furniture, creamy walls and rugs. Over to the left was a kitchen area with barstools at the counter where an open bottle of Macallan sat, and a little table in the far corner. To the right, along the same wall was a fire place with a flat screen hanging above it. A plush sofa and comfy looking chairs arched around the fire place. There were several candles around the tables and mantel which she had not expected.

Along the adjacent wall were large glass windows that looked down into the club. Ryen was not surprised by that. It seemed natural for Cash to continue to be "at the club" even after he left, but she couldn't hear music or even the bass. She concluded that the walls must be super sound proof. As she looked past the sofa area Ryen's breath caught as she took in that part of the apartment. A large bed was raised up a couple of steps from the main floor. Her imagination immediately went to what had most likely transpired in this apartment on numerous occasions, jealousy washing over her. Just then, from some room or opening she hadn't yet seen, Cash emerged.

He was wearing pajama pants and a white t-shirt. Again, Ryen was struck by how gorgeous he was, but she hadn't allowed herself to really see his physical beauty before. Now her assessing eyes took in his black hair, damp from a recent shower. The longer hair on top was tousled from a towel-dry. Images of how he had looked during their previous encounters flooded her memory: always dress pants, nice shirts, suits and ties, professional, sophisticated playboy, *muy suave*. But this was a completely different look tonight.

It was no secret that girls, women, hell, probably even guys, threw themselves at him on a daily basis, and she admitted silently that she didn't blame a single one. Ryen was surprised that the thought of the ones who had caught his eye caused another pang of jealousy...

When he returned to the club after their dinner, he had been in such a foul mood. After his failed encounter with the models, Cash had gone upstairs, had a couple of drinks and took a shower. The shower had not helped and once again he was drowning in the memories of tonight. Ryen was well on her way to Florence now and he needed to forget about her and get back to his old self. Perhaps it was finally time to throw in the towel with this one. He didn't know how to process that.

He was getting dressed when he heard the knock on the door. The guys had been well aware that he was irritable, so they would know to steer clear of him for the rest of the night. Maybe something important had come up that needed his attention.

As he walked out of the bathroom he was visibly shocked by who was standing in his apartment. He didn't even attempt to disguise his surprise.

"Ryen?"

"I hope I'm not interrupting anything. Do you have company?" She was clearly trying to confirm that they were alone. Did she think he had a woman up here? The backroom downstairs was reserved for that business. This was his personal space.

"Nobody else is here." Cash wanted to come out and ask her what *she* was doing here, but she looked like a cornered animal deciding on fight or flight. If he said the wrong thing she would very likely run for the hills. Her behavior had never really given him any reason to pursue her, but glimpses into her emotions did. That was probably the reason he wanted her so badly. He didn't understand why she was here, in his apartment, instead of on a plane to Italy, as she had insisted was necessary. Someone had to have let her into the upstairs hallway, so she wasn't here by accident. Who had let her in without notifying him? He'd figure that out later. She looked good standing there. She looked the same as she had at dinner but her hair was down now and her mood was different. Normally extremely calm and collected, Ryen's pulse was now racing. She seemed terrified or nervous, or nervously terrified. Instead of asking her why she was here he merely asked, "Didn't you have a plane to catch?"

"I missed my flight," was all she offered as a response.

Cash moved slowly towards the kitchen. He didn't want to startle her into fleeing. The last thing he wanted was for her to leave. "Can I get you a drink? Glass of wine? Whiskey?"

Ryen gave a little nervous chuckle, "Maybe some whiskey." He should have known then that she wasn't herself because she made no attempt to demand he open a new bottle in front of her. He noticed she kept looking towards the windows that looked out over the club.

"They're one-way windows, mirrors on the other side, so I can keep an eye on things." He had gotten out the glasses, but instead of pouring, something made him move towards her.

Careful, no sudden movements to startle her, he told himself. He stopped when he was right in front of her. Although it didn't seem possible, her heart rate increased even more. He looked into her eyes, searching for understanding. After so many rejections, what was she doing here? Why was she so terrified? He let a few moments of silence pass while he stared into her eyes. Then he slowly lowered his lips to hers.

Slowly, this got you slapped before, he reminded himself. But something was different this time. Something had changed; he just didn't know what it was.

Their lips met in a gentle kiss, lasting only a few moments, holding back the intensity that Cash longed to unleash. Ryen didn't pull away or resist. Cash tried not to get hopeful. When he slowly pulled back he looked into her eyes again, still searching for answers, now to even more questions. When he touched her he felt that electricity that he had felt when he had first kissed her at the club and the times their hands had touched, a subtle tingling that started at the point of contact but then spread to his entire body. There was that mental pull as well. He hadn't been able to describe it the first time he kissed her; so many other emotions and noises had been interfering. But now that it was completely silent, except for Ryen's thundering heartbeat, he could focus more on that pull in his head. It wasn't him trying to breach her mind, nor the other way around. It was as if an outside force was pushing or pulling them together.

Now what? Cash knew what he wanted to happen; he wanted her, every part of her. Never before in his life had he experienced what was stirring inside of him now. There was never a shortage of women lined up for his enjoyment, but he had never really cared about them. Every drop of blood, every sexual pleasure had ultimately been for his selfish desire. If this were a normal situation, Ryen would already be throwing herself at him and he would take her in his arms, kiss her so thoroughly while sending mental suggestions of what he wanted and what she wanted from him, that she would practically be opening up her neck for him herself.

Nothing about Ryen was normal, nor was anything about this situation. Cash had been throwing himself at *her* over and over, but now it was Ryen's turn to give a signal. She slowly turned to leave. Cash felt himself internally collapse from crushed hope he'd allowed to exist. But instead of putting her hand towards the doorknob, Ryen reached slightly higher, and locked the door.

Chapter 40

Ryen knew what was coming as Cash stood before her. She could really use that drink he had left on the counter. The first time he had kissed her, on the dance floor, she had been caught off guard and definitely not expecting how it would affect her, but now she prepared herself. He moved so slowly, like he was giving her time to stop him. She had no intention of doing that! This was the whole point of being here. Regardless of how prepared she thought she was, when his lips touched hers she was metaphorically knocked off her feet by the electric current that shot through her. This kiss was different from the last. It was soft and gentle, but Ryen could sense the power Cash was holding back.

She wanted to protest when he pulled away, but she was frozen into place. His eyes searched hers, wanting her to answer questions she couldn't hear, but she knew them anyway. Words would not come to her, so she turned to lock the door.

When Ryen turned back around she looked at Cash. A fire filled those icy blue eyes, and Ryen saw the white blue center of a flame. Before she even had a chance to smile at him, Cash's lips crushed hers as he unleashed the passion he had been holding at bay. Ryen was afraid she would struggle to keep up, but her passion matched, if not rivaled, his.

Cash's hands grabbed her hips and pressed his body to hers as he backed her up against the wall. Ryen had her hands pressed to the wall to steady herself, but when his mouth threatened to leave hers she wound her fingers through his hair, preparing to hold his head in place. However, when his lips moved to her jaw she didn't resist. Cash blazed fiery kisses from her jaw line down her neck and across her collar bone. A hand left her hip to move aside the neckline of her dress, exposing her shoulder to more of his kisses. Then slowly, his mouth started to retrace its path.

When he reached her neck Ryen felt his tongue caress what she knew was the soft skin covering the veins. Her whole body went tense with fear and she knew it was radiating out of her so Cash could feel it too. His lips pulled away from her neck, and she could feel his breath on her ear as he spoke, his voice deeper than usual, conveying the dueling hungers he was feeling.

"I won't bite you unless you ask me to."

Ryen didn't relax; her mind racing. *What was that supposed to mean?* She would never ask him to bite her. Was he crazy?

She felt his breath again and his voice caressed her senses, "You have my word. Do you trust me?"

Two weeks ago, hell two hours ago, she would have said no without a moment's hesitation, but now... She could feel his mind reaching out to her. She could feel his emotions as if they were hers. Everything told her that in this moment he wouldn't hurt her; he couldn't. "Yes," she said, barely a whisper.

His mouth returned to her neck as if to prove to her he could be trusted. This time as his tongue caressed her skin she let the tension fall from her body. Now her hand sought the skin under his shirt. It was warm and smooth, and she could feel his tight muscles moving beneath it. His mouth found hers again, only to pull away just enough, as she pulled his shirt up over his head. Free from his shirt, Ryen placed her hands on his chest, feeling the electric current flowing up her arms as she knew he could feel it flowing into him. His eyes closed at the pleasure of her hands moving their way from his chest over his abs and up to his shoulders. Ryen leaned forward and softly kissed the hollow of his neck, and she felt a shiver of ecstasy ripple through him.

Cash's hands went to her hip and undid the tie of her dress. As it fell open Ryen froze again, this time out of embarrassment of standing before him. Panic shot through her and the lights dimmed.

Oops! She thought. She would have to hold her powers in check. Cash looked up at her questioningly. She gave him a sheepish smile. Cash's eyes shined with admiration. If he was impressed by a little light trick, Ryen would definitely need to watch her powers, lest *she* frighten *him*.

Ryen watched his eyes leave hers and drop lower. His hands moved over the strapless black bustier that covered her stomach. He dropped his head to the exposed skin of her chest, the skin that even the deep V of her dress had covered. This time it was Ryen who shivered at his touch. Ryen arched and let her head fall back against the wall. Cash's hands brushed her dress from her shoulders. As it fell to the ground he lifted Ryen into the air so her mouth was level with his as he stood. She wrapped her legs around him and an ache filled her center as she felt the hardness barely covered by the cotton layer of his pants.

Cash carried her with her legs still wrapped around him across the room to the bed as if she weighed no more than her dress that was lying on the floor, his mouth never leaving hers. Before he lowered her to the bed, he skillfully unzipped the back of her bustier and flung it to the side. As she lay on the bed, his mouth again moved from hers to her neck, and this time it continued down, and again Ryen wound her fingers through his hair that was still damp from his shower. Cash took his time, stopping to caress each breast with first his hand, then his mouth, and lastly his tongue. Fire blazed through Ryen as if she were burning from the inside out. No man's touch had ever made her feel even close to this.

She was so caught up in his kisses and the fire burning within her, she didn't even notice that his hands had removed her panties until his fingers touched between her legs. Shock and pleasure shot through her and there was a whooshing sound throughout the apartment.

Cash stopped kissing her to look around at what had made the sound. All of the candles around his apartment were ablaze with foot high flames. Ryen took a deep breath and lowered the flames. An impressed smile crossed his face, and Ryen bit her lip guiltily.

"I'm glad I haven't pissed you off enough to use your powers against me," he said as he stood over her staring hungrily.

If only he knew what I am capable of, she thought. Ryen was acutely aware of her nakedness, but the look in Cash's eyes erased any guilt, fear, or insecurity that threatened to creep in. The lack of his touch was depriving

197

her of the electric current that had been feeding her, and she felt a chill without it. She looked up at him, imploring him with her gaze. She wanted him to touch her again; she needed him to touch her.

When he didn't move, Ryen sat up, letting her legs fall over the side of the bed. She reached out and untied the waist string of his pants and gently tugged them down. Another wave of warmth filled her as she looked at him completely naked. She reached out and touched him, eliciting a moan of pleasure that seemed to originate in his very core. Cash's emotions washed over her. Knowing she could not do it justice she moved her head towards where her hand was and took him inside. The moan turned into a deeper groan and his hands grabbed her hair, holding her head in place as he rocked back and forth.

Cash mumbled a protest when Ryen pulled her head away, but his eyes burned with the fire she felt as she laid back and pulled him to her. As his bare skin touched every inch of hers, urgency filled both of them. She let out a cry of pleasure as he entered her. Pulling her mental shields back, still concealing her darkest secrets and things not hers to tell, she let her emotions leave her freely. Ryen felt Cash's reaction when he realized she had opened herself up to him willingly for the first time. His mind mingled with hers and the thrill it brought caused his movements to increase, as his hands urgently sought out every inch of her body, igniting flames of electric heat on her skin. She couldn't get enough of him either, her hands moving over him, pressing him to her. His mouth traveled from hers to her neck and back, the burning consuming both of them until it exploded into unimaginable bliss.

With neither of them wanting to sever their connection, soft caresses and gentle kisses followed until they lay side by side on the bed. Ryen had her eyes closed and focused on catching her breath. She was very much aware of Cash lying next to her. In this moment everything seemed perfect. She didn't care about the "what ifs" or the "what happens next". The only thing she could think of was how she didn't want this feeling to end. She was afraid to move or speak for fear of shattering the delicate balance, so she did neither. She laid still and quiet for a long time.

Ryen felt Cash move his arm and she silently begged him to be still, but she could tell he had rolled onto his side and was looking at her. His hand encircled hers and squeezed ever so slightly. "Are you ok?" he asked just above a whisper.

Ryen sighed softly. The answer was very complicated. Ok was merely a shadow of how she was feeling, but she wasn't sure she could put it into words. She felt Cash's anxiety increase at the amount of time it was taking her to answer.

"Do you need to run for the door now?" He was trying to sound like he was joking, but Ryen could feel his worry and uncharacteristic insecurity, the latter so out of place with the obnoxiously confident Cash she knew.

She smiled and then opened her eyes as she turned towards him, "No need to run just yet. I'm content here." That was at least enough of the truth to calm his fears. She let some of her emotions wash over him again and he smiled back at her. With his free arm he pulled her close and kissed her forehead and then her mouth. He continued to hold her close, so Ryen laid her head on his chest and relaxed. When she heard Cash's breathing slow and even out, she allowed herself to fall asleep.

Chapter 41

Cash wasn't sure for how long he had dozed off; at some point Ryen had moved. She was no longer in his arms, and laid with her back to him. The sheets covered her legs, but her hip and back were exposed. He wanted to touch her but he was afraid to disturb her. He let his eyes wander over her, memorizing her every curve as he thought about how they had gotten here.

This had been his original end game, to get her to give herself to him, and now he didn't think he could ever let her go. He had never experienced what he had tonight. Everything before seemed so empty compared to now. He had relished in his bachelor status and he had never wanted for female attention, but he had never encountered anything, on any level, close to the connection he felt with Ryen. The physical contact was incredible, but when she had willingly dropped some of her defenses to let him in, that emotional and mental connection had been the most intense feeling he had ever experienced. He wanted more. He wanted to know everything about her, and he wanted her to know everything about him.

He wanted to bite her. Sure, he could use a drink, he hadn't had any blood for a couple of days, but he wanted to see if that myth he had heard all his life was true, that a bite between two people who loved each other was the most powerful connection and feeling there was. But he had given his word that he wouldn't bite her unless she wanted him to. Well, he smiled to himself, he had her practically begging for other things earlier, maybe he could get her to beg to be bitten.

Thinking about their previous activities, and imagining biting her combined with her bare skin within reach stirred Cash's desires. Very slowly and gently he leaned down and placed a kiss on her hip. Not caring that he was disrupting her sleep, he continued to sensually forge a path of kisses up her side and back. He heard her heart rate increase and he knew she was awake, but she stayed still and quiet. He brushed her hair aside to kiss the back of her neck and noticed her tattoo for the first time.

Cash's dad had an almost identical tattoo on his arm, but Ryen's had a portion filled in. His dad had told him that all witches had this tattoo, but he had never mentioned any of them looking different. In fact all of the witches Cash knew had tattoos just like his dad's. His thumb moved across Ryen's tattoo as he wondered why hers was different. He decided to break the silence and ask, "Why is part of your tattoo filled in?"

He felt Ryen's body tense, but her voice sounded calm when she asked her own question, "What do you mean?"

"My dad and other witches I know have this same tattoo, but yours is different. Does it mean something?"

Her actual thoughts were blocked from him but she hadn't closed her mind completely. He could feel them racing. Still she sounded calm when she answered, "It's just a rite of passage kind of thing."

Cash could tell that she wasn't willing to give anything further, so he resumed his kisses. He had no intention of this being his only night with her. There was time to learn her secrets. As he continued to kiss her he felt her relax once again. With his thoughts returning to the things that had started his kisses, he nuzzled her neck. He could feel the blood flowing under his tongue, his need for her causing his canine teeth to extend slightly. He had no plan of biting her, but his teeth were very sensitive, and brushing them along her neck elicited an unbelievable sensation. The feel of his teeth caused Ryen to go rigid again. Cash pulled back slightly and sighed, saddened that she really didn't trust him.

Maybe she should be afraid of you. Cash mentally kicked at his inner voice for reminding him of his recent lapse in control. Things were different now though. Being here with Ryen felt *right*. He realized that he wasn't worried about hurting her, and he wanted to reassure her as well. "You don't need to worry, I said I wouldn't bite you and I meant it. I was just enjoying the sensation it created. I'm sorry I made you uncomfortable."

Ryen rolled onto her back to look Cash in the eyes, "I'm ok. It's just hard. I forget that you're a vampire until moments like that."

There were so many things he wanted to ask her. He knew she hated vampires, but why? With the mere glimpse of her powers tonight no vampire would be a match for her. Instead of prying into her thoughts he opted to be honest with his, "Maybe if you understood what I was thinking. There are three or four reasons a vampire bites someone." He saw concern fill her eyes, but he continued, "Blood is the most logical, it's the basic way to get nourishment to fuel our supernatural abilities. Obviously a bite can be used as a defensive weapon, and there are some who use it as a way to exert their power or to purposefully cause pain." At his third reason the concern in Ryen's eyes switched to terror.

"Hey," he caressed her face, completely confident in his word, "I won't hurt you, I promise." *What happened to her?* "My point for telling you this is actually for the final reason. It's one of those things, kind of like saving yourself for marriage, which vampire parents tell their children, but I've heard about it from more than just my parents. They say that when two people are truly connected, a bite can raise that connection to an intensity beyond imagination. Someday I will ask to bite you. I want you to know why and have time to consider it."

She started to say something. Fearing she was going to shoot down any future questions on the subject, Cash placed his finger on her lips, "Shh, don't say anything now."

And then he kissed her mouth until he was sure she would no longer offer protests. In order to keep her mind off of being bitten he had another plan, "Now, last time you almost set my apartment on fire, so please prepare yourself." He knew the smile he gave her as his hand reached below the sheets conveyed the wickedness he intended. His smile widened to a chuckle as her eyes widened in understanding.

Chapter 42

Cash was irritated with himself for falling asleep again. Even before he opened his eyes he knew he was alone in bed. He wouldn't admit it out loud, but panic ran through him, thinking Ryen had snuck away without him knowing. There was no need for his panic, and he realized that as he heard the water running in the shower. Her suitcase was open on his sofa, so she had clearly found Rafa's delivery. Cash had asked him to bring up her things after she had fallen asleep. Cash wished he could have seen her face when she realized that someone had entered the apartment while she was here.

Cash contemplated joining her in the shower, quietly sneaking in behind her and wrapping his arms around her wet soapy body. Instead he decided to give her some privacy and enjoy the version of events in his head. This fantasy was better than any he'd had before tonight because now he knew exactly what her eyes looked like when he touched her, knew the feel of her skin. He was enjoying the show in his head so much that he almost didn't notice the crashing sound that came from the bathroom. Amused, he smiled. It sounded like the contents of the countertop met the tile floor.

The club usually didn't close down until around six, and although it was getting close, the music and patrons were still going strong. The lights flashed through the windows along the wall. Cash wanted to make Ryen feel more at ease so he grabbed the remote control from his night stand and pushed a few buttons. The view to the club disappeared, replaced by a nighttime scene of Florence, the Duomo with a full moon shining behind it.

Cash heard her before she had fully emerged through the door, "How was the shower?"

He held back a laugh as she started, clearly not expecting him to be awake. Admittedly, Cash was disappointed her towel had stayed firmly in place. A look of realization crossed her face, "Sorry if I woke you. I accidently knocked some of my stuff on the floor with my towel."

All of this time Ryen had been a mystery to him, and still was for that matter, but she seemed so other worldly, beyond comprehension with the way she

203

affected him. Yet the simple act of dropping a hairbrush made this maddening woman normal.

"It appears you found your belongings." Cash couldn't help laughing at the look that crossed her face. He imagined it was a mix of embarrassment and incredulity. "Don't worry. It was delivered with the utmost discretion."

He watched her rush over and start digging through her bag. "Did you lose something?"

"No," she said with frustration, "I'm looking for my phone. Thanks to your friend, I'm sure I have several missed calls and texts from Sophie."

"Again, don't worry. He was told to keep your presence to himself."

Ryen shot him a look that said *he* might trust Rafa, but she did not. He watched her find her phone, make a face about its dead battery, scavenge through her bag more until she found her charger, and then look around for an outlet. Cash, thoroughly enjoying these trivial behaviors, pointed towards the wall. He watched her face as she saw the windows to the club. "That's beautiful. It looks so real. How'd you do that?" she asked.

"It's sort of like a digital picture frame. I spend a lot of time here, so I have different images uploaded to mix up the scenery. I thought you'd like this one." A warm smile played across her lips. He could tell she considered Florence her home as much as he did.

"I'm sure all your ladies are impressed with it as well?" She was trying to be light, but there was something in her voice. She was obviously fishing, but was that jealousy Cash was picking up?

"I'm sure they would be, but this is my sanctuary. I don't bring people up here." He hoped that the magnitude of her presence here would be conveyed. Besides Rafa, and his sister when she had visited, no one else had been in his apartment in the three years he'd lived here.

"I guess I wasn't invited here either. Sorry for invading your privacy." Her tone was only slightly sincere. Now she was definitely fishing for validation.

She was still wrapped in her towel, and Cash closed the distance between them. Ryen didn't seem to mind that he was still completely naked.

"If I didn't want you here, you wouldn't be here." He was all seriousness as he looked into her eyes, letting his emotion flow over her, imploring her to know with all of her senses that she was exactly where he wanted her to be.

He decided to play with her a little, "So, you currently don't have a job to rush off to," she narrowed her eyes at him, "and I'm assuming no one is expecting you immediately in Italy?"

She seemed concerned or confused at the direction of his questions, "No, not immediately."

"Hmm, you certainly make it easy for someone to kidnap you without alerting anyone to your absence."

Ryen glared at him. He had said it only half seriously, but her irritation was mixed with something else, fear maybe. However, her voice was even when she asked, "And who might be kidnapping me?"

In a matter of fact tone he said, "Me, of course. You didn't think I was just going to let you run away and chance you never coming back?"

Ryen laughed a little and said with a wink, "That depends on how good you are at making breakfast."

"Before we worry about breakfast, I have a field trip." Cash pulled on his pajama pants and walked into his closet over by the bathroom. He emerged wearing a light sweater and handed Ryen a pair of pants and a sweatshirt. She looked at him questioningly.

"We're going up to the rooftop."

"Aren't there people up there?"

"No, Rafa closed down the rooftop dance floor earlier when an unexpected rain shower came through."

"It wasn't supposed to rain, was it?"

"No." He watched as shadows of thought played across her face. Ryen looked like she was thinking hard about something, but she put on the clothes he handed her without further comment. He had grabbed the smallest things he knew he owned, but they were still a little baggy on her. Still, he liked seeing her in his clothes. He grabbed a blanket on the way out the door.

"What are we doing on the rooftop?"

"Watching the sunrise." Ryen linked her fingers with his, and Cash felt the electric current. After all of the touching the past few hours, it was no longer shocking, but its intensity had not diminished. He smiled at her and thought how, after all of the stress and aggravation over this woman, everything seemed as it should be now...

A shiver ran through Ryen. She was glad Cash had given her a sweatshirt and brought a blanket. She wondered about the unexpected rain. Had she had something to do with that? What little control she had tonight had gone towards protecting things in her head from Cash. She had let her powers slip more than once. Could the intensity of everything she had been experiencing have caused the rain? Oh well, no one thought anything of it, so she wouldn't dwell on it either.

Little puddles here and there from the rain reflected the lights draped above them. Tables, high and low, were positioned around the outskirts of the dance floor, that wasn't quite as big as the one downstairs, and there were two little sheds opposite each other. She figured they must be the DJ booth and the bar covered for protection. Ryen sat between Cash's legs on a lounge chair and leaned against him. Some of the clouds still lingered in the sky, and as the sun came up, she marveled at the beautiful colors before her eyes. Cash rested his cheek against her head and had his arms wrapped around her with her hands in his. Every once in a while he would bend down to kiss her cheek or her neck, or bring her hand to his lips. She was awed by the sense of peace she felt. Even more incredible was how safe she felt in the arms of a vampire.

"The other day you told me you'd been having dreams about us. Would you tell me about one of the ones that ended happily?"

Ryen knew he smiled even though she couldn't see him. Maybe she felt it in his face. "I will," Cash paused, "if you promise to answer a question for me afterwards."

"If I have an answer, I will." Making a promise to answer an unknown question made her apprehensive, but if necessary she was confident she'd be able to evade him.

Still holding her hands, Cash raised his to Ryen's head. On either side of her temples his index fingers rubbed gently, "If you open yourself up, I'll show you as well as tell you."

Ryen was very tempted by his offer to see what he saw, but the more she withdrew her shields the more vulnerable the information in her head became. Sensing her inner struggle Cash tried more persuasion, "As much as I'd love to be inside your head, to know what makes you who you are, I'd rather you show it to me or tell me willingly than to invade your head unwelcomed. I'll only show you what's in mine."

Ryen didn't respond. She was still debating whether or not the temptation outweighed the risks. Cash didn't wait for her to answer, probably because he didn't expect her to say yes, "I don't know where we were exactly, but I knew that it wasn't the present. There was a little house built out of the earth, and as we looked out there was nothing but rolling hills for miles in every direction. I had on boots, pants and a long sleeved shirt with the sleeves rolled up. My hands had a trace of dirt, like I worked so much that it didn't matter how much I washed them, they would always look that way. You wore a long skirt and a long sleeved shirt as well. Your sleeves were rolled up too, and the top few buttons were undone because it was warm. It was windy. It blew your hair around your face, and looking out at the tall green grass all around us, it moved in the wind and looked like rolling waves on the ocean. I remember you holding my hand and squeezing, and although we didn't speak I knew I was happy and so were you. There was this sense that it had been a struggle for us to get where we were, but we had made it, and everything that lay before us was ours."

As Ryen listened to Cash's words she slowly pulled back some of her defenses, letting in the images he wanted her to see.

The warm sun shone down, warming her face. Cash held her hand and looked at her with the biggest, happiest smile. The breeze danced around the bare skin on her neck, and she could feel the sweat on her back and legs. It was so real. She could smell the fresh air, the wild flowers mixed with the grass, the upturned earth by their little house. When Cash spoke of the feeling of accomplishment, she felt it too.

"Hey," Cash turned her to face him and held her face between his hands, his thumbs wiping at her tears, "What's wrong?"

"That's all you saw?" Cash nodded, and she continued, not satisfied, "How do you know it had a happy ending?"

With concern for her in his eyes he answered, "Because to me it felt like the end of something, like we had already conquered the hard part and we could relax and be at peace."

Ryen smiled, but she let out a jagged breath as a few more tears fell. Instead of using his thumbs again, Cash kissed them away. "It's ok. It was just a dream, and it was happy."

She didn't know how to explain. After all of the heartache she experienced from glimpses into Zeta's and Afton's lives, this brief peek into an experience that ended happily was responsible for her tears of relief. It sparked hope within her that she wanted to ignore. Ryen took a deep breath, closed her eyes, and leaned forward to kiss him. There was an urgency in her kiss, but not like earlier in the evening. This urgency came from the need to know this moment was real, and an urgency to freeze time.

Cash had been taken aback by the need in her kiss, but he kissed her back with the same fervor until she relaxed and he could easily pull her head away to look in her eyes. "You had dreams, too."

It wasn't a question but Ryen felt the need to answer it as such. She lowered her eyes from his as she whispered, "Yes, sort of."

"I thought as much when you seemed so interested in the fact that I had. So, here's my question, and I know you have an answer, what does it mean?"

Not wanting to look at him as she answered, Ryen turned back around and leaned her back against Cash's chest again. She allowed his arms to encircle her once more. As she spoke she looked at the brightening sky. "I had no idea where it was going to lead, but several weeks ago I did a spell to connect with my past lives. As a result, I had these dreams or visions. They weren't like yours. I was watching them happen like a movie though I could feel what my counterpart felt. I didn't see *us* either. The people I saw were different each time. I made the connection when you kissed me. I hadn't put it together that the same blue eyes that I see when I look at you were the same blue eyes I saw in my dreams. When you kissed me it all fell into place. I would have run from you anyway, for kissing me, but that realization was why I left and why I avoided you after that."

Cash didn't speak but Ryen thought she felt his body tense. Her curiosity broke the silence, "What were some of the other dreams you had?"

There was a huskiness in his voice as he spoke, fighting through his emotions to be able to speak, "There was one that was sad. It was sort of medieval but more modern. I betrayed my best friend to be with you, and I didn't care. Then I left you, to save him from knowing."

"Afton and Shaw," Ryen whispered. She felt Cash nod ever so slightly.

"The most disturbing was in Egypt. I had to watch you be tortured, and then I was killed trying to save you." Ryen could hear the pain in his voice as he spoke of the dream.

"That was the beginning, Zeta and Tarik. They killed her too, after him. I spoke with Zeta and she said that she would have killed herself anyway to search for him in the afterlife."

"So, what does it *mean*?" Cash was almost pleading with her to give him an answer that he could understand.

Ryen was glad she was facing away from him. She had never said it out loud, and something about doing so gave her a sense that it would lock it into existence, that she wouldn't be able to ignore or avoid it anymore. "We're soulmates," she whispered as she let out a sigh of defeat.

After a long silence Cash finally spoke, "Well, at least it makes sense now."

The relief in his voice caused Ryen to turn to look at him with a "how?" expression on her face. Somewhat lightly he said, "I mean, all this time I've been crazed. I couldn't get you out of my head no matter how much I tried. You not wanting anything to do with me, and having open hostility towards me, just made me want you more. Everyone around here has been dealing with my sour mood for weeks. I've destroyed my office; I haven't had any blood for days, all because I thought I was going crazy. I have been in love with you since I first saw you in Paris, and now at least I know I had no control to make it otherwise."

Did he just say he was in love with me? Ryen felt her heart race along with her mind. She was stupid to think she could come here, get something out of her system, and then just walk away. What had she done? She didn't think she could be as strong as Afton and leave him, and now there really was no turning back.

Either he sensed the turmoil inside her, or he wanted her to say something in response. Cash roughly turned her face to his with both hands. Ryen grabbed his wrists to protest as he looked fervently into her eyes, "I love you! Does it scare me? Yes. Did I ever expect it? No. Do I want to change it? No. I love you."

Ryen felt her body shaking. If Cash wasn't holding her head in his hands she thought she might slump to the ground. She searched his eyes as she wrestled with her mind and emotions. Barely more than a whisper, she confessed, "I love you."

Instead of the increased internal destruction she thought she would feel, saying those words ignited a small flare of strength. She didn't have long to think about that as Cash's mouth bruised hers in his insistence at being as close to her as possible. She succumbed to the desire that overtook them both.

Chapter 43

Ryen was distracted by Cash as they reentered his apartment and didn't notice the delivery on the counter until he led her to his little kitchen. Similarly to when she discovered her luggage in the apartment, a shot of panic ran through her thinking about someone else being here with them.

"Rafa?" she asked a little annoyed.

"Yes, but don't worry. He's gone home to get some sleep." Gesturing to the items on the counter he continued, "I realize that I didn't actually make this, but since breakfast was one of your stipulations for staying..."

There was a pitcher of fresh squeezed orange juice and a bowl of more oranges. Next to that was a tray of delicious looking fresh pastries. Ryen sat down on one of the bar stools while Cash went to the other side of the counter to retrieve plates and glasses from the cupboard. Ryen's stomach growled as she eyed the pastries. She hadn't realized how hungry she was, but then again, she had burned a lot of calories since dinner last night. Her hunger beat out her patience and she grabbed a roll and started devouring it before Cash could put a plate in front of her. Her behavior caused a gentle laugh from Cash, but she wasn't ashamed.

"I'll go to the store later, or have Rafa stop on his way back to work. I usually just eat something downstairs, so there's not a lot here." Then with mischief in his eyes, "If I'm planning to hold you hostage I should have quality food to feed you so you can keep your energy up." His wink and grin brought a blush to Ryen's cheeks.

Ryen focused on another roll and her glass of juice, but she could feel Cash watching her. Although very subtle, she felt the tingling around her mind a couple of times letting her know he was still trying to get in. "As I told you last night, if there's something you'd like to know, you can always ask."

"Will you answer?" His interest was definitely piqued, but he raised an eyebrow in doubt.

"I might. But again, asking will get you more than attempting to trespass in my head." The idea of him forcing himself into her thoughts and secrets brought back that aggravation she had felt with him for the past few weeks, but she didn't blame him for trying.

"Ok," he started. "Will you play a game with me?" Ryen didn't answer, but her head tilt and raised eyebrows questioned what he had up his sleeve.

"It's called truth or strip," a wicked grin joining the twinkle in his eyes.

"Interesting. What are the rules?" Ryen figured it was pretty self-explanatory, but she was willing to play along for the time being.

"Well, one of us poses a question to the other. We can either answer it or remove an item of clothing."

"The first one naked is the loser?" she asked.

"Well, I don't know if I'd consider it losing, but yes."

"It may be a short game then, seeing as both of us are only wearing two pieces of clothing."

Ryen watched as Cash contemplated something, "That does pose a problem. How about if once the clothing is gone the questioner gives the option of a consequence instead of an answer, like you have to do the dishes if you don't want to give your truth? After that it would be whoever concedes first."

Ryen liked the idea of having another option, but she worried about the consequences Cash might dream up. She didn't think they would be as innocent as doing dishes. On the other hand, there were some things she'd like to ask him, and this would provide a fairly easy way to do so. "Conditions accepted. You start."

"We'll start with some easy ones, when's your birthday?"

She didn't think they would stay this easy for long, "February 5. Same question to you."

213

"June 23. What's your favorite color?"

"Blue," Ryen didn't look at him when she answered. Her favorite color had always been some shade of blue, but now it was definitely an icy blue. She blushed at her own silliness as her mind wandered to images of his eyes. "What's yours?"

"You know you can come up with your own questions, right?" He was teasing her. She looked up at him to give him her best irritated glare, but his intense stare held her. "My favorite color is a golden green. Green like the forest, but with golden sun light laced through it." He seemed to have understood her reference to his eyes and thrown it back to her in all seriousness. Ryen's cheeks warmed again, but so did the rest of her body.

Cash playfully asked, while eyeing Ryen seductively, "Are you a good witch or a bad witch?"

Although it had been meant as a sexy joke, Ryen's blood ran cold. Maybe this game was more dangerous than she had previously thought. She'd be lying if she said she hadn't contemplated that same question a thousand times. Aloud she answered as calmly as she could muster, "Aren't we all a mixture of both? Sometimes the balance shifts one way or the other."

Then she threw the question back at him. "Are you a good vampire or a bad vampire?"

She laughed in her head at how until recently she hadn't even considered that the former existed. Ryen watched as a shadow passed across Cash's face. She hadn't been as successful in matching his seductive tone, and judging by his expression his mind was a million miles away. His answer wasn't at all what she had expected. "I'd like to say mostly good, but I'm sure there are different answers, depending on who you ask."

The mood in the room had shifted and Ryen watched Cash briefly shake his head after a couple of silent moments, as if to clear it of something he didn't want to see. His next question let Ryen know that the easy ones had definitely concluded. "How many relationships have you been in?"

"Actual relationships? One," she answered looking him in the eye. He knew who she was referring to; he had been inside Demitri's head.

He didn't give her a chance to ask her own question, "Did you ever tell him you loved him?" Something in Cash's eyes made her shiver.

"No," Ryen held his gaze as best as she could with this new emotion flooding it.

"Did you love him?"

"That's three questions," she tried to sound annoyed at his breaking of his own game's rules, but his eyes almost frightened her.

"You can catch up if you'd like, but you should also answer the question," then after a pause he added, "or take off an article of clothing."

"No." As she said it she saw whatever that emotion was leave his eyes. Was it possessiveness? Was it jealousy? Whatever it was, she didn't like it. She wasn't sure she wanted to know the answer, but she asked anyway, "How many relationships have you been in?"

He smiled amusedly, probably from her lack of originality, and mocking her he started with her own clarification, "Actual relationships? None, but you already deduced that when you judged my character weeks ago." His words didn't completely match the playfulness in his voice, but the sparkle in his eyes let Ryen know that his feelings had not been seriously hurt.

Still wondering if she really wanted to know more she asked her next question to catch up, "How many girls have been told that you loved them?"

"Four." There was a little playful challenge in his eyes now, and Ryen felt a little punch in her gut. She shouldn't be surprised. He probably said it all of the time when he was coercing girls to let him bite them. Four was lower than part of her had expected. He started to elaborate, and she wasn't sure if it was due to the hurt he could most likely see in her face, or just because he wanted to, "My mother, my sister, my niece," after a pause he added, "and you."

Ryen swallowed hard at the significance of his words. Four had been his honest answer but he hadn't wanted her to think that there had been someone else in his life like her. He gently squeezed her hand from across the counter. Although she was far from being an expert on Cash and his behaviors, he was definitely surprising her. His cockiness came and went, briefly replaced by something tender and sincere.

She took a deep breath and continued, "So I have one more in this round, this isn't really a question, but will you tell me about your family?"

"I think this is worth at least four questions." Ryen nodded in agreement. "My mother, Calandra Di Marco, is a vampire. She's smart, powerful, controlling, and not the least bit subtle. My father, Luca, is a witch as I've said. He's kind and gentle, a good balance to my mother. I have an older half-brother. My mom was married to a vampire long before she met my dad. He died when my brother was little. He was an adult when my parents met. He has never liked my dad, and I think because of that he has never liked witches in general. He got into an altercation with a witch a long time ago and it really messed him up. He's sort of a recluse now."

"Why? What happened to him?' Ryen could sense the sadness the conversation about his brother was causing Cash, but she wanted to understand.

"I don't know what he and the witch got into, I only know she cursed him. And not just any curse. She somehow got her hands on the secret spell that strips vampires of their immortality. That, among other things, was the curse she inflicted on him. As you can imagine, that didn't soften his heart towards witches at all."

That was some serious spell work and Ryen wondered why they hadn't heard about this rogue witch in the Coven. She didn't want to be distracted from Cash, so she focused her attention. Ryen filed away another question for her next turn about why, or rather how, some people in his family were vampires and the others witches so as not to interrupt him again. She watched a softness come over his face as he continued to talk about his family. She couldn't help the smile that formed in response on her face.

216

"I have a twin sister, Calla, who is also a vampire. She is married to a human. That was quite the family scandal," the last comment was filled with sarcasm.

"They have two children, five year old twins, Lilia and Ford. They are night and day. You'll love Lil. She is already planning to be a witch. My sister doesn't know what to do with her, but I think it makes my dad happy."

Ryen's heart squeezed at the casual way Cash mentioned her with his family. Although something most girls would love to hear, Ryen hadn't let herself think that far into the future. She knew she had gotten in deeper than she had intended, but to what extent she wasn't sure. Cash kept talking so Ryen pushed those unpleasant thoughts from her head.

"Ford is vampire all the way, pretty much since he was born." Cash stopped and seemed lost in his thoughts. Ryen hadn't expected him to divulge so much information, but then again, he was not the one who was unwilling to share.

"Are you and your siblings close?" Both lost in the conversation neither commented on how Ryen's question was out of turn.

"My sister and I are. My dad says we have been connected since before birth, because of the twin thing."

"And your brother?"

Cash let out a sigh and a cloud of emotion covered up the warmth that had been on his face the last few minutes, "Not so much. When I was little I looked up to him a lot. I was always trying to get his attention, or get him to hang out with me. I thought maybe when I caught up to him in age things would be different, but they weren't. Now I think he has resented me this whole time for the fact I have a dad when he doesn't. Not that we ever did, but he doesn't really talk much to me since his accident. I guess I still hold out hope that he'll come around someday."

Ryen could tell that the situation was upsetting to Cash, but she wasn't sure what to say. She gave his hand a squeeze to offer her support, and he gave

217

her a lopsided smile. After a few moments she heard him ask her the next question, "Do you know if you have any siblings or half siblings I guess?"

Immediately her paranoia kicked in. Had he seen or heard something about Elijah in her head? She recovered quickly though, "There were no siblings before I ran away, and I don't really know what happened after that." She felt a little guilty being dishonest, but her actual words were truth.

"So I get three more now, what are you most afraid of?"

Yeah right. There were several answers to that question, but none of which she was willing to share. Without hesitation she removed the pants she had on.

"We're done sharing already? Not that I mind the new development, but I was just getting started." His wicked little smile resulted in another glare from Ryen. "Let's see if we can get the shirt to come off. Why won't you let me in your head?"

Ryen gave a snort of laughter. "That I will actually answer. Originally the sole reason of not trusting you was enough, but truthfully, there is information in my head that is not mine to share, and there are things that aren't public knowledge that affect more than just me." *Ha! So there! I kept my shirt on!*

"Why did you quit working at the museum? It wasn't because of me, and I know 'family issues' was a fake reason since you didn't leave last night and don't seem to be in a great hurry."

"It was time."

"So what are you going to do now?"

"I think you're out of questions."

"Are you refusing to answer?"

"Fine," a little frustrated Ryen removed her shirt, but held it in her lap. She ignored the victory in Cash's eyes although he was disappointed she didn't answer his question. "When you came to the museum after calling Demitri, what was your intention?" She noticed a little flare of that previous emotion at the mention of her ex-boss/ex-boyfriend again.

Cash removed his shirt, prompting Ryen to ask, "Are you refusing to answer?"

He gave his shoulders a shrug, "I already told you that I was going crazy this whole time. I don't want to tell you what I thought I was doing because I don't want you to be mad."

"You intended to get me fired."

It hadn't been a question, but Cash felt the need to defend himself, "I wanted you to think that. But the truth is, I wouldn't have had the power to do so without confessing what I was up to, to my mother, and that was never an option. It was just a scare tactic."

Remembering that day, feeling cornered by Cash, called names by Demitri, having her capabilities questioned, Ryen asked another question, "Earlier when you asked me about my previous relationships, you already knew about Demitri," she paused because that same look flashed in his eyes, "What were you thinking, or what are you thinking now that does that to your eyes?"

"Seriously?"

"I wouldn't have asked if I didn't want an answer."

"No, I meant, you don't know?" Ryen knew she looked confused. Cash sighed and continued, "It makes me insanely jealous to think about you with him, and believe me I have the visual to go with it. That dolt is still in love with you and he can't keep his thoughts off of your *past* when he's around you."

"Why do your eyes still do that? I told you I didn't love him."

"You may not have loved him, but seeing his memories, even before I knew what was going on between us, made me want to rip his throat out. That, and despite being in love with you he also considers you a tease and a bitch. I don't like him thinking any of those things."

219

The bitch part she knew, but hearing these things made her see Demitri in a completely different way. She had always thought he was sweet and nice. Was she really that naïve or had she hurt him that much when she ended things? It didn't really matter, but it did make her question her perceptions.

"Since you are out of clothes, my consequence is coming to the club with me tonight. Is there anything that makes you jealous?"

The pictures of all those girls from her internet search flashed through her head, thoughts of him drinking blood from girls at the club. All she said was, "Yes."

"Elaborate?"

"Is that another question? Same consequence?"

"Yes to both," he said watching her carefully, like he was trying to hear her answer before it passed her lips.

Ryen refused to meet his gaze as she answered, "I know you've been with *a lot* of girls, and I'll believe you if you tell me you never had feelings for any of them, but I still don't like it. And I know it's necessary, but I don't like the thought of you drinking blood from them."

"Because you're afraid I'm going to hurt them or that I'm doing it against their will?"

"Maybe initially, but that's not the reason anymore," she said quietly still avoiding his penetrating stare. Ryen was sure that look she had seen in Cash's eyes was now flaring in hers.

Cash came around the counter and wrapped his arms around her from behind. Ryen could tell he was choosing his words with caution, "I can't stop drinking blood, but know that I haven't had sex with every person from whom I have drunk. Selfishly it pleases me that you are connecting the blood with intimacy. I think it helps you see that part of me as less of a monster. But would it help if I only drink from somewhere with less of an intimate association? And if I promise not to fill any heads with seductive thoughts or memories? Besides, I haven't been taking anything other than blood for a while."

"Thank you," was all she could say. His words were conflicting with what she had always believed about vampires. She was still struggling to reconcile the two. This seemed like a fair compromise, but she would try not to think about it. No matter how he was making her feel, she still didn't know what she was going to do. His willingness to change to please her mixed guilt with her other emotions, and she wasn't sure what to make of his confession at the end.

Cash stood her up, her shirt falling from her lap, and turned her to face him, holding her at arm's length, "I love *you,* no one else. I'm not interested in anyone else either. You have no reason to be jealous of anyone. I'm not claiming to know how relationships work, but I promise not to hurt you that way."

Ryen gave him a small smile, feeling silly at her jealousy after what she had felt from him over the past twelve hours. His words and his hands on her did crazy things to her insides. While Ryen was pondering her sanity or insanity she wasn't aware of how Cash's gaze was focused on her stomach. She wasn't expecting his keen observance.

"Last night I passed it off as a play of shadows, but are those scars on your stomach?"

Ryen turned away, frantically grabbing for the shirt she had dropped on the floor, "I'm not playing anymore."

Cash pulled the shirt from her hands, still analyzing her scars despite her efforts against it, "Oh my god, are those bite marks?"

"I said I'm not playing anymore." Ryen hated how her voice was shaking and how vulnerable she felt. Still trying to get away from his prying eyes, she searched for something to use as a cover. She did not want to talk about this with him now, or ever.

"Neither am I." Cash swept her up and carried her to the sofa despite her protests. "Please just let me see."

Chapter 44

Cash had seen the scars last night, but he didn't look close enough to really see them. Admittedly he was focused on other parts of Ryen's body at the time. Now, in the light of his kitchen he could clearly see that there were bite marks among others. "Were you attacked by an animal?"

A "humph" sound came from Ryen and her eyes glazed over before closing, "Something like that."

"What happened?" Cash figured she probably wouldn't answer, but that didn't mean he didn't want to know.

"It doesn't matter. It happened a long time ago. It's in the past and that's where I'd like to keep it."

Under closer inspection Cash recognized the shape of the marks, "Oh my god, a vampire did this to you?"

Cash was hoping Ryen would contradict him. However, her increased breathing and the pain in her eyes proved his assumption had been correct. Anger flared in him. Had she been just a teenager when some vampire had attacked her? That would explain her aversion to vampires. He didn't understand; the stomach was an awkward feeding place, no matter the situation. Ryen must have sensed his confusion, "What? You don't believe me?"

Cash's head snapped up, "Of course I believe you. I was just thinking that they are in a strange location."

A sort of understanding spread across her face, and she clenched her jaw. Her nostrils flared as she let out a sigh and made an internal decision, "The scars are what were left over after a healing spell. They are a karmic reminder that I crossed a line with my powers."

"What do you mean? You did something and you think it resulted in being attacked? "

Ryen turned away from him as she answered, unwilling to look him in the eye. "No, I reacted to the attack in a vengeful and inappropriate way, and that is why the scars remain."

Cash was quiet as he pondered this information, and then something crossed his mind that made his stomach turn, "Wait, you said the scars were 'left over' from a healing spell? That means the healing spell worked?"

Ryen was nodding her head though still not meeting his gaze. He thought he understood, but he needed to know for sure, "So you weren't just bitten on the stomach."

Her voice was barely louder than a whisper, "No."

Part of him didn't want to hear it, but again, he needed to. His voice was not much louder than hers, "Where else?"

"Pretty much everywhere."

Hearing her confirm it, picturing the marks that created those scars all over her soft beautiful skin, rage filled him. He wanted to know who did this. He wanted to rip his throat out. When he felt in control enough to speak he asked, "Who did this? Did you turn him in?"

"They were dealt with."

They? More than one person was responsible for this? Surely she had turned them in and their families had done the noble thing to hold them accountable for the disgrace. He didn't know of any vampire family that would have allowed attacking someone, especially a witch, to go unpunished. Again, he had to know for sure. If they weren't dead, he would take care of it, "Surely their families or the Elders sentenced them to death?"

That question caused Ryen to finally look at him. A new emotion clouded her eyes at his question, "I didn't turn them in. I only knew a couple of first names, and it was too late at that point anyway."

"What do you mean 'it was too late', and just how many people attacked you?"

Pain filled her eyes again, and she looked down as she said, "Four."

Four? A growl escaped him, and Cash barely contained his fury. He focused on deep calming breaths. Ryen continued cautiously, no doubt feeling some of his anger seeping out of him, "I already told you I acted out of vengeance, almost without knowing it."

Cash thought he saw guilt in her eyes as she kept going, "Three of the four ultimately got what you think their families would have deemed appropriate."

"Even with all of your answers you are good at being impossibly vague. If it's even possible I think I'm even more confused. Would you please start at the beginning?"

Cash could tell Ryen was struggling with his request. She had already shared more in the last few minutes than he had been able to get out of her for weeks. He knew he was asking a lot of her. This was clearly a painful memory and he didn't want to cause her any unnecessary pain, but he needed to know, to understand. He realized how exposed she must feel emotionally, and physically, as she sat before him naked, telling him about this horrible experience. He took the blanket off the back of the sofa and wrapped it around her shoulders. He remained a slight distance from her, not knowing if she needed or wanted physical comfort from him, a vampire, as she recalled her past.

She took a deep breath before starting at the beginning, and Cash swore to himself he would sit quietly and listen, "I was fifteen and basically had a crush on this older guy that I'd seen around. I didn't really know anything about him except his name, and I thought I was in love with him without even talking to him. After following him around with puppy dog eyes he asked me out on what I considered a date. At some point he drugged me and I woke up in an abandoned building with him and three of his friends."

Cash clenched his jaw in an effort not to picture fifteen year old Ryen with the bastards that attacked her, and he worked on controlling his breathing. Hesitantly she continued, either sensing Cash's struggle with his emotions, or struggling with her own, "Whatever he had drugged me with was some sort of paralytic; I heard the doctors discussing it at the hospital later. I couldn't move anything except for my eyes and eyelids. All of the involuntary functions worked like breathing, heart beating, swallowing, but it had somehow blocked my ability to access my powers too. I was in and out of consciousness a lot, but I'm sure we were there for several hours. They apparently left me for dead. I woke up as the drugs were starting to wear off, and I somehow got out of the building."

Again Ryen paused. At some point during the recounting of her torture Cash had moved closer to her, and now he took her in his arms. What if she had been lost to him all those years ago? The thought was more than he could bear right now and he pushed it aside to continue listening.

"Someone found me and called an ambulance. The first nurse I saw recognized me as a witch and did a quick healing spell. It wouldn't have healed me completely, but it saved me from dying before the doctors could help me or others could get there to do more powerful spells. I had heard the guys in the ambulance talking about how they weren't sure I'd even make it to the hospital."

Cash tightened his embrace. As she went on, she pulled away from him to look in his eyes. Cash wasn't sure what the driving force was, but it was like she was pleading with him to see her side as if he wasn't already behind her. "You have to understand, the whole time I was in that building I was thinking of any spell I could to stop them, to punish them. My mind kept going the whole time. I don't know for sure when the drugs started wearing off and the healing took over enough for my powers to work, but at some point, even without me saying it aloud, one of the spells took flight. I felt it as soon as it happened and I tried to take it back, to stop it, but it was too late."

"What do you mean?" It was the first thing Cash had said since she started her story, and his voice was strained with emotion.

"I sent a spell of vengeance and retribution to all four of them. If I had been in my right mind I know I could have turned them in, to the police or to their families, but at that time it was too late. Two of them were traveling, one by

226

motorcycle and the other by car, when the spell hit them. As a result they crashed and both of them died. Another one killed himself a few days later. I don't know what happened to the last one."

Cash was shaking his head. He could feel her emotions, "Don't you dare feel guilty about what happened. You didn't intentionally kill them, and if they hadn't died I'd kill them now."

Cash was completely serious, but Ryen brushed aside his murderous comment, "Cash, it wasn't my place to seek vengeance; I should have turned them in."

"As the victim, it sure as hell was your place. If you had turned them in, their families, if they were even the least bit noble, would have sentenced them to death for their abominable acts. What you did may have even been merciful."

"Even if vampire law says that, I violated our witch principles. I accept that."

Cash didn't argue with her further. He sat quietly again, lost in his thoughts and emotions. He marveled at her power level, to inadvertently take down three vampires. Clearly they had been made and not born, but the bottom line was that most of them were dead. Then something else occurred to him and bile rose in his throat. He couldn't bring himself to say it out loud so he sent an image to Ryen, an image of her experiencing someone else's life, a punishment inflicted on Zeta.

Ryen's body slumped as she nodded. He crushed her to him then, enveloping her body in his protective embrace. He knew she could feel the array of emotions emanating from him: anger, pain, fury, sadness, helplessness. "You have no idea how much I want to erase this for you. No wonder you hate vampires and the idea of being bitten or how vampires treat humans."

He didn't want to believe any of what Ryen had just told him. His voice was laced with malice when he spoke again, "Do you know who the last one is? I'll kill him for what he did to you."

Ryen turned sharply and took Cash's face between her hands. Her eyes were wide with panic, and Cash wasn't sure if it was due to the idea of him getting in trouble or getting hurt, "You will do no such thing. I told you that I sought my vengeance. I will not have another death at my hand. If he's still alive, he's been living with what I did to him as long as I have. In my mind we're even."

He didn't believe that for a second. It still caused her so much pain to remember what happened. There was nothing that anyone could ever do that would make it even. Rage filled him, but he kept it hidden. He vowed that somehow he'd find the last bastard and make him suffer for even looking in Ryen's direction. He took a deep breath and heard his desperation as he spoke, "What can I do? I need to do something."

"You can hold me right here," Ryen said, and she kissed him gently before laying her head on his chest and snuggling in. "You're already changing my mind about vampires. Thank you."

Cash gave her a tight squeeze. He eventually loosened his hold, but not by much. Ryen slowly relaxed and drifted off to sleep. Cash wasn't sure how long he sat there holding her, wondering about justice, questioning the purpose behind such events in people's lives. He was guilty of thinking of humans as merely his food and pleasure, and he knew that accidents happened occasionally when someone was caught up in the bloodlust. Luckily he had a friend whose quick thinking had saved him from knowing firsthand what crossing that line felt like. He knew others who had crossed it, both by accident and intentionally. But to purposefully torture someone without just cause was punishable by vampire law. It could threaten secrecy and if it was being done against witches it could start a war. He could justify his plans by claiming rightful justice, but that wasn't what his real motivation would be.

The depth of his feelings for Ryen was more than he could put into words. He wanted to protect her and ensure her safety. He had watched Ryen as Zeta, be raped over and over. He couldn't erase it from his mind. It was hard enough when he thought that was just a nightmare. To know it actually happened to Ryen was more than enough to make him want to tear the guy limb from limb. It was more than he could handle, knowing that they beat her, tortured her, and bit her for hours, leaving her for dead. He would hunt down the last mother fucker and make sure he experienced the same fear, pain and humiliation he had inflicted on Ryen before he took his head and ended his miserable life.

Chapter 45

She hated to admit it, but the week passed faster than Ryen wanted. Cash had convinced her to come to the club with him each night; he even had clothes delivered for her when she argued that she didn't have any club appropriate clothing. Most of the time she sat at the bar and watched him in his element, but a few times he dragged her onto the dance floor. Part of her enjoyed the envious looks she received, especially when she and Cash would sneak away for more private moments.

She had allowed herself to fall into a comfortable routine; each day they shared brunch on the roof talking and then going to bed for a few hours before Cash headed back to work in the late afternoon. They even got a little bit of sleep. Ryen knew when Cash went to work, he also used the time to get himself something, or rather someone, to drink, but neither of them spoke of it, and Ryen tried to ignore her knowledge of the inevitable. Cash felt guilty about holding her captive within his space and offered several times to take her out, but Ryen didn't want to chance being seen with him out and about by anyone that might recognize her. It was even more of a risk since he was a favorite target of the paparazzi. She went to a great deal of effort to keep her image from the public eye, and even though she was currently in a make believe world, she refused to be that reckless. She told him as much, and he had said he was happy to keep her to himself. There was also something to be said about not leaving here, the secret place that had witnessed the union of their souls.

Was it possible to really know someone in only a few days? Ryen was sure she knew almost everything about Cash, not just answers to questions, but how he mumbled when he was dreaming, how his facial hair was ridiculously soft no matter the length, the scent of mint in his hair from his expensive shampoo, his obsession with always using coasters, and how the dishes had an exact way to fit in the dishwasher. Yet he didn't mind the clutter of her things in the bathroom. She couldn't ignore the way his hand locked perfectly with hers, how the nape of his neck was the exact right fit for her head, no matter where she fell asleep she always woke up with a blanket, how he loved to tease her until her eyes flared in indignation only to smile his seductive smile for her forgiveness. And although she never would have predicted it, she had willingly shared things, allowed him to know her, at least most of her. She had even contemplated telling him about the Triumvirate and her place in it. That was the danger of spending so much time with him; he made her feel so safe and complete that her heart was tempting her with a future that could not be.

Reluctantly her bag was packed once again for the trip to Florence she had postponed. Cash's bag sat next to hers by the door, but he was headed in a different direction, to Barcelona to check out some real estate suggested to him by an old friend. Over the past week Ryen had shut out the real world, with its responsibilities and incompatibilities to her current dilemma, but now it was time to say good-bye to Madrid, to her perfect make believe world, and go home. She could already feel the clouds moving in, and it would be raining soon as her sadness became overwhelming.

They would be leaving for the airport shortly. Rafa was going to drive them and whatever moments they shared in the apartment before their exit would be their last moments alone. She hated what she had planned, what she knew had to be done. Cash would say good-bye to her thinking he would see her in a few days, but in truth, this was the final good-bye. It would be far less dramatic than Afton and Shaw, but no less painful on her part. She knew that Cash would come looking for her when she went off the grid, but with the compound cloaked, she would have no trouble avoiding him. Then again, she wouldn't put it past him to stalk her favorite places in Florence, especially the Uffizi, until he tracked her down. Part of her, a part she would lock away when she left this apartment, hoped he would, but that part was soon to be overruled by reality. If she was honest with herself, neither running away nor continuing as is was fair to Cash. He wouldn't understand why she left, and as it were he would be hurt to know that she had been lying to him this whole time, pretending that they were starting something that could never be, hiding who she really was from him.

Ryen had been so lost in her sad thoughts she hadn't heard Cash come back from downstairs, "It shouldn't affect travel time, but it's raining out. Rafa is here, so whenever we're ready to go down…"

Ryen jumped a little at his voice and quickly wiped the tears from her eyes before turning to face him, "I guess we can't linger too long, or we'll miss our flights."

Despite Ryen's efforts to hide her tears, the concern that rushed to Cash's face was proof she had failed. He closed the distance between them and cradled her head in his hands, "Please don't be sad. It's just a few days, and I'll join you in Florence."

At that Ryen shuddered and collapsed into sobs in his arms. She could feel the impact of her strength of emotion on him. From his mind she could sense his bewilderment followed by his own anguish. Before she had time to gain control of her sobs Cash swept her up into his arms and carried her over to the bed. He shed his clothes quickly and Ryen's did not put up much of a fight when he refocused his attention on her.

Their impending departure gave a cloud of urgency to the moment, but each kiss, each touch was slow, deliberate and gentle. Ryen could sense that Cash was being driven by his desire to erase her sorrow as well as his need to claim her as his own once again. For Ryen it was a final moment to experience the euphoria she felt when she let herself go. It was the final moment of the fusion of their souls. Cash's mark was so thoroughly branded on her heart that she knew she would never be the same person again. She could not keep the tears from falling as they simply held each other in the end.

Cash continued to touch her as they dressed in silence, a kiss on her shoulder, a brush of his hand on her cheek. Ryen cherished them, although each one was a stab to her heart.

They were about to walk out the door when Ryen broke the silence. She stopped before crossing the threshold and grabbed Cash's arm, pulling him back inside. She placed her hands on either side of his face, tilting his head down so she could look in his eyes, "I love you. No matter what happens after we leave here, I want you to know that right now, in this place, I love you more than I ever thought possible."

He took both of her hands in his and squeezed them gently, "I know what you mean. This whole week has been surreal, but leaving here doesn't change anything. I love you. I love you here; I love you outside; I love you in Barcelona; I love you in Italy; I love you everywhere."

Cash was obviously confused by the seriousness and sadness in her voice and face, and he clearly didn't fully grasp the reason behind it. This was their last private good-bye. Rafa would drop Cash off at his terminal first, so they wouldn't even have a good-bye inside the airport. Ryen couldn't explain any further without giving herself away. So instead she smiled and squeezed his hands back. She kept a firm grip on one of them as they walked down to the car.

It was indeed raining, and Rafa did not look too pleased as he helped load their bags into the car. Ryen and Cash crawled in the spacious backseat trying to stay as dry as possible before their flights. Ryen wished she could make the rain stop, but with her emotions so frazzled she couldn't hold back her sadness. Alas the rain would continue to fall, at least until her plane left Madrid, then Madrid could experience the sunny day that had been forecast.

Rafa shook his head when he got in the car, sprinkling the back seat as intended. He winked as Ryen gave him a little glare. He was still seeing Sophie and that continued to make Ryen uneasy. She knew that he was like a brother to Cash, and in all honesty she liked Rafa. He had been discreet about this past week, even with Sophie, and he always seemed to have Cash's back. Maybe it was just because she knew he didn't really have feelings for her friend, or the fact that despite his claim to like Ryen, he took every opportunity to push her buttons.

Cash attempted to scold Rafa, "Careful hermano, or instead of letting you run the business on your own I'll send you to Barcelona."

"Esmeralda's invitation was to you, not me. I don't think she'd be very happy if I showed up in your place."

Even though it didn't matter after today, Cash would be free to do as he pleased, jealousy flared within Ryen. It was so unexpected she didn't get her emotional blocks up in time to stop some of it seeping out, alerting the other occupants of the car to her feelings. Taking what she knew was Rafa's bait she asked, "Esmeralda?"

"What? Cash didn't tell you he was going to see his gorgeous ex-girlfriend?" Rafa was working at controlling the laughter that was threatening to erupt. That is, until Cash leaned forward and smacked the back of his head. His laughter subsided, but he shot a "what?" expression at Cash through the rear view mirror.

Ryen hated that she was reacting the way she was. It shouldn't matter if Cash's friend was a girl, or if she was beautiful, or if they had a history together. She was walking away from him today and maybe this friend would be there for him when she couldn't be. She didn't want to think about him going back to his old habits, but she was choosing not to have a say.

Cash took her hand and shot an annoyed look at Rafa before he started, "Esmeralda was never a girlfriend. My sister set me up on a blind date with her when we were in boarding school. As it turned out, she would rather have been on the date with my sister. We became pretty good friends, I think because she had ulterior motives, but I never could convince my sister to go out with her."

"Ay Dios!" Rafa snorted. "I think they both dodged a bullet there. Can you imagine those two together? Crazy emotional artist and level headed control freak?"

Ryen wasn't really paying attention to the conversation anymore as the guys mused on about what could have been. Most of the jealousy had subsided with Cash's explanation, but some of it still lingered. Her emotions were in a jumble, and she wasn't sure how spending the next few hours in an airport and plane was going to help clear her head or calm her heart.

Chapter 46

Leaving Ryen at the airport had been harder than Cash had expected. Maybe it had to do with the rain that added extra dreariness to the situation or how upset Ryen had been. It had been strange and unsettling. Cash had seen her frustrated, irritated, scared, secretive, jealous, sad, shy, relaxed and inflamed with passion, but he had never seen her in the state she had been in today, and he hoped he wouldn't have to again. It made him feel helpless when he couldn't cheer her up. Even when they were making love she had been filled with a sadness he couldn't touch. He thought he understood at least part of it, if she felt the same way he did. He didn't want to be away from her. Although he had never known that he was missing something, the part of him that Ryen completed felt empty now in her absence. He was excited to see Esmeralda; she was always fun, but he hoped his time in Barcelona passed quickly. He was even contemplating flying straight to Florence instead of stopping back in Madrid to check on things as planned.

Barcelona was a sunny, warm change to the unexpected rain he'd left behind in Madrid. He was meeting Esmeralda at the airport. He knew that they would have dinner and planned to check out the club scene tonight, but it was still pretty early. Knowing her, she probably had plenty of ideas for things to do.

Cash grabbed his suitcase off of the baggage carousel and headed towards the exit where the general public was allowed to wait for passengers. The airport was fairly crowded with tourists, and he wasn't sure what to look for. It had been nearly two years since he last saw Esmeralda and at that time she had short spiky bright red hair. The likelihood of it still being that color was not good. She changed her hair color almost as often as her clothes, part of her artistic nature. Her passion was art, painting and sculpture mostly, but to appease her parents she was working on her master's degree at the university, strangely enough in genetics. Cash had known her since they were teenagers and she had always been really smart, although her artistic personality, including disregarding deadlines and due dates, got her into bits of academic trouble. That, and her own reluctance to spend time on something she viewed as mundane as science, she was still working on her degree when others her age had completed it years ago.

A tap on his shoulder caused Cash to turn around, where he was greeted by a fountain of bright blue hair atop Esmeralda's pixie face. With a huge smile she flung her arms around him. Even though she was slender, she was almost as tall as Cash, and the force of her hug nearly knocked him over.

"Oh Cash, it's so good to see you! I can't believe you're finally here! You know it's customary to return an invitation to visit before a year *or two* pass!"

"Easy Es, you're cutting off my circulation." She let go of him and gave him a narrow gaze as he continued, "I'm sorry it's been so long, but with the bar opening, and then the club, I haven't really had a chance to get away."

"Fine, I forgive you, but that means you have to do everything I say while you are here," she gave him a mischievous wink. Knowing her, there would end up being police involved.

"So what's on the agenda for today?" he asked.

"Well, we can take your bags back to my place. Then I was thinking we could catch up at Park Güell, and you haven't been to the aquarium, so we can go there before dinner. How many clubs do you want to check out tonight? I have about seven on the list you might be interested in," she rattled off all in one breath.

"Did you only want me to stay one day? Why don't we check out two or three tonight and then a couple more tomorrow night?"

"Of course I want you to stay! I certainly don't think a one day visit is sufficient after two years! Besides, I already have some plans in the works for your birthday." She winked at him. He had never been cautious, but Esmeralda had always been in a class of her own. If he stayed too long he would end up in some kind of trouble or at least have something to regret.

"Go easy on me, Es. We're not as young as we once were," he told her half joking and half serious.

She waved away his concerns, "Do you want to come up the mountain with me tomorrow?"

"Tibidabo? What are you going up there for?"

"Yes, tomorrow's the solstice, silly! I'm meeting some people on the mountain for a celebratory ritual. Guests are always welcome."

He was usually aware of Wiccan holidays because of his dad, but when he wasn't around witches he didn't pay much attention to them. Now hearing Esmeralda talk about the summer solstice automatically drew his mind to Ryen. That must be why she wanted to get back to Florence, so she could celebrate the solstice with the people she considered her family.

Snapping fingers in front of his face along with Esmeralda's voice brought his attention back, "Hello? Where'd you go? I'm pretty sure you weren't hearing a thing I just said." She sounded fairly annoyed.

"Sorry. Your mention of the solstice just caused my thoughts to drift. I'll pass on the mountain hike tomorrow, but thanks." The wheels in Cash's brain were turning. With Esmeralda being a witch, maybe she could answer a few questions he had that might help him understand Ryen better. He could obviously ask his dad, but he always felt guilty talking to his dad about witch stuff. His dad said it didn't bother him, but it was yet another reminder that neither of his children chose to follow his path.

She was shaking her head at him, "There you go again, off in another place. And people say I'm spacey!"

"Sorry! You have my full attention now! Let's go to your tiny little flat!" He said it as a teasing dig, but she thoroughly ignored it.

"Let's! But I'm more interested in where your mind keeps going. You're not usually like this."

He gave her an innocent shoulder shrug that didn't pacify her curiosity at all, but she dropped it for the time being.

Esmeralda's apartment was a small, somewhat cramped, one bedroom loft, if a curtain separating the bed from the kitchen table qualified as one bedroom. Cash really didn't mind spending a couple of nights on the couch, but he was baffled by his friend. Her parents were very well off, and he was sure they'd be glad to buy or help buy her a bigger apartment, but Esmeralda was independent and stubborn. She loved her tiny apartment. She rented space closer to the university where she spent her free time working on her various art projects. Cash wondered if her parents wouldn't help because they knew a bigger apartment would give her space for the art they'd rather she not let consume her time. The best part of the place was the patio, arcing in a semicircle around her apartment. It was almost as big as the apartment itself, and had a view of Park Güell, la Sagrada Familia, and the harbor in the distance. Cash thought he might take advantage of that view tomorrow while Esmeralda was in the mountains for some of his own meditation.

He spent a couple of hours with Esmeralda rattling off facts about Gaudi, the park, and the architecture around the city. Cash half listened and half day dreamed. He thought Ryen would like the art here and wondered if she had ever been to Barcelona. Maybe he'd bring her here to meet Esmeralda someday, just not anytime soon. Esmeralda could be a lot to take in, but Cash was certain she and Ryen would get along great. With art and witch stuff, they at least had a few things in common. He considered calling her, but it had only been half a day since they had parted, plus it would cause an onslaught of questions from Esmeralda. None of that stopped him from checking his phone repeatedly for texts and missed calls.

"Ok, you're not paying attention to me again, and I'm starting to get offended! Why do you keep looking at your phone? Am I not interesting enough company for you? Are you worried about Rafa handling things in Madrid?"

Esmeralda's eyes bore into him and Cash felt her trying to search his mind. He wasn't quick enough with an answer or in blocking her mind meddling, "What? You're thinking about a girl? You've never even bothered remembering a girl's name before! Who is she? How'd you meet her? What's she like? Spill! Now!"

It had been awhile since he'd been in Esmeralda's presence and he had forgotten how much her high energy flooded every aspect of her being, especially when she was excited. He figured he'd better start talking or she wouldn't have time to come up for oxygen, "Calm down. It's very new, and believe me, I'm as shocked as you are."

"New? How new?"

"Well, I met her weeks ago, but we've only been seeing each other for a couple of weeks." Cash thought he'd count their business meetings as dates.

"Where'd you meet her? I'm assuming she's not your typical club fixture?"

"Why do you say that?"

She gave him an eye roll, "Since I've known you, you've never given any girl you've picked up at a club a thought past how their blood tastes. Frankly, aside from me and Calla who don't count, I'm not sure there's ever been a girl that held your interest longer than an evening."

"That's true." He didn't want to share too much, but he was excited to be telling someone. He laughed at how giddy the idea made him. His laughter caused quizzical looks from Esmeralda. "You're right. I didn't meet her at a club. I met her at a museum fundraiser if you can believe it."

"You hate those," she commented flatly while she continued to eye him with suspicion and curiosity.

"Yeah, I know. I was planning on leaving as soon as possible, but then I saw her, and I spent the entire night trying to get close enough to talk to her."

"And?"

239

"And I didn't. I didn't even know her name until she miraculously wandered into my bar a few weeks later."

Cash knew Esmeralda would eat that story up. Her eyes were huge and she leaned closer waiting for more, "That's so romantic. So, then you swept her off her feet with your charm and good looks?"

Cash laughed again. If only it had been that easy, "No. She didn't want to give me the time of day."

Esmeralda smiled, "That's my girl! Playing hard to get! I bet that drove you crazy."

He didn't want to admit just how crazy he had been, so he attempted to distract her. They had been traveling on the metro as they were talking and were almost to the aquarium stop, "Don't we need to get off at 'Drassanes'?"

"Yes, but don't think I'm done with you. I'm sure there's much more to tell."

Thankfully she laid off the conversation for a while as they walked the rest of the distance to the aquarium and bought their tickets. It was open for another hour or so, and it was dark in the underwater passageways as they meandered around.

"So how's Calla?" Esmeralda asked casually. Cash knew that she still thought of his sister as the one who got away, although Calla had never given her any reason to think she was interested in her that way.

"She's good. You should give her a call sometime. She could probably use your help soon. My niece is headed down the witch path and Calla is lost as to what to do with her."

"I'm sure your dad is thrilled. Isn't he helping?"

"Yes, of course, but you know Calla. If she doesn't thoroughly understand and feel like she's in control then her world is out of sorts. Plus, having a friend's help might go over better than a parent's." Cash was hoping that Ryen could help there, too. He knew his dad and niece were going to love

Ryen, but he hoped the vampires in the family would be just as powerless to her charms as he was.

"There you go again, drifting away. Thinking of your girl again?" Cash just gave her a lopsided grin in confirmation. "Wait, is she a witch?"

Feeling almost like he was giving away sacred information he answered, "Yes." He felt Esmeralda's fingers dig into his arm as she grabbed him in interest and excitement.

The path they were walking was nearly deserted, and she pulled Cash over to the side to sit on the bench that lined the path, "Are you going to make me beg for the slightest piece of information?"

Cash watched a group of teenage girls walk past, taking the opportunity not to answer right away. He was torn between confessing how hopelessly in love he was with every detail and keeping Ryen to himself. In the end he knew that Esmeralda would never give up if he didn't give her something. "She's incredible, Es. She's gorgeous, and smart, and feisty," he smiled as he remembered just how feisty she could be. "She's strong and fragile all at the same time. She's loyal and protective, and there's so much more I don't even know. What can I say, Es? I love her."

Esmeralda stared at him with her mouth open in disbelief for several moments before she responded, "I am in awe of this woman. I never thought my little playboy would ever find someone who could tame him. So when do I get to meet her?"

"Maybe never," he said with as much seriousness as he could muster while hiding a smile. Her hurt expression changed with his next sentence, as he let the smile breakout across his face, "I wouldn't want you to try to steal her away from me."

"Well, if she is half of the greatness that you claim I most certainly would try, but then again, if she cares for you even half as much as you care for her, I'm afraid I wouldn't stand a chance. Do you have a picture?"

"No, sorry." That wasn't entirely true. He did have one picture on his phone he had snapped when Ryen was sleeping, but she would kill him if he showed it to anyone, let alone if she even knew it existed. He fought the urge to take it out and look at it now. He wanted to hear her voice. *I'm worse than a lovesick adolescent!*

The announcement that the aquarium would be closing soon had them wandering towards the exit. Cash sighed, realizing that even a little information wouldn't cease Esmeralda's questioning. "So is she from Madrid?"

"No, she actually grew up in Florence if you can believe it."

"Just think, if you had gone to school at home you may have met her sooner, but then you would have missed out on meeting your bestest friend in the whole world."

He couldn't help himself, "Yeah, I don't know what my life would be like without Rafa." That earned him a punch in the arm. "Or you, of course," he added as he feigned an injury from her assault.

"So if she's from Florence she must have gone to school at the Universal Coven Headquarters."

"Yes, I think she lived there while she was growing up," Cash was hesitant to share details of Ryen's life. He felt as if he would be betraying her confidence, especially since she had made him work for every morsel of information.

"Wow, I've never been there. That means she has probably taken classes with the Triumvirate."

Cash saw the opening he was hoping for, "They're like your leaders right? My dad has spoken of them before."

"Yes, the Maiden, the Mother and the Crone, representing the stages of womanhood, serve as our leaders, spiritual guides, links to the Goddess; they

242

are our royalty. They are the three most powerful witches in the world; together they are essentially unstoppable."

"So are they immortal or elected? How does that work?"

"No, they age, though maybe more slowly than the rest of us, well, except maybe vampires," she winked at Cash. "There's a special ceremony that's held every few years in order to conceive a new Triumvirate member. The Goddess decides when that ceremony results in a baby. When the current Crone passes everyone moves up in title, and the new Maiden is crowned for lack of a better description. In fact, this year's ceremony created our next Maiden."

That was more or less what Cash already knew, but he still wanted to understand more. He waited until they were seated at their table at the restaurant before he continued, "What makes these women so powerful?"

"Each is said to be a wizened soul and flesh of the Goddess herself. Most born witches can manifest some sort of power, the stronger ones can tune into nature and the elements. The Triumvirate are in tune with all of the elements; they can even command them at will. Because they are a direct link to the Goddess, it's said that they can command her power as well. It's actually rumored that the current Maiden is the most powerful witch there has ever been."

He was intrigued. Some vampires sought out power more than anything else. Power within vampire bloodlines was inherited, but it could also be stolen or freely given to a made vampire through complicated blood magic. He assumed that witches would have the same concerns as vampires, "No one worries about the dangers of people having that much power?"

"No. They are servants who have taken an oath. They are governed completely by the Goddess. If a witch were to do something unethical or against witch principles, he or she would be held accountable and judged by the Triumvirate. With minor things we just worry about karmic retribution. Major things have resulted in the binding of powers and/or being banned from the protection of the Coven. I've always been taught that the Goddess reprimands the Triumvirate herself. There are stories that things like that have happened before. Apparently the Goddess will remove one of them herself if they abuse their power. There's at least one story where the Crone was not the first of the three to move on to the next life. That's your basic witch judicial system."

"You mean the Goddess killed one of them?"

Esmeralda shrugged her shoulders, "In essence She and they are one in the same. But remember these are stories passed down through the years; who knows for sure if they are true?"

"So they run the compound outside of Florence?"

"Yes, it's their home, and where they help Coven members with spells and such, but it's also a place of learning. There's a school there, not unlike the boarding schools we attended. The Triumvirate leads rituals and ceremonies for the major holidays that attract visitors from all over the world, and new inductees to the craft can spend their year of learning under the instruction of the Triumvirate and the other teachers there. Your niece should go there since it's practically in her backyard."

"Maybe she will." Cash was lost in thought. Something Esmeralda had said about karmic retribution made him think back to things Ryen had said along similar lines. He took a moment so they could order some food, but he wasn't finished with this conversation, "So what's considered unethical and how does karma fit into it?"

"Well, the basic principle of the Coven, of all white magic, is 'harm none'. There would be varying degrees of that, like taking someone's will from them, or causing actual physical or emotional harm. Basically the Universe or the Goddess or karma, whatever you want to call it, sends back to you what you've done, times three."

Cash had heard his dad talk about the rule of three before, but he'd never asked him to elaborate, "Does that apply to every action or just magical ones?"

"Well, the Triumvirate would be involved with the consequences for magical ones. Both would have karmic retribution though, like taint your soul, possibly setting it back in its journey through time. The non-magical decisions or actions might have more apparent consequences. You know, like think something bad about someone, get a splinter in your foot."

"Would the Goddess consider it unethical if someone were to accidentally cast a spell? And what if it was to punish someone who caused physical and emotional damage to him or her?"

"Well, I'm not sure about accidental spells, but if it was a spell that meant to punish and/or cause pain I'm not sure how it could be accidental and successful at the same time. The person would have to be pretty powerful for it to be an accident. Most witches would have to go through a formal spell casting for a major spell to work."

Cash already knew that Ryen was powerful. She had lit all of the candles in his apartment simultaneously, and she was extremely good at keeping him out of her head. He didn't care how powerful she was, but it was something he was curious to discuss with her, if it would be a topic she was willing to talk about. He didn't think it was unethical for her to punish the guys that tortured her, but he knew she felt differently. Luckily, Esmeralda didn't seem suspicious about anything they had been discussing. Cash wasn't prepared to tell her why he had these questions about ethics and karma. He turned the conversation to less serious matters for which Esmeralda looked happy. "So, where to next?"

"Let's hit some of the beachside clubs first and then make our way back into the city. But first, I need to use the lady's room."

Once Esmeralda was out of sight Cash took out his phone. Still no messages. He frowned in disappointment and dialed Ryen's number. More disappointment, it went straight to voicemail. At least he got to hear a recording of her voice. He thought about calling back later, but he wasn't sure how late they would be out. He had time to leave a quick voicemail before Esmeralda returned. She would tease him mercilessly if she overheard his words or the insecurities in his voice. "Hey. I miss you. We're heading to check out the clubs around here, so I probably won't hear you call back. I figure you'll be busy tomorrow, but I wanted to tell you good night, and I love you."

Ryen awoke in a puddle of sweat. Her dream had started out with her and Cash in that wide open field, but then it turned into the vision of Shaw and Afton saying their good-byes. This time Ryen was seeing through Afton's eyes and looking into Cash's face. As if that experience wasn't painful enough, her dream took an even darker turn, to Zeta and Tariq's final scene and then to her all so familiar nightmare. Instead of reliving the exact details of what happened, Ryen was trying to call out to Cash for help. The look on his face was so full of anger and pain; he just stared at her before turning his back.

Ryen knew it was just a dream, but she couldn't shake the feeling of dread it caused. It didn't matter anymore anyway; Cash was out of her life now. She had cried her tears on the plane and also on the train she took from Rome to Florence. She wasn't sure how long she had been asleep so she grabbed her phone to check the time. She needed a good night's sleep for tomorrow's festivities. The "missed call" message appeared on her screen. Ryen wondered why she hadn't heard it ring, but remembered she had turned it to "do not disturb" before getting on the plane and must have forgotten to change it back.

She was so out of sorts she didn't even bother checking the number before hitting the voicemail button. That was a mistake. The sound of Cash's voice, so much more real than it had been in her dream, assaulted her eardrums. It felt like there was a vice grip squeezing her heart. Fresh tears fell from her eyes. Her finger hovered over the delete button, but she couldn't bring herself to push it. The narcissistic part of her wanted to hold on to the last piece of their happiness. There wouldn't be time tomorrow, but getting a new phone was the first thing on her personal to-do list.

246

It was after six, and the sun was already lighting the sky when Cash and Esmeralda made it back to her apartment. They had visited five clubs, and she had plans for them to go to a couple more this evening. So far, from what Cash had seen, the Barcelona market was wide open for his brand of business venture. However, while they were waiting outside one of the clubs he'd noticed something peculiar down the street. There was a building with no door on the street side, but people would approach a window, and then after a few moments they would slip in a side door. He never noticed anyone come out. He could tell, even from the distance that the people going in were vampires. He wanted to check it out again today.

Cash let Esmeralda shower first. She was hoping to get an hour or two of sleep before heading to Mt. Tibidabo for the day. Cash had a meeting with a realtor later this morning to look at the property Esmeralda had contacted him about, and then he planned to stop by that mysterious building.

He couldn't help checking his phone again while he waited for the shower. Still no messages. Ryen probably hadn't woken up yet. He reminded himself that she would be occupied today so he shouldn't expect any communication, but he still hoped. Being at the clubs last night, girls dancing all around, and not having any blood for a couple days had made Cash thirsty and longing for Ryen above any other girl. He pulled up his picture of her. It was crazy how much he missed her when it hadn't even been twenty-four hours since he'd seen her. The picture had captured her when she looked completely peaceful. When she was awake she never quite relaxed. Every day she had stayed at his apartment he had tried to memorize everything about her because he was never sure if she would bolt unexpectedly. Right now he could imagine her eyes opening and looking up at him as she smiled. Then she would realize how open she was and slam her shields up around her mind.

He was willing to be patient and wait for her to fully trust him, but it still stung like a slap in the face every time she closed herself off. She had told him about her mom and about being tortured. Cash thought those things would have been difficult enough, although he did pretty much force both

247

out of her. Was there something even worse that she was afraid for him to see? He couldn't imagine anything that would change how he felt about her.

Esmeralda's loud throat clearing brought him back to the present. "The shower's free." She smiled a knowing smile and shook her head. "I'm not sure I can leave you to take care of yourself today. You may start daydreaming and accidentally walk in front of a bus."

Cash gave her a little glare as he headed to the tiny room that held the shower, "I'll be fine, thank you! Maybe I should be worried about you falling off a mountain or spraining your ankle?"

"I'm much more in tune with nature than I used to be. You'd be surprised; I've even slept outside in a sleeping bag."

"What, on your balcony?" he asked sarcastically. He didn't wait to hear an answer. If she tried to argue, she was drown out by the sound of water. He shook his head. Although their relationship had never been anything other than platonic, Esmeralda was probably the closest thing he'd ever had to a girlfriend. She knew him just as well as his family and Rafa. Suddenly he really wanted her to meet Ryen, to have her approval. He knew that he didn't have to worry about that, but it also made him decide to call home later and tell his family about Ryen. He wanted to introduce them as soon as he got to Florence, well maybe not before he reintroduced himself to her first.

It was close to thirty degrees out, but the afternoon sun was obscured by puffy clouds and a breeze made it feel less warm. The property Cash had looked at was decent. He wasn't quite sure he wanted to open another club when La Noche Oscura had only been up and running for a few months. He hadn't opened more than one in a country and he liked the idea of keeping it that way, plus despite Ryen's warnings, he still wanted to check out the U.S. market. They'd be stupid not to at least look into the possibility.

Now he approached the street where he had seen the vampires last night. He didn't have a great feeling about this, that's why he had emailed the address and his apprehensions to himself. He had also texted the address to Esmeralda and told her that if she didn't hear from him by tonight to give the address to Rafa and his mother and to tell Rafa to open his email. Under no circumstances was she to check out the address herself. If this was a secret vampire club they certainly wouldn't welcome a witch poking around. They may not like him doing it either, especially if they knew who he was and that he was in a similar business looking to branch out in the area.

As he had seen several people do last night, he stood in front of the window and stared intently. He figured whoever was on the other side was trying to confirm his vampire status. He let his canines grow and opened his mouth slightly. He heard a click from the door on the side of the building, and went to open it.

The darkness of the interior was such a contrast to the daylight outside that it took his eyes a moment to adjust. When they did he was greeted by a vampire at what could only be described as a hostess stand. She welcomed him and asked for his name. He certainly couldn't give them his real one so he grabbed whatever came to mind the fastest. His sister would be pleased with his *Interview with a Vampire* combo of the Vampire Armand and an actor from the movie version.

"Soy Armando Cruz."

"There's a two hundred euro cover charge which covers the basic communal drink. Other services you may desire are extra."

Cash handed over the money and the girl led him to an open foyer where a human girl was tied to a table. There were a handful of other vampires standing around and she had several bite marks covering her. Anger rose in him as the image reminded him of Ryen's story, but for his own safety he pushed it back down. He was a guest here and didn't need to cause a scene while he was gathering his information. He guessed that the girl was not here of her own free will, but the restraints could be for show. As he got closer though, he could smell drugs in her blood; she was heavily sedated. Cash deduced that vampires in the area must be desperate to pay two hundred euros for tainted blood.

Despite the vulgarity of the situation, the smell of her blood combined with his hunger caused his teeth to grow again. He hated that he could react in such a way to a scene that turned his stomach. This place was exactly what he never wanted his clubs to be. He bent down by the girl's head. To the others it would appear he was going for her already overused neck, but he whispered in her ear what the others couldn't hear, "I'm sorry. I promise you, this place will not last."

He couldn't save her now. He was well outnumbered. But he could report this place and have it shut down. The proprietors would not take kindly to that, but hopefully they would never find out that he was responsible for their demise.

He raised his head and a man approached from across the room, "Is she not to your liking?"

Cash held his anger back as he responded to the man who appeared to be in charge. The drugs wouldn't affect him, but they would alter the taste, and of course he couldn't bring himself to bite this girl that reminded him of what had been done to Ryen. "I would prefer clean blood if you have it."

"Certainly. A private room is an additional two hundred euros. We have other services available as well."

As Cash handed the guy more money, he withheld the disgust from his voice. "Just a drink today, thanks."

"This way." Cash followed him deeper into the building. He passed several doors, and he noticed several noises coming from the activities behind them. Some sounded consensual, others not so much.

"I don't believe I've seen you here before."

Cash tried to keep panic from being a visible read to this other vampire. He calculated his answer to sound respectful and with the least amount of suspiciousness, "Just passing through *your* city. The place was recommended by a friend."

The other vampire seemed satisfied with Cash's answer. "Here is your room. This is Julia. If you change your mind about anything else there's no need to notify us first. We can take care of additional payment before you leave."

Cash swore to himself. He hadn't been looking when he came in the building but there was clearly a camera in this room, and he'd bet there were others at the entrance and main room as well. Fake name or not, they now had his face on record. He wondered if it was for insurance or blackmail. Well, if he didn't go through with it he would appear too suspicious to leave of his own accord. He wasted no time. He walked over to Julia and pulled her up to stand in front of him. She was aware, but it appeared she was under some mind manipulation. He'd apologize to Ryen for breaking his promise later, but he didn't want to add more suspicion. He whispered an apology into Julia's ear before biting into her neck.

Chapter 48

Cash took an extended journey on his way back to Esmeralda's. He wanted to make sure he wasn't followed, for his sake and for Esmeralda's future safety. When he arrived back at her apartment, content that no one had pursued him, he sent her a text letting her know he was ok, and to disregard his previous message. Before placing a phone call, he sent an email with the information he had gathered about the club to the one person he knew could handle the situation, his mom. He had been planning to call his parents anyway, but now he would get his mother's assistance in reporting the club. Being a member of the Council of Elders, she would see to it that the place was shut down, and she would help in creating a trail that wouldn't lead back to him.

After he'd finished his business with his mother, his father came to the phone. He quickly changed his mood, hoping to push everything that he had seen today to the back of his mind. "Hey dad, Happy Solstice! Did you go to the compound to celebrate today?" Cash wondered if his dad had run into Ryen.

"Thanks, son, and no, I did not. I had a private celebration earlier here at home. Lilia joined me."

Cash smiled, thinking of his bright and determined little niece, "Well, you can let mom know, I forgot to tell her, but I'll be in Florence in a few days." Cash heard his dad snort. Apparently he had not been convincing with his declaration of forgetfulness. It was true he had avoided telling her directly. He also didn't want to tell her that he was bringing Ryen home. She was distracted enough by the news he was relaying, about the filth in Barcelona, that she hadn't commented on his failure to make it to their scheduled meeting to discuss his recent interest in the family business. He counted that as a win where conversations with his mother were concerned.

He didn't hold the same reservations about telling his dad. "And while I'm home, there's someone I'd like you guys to meet."

His dad's voice was filled with intrigue as he responded, "Could this 'someone' be a girl?"

"Yes, she is, and maybe you could warm mom up first."

"I doubt that is necessary. Your mother will be happy that you have finally found someone you're willing to share with your family."

"Well, I don't know that mom will necessarily agree. This isn't someone who hails from the sacred vampire power hierarchy. She's a witch." As with most things concerning her children, especially Cash, he felt his mother operated under a double standard when it suited her. It was acceptable for her to love a witch and for a witch to father her children, but Cash figured a connected vampire love interest would more easily gain her approval for the son who would be the biggest heir to the family fortune and power.

"Funny," his dad said, "not that she's a witch, but that you want me to have that conversation with your mother. I think you can handle it when you get here. I won't spoil her surprise." Cash could hear his dad's silent laughter in his tone. "So, a witch, huh?"

Cash was annoyed at his dad's laughter, however quiet, but talking about Ryen made him smile. He had never been able to stay mad at his dad either, "Yeah, she's actually from Florence. It's possible that you've seen her or even met her before. Her name is Ryen."

Something in his dad's voice changed, "Ryen? That's unique. What's her last name?"

"Cardona. She grew up at the compound, but she's been working out of town and she hasn't been there recently. Do you know her?"

Cash heard his dad stumble over his words and thought he interpreted something disconcerting, "Um, no. I don't think I do. That name doesn't sound familiar, but I look forward to meeting her. And honestly, your mother will also be excited that you're willingly introducing someone to your family."

"Well, you'll meet her soon. I'll see you in a few days." They said their good-byes and hung up. A lump of apprehension settled in Cash's stomach. His father knew that he avoided serious discussions with his mother at all costs. They were always a battle. Calandra Di Marco hated to be challenged or defied. Although his dad was always amused to see someone attempt to stand up his wife, he seemed proud when that person was his son. Cash hoped his dad would lay some ground work for him. His father was the only person Cash had ever witnessed not be intimidated by his mom, and he had never seen them have a major argument. Coming from his dad maybe his mother would be less critical. Then again, maybe his mother would fall in love with Ryen all on her own and he'd have no need to worry. *Here's to hoping.*

Cash had fallen asleep and didn't hear Esmeralda until she squirted her water bottle in his face. He responded to her assault while drying off with his sleeve, "That was not very nice."

Her voice was dripping with annoyance, "Neither was that cryptic text you sent me earlier! I hope you know I was worried about you for hours, even after you said you were fine. What was that all about?"

Cash relayed what he had seen the past night and afternoon, and made it very clear that Esmeralda was never to go snooping around. Hopefully it would be shut down in the next few days, and if he was lucky, it wouldn't be traced back to him. He wished he could somehow erase the video footage of his face, but that was impossible without going back. He also made sure Esmeralda would be diligently observant about her surroundings in case it did come back to him and those he'd crossed came looking for people to whom he was connected. She seemed horrified enough to heed his warnings.

"I know you had to, to protect yourself, but I'm sorry you had to participate in that. I know it's against everything you believe."

"At least I was actually thirsty, or I may not have been able to force myself."

"Yeah, I was a little concerned after last night. I noticed you didn't get anything to drink while we were out." Half joking she added, "I was worried that I'd have to offer you my neck tonight, and I'm pretty beat."

"I would have declined your beautiful neck anyways." He reached out for her arm and flipped it over so his thumb rested on her upwards turned wrist, and winked with a devilish gleam in his eyes, "Although I had to break it today, I made a promise to a lady. I'm strictly a wrist man now."

"How would she feel to know I'm a repeat donor?" Her question was light, but Cash wondered, how would Ryen feel? Esmeralda was the only person he had drank from more than once in his adult life. As a child the house had "wet nurses" for him and his sister, but once he went off to school he'd realized it wasn't necessary to have one person stick around. He preferred it actually. It had made it easier. As a response to her question he just shrugged.

He still held her wrist and as he moved his thumb he looked at Esmeralda's witch tattoo, "All witches have the same tattoo, right?"

"All witches that are part of the Universal Coven at least. It stands for the three aspects of the Goddess, of womanhood really: maiden, mother, and crone."

Cash nodded thoughtfully. His dad had told him all about it when he had asked as a child, "When did you get yours?"

"When I was ten and had my initiation."

"And they all look exactly the same?" Cash was still wondering about Ryen's tattoo. He had let her vague explanation go, and hadn't returned to the conversation in the remainder of their week together.

"Yes."

"Could you change it if you wanted, fill it in? Color it?"

"NO! It would be sacrilegious to alter this symbol of the Coven and the Goddess!" Her adamant tone was shocking, but what she said had the wheels in Cash's head spinning. She continued when he looked confused, "There are some circles that use the symbol as the center of a more intricate design, to show unity and loyalty amongst themselves. But as for the symbol itself, there are only three living souls that would have any part of it filled in. That would mark the Triumvirate, the Maiden, the Mother, and the Crone."

"What do you mean?" Cash almost lost his composure. His head shot up from looking at her wrist to look in her eyes. What Esmeralda was saying couldn't be correct. That would mean that Ryen was some sort of heretic against the Coven, or... "What are their names, the Triumvirate?"

Esmeralda clearly didn't understand the severity of his reaction, "Lady Celeste is the current Crone, Lady Luna is the Mother, and Lady Reina is the Maiden."

"Those are their names?" None of this was making any sense to Cash.

"Well, I mean, they have regular names too, but I don't know what they are. All Coven members address them with their respectful titles. Those that live at the compound would probably know their other names, but they would use their titles as well."

His mind was swimming but he still wanted more information, "And you're sure about the tattoos? You said you've never met the Triumvirate."

"Yes, I'm sure. As they enter each stage of their service a phase of the moon is filled in. The Maiden would have the waxing crescent filled, the Mother would have the waxing crescent and the full moon, and the Crone would have all three filled."

"And you said they live at the compound?"

"Yes, it's where they live, conduct their business, do spells, hold rituals and ceremonies. They hardly ever leave. But, it was rumored that all three of them left to retrieve the vessel of the newly conceived Maiden, the pregnant girl," she clarified.

"That's what their life is like? Do they have outside jobs, families?"

"No jobs and they obviously came from families. The parents are invited to live their lives at the compound but most don't stay forever because they have their own lives and other children. But the Triumvirate don't have families of their own. They consider all of the witches they represent their children. Plus they raise the future Maiden as if she were their own child."

Cash tried to control his voice as he continued to ask questions, though he was sure Esmeralda could sense his emotions going haywire. He was doing his best to gather information without coming right out and asking what he really wanted to know. "That must be lonely for them. They're like nuns or something?"

"Well I don't think it goes quite that far. Witches aren't frightened by physical connections. I'd imagine that none of them are celibate, unless it's by personal choice. They just don't get married or have serious relationships, that sort of thing because it would distract from their purpose."

Outwardly Cash tried to seem superficially thoughtful, nodding his head and looking like he was considering the information he'd been given like a student, but on the inside he was in turmoil. The way Ryen talked about Florence and how the Coven had taken her in, there was no way she would get a tattoo that would betray those who had raised and protected her, unless she was working with her mother, but that wasn't possible either with how he had felt her fear about what was going on in the U.S. But the other things didn't fit either. She had a job, she was hardly ever in Florence, they were meant to be together, or had she just been pretending? He didn't think so. He knew that what was between them was real. Could this be what she had been fighting so hard to keep hidden from him? What did this mean for their future? He needed to talk to her. He needed to see her, to see her eyes when she answered him, to feel her emotions that she could no longer completely withhold from him.

Esmeralda was watching him, and he knew she was wondering why he was so quiet. He took a deep breath, confident his tone wouldn't give him away. "That's pretty interesting. Thanks for the cultural lesson. Now I'll feel more educated when I hear Ryen talk about things."

"Ryen? Is that your girlfriend's name?" Cash cringed at her question. He didn't mean to let Ryen's name slip.

He wondered if it was smart to tell her that. She was intelligent and perceptive, and given time to think about his questions and reactions, she would no doubt figure out who his girlfriend was. "Yes." *But you may know her as Lady Reina.* "Why don't you shower? You stink," he pushed her gently in the shoulder. "I'm going to get some fresh air on your balcony for a bit."

He needed the fresh air for sure, and he wanted some privacy to place a much needed and also dreaded phone call. Just like the last time it went straight to voicemail. This time his tone was different, pleading and demanding at the same time, "Ryen, please call me immediately. I really need to talk to you."

He paused, wanting to tell her that he loved her no matter what, but if all of this was true, could he forgive her for keeping it from him? And if there was no future for them, was she just stringing him along for her selfish pleasure? He hung up without saying anything more and sat down on a bench with his back slouched against the building's exterior. He felt deflated, confused, hurt, and he questioned the truth of what had transpired these past weeks. Part of him wanted to show the picture on his phone to Esmeralda and have her confirm his suspicions, but maybe she didn't know what the Maiden looked like since she'd never met her. The other part of him wanted to hold on to the hope that this was all a misunderstanding, though that part was shrinking by the minute.

He placed a call to the airline, changing this ticket from a few days from now to tomorrow, with a direct flight to Florence instead of heading to Madrid. He sent Rafa a text telling him his plans as well. Though not for lack of trying, he couldn't get an earlier flight, so it would be evening before he arrived. That gave him plenty of time to figure out how he was going to confront Ryen about all of this, but it also gave him more than enough time to second guess every thought and feeling he'd had about her.

Chapter 49

Ryen had another voicemail from Cash, but this time she decided not to listen to it. She had a few appointments with Coven members today and she wanted to discuss the issue of her brother with Chesna and Kora. They were supposed to be looking further into the matter over the past week, and Ryen was anxious to hear what they had found. She wondered if they would agree with her that something needed to be done soon in the States. Too many witches had already fallen victim to her mother's murderous group.

As soon as she could get away she'd be changing her phone number so she could avoid any more calls from Cash until he gave up. Ryen wondered how long that would take. She also wondered if "working" today was really a good idea. Was her head really in it, or was she too distracted to pay attention? Her next visitor was a longtime acquaintance. She didn't know him extremely well. He was a local witch who had been coming for private spell work since before Ryen had become Maiden. Just then there was a knock on her door.

"Come in" she said.

Brother Luca Solano opened the door. "Lady Reina," he greeted with a slight bow, "thank you for meeting with me today." In actuality he was in his early fifties but the spell work had been doing its intended purpose; he looked younger than forty.

It wasn't necessarily Ryen's preference to assist in spells of vanity, but the commitment had been made before her time, so she followed through with her duty. Luca wasn't here for his spells today. Those were special ceremonies, involving special preparation and the strength of the full Triumvirate. Today was just a meeting at his request. She had never met with him privately before.

"What's on your mind, Brother Luca?" Ryen asked as she smiled and motioned for him to take a seat.

"Actually Lady Reina, I'd like to speak with you casually today. It's not really witch business." Ryen's face surely showed the confusion she was feeling. As

Luca continued he watched Ryen closely, "You've always known me as 'Brother Luca', hopefully a nice guy, but you don't really know much more, do you?"

Ryen immediately felt guilty at his question. Of course she knew it was impossible to know every single witch in the world on a personal level, but to be called out on it was embarrassing. This was now the second time in recent history that she had felt like she wasn't doing a good job as a leader, at least in knowing the witches for whom she was responsible. Luca read the look on her face, and took it for offended shock instead of guilt, "Please forgive me, my lady. I didn't mean that you *should* know more about me. I was just curious. It's why I'm here today."

Still more confused Ryen apologized, "I'm sorry. I'd like to say yes, but no, I don't. I've never taken the time to ask."

"I knew this encounter would be awkward for both of us. That's why I wanted to talk to you ahead of time. You know me as Luca Solano, but you don't know my family because they aren't witches."

Oh, that much she did know. She mentally chalked up a point for herself to relieve some of her guilt.

"My family, well my wife, is the reason I come for the spells. She's a vampire."

Ryen was taken off guard. How strange, or ironic really, that he was confessing this to her, the witch leader currently in love with a vampire? Ryen wondered if Kora or Chesna had arranged this meeting because they were concerned about her relationship. She had told them she had ended it when she arrived the other day, at which they had exchanged glances that could have been doubt or concern. Whichever it was, it had irritated Ryen.

Luca continued when Ryen stayed quiet, still looking at her like she was missing something, "My wife's name is Calandra Di Marco."

Ryen's eyes widened, possibly to the point where they could not open any further, and she knew all of the color and animation had drained from her face. Her head was racing with so many thoughts. When she still didn't speak, Luca kept talking, stating the obvious in case she hadn't understood. "I'm Cash's father."

Of course, it fell into place now. Cash had said his father's name was Luca. Why hadn't she put two and two together? Right now she felt like a child caught doing something wrong instead of the powerful witch leader she was. "Wow," Ryen managed, marginally recovering from her shock, "that is not what I was expecting."

"I know," Luca apologized, "I thought it would be better to do this, you and I, in private."

"Agreed," Ryen said. She had no intention of seeing Cash again, but now she knew that she would at least have to break things off officially, out of respect for everyone involved and respect for her position. Although others' opinions of her shouldn't matter, she didn't want to have to face this man in the future and have him see her as a heartless bitch that had hurt his son. She wondered if that could even be avoided at this point, "How long have you known?"

"Since he told me your name yesterday and that you were a witch from Florence. When he said 'Ryen', I knew it couldn't be a coincidence. When I asked your last name, my suspicions were confirmed."

"I didn't make the connection." Ryen felt foolish and naive. "Cash told me you were a witch and that your name was Luca, but I kept thinking your last name was Di Marco, like his, and maybe you didn't associate strongly with the Coven."

"Vampire surnames carry on in the vampire line," Luca stated without any subtext. After a pause he asked, "Does he know?"

Ryen knew what he was asking, and seeing him look at her as a concerned parent made her feel ashamed. When she answered it was little more than a whisper, conveying her shame, "No."

Ryen noticed a crease form on Luca's forehead. She wondered if it was in disapproval of her withholding such information from his son, "I thought as much when he asked if I'd ever met or seen you. When are you planning to tell him?"

He wanted to know when, not if. She couldn't very well tell Cash's father that she had never had any intention of telling him, since until this moment she had no intention of seeing him again, and therefore there was no reason for him to ever know. Their relationship could never work. There was no way to reconcile a soulmate with being one of the Triumvirate, let alone a vampire soulmate. Surely his father could understand that. If only Luca wasn't Cash's father, he might be a good person to confide in. "Does anyone else know?" she asked, avoiding his question.

"No, no one else made the connection with your name. Calandra knows witch basics, and of the Triumvirate. She doesn't involve herself in witch business, but believe me; she will take an interest when Cash confesses his feelings. No one else is really that interested either, except for my granddaughter, so it wasn't something I needed to share. The look he gave her conveyed that it was *her* business, but that it should be shared in the future. She gave him an understanding nod.

"So, how do we go about this?" Ryen asked, unsure if they should conceal today's meeting. "Shall I call you Signore Solano?"

"Um, no, you can call me Luca. I won't hide that I know you again. If he says something to me, I won't lie to my son a second time. But for future personal encounters may I ask your permission to address you informally?"

"Definitely. You may address me as Ryen outside of the compound."

"Thank you, my lady," Luca responded respectfully. "Ryen," he said, testing it out, "I'm looking forward to getting to know you personally, as my son's girlfriend." Luca's eyes were sincere and full of genuine care, and also something of a warning, "But you didn't answer my question."

Ryen set aside the Coven pretense and saw Luca only as Cash's father. She wasn't quite sure how to answer without it being clear that a conversation about her responsibilities was only necessary now because of his knowledge.

He continued speaking when she still didn't provide an answer, "He's planning to introduce you to us in a few days when he arrives in Florence. If you know anything about my son, you know that action is something neither he, nor his family takes lightly."

Ryen heard the unspoken words cautioning her to tread carefully. What he was really saying was that Cash was in deep, and if she didn't feel the same she had a responsibility to him to be honest, and soon.

"Understood." Ryen responded. "Before you go, do you mind if I ask about your spells?"

"Of course not. I already alluded to the fact that it is because of my wife. I'm assuming you'd like to know why."

"Yes," was all Ryen said.

"In the beginning Calandra was willing to age with me. She still is, but that's not what I want for her. Someday I'll be gone. I don't want her stuck as an old woman, searching for a new love."

This was perplexing to Ryen. She knew a few things about vampires, but as questions fired off in her mind she was surprised that she didn't know as much as she thought. One would think, with her hatred of vampires for so many years, that she would have acquired as much knowledge as possible. The whole "know your enemy" thing, but maybe she had inadvertently avoided learning about vampires. *Wow!* As a leader of witches around the world she should really know more than she did. She chastised herself for her irresponsibility.

Her face must have conveyed the confusion swirling in her head because Luca quickly continued, thinking her expression was due to his explanation and not where her own thoughts had traveled. "I won't ask for intervention if I should have an accident or an illness that shortens my life, but if magic can help me stay younger awhile longer, it's not harming anyone."

This scenario had never occurred to Ryen. She had always assumed he had been getting the spells out of vanity, but it was for love. She decided to ask what she thought was the obvious question he hadn't answered, but she phrased it as a statement. "You don't want her to change you."

"I thought about it for several years, especially when the children were little and they both were leaning towards the vampire life. Ultimately I knew my answer was no. A changed vampire is so different from a born one. Our lives would not be of equals. As I said, Calandra was willing to grow old with me, but I wouldn't allow her to be stuck as an elderly woman when I'm gone. So this was my only option."

Suddenly there were so many things Ryen wanted to know. The perfect opportunity to get those answers was sitting right in front of her. She was hesitant to ask, fearing her ignorance would make her appear weak, but Cash's dad might be the best person to whom to expose this weakness. "Can I ask you a couple more questions about vampires?"

Luca frowned slightly, contemplating her question, before he answered, "Of course, though I hardly think I'm an expert."

Ryen thought that she understood his unspoken question of why she didn't ask Cash, but she soldiered on, "You said that born and made vampires were so different, what did you mean by that?"

"Well, I'm sure you already know that made-vampires don't age past the day they are changed. They are in fact dead; the blood that is consumed is what allows them to function. There are limitations of course; made vampires obviously cannot reproduce naturally nor make others. The removal of a born vampire's birthright means he or she can no longer age either. At that point both are equal in susceptibility of being truly killed."

Side tracked, Ryen jumped in with another question, "I know that the removal of a vampire's birthright is not something that is taken lightly. How is that determined?"

"Well, if something horrendous occurs, the family and the ruling vampire council come to that decision as a last resort. It's a fairly secret ceremony. A witch that the council employs completes the spell to which she is the sole person outside of the vampire council to know the ritual. It doesn't happen very often."

Ryen's thoughts drifted to what Cash had told her about his brother, and she wondered who the current witch was, privy to such powerfully information. She filed away her tangent thoughts to continue listening to Luca's explanation, "But the biggest differences are within vampire society itself. Born vampires pass down their power with each generation, growing in strength. Made-vampires are all the same in power, and it pales in comparison to the inherited power that some families have built up. There is dark blood magic that can transfer power, but not many respectable people would even consider it. And it's really only a temptation if there isn't a born heir. The Di Marco line has been around for a long time. Calandra is a powerful woman, in strength and social status. As a made-vampire I would be looked down upon regardless, but next to her the difference would be laughable. She wouldn't care, but I would. Not for myself, but for her."

Ryen absorbed the extensive information as best she could. It caused more questions and conflicting feelings within her, but she pushed those aside for the question that she had planned to ask Cash but hadn't gotten around to, "How does it work in your family, with your kids and grandchildren? How do they choose between being a vampire and a witch?"

He gave her a lopsided smile before he continued, and she hoped he wasn't reading too much into her question, "Well, my children are fifty-fifty, so technically it could ultimately come down to a basic choice. But as I mentioned inherited power before, that factors in as well. Di Marco blood is full of power. I am a very average witch as you know. So, with my children the pull towards being vampires was much stronger than towards being witches. I expected as much, so it wasn't a surprise when they leaned that way at an early age. The same goes for my grandchildren, but having the weaker witch blood even further diluted with human blood, Lilia's strong inclination towards being a witch shocked everyone."

"Thank you for sharing that with me. And though it may not have appeared so, I do appreciate you coming to see me today." She reached over and squeezed his hand. Then she rose, abruptly indicating that their meeting was over. Ryen had so much to sort through emotionally with all of this new information. She needed space now to clear her head and think.

"Of course. I meant what I said before; I do look forward to getting to know you. You're obviously special to us," he gestured around him, indicating the witch world, "but I think it's safe to say that you are special to my son as well." He bowed slightly before leaving her office.

Luca's argument for his spells made sense to Ryen. It was sweet, romantic, unselfish, and honest. And it hit way too close to home. Ryen would be lying if she said those thoughts had never entered her mind, but hearing about the Di Marco line and vampire society seemed to solidify her resolve. This was yet another reason on the ever growing list that their relationship was a bad idea. There were aspects of her future that were not up for debate, she had responsibilities to the Coven, to witches all over the world, becoming a vampire was not an option, and neither was having a serious relationship with one.

She had chosen to be a coward and ran away, avoiding a conversation she really didn't want to have. She had known all along that it wasn't fair to Cash, and she was surprised that she thought it would work or that she wouldn't be affected by how it would hurt him. Now with his dad knowing who she was she had to suck it up and face Cash. The problem was that she wasn't sure she had the strength to walk away from him again.

Chapter 50

After Cash's father left, Ryen knew that she would be useless the rest of the morning, but she was relieved when her next appointment walked in. Elise and Gelina both had sheepish smiles on their faces, and Ryen was thrilled. She had seen them yesterday but didn't have a chance to speak with either one. Now she laughed that they had actually scheduled an appointment with her. She could definitely use the pleasant distraction from her new predicament.

"Welcome ladies. What can I do for you? Gelina, how are you feeling?"

Gelina answered first. "I'm feeling pretty well. The yoga sessions have really been helping with morning sickness."

"And you're feeling at home here? Did I see your dad yesterday?"

"Yes, my dad and sister came for a visit. My mom is taking them to the airport today."

"How's Holt holding up?" Ryen hoped that their relationship wasn't suffering because of the role Gelina had been chosen to play. The situation with Cash had given her a different perspective on relationships that she had never had a real understanding of before.

"Great, actually. He talked to his recruiting officer, and he postponed his enlistment. He wants to be with me throughout the pregnancy and whatever comes afterwards. He's made some friends, and he has enjoyed getting to know the city. He's even trying to learn Italian."

"And you've been enjoying your classes here?"

"Absolutely. I have such a more thorough understanding of things here, and all of the teachers are so talented. Elise and I have both received confirmation for attending university here in Florence as well."

"That's great! I'm glad both of you will be sticking around for a few years at least." Ryen really did feel that way. She hoped that Gelina would continue to be a part of her baby's life, even though that life would be dictated by others.

Elise, who had been quiet so far, spoke up, "Don't forget to tell her about discovering new powers." She nudged Gelina as Gelina blushed.

"It's not really a big deal. It could just be because of the baby. Lady Luna said that eventually I could tap into her power without even realizing it."

Although it didn't read on her face, tension appeared in Gelina at the mention of the baby's powers. Ryen noticed the subtle difference but rather than draw attention, she let the girls continue. Elise was quick to argue, "But she also said that probably wouldn't happen until at least the second trimester. Stop being modest, and accept that you have power you never knew about."

Ryen was very intrigued by these developments, but she tried not to let her interest seem to be more than what would be expected, "You were able to manifest powers before though, right?"

"Yes, but nothing major: light a candle, get a rose to bloom, pop some popcorn if I concentrated enough."

"Hmm, fire. How has that changed?"

Gelina blushed and looked down so Elise answered for her, "She lit up an entire fireplace."

Ryen couldn't hold back her surprise. That actually required a significant amount of power, "Impressive. Was it intentional?"

Elise giggled and Gelina's blush became deeper. Gelina only muttered, "No," still staring at the floor.

So Elise helped her out, "Let's just say it was the fireplace in her bedroom, and she was there with Holt."

Ryen felt immediate sympathy for Gelina, because she knew firsthand how those things could happen and also because she could see how mortified she was to have this information become known to Ryen. Ryen tried to make her feel better, "Oh sweetie, don't even worry about it. It happens to the best of us."

At that both girls' heads shot in her direction, but she kept talking. "Have you tried intentionally using this new strength? Lady Celeste, Lady Luna, and I could do a power searching spell on you to see if it's connected to the baby if you want."

This time at the mention of the baby something briefly flashed across Gelina's face, but her voice remained steady and unchanged, "I've been experimenting successfully with multiple candles, but if you would be willing to help answer that question I'd appreciate it. I don't want to use my baby's power, and I would like to learn how to control it."

"I have a meeting with both of them in a little while, so I will mention it to them. I'll find you later and let you know when we can do the spell. It shouldn't be that big of deal. But are you sure you are ok? Something feels a little off."

Concern flared in Gelina's eyes, but she readily provided a sensible explanation, "I'm sorry. My hormones are everywhere. I'm still sorting them all out."

Ryen let it go. She made a mental note to keep an eye on Gelina's stress level. Maybe she wasn't handling this unusual pregnancy as well as everyone thought. The three of them continued to have a pleasant visit, discussing the season and Florence. Ryen was feeling reenergized. As the girls got up to leave, Ryen said very sincerely, "Now that I'll be around here more, I hope we can spend more time together."

Both girls responded with statements of agreement. Ryen smiled. She wanted to be someone both girls, but especially Gelina could turn to. She knew firsthand what it was like coming to the compound without any friends. Being someone "special" only made friendships harder to come by. Selfishly Ryen had a feeling that she could use someone to help fight her own loneliness. With Sophie working in Madrid for a few more weeks Ryen didn't really have anyone other than Chesna and Kora. And who knew if Sophie would choose to come home now that she was in a relationship with Rafa. Elise and Gelina's visit had initially cheered her up, but now Ryen was overcome with a sense of loneliness.

Chapter 51

Ryen was still rattled from meeting Cash's father, and she felt unsettled after talking with the girls, but she had more important things to think about than her personal feelings. She collected her folder of information the private investigator had found on Elijah Turner and prepared herself for the conversation ahead with Chesna and Kora. She was torn about whether or not she hoped they had found out more over the past week. More information could confirm her fears that either her mother knew she was still alive, that they were bringing their war to Europe, or both. No information would mean that either there was nothing to worry about or they just needed to keep digging.

For years Ryen had thought they should be doing something about what was happening in the U.S. Kora and Chesna kept insisting that they needed to wait until her mother's fanatical group crossed the Atlantic, or at least spread to another country in the Americas, but Ryen had never agreed. Maybe she felt more strongly or even responsible on some level because it was her mother who was part of the murdering. Maybe she felt guilty now because she had been removed from the daily workings at the compound for so long, or subconsciously she was trying to find something else to throw her energies into rather than think about or deal with the Cash situation.

Kora and Chesna were waiting for her when she walked into their shared space. Before they got down to the dirty business of her family, she mentioned testing the origin of Gelina's newly developed powers. The look the other two women shared did not go unnoticed by Ryen, but she figured they, too, were noting the one hundred percent engagement she was giving to business at the compound. Kora had her assistant arrange a time later in the week and sent word to Gelina. They chatted about yesterday's festivities and what would need to be done before the next full moon ritual and the celebration for Lammas which would take place in just over a month. Kora updated Ryen on the classes currently in progress and those approaching in the near future so she could decide where she'd jump in with instruction. Being able to study under the Triumvirate was a major reason for attending school here.

Ryen was getting a little antsy, and she felt like they were purposefully avoiding the topic that had generated this meeting in the first place, but finally all other business seemed to be concluded. When she had an opening she jumped in, "Did you guys find anything new about Elijah Turner?"

Kora answered her question, "Aside from a blood test, we've pretty much concluded that he is in fact your half-brother. We were able to find hospital records of his birth and spoke to some nurses who remembered your mother."

Ryen had already been confident in who he was, but it was nice that Kora and Chesna had found their own proof. "Were you able to get more information about what kind of internship he is doing at the Vatican?"

She watched the other two women exchange a worried look. Neither of them seemed willing to speak up to answer the question, "Well?" she prodded again.

"Do not overreact," Chesna's words resulted in alarm rising inside Ryen, "it hasn't been confirmed without a doubt yet, nor is it a definite cause for concern."

"What?" Ryen was about to crawl out of her chair with dread. She could tell it was bad at Chesna's reservations in telling her.

"Our sources think he's studying demonology."

Ryen thought she may get sick. There were too many things to make it coincidental. Demonology was not a largely pursued topic within the Catholic Church, but a small faction remained. That, combined with who Elijah's parents were, made the situation serious. "Are you two ready to agree that they have crossed the ocean now?"

She couldn't believe what she was seeing. Before either of them answered, she could see that they still weren't ready to engage in a defense. "Ryen," this time it was Kora, "you need to calm down. He has not acted against us in any way. Right now he is simply being educated at the Vatican. It's entirely possible that his parents' interactions with the supernatural have generated

272

a legitimate interest in actual demonology. It doesn't mean that he's going after witches. The Pope has never sent his people after us." After the heads of both of the other women in the room turned to her in disbelief, she quickly added, "Ok, in the past, yes. But at least not *this* century, and certainly not *this* Pope."

Anger was filling her, and she had to direct some of her energy to control her emotions so her powers didn't respond. She could feel tears flooding her eyes as she struggled to keep her frustration in check. When she was calm enough to speak, she asked accusingly, "How many witches have to die before we do something? Over the past thirty plus years hundreds of witches, mostly powerless humans who have heard the call of the Goddess and have no means to protect themselves, have been murdered, and we sit over here in our safe, hidden compound and refuse to help them. Have you forgotten that this place was created in response to thousands of deaths at the hand of the same Christian "God" and the Inquisition? Witches all over the world, those witches who are in danger in the States, look to us for guidance and protection, and we've done nothing!"

They let her get out everything that she wanted to say. No one commented on the rumble of thunder outside with not a cloud in the sky. They didn't tell her to calm down again, nor did they argue with her. When she finished her rant they looked at each other and shared a quiet, private conversation that Ryen could hear, but didn't understand.

"I think we should tell her. It's time that she knows," Kora said.

"You are probably right. We can't keep it from her forever, especially now," Chesna agreed.

"What are you two talking about? What should I know?"

Chesna spoke, "We understand your anger, and we too, want to stop what is happening. But child, it simply isn't time yet."

"What is that supposed to mean?"

Kora got up from her chair and walked over to the large painting of a witch worshipping under a full moon. Ryen had always loved that painting, and it was still as imposing as it was when she was nine. Even as an adult it was bigger than she was. The witch in the painting had long blonde hair hanging down her back and she wore a simple white dress like the one Ryen wore for ceremonies and rituals. The witch stood on the grassy shore of a lake. She held her arms up, reaching for the full moon that occupied the top half of the painting. The contrast of the white of the witch's dress and the moon with the dark blues and grays made them look luminescent and alive. It was difficult to discern details of the witch's appearance, but her eyes were closed as she raised her face to the sky, soaking in the power of the light as Ryen had done on numerous occasions. Kora swung the side of the picture outward revealing a door to a safe about the same size as the painting. Ryen inhaled in surprise. She had never known that a safe existed there.

Kora typed in a combination and took a folder out of the safe. When she opened it on the table in front of Ryen it held very old-looking parchment paper with curly writing. Kora motioned for Ryen to take a closer look. Ryen read the paper once, and then again. Things were fluttering inside of her, and her head was swimming. She understood the words, but her mind wouldn't let her believe what they said. She looked up at the two women in front of her; they, who had been her family for more years than not, "What is this? And how long have you had it?"

Chesna took the responsibility of answering, "It's a prophecy, and it has been in existence here since anyone can remember."

"You believe it is about me?"

"Yes," Chesna stated flatly, lacking emotion as she so often did.

"And you didn't think it was necessary to tell me before today?"

Kora looked close to tears, "We understand if you feel betrayed, but you have to understand that when your mother disappeared we thought we would never see you. We feared you were dead too, like all of the others. Then when you contacted us we were ecstatic to have you back. It was between your contact and your arrival that Maggie made the connection between you and the prophecy. You were just a child, so we decided to wait until you officially became the Maiden to tell you. Then you were attacked, and Chesna and I couldn't bring ourselves to add it to your plate. We wanted to protect you. You have always been like our own daughter. You had been through so much, so we indulged you more than maybe we should have. We kept this from you, not wanting to burden you with the responsibility until it was necessary."

"So this is why I've been given more freedom than any other in my position? Because you feel sorry for me and what my future ultimately holds?"

They didn't need to answer. Ryen could see the confirmation of her accusations in their faces. Damn right she felt betrayed. She picked up the paper again. Normally with her Art History education she would be more careful with a document that was so old, but right now she didn't care. She began to read aloud:

> Presumed tolerance and acceptance will mask a war waged against the Goddess and Her children. One of the Goddess's own will betray her and be lost to darkness.
>
> In this time, one who bares the mark of the Goddess will come from darkness lost and will wield great power, before unseen. She will be known as the Warrior Maiden.
>
> The Warrior Maiden will be aided by elemental warriors manifesting strength in each power.
>
> When the powers arise, the Warrior Maiden will lead them against the enemies of the

Goddess. Only united can they defeat the blood enemy who seeks to destroy.

The room was completely silent when Ryen finished reading. She looked up from the parchment, "So you think the one who betrayed the Goddess is my mother."

Chesna nodded, all emotion lacking from her wizened face. Kora just sat with an expression of pity and sadness.

"And you think I am the Warrior Maiden." Again it was not a question but Chesna nodded in confirmation. "Why?"

It was Chesna who spoke, "We interpreted that 'darkness lost' referred to you being lost to us, being raised in darkness. Of course there is also the part about your powers. No one would argue that you are by far the most powerful witch that anyone has ever seen. Even before you knew what you were, your powers were manifesting themselves. Your mother wrote of her fear in her journals, remember? She was afraid of you and for you. You don't lean towards one element; you are incredibly strong with all four."

"So what or who are these elemental powers?" Ryen asked, not commenting on Chesna's interpretations.

"We believe that the Goddess will show us four witches, each with a strong inclination towards one specific element when the time is right to train them."

"And since these 'powers' haven't yet been raised, that's why you say it's not time to defend our brothers and sisters?" Ryen was trying as hard as she could manage to keep emotion from her voice, but everything was swirling inside. If she closed her eyes she was sure she would pass out.

"We could try, but we feel that it would be futile until the prophecy is ready to be fulfilled."

"So we sit back and allow them to be murdered. That makes perfect sense." Her sarcasm could not be contained.

A disturbing thought had been forming in Ryen's mind since the conversation had begun. She wasn't sure that she really wanted to know, but she had to ask, "You've admitted to allowing me freedoms, school, the museums, out of pity or love, whatever you want to call it, because of this," she pointed down at the parchment almost in disgust. "So, last week when you told me to be selfish and basically gave me your permission to choose Cash, was that out of this same love and pity?"

Kora began crying and Chesna just looked at her, neither verbally denying nor confirming it.

"Do you realize what he is to me? In light of all of this it would have been better if he had never met me." She could no longer hold back those emotions she had been fighting. Anger, sadness, helplessness, all spilled out in her words as more thunder boomed outside. Dark clouds were moving in. "I may understand, maybe even expect you to manipulate and mess with my life, but I can't forgive you for disregarding his."

"Ryen, everything is about free will, even this. No one forced you to go to him, and frankly no one can force you to fulfill this prophecy. Maybe we were misguided, but neither of us will apologize for loving you enough to let you have a life." Chesna had never raised her voice in Ryen's presence before and if she wasn't being fueled by so much anger, she might even be frightened by the tone. Although Chesna did not mean it in a threatening way, Ryen could feel the power emanating from her.

Ryen released her own power, dwarfing Chesna's, "You're right. I alone made the decision, regardless of my counsel, to get involved with Cash. I can take responsibility for that. But hindsight or no, I can tell you for certain, that if I had all of this information I would have chosen differently. I wouldn't have even been in a position to meet him in the first place. I can claim my responsibility; can you?"

Silence hung in the air, and then Ryen continued with less aggression, "I'm going to walk away now. I don't want to see you or hear from either of you until I decide I'm ready. In case of an emergency Sophie will know how to reach me." She paused and then released her power again, "But do not pressure or manipulate her into telling you where I am unless it's a necessity."

She walked out of the room, and was too preoccupied and far away to hear the conversation continue in her absence. Through her tears Kora asked, "When do we tell her we've already located two of the four powers?"

"She'll discover them soon enough and we still have two more to go. There's no rush. Right now she needs to calm down." Chesna seemed indifferent except for the cracking in her voice.

Ryen went upstairs to her bedroom, threw a few things into a bag and left. On her way into town she made two phone calls. The first was to the Hotel degli Orafi to get a room; the second was to Sophie, to tell her that she could be reached at the hotel in case of an emergency. She had two more missed calls from Cash, but she forced herself to ignore them and turned off her phone.

Chapter 52

It had now been over forty-eight hours since Cash had talked to Ryen. Her phone was still going straight to voicemail and she hadn't responded to any of his messages. He was torn between fear that something had happened to her, and anger that she was purposefully ignoring him. Had she figured out that he had discovered her secret? Is this just what she did when she was done with a relationship? She had at least given that museum dork a face to face breakup; she owed him just as much. He was pissed, but he wasn't going to simply let her walk away. In the very least she would admit who she was and what she intended to do.

Esmeralda had broken him down earlier while he waited at her apartment for his flight. He ended up telling her the entire story, everything. She had been shocked, but had confirmed that the picture on his phone was indeed the Maiden of the Universal Coven. She wasn't sure what to make of the situation though. Esmeralda felt that the soulmate principle superseded the role of the Triumvirate since it was a law of the Universe, but she really didn't know. Her emotions bounced between being wrapped up in what she found to be a romantic story and concern that Cash was going to get hurt. Cash left early for the airport when he could no longer take seeing the look of pity in her eyes.

He had tried to call Ryen multiple times before he boarded the plane without success. His direct flight had only lasted two hours, but he had used that time to contact the one person who had always been able to assist him with Ryen. Sophie was reluctant, but when Cash told her he knew who she really was, Sophie told him where he could find her. She promised not to tell Ryen ahead of time as long as Cash promised to hear her out. He knew Sophie had always been on his side though her loyalty was to Ryen.

Now he stood outside the hotel entrance, the Arno River at his back. Ryen had wreaked havoc on his life since the night he set eyes on her, but she had also had his heart since that night. As angry as he was that she had lied to him, and then tried to disappear, he was still excited to see her, to be able to touch her. But his longing couldn't erase the hurt he felt. He had never felt like this before, and he wasn't sure if there was anything Ryen could say or do to make it better, but he would at least give her the opportunity to try...

Even after a shower, some room service, and a short nap, Ryen was still agitated. She could mark this on the top-ten list of bad days for sure. She felt as if she was being torn in opposing directions, towards her heart, towards her responsibilities as the Maiden, towards the battle brewing. She was emotionally exhausted. She wasn't sure how long she would stay at the hotel. She was so angry at Kora and Chesna for keeping such important information from her, even if they claimed it was out of love. Didn't they realize that by keeping it from her they had caused so much more pain, not only to her but to others that were now involved in her life? Her heart clenched. Oh how she wished that Cash was here with her, to hold her in his arms and make her feel safe. But that was selfish, and not possible.

As the sun was setting she sat on her balcony and took in one of her favorite views: the Palazzo Vecchio and the Duomo. For the first time all day she started to physically feel at peace. Emotionally she would require a great deal more time. She was extremely pleased with her suite. From the other side of her rooms she had a view of the Arno and the Ponte Vecchio. It also made her feel at home with the hotel practically next door to the Uffizi Museum. Maybe she could hide here forever, with no one to reach her other than Sophie.

Her peace was interrupted by an unexpected knock at the door. She choked on the sip of water she had just taken as she looked through the peephole. As if answering her unspoken prayer from earlier, Cash stood on the other side. Ryen's first thought was to hide and pretend she wasn't here as she physically put her back to the door and dropped to the floor, followed by thought number two, which was to curse Sophie for not being able to keep her mouth shut. So much for staying hidden forever, but the longing that ached in every part of her body empowered her to get up and open the door.

She knew this was the face to face confrontation she had tried to avoid, but she had to follow through, especially now that he was here. For that reason she refrained from throwing herself into his arms. He too, hesitated. Although he smiled with some relief, Ryen noticed the hard set of his jaw, and the warmth of his smile didn't penetrate the depths of his eyes. She held onto the door to prevent herself from collapsing under all of the stress and anxiety she was feeling.

Ryen tried to sound light, but sarcasm edged her greeting, "How's Sophie?"

"Always the cheerleader, even when the team has no hope of a comeback." His voice was fearfully passive, "I'm glad you are ok. When I couldn't reach you I was afraid something had happened."

Was his sports reference a metaphor for how he saw their relationship? It broke her heart that he had been worried about her. If he only knew what all had happened since she had last seen him. She knew he would be able to tell she was lying, but the words came out anyway, "Sorry, I shut my phone off because there was a lot going on."

The tension around them was so thick; it was difficult to breathe normally. Cash wasn't trying very hard to conceal his emotions from her, and she could feel hurt and anger radiating from him. His voice wasn't the confident, arrogant sound she was used to when he asked, "Can I come in, or would that be too inconvenient?"

Ryen flinched at his harshness, but gestured for him to enter. "Would you like to sit down?" She motioned towards the couches in the sitting room, "Or the balcony has a nice view."

He walked towards one of the couches as his icy words pinched her heart, "This is awkward. Walking on eggshells is ridiculous. I thought we were far past this." He sat down, and Ryen followed suit on the couch opposite him. After a moment of silence, Cash rose to his feet and started pacing, "I knew there was something off before we left my apartment. You were acting strange." He turned to look at her, "You were running weren't you? You never intended to see me again. What I can't decide is if you were being cavalier with my feelings or if you were running because of your own fear. I don't know which would be worse at this point."

A hurt expression cracked his smooth face causing Ryen physical pain, "Look, Cash,"

He shook his head, "Don't bother. The guilt is evident on your face, and it's seeping from your emotional shields."

Wanting to be close to him, she crossed the room until she was standing in front of him, "You don't understand. Regardless of how I feel about you, there are things you don't know."

Cash cut her off, "Oh, I think you'd be surprised, Lady Reina, or is there more?"

Ryen closed her eyes in guilt-filled defeat. She had been trying to protect herself, and then maybe both of them, but that didn't matter anymore if he knew the truth. His pained look from her betrayal was a punch, knocking the air from her lungs. She was speechless for a moment as she recovered from the shock of his new knowledge. She had been preparing herself to break up with him rather than tell him who she really was. Now he knew, but she was unsure how much, "Did your dad tell you?"

A new flash of pain crossed his face, and his confusion clearly stated that it had not been his dad, "Wait, my dad knows you? I asked him yesterday and he told me no." More hurt filled his eyes, and he sat down in a chair nearby, "You've spoken to him? You know him?"

She hated that he was hurting, and even more so that she was ultimately responsible for it. Ryen thought about putting her hand on his shoulder to comfort him, but decided against it, "I didn't know he was your dad. He came to see me this morning because he realized when he talked to you yesterday that it was me whom you were telling him about, and that you didn't know who I was. He made it clear that he would not lie to you again, and that I had to take care of things."

"So, what was your plan when I showed up? Were you going to tell me the truth, or end things?"

That was a good question. She hadn't been planning to see him so soon, but the plan had been to end things somehow. Now that he was here her heart was going to do its damnedest to change her mind. Every cell in her body was calling out for him. She was so beaten today; she needed him to be here, to be strong for her, to help her understand what all this meant. Only one word came out, filled with all of the remorse and longing she felt, "Cash…"

Chapter 53

Cash knew as soon as Ryen opened the door that he wasn't going to be able to hang on to his anger, partially because the mere sight of her did things to his insides. But he could also tell, though her shields were firmly in place, that she had been through an emotional wringer.

His heart leapt when she whispered his name and fell into his arms. As always when their skin touched, electricity traveled from the point of origin all over his body. Her remorse for lying to him and hiding things washed over him and pulled at his heartstrings. He allowed himself to kiss her. She was soft and warm, and her kisses were eager. He fought every urge he had to rip off her cotton sundress and claim her as his right there on the floor. Instead, he gently pushed her to arms' length.

"Ryen," he whispered, filled with his own longing for her touch. He shook his head slightly to focus his thoughts, "I may know the truth now, but I'd still like to hear it from you."

She hung her head in resignation and nodded. Cash took her hand and led her over to the couch. She looked up at him, "I'll tell you everything, but first will you tell me how you figured it out?"

Cash knew a guilty look crossed his face, but he told himself there was nothing to be guilty about. She didn't trust him first, "I didn't intend to uncover any big secrets. I had a few conversations about the Coven with my friend, Esmeralda. I didn't mention before I left that she is a witch. At first I was just curious. I wanted to know more, to be closer to you, but some of the things she told me made me more curious; they didn't add up. Ultimately I asked about your tattoo."

"So she knows?" He didn't sense anger in her voice, but maybe some fear.

"She does now. I didn't tell her until just before I left. I couldn't reconcile you with the things she was telling me. I was hoping that maybe she was mistaken in her information. I have a picture of you on my phone, so I showed it to her, and asked if you were the Maiden. After that she put it all together, and I told her the whole story. I'm not sorry that I know the truth, but I really wish I had heard it from you first, that you would have trusted me enough to tell me."

He felt Ryen's remorse again before she spoke, "I'm sorry, too. You've been the only person I've ever truly cared about who hasn't betrayed me, but I still couldn't put my trust in you. I've told you some things already; I just left out some details. I'll start over at the beginning now."

Cash sat on the couch next to Ryen as she told him about her mother, who she was, and what she did. He held her hand as she told him about finding her mother's journals, discovering the truth about being a witch, and then finding out who she really was, or would be when she arrived in Italy. When she spoke of Maggie's death, becoming the Maiden and being held captive and tortured all within days of each other, he held her in his arms. He had already heard parts of her story, but hearing it again, all at once, in its true context made his heart break for all the traumatic things she had endured by the time she was a teenager, and he told her as much. "That's a lot for one person to handle," Cash's voice was thick with emotion. "Even though you had already told me pieces, hearing it all at once, with all of its significance, you've been through a lot."

"Yeah, apparently that's what Chesna and Kora thought too," the sarcasm and anger in her voice was apparent even without the feel of her emotions as they drifted past him.

"I'm not sure I understand," Cash wanted her to elaborate. He almost felt he could demand it at this point, for keeping things from him, but he waited to see if she'd continue on her own.

"I don't know exactly what Esmeralda told you about the Triumvirate, but usually they, we, do not have the freedoms that I've experienced: going to university, having a job, traveling on non-Coven business. They indulged me because of everything."

"Is that why you didn't tell me, because you're not supposed to have relationships?"

"Sort of. Relationships aren't forbidden, at least not casual ones. Hell, Chesna has had a secret lover stashed away at the compound for as long as I can remember. Honestly, part of the reason is because you scare me."

"I told you that I won't hurt you. I won't bite you unless you say it's ok, and even then I won't hurt you." Cash silently pleaded for her to hear his words and understand the deep meaning behind them.

Her gentle smile eased some of the defensiveness he felt. "It's not that. I'm not afraid of physical pain. Soulmates are sort of a law of nature, from the power of the Universe. That seems bigger than the Goddess, or anything. Does it supersede everything that runs my life? I don't know how this," she motioned between herself and Cash, "works with who I am. I don't know if it can. I can't turn my back on who I am, and the power of what's between us is what scares me. That's why I didn't tell you. That's why I tried to walk away."

Cash felt like he was a ball being bounced off walls of various emotions. He had never had to deal with so many all at once before. Anger edged his voice, but it was barely a glimpse of what he was feeling, as he stated his accusations for more confirmation, "You walked away, without saying good-bye. You were going to try to disappear on me."

"Because I knew if I tried to tell you I was walking away I wouldn't be strong enough to follow through."

"And I wouldn't have let you," he didn't care about how possessive that sounded in a semi-psychotic way. Ryen had turned his world upside down, but he could never go back to how things were before her. There would be an emptiness in him that he'd never be able to fill even if he tried.

She gave him a lopsided smile, and then she cringed causing his chest tighten in response, "I'm not sure any of that matters anymore. There's something more I should tell you that I found out today. It's actually why I'm here at the hotel without any plans to go back anytime soon."

Cash could tell she was still reluctant to share. He didn't want her to tell him just because he was mad at her or because he'd discovered her other secrets. He wanted to know, but he wanted her to tell him because she trusted him and wanted to share it with him, even if it was bad. He stroked her cheek with his hand in an attempt to show he was supportive, but her words had awoken new curiosity. What more could have happened? He implored with his eyes that she could trust him no matter what it was.

Ryen took a deep breath, "Chesna and Kora confirmed that they had indulged me. Even though I knew it was irregular, I never really questioned my opportunities. I don't blame them, but we wouldn't be in this situation if they had just followed with the traditions and expectations that have always been. I would never have been in Paris for you to see me, or in Madrid, or at the museum."

Before she could continue he interrupted her, "Then I should thank them. Do you really wish that we had never met?" He could hear a tortured tone in his voice when he asked, but he couldn't believe she really felt that way. He certainly didn't, even with all of the upheaval that had occurred since he'd first seen her.

"No, I don't, but it would be so much easier if we hadn't, especially with what I found out today." There was so much dread and sadness in her voice. She was slowly chipping away his anger. Cash tightened his arms around her. He wished he could erase all of the negative emotions she was feeling. She took another deep breath before she continued, "Well, as if me being the Maiden wasn't enough of a challenge for a relationship, apparently I'm the answer to some ancient prophecy. Kora and Chesna, and Maggie before she died, believe I'm some Warrior Maiden that's meant to fight an epic battle with my mother to protect the future of witches."

Ryen sat still and quiet, waiting for him to react. She remained facing away from Cash until he turned her around. Cash wasn't sure what to say, "What does that mean?"

"I'm not really sure. Prophecies don't spell everything out. It doesn't really give a timeline or say what the final outcome will be."

He didn't really understand, but he knew this information, and how she had found out, was quite upsetting to Ryen. He would be lying if he said it didn't scare him a little bit. Was it enough to turn his back on her? Absolutely not. He attempted humor to lighten the heaviness that hung in the room, as well as the fear within him for her safety, "I've always thought you were extraordinary, but I guess this confirms it."

He watched her roll her eyes and shake her head at something she was thinking. After a couple of moments her expression turned serious again, "Can you forgive me? For not being honest with you?"

"Yes," he said almost automatically. He knew that answer before he'd even shown up at the hotel. The only problem now was that he would struggle with trusting her, not nearly as much as she, but enough. Then he thought of all that had transpired in Barcelona, "For the sake of being equally transparent, I have a couple things to tell you about my trip."

She wasn't facing him anymore, but he felt her body tense. *And there's the trust issue again.* He told her the story of visiting the secret vampire club without leaving out any detail. He emphasized how he had to drink from someone there and it had to look as genuine as possible, but he knew that she would be disgusted about the whole thing.

When she spoke he realized he had been holding his breath, waiting for her response, "Is it shut down now?"

Of course her first concern would be for the girls trapped inside. "Probably not, but soon. My mom had to work out a false trail so it wouldn't lead back to me. If they are resourceful, with the video footage, they could probably figure out who I am. It will look suspicious enough that I'm a club owner myself, but if they link me to their closing, it could get ugly. These weren't really respectable businessmen."

Terror filled her eyes and rushed out from her as she grabbed his arm, "Would they come after you?"

This had not been where he thought his confession would lead. He expected to be trying to get her to understand why he had "willingly" participated in the depraved activities there and the ones he'd promised he wouldn't do, but was it wrong that her concern made him happy? "Most likely, that's why

I went through my mom. She has powerful connections that can get it shut down without me appearing to be connected. You don't need to worry, but it's also why I had to be as convincing as possible while I was there. Can you forgive me for that?"

He held his breath again, this time consciously. He could tell several things were playing across her mind, and it was killing him not to know what they were. "So, you really think that they won't connect it to you, proof or no proof?"

Cash was about to burst, "Woman, you're killing me." The look she gave him conveyed that she didn't understand, so he answered her question, "That's what we're hoping, but ultimately we'll just have to wait and see how it plays out. Please don't let that worry you. But PLEASE, will you answer *my* question?"

Ryen looked confused again, and Cash was about to ask her for forgiveness again, but finally she landed on the question that he had been referring to, "I understand why you had to do what you did. I'm glad that you went there otherwise who knows how many more girls could have been tortured and killed. I forgive you, and thank you for telling me, all of it."

At that Cash allowed the longing that he had held off earlier to take over. He dropped his mouth to hers. He wouldn't apologize for the passion that spilled forth. She willingly parted her lips, inviting him in. The eagerness she had shown earlier also returned in full force. Neither of them wasted any time in removing clothing from the other. They were still sitting on the couch and Cash pulled her onto his lap. Ryen worked her hips back and forth with her fingers laced through his hair as his mouth burned kisses from her neck down to her chest. He could feel her heartbeat under his lips as it pounded almost in rhythm to their movements, sounding like a drum in his ears as well. He savored the taste of her that he had missed for what had only been a couple days, but had felt like a lifetime.

Cash allowed her to be in control for awhile longer, until he feared he wouldn't be able to restrain himself from reaching his limit. He contemplated carrying her to the bedroom, but that seemed like a waste of precious time.

Instead he grabbed her hips and lifted her as he stood and laid her down on her back. Her eyes were open wide staring up at him. He looked deeply into them and then something he never expected happened; he felt her protective shields dropping. Finally she was truly opening up to him, now that all her secrets were out. The significance of her action hit Cash hard, as did the incredible feeling of her emotions and thoughts washing over him. He could not contain the satisfaction and wonder that filled him. His emotions and mind were already wide open to her, but he wanted her to know how much he appreciated her trust. He guessed he would have to show her. He smiled as she gasped in pleasure...

Ryen wondered how people could go through life never feeling as she did now. She had built up protective walls around herself for so many years, arguably for good reason, but now it seemed ludicrous. She had nothing left to hide, and she wanted to remain in the blissfulness of this feeling forever. Cash was doing his damnedest to make sure she knew how he felt about her, and if she could freeze time she'd never leave this moment.

Somewhere between opening the door and laying here on the couch, Ryen had an important revelation. She had always been a fighter. That drive inside her had helped her navigate through some pretty crappy things, and it would continue to be put to the test. But for the past few weeks she had been using that strength to fight against a relationship with Cash. What she realized was that she should have been fighting for their relationship. She made a silent promise to herself to do just that, and she knew that Cash could hear her thoughts. She felt his smile against her neck before his tongue traced a sensual trail under her ear, contining to elicit sounds of gratification from her for his actions.

Deep in her mind where she was hoping he couldn't access at the moment, a thought occurred. Cash deserved her trust. She had already dropped her shields, and he seemed to have been overjoyed by that, but she wanted to do more. She couldn't believe she was even considering it. Even though part of her was terrified, the other part of her really wanted to.

As she felt another orgasm rock her body, she made sure her mouth was right next to his ear, "Bite me."

Chapter 54

Ryen's body protested as Cash's stopped moving. He stared at her in disbelief. "What did you just say?"

She felt a little embarrassed as he looked at her, but it didn't change her mind about what she had said, "I said that you could bite me," and then after a slight pause, "if you want to."

Not necessarily what one hopes to hear in their current position, Cash let out a hysterical laugh, "Of course I want to. I've already told you that. But do *you* want me to?"

Ryen didn't hesitate as she looked into his eyes, "Yes."

Cash's lips crushed hers as his body began moving again. His mouth slowly left hers and traveled to her neck where he kissed and licked predatorily, coaxing the desired vein closer to the surface. Even though she wanted it, Ryen tensed, and she knew he could hear and sense the slight edge of fear that crept over her.

Cash lifted his head and looked in her eyes again and she felt the sincerity behind his words, "It won't hurt like before, I promise. I love you."

"I love you, too."

"Trust me?"

"Yes," and she truly meant it.

Cash lowered his lips to her mouth again and thoroughly showed what her concession meant to him. Ryen let Cash's feelings of anticipation and excitement wash away any tension that had snuck into her body. True to his word, there was no pain when his canine teeth broke through her skin. Instead, the same fire that filled her when he touched her bare skin ran through her veins as he gently sucked. Then she didn't just feel his thoughts and emotions emanating from him, she was inside him, feeling them first hand. Everything she had felt before was immensely magnified. Sensations were hitting her from inside and out and she couldn't tell if they were hers or

Cash's, or a mix of both. Most incredibly, she saw him, she saw his soul, what he was when everything else was stripped away, and he was beautiful...

Cash had imagined biting Ryen since he laid eyes on her in Paris. Over the weeks the reasons for wanting it had changed and evolved from mere desire to taste her, to wanting to experience that mythical sensation that he never knew if he believed existed. Although he had bitten hundreds, maybe even thousands, of necks he was never more anxious than this moment. He wasn't afraid he would hurt her. It was the not knowing what to expect. As his canine teeth extended and brushed over her flesh, chills went through him. He continued his previous sensual movements, and Ryen arched in response.

He almost lost control of his body when he felt that pop of her skin breaking under his teeth. The sensation that came over him was so unimaginable he knew he'd never be able to put it into words. He started to send that feeling to Ryen and realized she could already feel it, or was it coming from her? He couldn't tell.

As her warm essence filled his mouth and throat, he clung to her desperately. Cash had thought that he had truly seen Ryen when she dropped her shields earlier, but now it was as if he was walking through her mind. He could sense her feelings and thoughts, but it was more than that. He was walking through a hallway, and behind each door was a memory of something important to her. Each door was ajar for him to enter if he wanted, different emotions coming from each one. He could also see their past, all of them, trailing behind their present. Most surprising was the power he could feel within her that she had been holding at bay, and it was frightening.

Cash opened a door he knew was a memory of their first night together. She had withheld so much from him; he couldn't help himself from seeing it from her eyes. Ryen did nothing to stop him, but he knew she was aware of what he was experiencing. They relived those moments together and he allowed his release inside her as she cried out yet again in ecstasy. Cash knew he had taken enough of her blood, so moments later he slowly withdrew from her neck. Neither of them moved, just silently worked on catching their breath.

Cash didn't need to ask if Ryen was ok. He had felt what she felt and vice versa. When Ryen broke the silence Cash was dumbfounded by her question, "Is that what it's like every time?"

Cash rolled himself so that he was lying against the back of the couch and he held Ryen in his arms facing him. He kissed her forehead gently before answering, "I've never experienced anything like that in my whole life. I told you that caring deeply about you would magnify the intensity."

He watched her eyes flutter shut, self-consciously hiding from him, "No, I mean if you were to bite me again, is that what it would be like?"

He smiled at what he felt coming from her. The girl, who tensed every time his kisses got near any vein in her neck, was admitting that she was willing to be bitten by him again. "I honestly don't know, but I wouldn't mind trying again either." He made sure to put emphasis on the last word so she knew that he understood.

Chapter 55

Ryen had allowed herself to fall back into the safe cocoon of hiding out with Cash. Several days had passed since Cash had shown up at her hotel room, and she was in no hurry to go back to the compound. Although they were definitely enjoying their new openness with one another, they weren't staying holed up at the hotel. Florence was Ryen's home and if she was fighting for their relationship, she couldn't be afraid to be seen with him.

Although not new to either of them, they wandered around Florence as if they were tourists, visiting all of the sites. Seeing everything together was like seeing it with new eyes. Demitri hadn't removed Ryen's status at the Uffizi either, so they were able to enjoy private access at the museum, including the de' Medici chamber above the Ponte Vecchio. Maybe Ryen was avoiding reality; she knew that eventually she'd have to face Kora and Chesna again. As long as there was nothing pressing, she didn't see the need in doing that any time soon. She could argue that the foreboding visions she'd had the past couple of days were a good reason to return to the compound, but then again Ryen had become pretty good at convincing herself that it wasn't what she thought, and there was no rush.

She hadn't thought anything of the little brown haired girl with golden brown eyes the first time she'd seen her while sleeping, but as she appeared a second, third, and fourth time when Ryen was awake, she knew it had to be significant. There was no verbal communication, but the girl was clearly trying to reach out to Ryen. Part of her thought her visions were just a paranoid reaction to hearing about the prophecy, but realistically the girl in her visions could be one of these mysterious "powers" for whom they were all waiting. Chesna was the vision expert, and the way things had gone recently Ryen wouldn't be surprised if Chesna already knew all about the visions and what they meant, angering her further.

Ryen tried to push all thoughts other than Cash from her mind. They were enjoying a bottle of wine, some bread, and a caprese salad at a little restaurant with the Mercato Nuovo at their backs when Cash brought up their isolation, "I'm not pushing, but I think being the go-between is starting to wear on Sophie."

Ryen frowned, so much for avoiding Coven business, "Well, she doesn't need to call every day." The look Cash gave her felt like a reprimand. "Look, I know. I need to stop acting like a child and face them, but I don't forgive them."

He squeezed her hand and her whole arm warmed, "I'm not saying you have to, yet." Ryen knew the look she threw him was daggers, but he continued, "Ryen, they love you. They are your family. Was it wrong of them to keep something like that from you? Yes. But their intentions weren't bad. And I've already told you that I'm glad your freedoms gave us the opportunity to meet. I wouldn't have it any other way. Besides, when you do decide to forgive them, it will be for you, not them, so *you* can move forward."

"Fine, I'll think about it more seriously. But I'll be less accessible if I go back." She was trying to be seductive and play on his desires. She still wasn't very comfortable being flirtatious, but he winked in understanding.

"I'm always up for a challenge. I could scale the wall to your window or secretly meet you on the roof or in the gardens." He kissed the top of her hand, her fingers, and lastly her wrist where he added a little tongue while he spoke.

Cash was so much better at seduction than she was, and sometimes that was frustrating. Trying to control her own desires, and pretending to ignore how those scenarios sparked a fire inside of her, she attempted a bland response, "Or you could just come in the main gates and use the door."

"Or I can hold onto our hotel room." He was serious now, and Ryen didn't want to admit how appealing the idea of having their own secret place to sneak away to was.

"Talk about avoidance. Are you saying you don't want to spend quality time with your mother?" Cash had been preparing Ryen to meet his family for days. In fact, he was nearly insisting that they go before the week ended. Even though he had painted her in a pleasant light, meeting his mother ranked right up there with talking to Kora and Chesna. She was certain that

Cash was putting a positive spin on everything for her benefit, but she could tell that he was tense about her meeting his mother too.

She knew Cash could sense her own apprehension, "I told you, she is going to love you. She loves me too; she just shows it by reminding me that my career choices are a disappointment to her, even if I am very successful. At least with you here she can stop nagging about my personal life as well." He sounded confident in the last part, but Ryen still wasn't completely convinced. If she knew anything about Ryen as a witch, his mother probably wouldn't be campaigning for president of her fan club. If he was the heir to the Di Marco power, she doubted his mother would be content for him to be with a witch who had her own responsibilities that would ultimately have to come first.

When she hadn't commented aloud he prompted the conversation further, "How about dinner tomorrow night with my family, and then the next day I'll go with you to face Kora and Chesna?"

"Fine, but I don't know which of those scenarios is more frightening." Really, she did. Kora and Chesna already knew about Cash, probably more than anyone realized. She knew they would be welcoming, so introducing them was not a concern at all. She just didn't know if she was ready to talk to them yet. Dinner at Cash's parents' house was by far the most daunting.

"You are so agreeable today," he commented sarcastically. "Now, let's go back to the hotel and I'll reward you for your good choices." He slid his tongue over his lips in a way that had parts of Ryen clenching in anticipation.

She smiled with her lips tight and tilted her head, challenging his suggestion. When fire lit his eyes and he tossed more than enough money on the table to cover their meager bill, Ryen laughed out right. And when Cash's hand touched bare skin on her back, as he ushered her through the throngs of tourists, her whole body tingled.

Chapter 56

"Stop fidgeting! You look beautiful!" Ryen ignored Cash's words as she put two more bobby pins in her hair. True, this was close to the tenth time she had changed her hair from down to up or vice versa, but she was too nervous about meeting Cash's family to relax. If they weren't riding in the car she would probably be changing her clothes twenty more times as well. Cash had been impressed at Ryen's ability to power shop earlier, but she couldn't decide what would be the best "family meeting" outfit. She didn't like senseless shopping, but he had been a little shocked when she informed him that she would return whatever she decided not to wear. He was sure his sister would just add everything to her closet.

It was a private, casual dinner at the Di Marco estate, but it was imperative that Ryen was prepared in every way. After several wardrobe changes, from which Cash got thorough enjoyment, Ryen had left the hotel in a sleeveless orange dress that hung simply to her mid-thigh. The only jewelry she was wearing were her quartz pendent and a simple silver bracelet Cash had bought her. She gently turned it around her wrist and smiled at the memory of its purchase. Ryen had insisted on finding Cash a birthday present since she was hiding from him on the actual day, but of course he argued that she needed something special to wear tonight. He was wearing the silver and onyx ring she had picked out for him. It was still wrapped around his left ring finger where he had initially placed it. As it did the first time and every time since, Ryen's heart skipped a beat when she looked at the ring on Cash's finger. She returned her attention to her hair in the tiny mirror and smiled again as that ringed hand traced its way up her leg.

She slapped Cash's hand away from her upper thigh, where her hem fell while seated, "Well, this will have to do, there's your house." They had been driving up into the hills. There were still a few hours before sunset, but the sky had already taken on the hues of pink, purple, and orange. As they were driving up the tree lined road that led to the Di Marco Estate buildings, Ryen could see olive trees to one side and rows of grapes on the other. Both wine and olive oil were big exports for this region, and the Di Marco family had been in the business of both for a very long time.

The car parked in a circular drive in front of a sprawling group of stone buildings. If Ryen hadn't grown up in this area, seeing homes like this dotting the hills, the size of the structure might be shocking in its Tuscan opulence. However, being comfortable with the architecture didn't make the occupants of this particular house any less terrifying. The driver opened the door on Ryen's side and Cash grabbed her hand as they walked up the path to the entrance of the largest building, the main house. She knew she was being silly, but as Cash knocked on the door Ryen made a last minute alteration, pulling the pins out of her hair, stuffing them in her purse and giving her loose hair a toss with her free hand. Cash laughed as he brushed her hair back from her shoulder and planted a light kiss on her bare skin. Shivers ran down her arm and back up from his kiss as he whispered in her ear, "I'm right here. I won't let go of your hand if that will help."

His patronizing wink flared Ryen's determination, and she dropped his hand but grabbed it again when the door opened. A welcoming smile from Cash's father greeted them. Ryen was expecting the informal address, as discussed, but she was taken aback by the familiarity of Luca's greeting when he lightly kissed each of her cheeks, "We are very happy you could join us, Ryen. Son, it's good to see you as well."

Cash gave his dad a one armed hug, and he kept his promise and held tight to Ryen's hand. Ryen could sense a little tension between Cash and his father so she wasn't surprised at Cash's abrupt declaration, "For the sake of a peaceful evening, I forgive you, father, for not being honest with me about knowing my beautiful girlfriend."

The tension increased slightly, as Luca answered guiltily, "I didn't want to complicate things, and it appears to have all worked out in the end, but I am sorry, son."

Ryen gently squeezed Cash's hand. He let out a sigh and with it the tension washed away. Now that everyone, except Ryen, seemed relaxed, she looked around the foyer of the house. It was big, open and rustic. It was traditional Tuscan: ceramic floor, brick and stone on the walls, wood beams. But it wasn't what she was expecting. Somehow she was picturing something with a more ornate decor, she didn't know why.

300

The walls were an earthy yellow color and there were three large arched openings leading to other rooms of the house. Luca put his arm around Cash's shoulders again and started to usher them towards the largest of the openings when a tall gorgeous blonde, in a long, flowing dark blue dress came from the arch to the right. A slightly less enthusiastic male trailed closely behind her.

Ryen felt the joy emanate from Cash as he let go of her hand to meet the blonde halfway. She watched them embrace and kiss each other's cheeks. Cash nodded a greeting to her counterpart before turning back to Ryen. "This is Ryen. Ryen I'd like you to meet my sister, Calla."

Ryen smiled, and Calla smiled back as she approached. Physically Cash and Calla were like night and day. They were the same height and both in great shape, but where Cash's hair was black Calla's was light blonde, almost white. Cash's eyes were the lightest blue, and Calla's were a rich brown. But those striking differences aside, there was no denying they were brother and sister. Ryen could sense the connection between them, and she was intimidated, but not threatened. Ryen hadn't realized she was holding her breath until after Calla had given her a greeting almost as zealous as the one she gave Cash. Quietly, though not enough to keep it from Cash, Calla praised Ryen, "You must be quite remarkable to not only hold my brother's attention, but to also put up with him. I'm very pleased to meet you."

A little tension released from Ryen. Number two on her list seemed agreeable. Calla introduced her husband Nico. Ryen wondered if he had ever been in a rock band. He was an inch or two taller than his wife, long and lean. His shoulder length brown hair and scruffy face reminded her of a guitarist or maybe a drummer. She refrained from asking for the time being. He was very nice, but much more reserved than anyone else in the family so far. Ryen attributed that to his being the only human in a house full of supernatural beings. One thing was for sure, he adored his wife. Aside from a polite greeting to Ryen, his attention was fixed on Calla. Every once in a while she would glance at him or touch his hand or arm in some way. Each time Ryen witnessed it her heart warmed.

A little blurry figured came shooting past, before anyone had time to leave the foyer. Cash bent down and grabbed it. As it settled in Cash's arms, Ryen realized it was a little boy. She imagined that Cash had looked nearly identical as a child, messy black hair and gorgeous blue eyes. A little voice that sounded much too innocent for the look in his eyes said, "Put me down Uncle Cash. I'm chasing a monster."

Ryen giggled which drew the little boy's attention. With no pretense, just open curiosity, he asked, "Who are you?"

"This is my friend, Ryen."

"You mean your girlfriend?" mini Cash asked with his nose wrinkled.

"Yes, my girlfriend," Cash said back. To Ryen he explained, "Ford has an aversion to girls. He finds them, icky?" Cash turned back to the boy for confirmation. The little boy nodded emphatically.

With a wink at Ryen, Cash continued talking to his mini me, "You know, someday you'll change your mind about girls."

Ford's nose wrinkled again and he adamantly shook his head. Ryen tried to win him over, "You must be Ford. I've heard you are quite the monster hunter."

Ford looked at her appraisingly with his little blue eyes, "I'm a vampire. The monsters run from me in fear."

Everyone was holding back their amusement so as not to hurt his tender feelings. No one was expecting the honesty of the barrage of questions Ford asked next, "Uncle Cash, do you bite her? Does she taste good?" Then turning his head back to Ryen, "Can I bite you?"

Calla stepped in a little embarrassed. "I'm so sorry," she said to Ryen. She took Ford from Cash, "There will be no biting of guests, especially our friends. Now go on and chase those monsters before they hide under your bed." She put him down and swatted at this little butt as he ran off.

Sarcastically, Cash chided Calla, "Your son has great manners, sis."

302

"I really do apologize. He is getting curious about biting. We were hoping the blood bags would work until he's a little older and has a little more control."

"We never had blood bags," Cash reminded his sister.

"I know that, but we didn't actively drink blood when we were his age."

Ryen was lost. She hadn't asked a ton of questions about what it was like being born a vampire, and now the conversation was over her head. Cash sensed her questions, "A full blooded, born vampire would require a little bit of blood each day, like a vitamin. For Calla and I, and more so for Ford, since we aren't full blooded, we wouldn't necessarily need any blood. The blood is what brings out and enhances the vampire characteristics. Ford is resolute that he is a vampire. Since he is younger than we were, Calla has been giving him blood from blood banks. He'll eventually need to be taught how to feed directly so he can learn how to do it with little to no damage and most importantly, how to control it."

Luca interrupted the serious conversation, escorted everyone to a sitting room with plush chairs and couches. "Perhaps we'd be more comfortable somewhere other than at the front door?"

Ryen was filing away all of this information. She enjoyed learning more about Cash and his family and what made them who and what they were, but her nerves were fighting for her attention tonight. A distraction from both came as they entered the new room. One side of the room was lined with large windows looking out on a patio and garden with beautifully blooming flowers in every color. Ryen imagined sitting on that patio in the morning hours, the flowers kissed with dew as the sun rose in the sky. She hadn't realized she was projecting her thoughts until Cash whispered in her ear, "The furniture isn't that comfortable for a sunrise, but the view is pretty nice."

Ryen blushed, catching his thoughts of their sunrises in Madrid, definitely not something she would consider doing at his family's home. Her blush was washed away by the feel of power that entered the room from behind. "My darling son, it really has been too long."

Ryen turned as Cash did. Cash went to embrace his mother as Ryen stood in awe. Cash had described his mother to her, and she had done her own snooping on the internet, but nothing compared to the real thing. Ryen could feel her strength, not in a threatening way, but as a mere statement of who she was. She was over a century old, but Cash had explained that power in vampires didn't necessarily come with age, most of it was inherited. The Di Marco vampires had been around a long time, so the family power was part of their birthright. Ryen wondered when Cash would tap into that power. His mother looked almost identical to Calla except her eyes were the same as Cash's and her hair was dark brown, pulled up into a tight sophisticated twist. Everything about her presence said power and elegance.

After greeting her son, she turned intense, skeptical eyes on Ryen. Cash introduced them, "Mom, this is Ryen. Ryen, this is my mother, Calandra."

Wanting to please, and struggling not to answer the power challenge that she felt coming from Cash's mom, Ryen took the outstretched hands that Calandra offered, "It's nice to meet you, Ms. Di Marco. You have a very lovely home." Ryen couldn't help sending a small amount of power back to the hands that were tingling with their own. *Don't worry, I can handle myself, and I'm not here to hurt your son.*

Calandra seemed a little taken aback, but her smile was unwavering. Although there was some skepticism, approval glinted in her eyes, "Thank you. Call me Calandra. I am pleased to meet you. I wish I could say that I've heard a lot about you, but that would imply that my son had shared such details."

It was more of a dig to Cash than Ryen, but she was defensive nonetheless. She continued with politeness, "Perhaps he wanted to surprise you."

"Indeed." Calandra shot a look at Cash. Ryen felt a gentle squeeze of her fingers as Calandra turned back to her with sincerity, "Any girl Cash is willing to bring home is welcome here. You're from Florence? Could this be the reason my son has had a recent interest in coming home?"

304

Ryen turned an inquiring look towards Cash whose face had a moment of panic before he recovered quickly, meeting his mother's intense gaze. "Now's not the time to discuss that, mother."

To her son Calandra said, "Perhaps not, but don't think that all of your distractions have caused me to forget our previous conversation." To everyone she said, "Make yourselves comfortable, dinner will be at least thirty minutes. Carlo is making some hors d'oeuvres that he'll bring out shortly."

Calandra walked to one of the sofas and sat. Luca joined her. Calla and Nico were sitting on another one. All four started up a casual conversation as if this were any other day. Ryen wasn't completely relaxed yet. There were still more people to meet, but Cash's hand around hers definitely helped. "Carlo is the chef," he explained, knowing she was confused. Then he added in a much quieter voice, "and I'll explain what my mom was talking about later."

She smiled a "thank you" and then asked about the rest of her apprehension, "Four down, two to go right? Your niece and brother?"

"Calla said Lilia is at a slumber party, so you'll have to meet her another day. I'm assuming Caio will come out for dinner, but he's not very sociable, and I'm sure he's not overcome with joy to meet a girl I've brought home either."

Ryen remembered how Cash had described the animosity between him and his brother. She tried to recall if Cash had said his name before. Something about the name Caio sparked a twinge of recognition and distress in the back of her mind, but she didn't have long to contemplate those feelings. She heard someone else enter the room, and when she turned one word escaped her before everything exploded, "Cai."

Chapter 57

Literally everything exploded: Ryen's mind, her control, and the glass windows lining the room. Everyone hit the floor for cover, not knowing what was happening, everyone except Ryen and the guy that stood staring at her.

Strong winds blew in the window openings where the glass had been. In the flash of an eye the sky had filled with ominous dark clouds. Thunder rumbled, and lightening electrified the atmosphere. That face, now staring at her in the shock of his own recognition, was etched into her memory. For years it had haunted her nightmares. Thoughts were racing through her head: *This can't be right. Why after so long? He can't be Cash's brother. What have I done? Damn right, you should be scared. How? Oh god, Cash.* But nothing was more prevalent within Ryen than the blinding red fury. In that moment she wasn't sure she cared about retribution from the Goddess or the Universe. All of the healing she had done over the years felt like it had been ripped away, leaving her wounds open and bleeding, and she wanted to revisit every last ounce of her pain back on him...

What the...? Cash was cautiously looking around the ground for Ryen. It felt like a bomb had just gone off. Had someone just attacked their house? The room was a mess, broken glass everywhere, lamps knocked over from the blow and the fierce winds now swirling around. The feel of intensely strong power surging from nearby drew his attention. Unlike everyone else, Ryen was still standing with no visible injuries from the explosion. Cash's ear drums were healing and the cloudiness in his head made things hazy. His dad was standing near Ryen saying something that Cash couldn't hear.

As his head finally cleared, he could feel the rage coming from her. Her eyes were locked on his brother. Now Cash remembered her saying his brother's nickname, the one his friends used, just before he felt the explosion. His brother was also standing. His clothes had cuts from the glass and there were red marks on his face and arms where cuts weren't healing due to his cursed condition. Caio may have been standing, but his eyes showed the fear

306

that Cash could sense filling him. Cash didn't understand. His brother had never been afraid of anything, except maybe the witch who cursed him.

NO. Some level of understand began to sink in. Ryen couldn't be *that* witch. Could she? Cash looked at her and he almost didn't recognize her, the raw emotion pouring from her, the immense power. His dad's voice cut through the turbulence in his head, "Cash, get her outside! Her control is hanging by a thread."

Cash still didn't understand. He could feel Ryen's rage and her power, but was she responsible for this? He looked at the destruction around the room. It was like ground zero of an explosion. It couldn't have been her…

"Cash! Help me now!" His dad shouted again over the thunder and wind.

Cash shook himself to focus. Despite her power pelting him, he threw Ryen over his shoulder and went out the broken door to the garden. Rain was falling now, thunder crackling, and lightning charging the air. When they were out of sight from the disaster zone Cash sat Ryen down on her feet, "What the hell was that?"

It took a moment for Ryen to focus on Cash. Her eyes softened when she looked at him, and Cash felt some of her power ebb. She slumped slightly and Cash caught her elbow, saving her from collapsing. Still shouting over the thunder and wind he asked again, "What was that, Ryen? Did you just blow up my house?"

Ryen's breaths were coming in short gasps, "Oh god, Cash. I'm so sorry. I didn't mean to."

He was shocked enough by the confirmation, but he asked the next question that was burning at him, "Ryen, did you curse my brother?"

Guilt was written all over her face, and tears started to fall from her eyes mixing with the rain. She didn't say anything, but he got his answer loud and clear. He felt like she had just slapped him with the same force that blew out the windows moments ago. He had spent years listening to his mother worry about Caio's condition, his brother's humiliation at having to be IV-fed blood

307

because he couldn't feed, even from blood bags, his extreme pain that he couldn't or refused to explain to his family, and the fear over the fact that his vampire-born birthright had been mysteriously stripped from him, leaving him vulnerable to true death.

Cash felt Ryen mentally reaching out to him, trying to speak to him when it seemed words couldn't be formed. He was angry, and his anger was growing; he shut her out. She had just admitted to being responsible for hurting Caio, he didn't want to hear anything else from her. He had always loved his brother even if Caio never quite felt the same. Had this been her plan all along, to get close to him, to have him lead her to his brother to finish him off?

Ryen flinched at his reaction, and her eyes pleaded with him. He couldn't do this. Her hand slowly came towards him and he yanked his from her reach. Bred and nurtured family loyalty kicked in. His protectiveness for his brother and his still growing anger found an outlet, "Don't! Don't touch me! I thought you had finally been honest with me. I thought you had finally decided that you could trust me. Not only was that bullshit, but you've been playing me this whole time, trying to get to my brother again?"

Ryen's confusion was apparent on her face and deep within her eyes, but Cash was certain she was just being a good actress, "Don't look at me like that. Your guilt was plain as day on your face. Are you going to deny now what you did to my brother?"

"No," she whispered. It seemed a "but" was waiting to follow, but he didn't allow her to continue.

"Then we're done here. I can't look at you anymore. You need to leave." He could tell that she had blocked herself off from him as well, and she was very deliberate in keeping emotion from her face, but he swore he saw something break in her eyes. The thunder and lightning ceased, but the rain continued to fall as she turned and walked towards the car that had brought them earlier. Cash watched her disappear around the side of the house before he went back inside.

Chapter 58

A couple of housekeepers were sweeping up glass, and soaking up water with towels when Cash reentered the room Ryen had blown up. His anger was still boiling in him, and he was trying to figure out how to apologize to his brother when their relationship had never been a great one. His family was all sitting on the couches again. His mother had an icy glare locked on Caio, and her hand locked on his arm when he glanced at Cash. "What's going on?" Cash managed.

Calandra answered without taking her eyes off of Caio, "Sit down Cash, your brother has something he wants to tell us."

A defiant scoff came from Caio, followed by a power slap to the back of his head from his mom. Calandra altered her previous sentence, "He has something he's going to tell us, whether he wants to or not."

Cash had no idea what was going on. His mother seemed pretty pissed with Caio, but no one seemed to be upset about what Ryen had just done. Calla and Luca were also staring at Caio with shock and disgust. "Did I miss something?" Cash asked.

"Apparently we all have," Calla answered him. She was looking at Caio like she didn't know him and a shiver went through her. Nico was holding her arms tightly; he looked as confused as Cash. He knew that his wife was upset, not that his grip could physically hold her if she chose to move. It was more for emotional support.

Cash sat down next to his father, not caring that he was soaking wet. Luca looked questioningly between Cash and the patio, but didn't ask whatever he was thinking. Cash knew he was wondering where Ryen was. Cash ignored his dad and focused his attention on the couch where his brother and mother sat, "Well?"

Caio met his brother's stare. Cash saw loathing reflected there; he always had, but now it was mixed with something else. Was it remorse? "It's never been a secret that I don't like witches. Luca, I've never been a fan of yours for taking my father's place. And Cash, you know that I've always hated you for having both of your parents, and the life I was supposed to have. I make no apologies for feeling cheated out of certain things in life, nor for my hatred of witches, even more so due to my current physical state."

None of this was news to Cash, but he let his brother continue. Caio was almost smug, "I could tell you that what happened was my friends' idea, but it was mine. Years ago I decided to test an idea to actualize my hatred onto a person, a witch. I wasn't picky, and there just so happened to be a young witch girl who was infatuated with me."

Understanding clicked in Cash's brain. He felt his stomach flip before dropping to the floor. "No," he said first in disbelief, and then fueled by the anger that was so close to the surface, "You son of a bitch."

Cash's mind was spinning. It couldn't be Caio. *Do I not know anyone?* He had taken Caio's side and hadn't even let Ryen explain. As it turned out, she had already told him everything he had needed to know, he just didn't put it together. Although others in the room seemed to have figured out some connection. Why else was his mother asserting her power over Caio?

Yet everyone looked at Cash, surprised that he seemed to know more than they did. Luca grabbed Cash's arm, "Let him finish. He needs to say it. We all need to hear what he has to say."

Cash sat still, but with each sentence he was mentally beating the shit out of his brother, wishing he had a knife to run through his heart. He wasn't hiding his thoughts from anyone in the room either. He continued to listen, though he wanted to be anywhere but in this room. Caio's next sentence stunned everyone except Cash, "She was a little young and naïve, but it didn't matter; a witch is a witch."

Calla sucked in a horrified breath, but Caio kept going with Calandra urging him forward with her presence at his side, "I let a couple of my friends in on my plan. I asked the girl out on a date with the intention of making an example of vampire dominance, of my dominance, over witches."

This time no one seemed surprised when Cash spoke, his voice oozing with a new found hatred, but the information itself caused more gasps from Calla and Calandra alike, "So who's idea was it to drug her?"

"Again I could lie and tell you it wasn't mine, but it was. I knew a witch would be able to defend herself in ways a regular human couldn't. The drug itself was actually acquired from an acquaintance, but the idea was mine. It was perfect really. It holds the body paralyzed but allows the person to be conscious. It had already been through experimentation and proved to adversely affect witch powers."

"You are sick. All these years I've allowed you to spend time with my daughter, your niece," Calla said in revulsion. "She should have killed you." Cash was again surprised that Calla had connected this story to Ryen, when he, who had been closest to her, had been blind.

Cash thought of how innocent Lilia was and how much she loved her family, including her uncle Caio. How many times had he hugged her, spent time with her, the whole time hiding such a deep hatred for the very thing she wanted to be? Ryen was a victim of such an atrocity solely because she was the unfortunate witch to show an interest in him. If Cash didn't get out of here he was going to rip his brother's head off. He'd already heard the rest of the story so there was no need to subject himself to this any longer, "Make sure you tell them the rest, you fucking shithead. Ryen is too good of a person to take your life, but I'm not. If you want to keep breathing, stay far away from me."

Cash left the room. He didn't need to hear from his brother how he and his friends had bitten, beaten and raped Ryen. He knew now that the remorse he'd seen in Caio's eyes wasn't for what he did, but for being found out after all of this time, and yet there was also satisfaction that something so long ago could hurt Cash in the present.

It was still raining pretty hard. He knew that the car would be long gone by now, but he went to the front to check anyways. How could he have been so blind? That's what Ryen had been trying to tell him, that Caio was the guy that held her captive and tortured her. What had he done? He had accused

Ryen of not being honest with him when it wasn't true. Looking back at her reaction, she clearly didn't know that Caio was his brother until today. Hell, maybe she didn't even know the extent of what her curse had done. He needed to see her, to beg for her forgiveness, but how could he face her after betraying her like that? He had blindly defended his brother when it turned out that his brother was the worst evil he'd ever encountered. He understood what he had seen in her eyes before she left. She had finally been completely open with him in spite of all of her reservations and he had broken her trust and with it, her heart. That realization turned a fraction of his anger inward.

Chapter 59

The rain was pouring down, and if Ryen had been able to pay attention she would have been impressed with the driver's skills in this storm. But Ryen's head was not in the car, it was trapped in the events of the past hour of her life. She wasn't sure which was worse, coming face to face with Cai again, or the conversation, or lack thereof, she had with Cash. She could still feel the betrayal he felt and his anger, and she would be haunted by that look in his eyes. She didn't have anyone but herself to blame. Ultimately this was her fault. Why did she keep pushing for things she wasn't meant to have?

She was in a daze as she gathered her things from the hotel room, and called the compound for someone to come get her. If the woman who collected her asked her any questions they didn't register with Ryen. Nothing drew Ryen from her mind until she walked into the lobby entrance of the compound and saw the same little girl with brown hair and golden brown eyes that she'd seen numerous times over the past few days, standing next to Kora. The lights flickered and Ryen swore she felt the ground rumble, but she didn't look to see if anyone else noticed. She watched the girl as she rocked back and forth on the balls of her feet as if she wanted to run towards Ryen, but she stayed put. Her little round face held excitement and sadness.

As Kora took in Ryen's emotions she turned to the little girl, "Terra, why don't you find Gelina. We need to talk to Lady Reina for a bit. We'll come find you when we're done."

A frown took over her little face and she looked at Ryen with something like longing or disappointment, but she turned and moped off. When she was out of sight Ryen asked, "Who is that girl? I've seen her before, but I didn't know if she was just in my imagination."

"We'll get there, but first come, tell us what has happened. You look like you've been hit by a bus."

"More like a train," she responded dryly. Ryen wasn't thrilled about running back to the open arms of the women who had kept so many important

313

things from her, but she had nowhere else to turn. Reluctantly she followed Kora up the stairs to the space she shared with her and Chesna. The lights flickered again and then Ryen heard popping sounds as light bulbs overloaded.

Kora was usually the overly emotional one, and Chesna was probably the least warm of the three of them, but when she saw Ryen walk through the door her trademark stoicism cracked as her eyes welled with tears. She wrapped Ryen in her thin, yet strong arms, and Ryen didn't doubt her sincerity when she said, "My child, I'm so sorry, for everything. The last thing we wanted to do was hurt you, and look at you!"

Kora took a moment to magically light the candles in the room before she joined in on the embrace with her own tears flowing freely. After a few moments Kora broke the silence, "Let's sit." Motioning towards the windows when the rain pelted against the glass, "Ryen, perhaps you can explain our sudden monsoon?"

Both Kora and Chesna listened intently as Ryen recounted the events at the Di Marco Estate. Confirming Ryen's suspicions that at least Chesna had known all along, they didn't comment as she filled in the back story about Cai and her involuntary curse. She was a little shocked that neither of them scolded her, nor did they allow too much pity to color their expressions. She asked the question that had been growing in her mind, "How did I strip their immortality? Only one witch is supposed to know that spell, and I am certainly not her."

Kora and Chesna exchanged glances and Ryen knew they were communicating wordlessly. After a few painfully silent moments Kora answered, "We don't know. Maybe in your intense pain and trauma you connected on a different level with the Goddess? Somehow you accessed that spell through time and space? We don't have an explanation."

That wasn't the type of answer Ryen was hoping for. She wasn't content with the lack of information, but that would be an investigation for another day. She didn't have the energy to deal with it. With that unpleasantness more or less taken care of, Ryen brought the subject back to her curiosity from earlier, "So, Terra, is one of the powers, isn't she?"

"We believe so, yes." Chesna verified what Ryen's intuition had been telling her since the little girl started appearing.

"How long has she been here?"

"A few days. She came for her dedication and we thought it best if she stayed here within the safety of the compound."

"But you've known about her longer than that."

It wasn't a question, but Chesna nodded her head.

"She's not the only one either, is she?" Ryen wasn't sure what made her think that. Maybe it was some inner knowledge because of the prophecy, like how she knew the little girl she was seeing was one of them.

Kora answered this one, "No. Shortly before your return from Madrid, when her powers were increasing, we started to look more closely at Gelina."

Ryen closed her eyes and let out a heavy sigh for the young woman she'd already come to care for deeply. *Poor Gelina. Was one major sacrifice for the Goddess not enough*?

Ryen should have been upset by yet another secret that they had kept from her, but with everything that had happened, what difference did one more make? A loud clap of thunder seemed to shake the building. Despite how rattled she felt, Ryen started putting some clues together, "Gelina's power is fire. And the girl? Terra? Hers is earth?"

Both women nodded in confirmation. Ryen tried to let this new information sink in. The emergence of powers meant that the prophecy would be fulfilled sooner rather than later. So many emotions were working their way through Ryen. None of them was reaching too deep due to the numbness that she still felt from everything that had happened at Cash's house. Kora must have sensed some tension so she tried to defuse it, "She reminds me a lot of you actually. At her dedication she insisted on giving herself a new witch name, and she was adamant that you be her sponsor. And similarly to you, she has some stubbornness in her. Although she wanted you as her sponsor, she refused to wait on the ceremony. She wanted to skip right to her initiation like another little girl I once knew as well."

Ryen smiled at the tenacity in such a little person, but her fate as a power saddened her. "What about her family?"

Kora seemed conflicted in answering Ryen's question but haltingly explained, "Brother Luca and her parents were here for the initiation ceremony, but everyone agreed that she would be safer here with us until the two of you could be united."

"Brother Luca? Cash's dad? Why was he here?" What was Ryen missing? Nothing was making sense, and her head had been through too much today to figure out yet another puzzle.

Chesna closed her eyes and took a deep breath before answering. In trying to keep the pity from her voice it came out a little condescending instead, "Terra is Cash's niece, Ryen. Her family calls her Lilia."

And there it was, the final nail in the coffin of her relationship. As if it weren't enough that she had destroyed the image of his brother, whom he had practically idolized growing up, and been responsible for the curse that had ruined his brother's life, now her stupid prophecy condemned his innocent little niece to a dangerous fate, possibly her death. Ryen's head fell back against the chair and she closed her eyes as soft bubbles of disbelieving laughter gently shook her body. The lights that had gone out earlier flickered. Sarcasm oozed from her as she sighed, "Of course that's who she is. Why would she be anyone else?"

The other two women knew her well enough not to try to comfort her at this point. They just sat with her for a while in silence, listening to the deafening lighting strikes outside, and exchanging uneasy glances at the state of their surroundings.

"Are you doing this?" Kora asked Ryen quietly, gesturing to the window and around the room at the surges in electricity.

Ryen lifted her head, scrunching her forehead in confusion. Chesna felt the need to redirect the focus back to the other people involved, "As hard as this may be on you, you are responsible for that little girl's instruction. She already adores you. She needs you, as does Gelina."

Ryen took a deep breath before responding, "I'm aware of my responsibilities. Could I have a couple of hours first? I'd like to take a bath and attempt to clear my head."

"Of course," Chesna said. She patted Ryen's shoulder as she left the room. Kora stopped in front of Ryen and cupped her face in her hands. She didn't say anything, but gave her a concerned half smile-half frown, and her eyes were full of empathy. She kissed Ryen's forehead before leaving Ryen to her own thoughts.

Chapter 60

Nothing was helping. Cash had mutilated the punching bag, imagining it was Caio, and destroyed pretty much everything else that was in the room for the third day in a row. He assured the gym owner that he would replace everything, again. Luckily his name carried enough weight, and the fact that Cash handed over a wad of money each time didn't hurt either. He had picked up his phone to call Ryen more times than he could count, but he never dialed a number. What was he supposed to say to her over the phone? He'd be lucky if she even answered. Hell, she had probably changed her number.

After he left his brother's confessional he had taken the fastest car in the garage into town. He was still soaking wet when he arrived at the hotel, but no one gave him a second glance. The rain was still falling. He had been too late. He knew that she'd go back, and he had hoped to catch her. He could sense her pain still lingering in the room. It was only out of respect for what they shared here that he was able to contain his anger at himself and his brother, and not destroy the entire suite. Instead the room phone bore the brunt of his anger. He had called his dad asking for directions to the compound. He had never been there and since it was cloaked he wouldn't be able to find it on his own. He was speechless when his dad refused to tell him. That's when the phone met its end.

Not wanting to be anywhere near his brother, Cash decided to continue staying at the hotel. The hopeful part of him thought maybe Ryen would come back. He headed back there himself now, after leaving the gym. The rain was slowing, but the sewers were still struggling to catch up. The weathermen were dumbfounded. The front that held the rain over Florence had arrived without warning, and hadn't shown any sign of moving. When he entered the lobby the man at the front desk flagged him down, "Signore Di Marco, I have a message for you."

The faintest bit of hope rose in him until he saw it was from his dad: We need to talk. Please come over this afternoon.

The front desk clerk didn't respond when Cash wadded the paper up and threw it in the trashcan by the elevator. Cash knew there were many things he needed to discuss with his family, but he was still pissed at his dad, and he was sure that he wouldn't be able to control himself if Caio was there. Maybe his dad had changed his mind about getting him into the compound, or maybe Ryen had contacted his dad. If either of those things were even a remote possibility he knew that he would not risk being stubborn, but he would shower first.

Cash drove to his family's estate in the same car he borrowed a few days ago. By the time he got out of the car the sun was starting to peek through the clouds. At least the weathermen could relax, but seeing the sun wouldn't cheer up Cash until he saw Ryen standing in its warmth.

Luca opened the door as Cash approached but Cash didn't allow a greeting, "Did you change your mind? Are you going to tell me how to get there?"

A somber sigh escaped Luca as he answered, "You know I can't do that, son. I'm very sorry."

Cash asked the next question that he needed to know, "Is Caio still here?"

"He's locked in one of the rooms down below. Your mother still hasn't decided what she's going to do."

"Seriously? Tell her I'll take care of it," his vehement response caused a flash of fear in his father's eyes.

"Neither your mother nor I would allow that."

Cash cut him off, "Are you kidding me? Didn't he finish his version of events? Can't you see he is still reveling in the pleasure of the whole thing?" Cash knew it was a bad idea to come here. If this is what his dad wanted to discuss, there was no need. He had no qualms about punishing his brother, especially if that punishment was death. If it was even possible, Cash's anger increased at the thought of his mother's lack of conviction on the matter.

Whatever the reason, Cash always felt he was the sole recipient of his mother's high expectations. He felt this was another example of her double standards.

Luca tried to put his hand on Cash's shoulder, but Cash shrugged it off. "Son, I know this isn't as black and white for you as you would make it seem. Neither is it for your mother. She is honor bound, by her role as an Elder. This isn't just any crime; Caio attacked a witch leader. If they wanted, it could start a war. But even beyond that, as a woman, as the mother of a daughter, because of you, and because of Lilia she knows that something must be done. Her struggle is with whether or not she can do it herself, or if she'll turn him over to someone else."

Cash wanted to sympathize with his mother, but he honestly felt he couldn't. Partly due to his guilt over jumping to rash conclusions with Ryen and sending her away, but mostly because he loved Ryen more than was rationally possible, he was confident he could make the decision that his mother was struggling to make, "I stand by my previous offer."

Luca brushed that off, "Son, no one in this house would deny that you have reason, but your part is not up for discussion. That is a responsibility that neither your mother nor I would want you to bear. However, there are other things we need to discuss." Luca directed him towards the dining room, and then went back towards the front door.

While Cash was waiting, one of the house keepers brought a tray of food and a tea set. Cash wondered what was going on. He watched her fret over how many cups she needed. Calla came in a few moments later and sat down, "How are you doing?"

Cash just looked at her.

"I figured. What happened between you and Ryen, before you came back in?"

"I confronted her about cursing Caio and she didn't deny it. Stupid me, I didn't connect the dots until after I'd told her I couldn't stand to be around her. Now I can't get in touch with her, and even if I could, I'm not sure what I could possibly say to make up for how I reacted."

"You've called her?"

"I've come close several times, but what would I say on the phone or in a message? *Sorry, I put family loyalty before my soulmate without hearing a defense? I'm an idiot for not getting it? I don't deserve you?*"

Calla's pity washed over him. He let her put her hand on his forearm. He really wanted to hug her, to have her comfort him. She was the only one so far who didn't have some hand in how he was currently feeling. "All of that would be a good start. She'll forgive you," she said softly, though her voice didn't hold enough confidence to be convincing.

"I'm not so sure."

"She had told you about it already?"

"Yes, but she never mentioned anyone by name. I understand now what I didn't that day; she didn't know he was my brother. I had no idea she was the mystery witch that got a hold of the immortality stripping spell. Did he tell you about the others?"

"About what happened to them? Yes. She's powerful: to accomplish that spell towards not only one vampire, but to four, to make them completely vulnerable, not to mention the other aspects of her curse. I just can't believe this is really happening." Cash could feel her inner turmoil. Where Caio had held open animosity towards Cash he didn't seem to feel that way about Calla. Though they had never been close, he never seemed to be jealous of her the way he did with Cash.

"You and mom didn't look totally shocked when he started to talk. How did you know? Did he say something before I came back?"

"No. Mom and I could sense the source of Ryen's rage; we knew the gist of what was driving her. That's when mom stopped him from running, about the same time you took Ryen outside."

"The bastard was going to run? We should have just let Ryen finish it. She would have been sick with guilt afterwards, but at least we wouldn't have to deal with his aftermath."

"No one would have blamed her." Cash was surprised by Calla's resolve, but then again he knew she had already thought of someone treating Lilia in the same way.

Cash didn't continue the conversation further. He was distracted by someone new at the door. He walked back towards the foyer, but stayed hidden so he could listen without interrupting.

"Lady Luna, welcome again to our home," Cash heard his father's voice. Lady Luna was one of the Triumvirate. He recognized it from Esmeralda's stories. What did Ryen call her? Was this Kora or Chesna? He'd know when he saw her. He knew that Chesna was the older one.

"Yes, thank you for receiving me. Is your son here?"

"Yes, he's in the dining room, waiting for us. How's Lady Reina?"

"As I'm sure you have noticed from the weather, it has been very difficult for her. This has had a deep effect on her, reopening old wounds and the new hurt she's experiencing. Understandable with the complications wouldn't you say?"

A picture flashed in Cash's head. He had heard Ryen describe it, and he had seen her remaining scars, but the picture he now saw in his mind was of her when she had been brought to the hospital all those years ago. This witch in the foyer knew he was listening and she had intentionally sent the image to him. Why did she want to torture him? What did she mean about the weather? He ached at the sight of Ryen in that memory and it fueled his hatred for his brother even more.

He shouldn't have been surprised when "Lady Luna" spoke to him from her place inside the front door, pulling him from his head, "Young man, would you disagree that her pain is justified?"

Cash stepped out to face her. It was clear from the look in her eyes that she was challenging his feelings for Ryen, "I'd say she is more than justified. I know that a big part of it is because of me. I brought her here, I didn't let her explain when I jumped to the wrong conclusions, and then I sent her away. You are right to blame me. I deserve it."

Satisfaction flashed in her eyes before the anger left them, "Very well. I'm Kora by the way. Brother Luca, you may address me as such here at your home as well. Now, shall we go somewhere to sit?"

Luca ushered her past Cash into the dining room where Kora greeted Calla, "Nice to see you again, dear."

Cash wondered when they had met. He had been away from home for years, maybe it was normal for this leader of witches to visit. Cash had no idea what she was here to talk about, but before they changed the subject he had another question he wanted answered, "What did you mean before when you were talking about Ryen and the weather?"

Kora calculatingly eyed him before she answered, "Sometimes when Ryen's emotions get out of control she affects the weather. You haven't noticed?"

"The rain?" he asked quietly, thinking back.

"Yes."

The storm. All of this rain. The rain the day we left Madrid. He guessed he wasn't that surprised. He had tasted her power at different moments when they were together, and everyone sensed how powerful she was a few days ago. *If she could cause a blast like a grenade, why would the laws of nature be a challenge?* He was clinging to his inner sarcasm to avoid thinking about his part in it all.

Kora was speaking to Luca and Calla. Cash had been lost in his own thoughts and now he interrupted with another question, "The rain stopped. What does that mean? She's ok now?"

"That's partially why I'm here. As far as her emotions, time will tell. She's not a danger to anyone," she said looking at Luca and Calla in an assuring way. "She is no longer in Florence. Her plane left this afternoon."

He did not notice the concerned looks his father and sister gave Kora at that announcement. He gave his dad a look that he hoped conveyed the anger he had over not getting to the compound in time, as he cried out in a frantic voice, "Where'd she go?"

"She is attending to some sensitive issues and therefore her location cannot be disclosed."

"Is that a polite way of telling me that you refuse to tell me because this is my fault?"

"Young man, I was barely older than a teenager when Ryen came to us. She has been a daughter to me. Trust me when I say that personally I want nothing more than her happiness. I know what you are to her, and if my meddling would do any good I would help you. But regardless of that, she has business that needs her attention. What she's doing is sensitive. Secrecy is of the utmost importance. However, I will also tell you that she does not want *anyone* to know her whereabouts. I don't even know."

"But you could easily find out, with magic," he meant for his words to be a challenge, but Kora did not take the bait.

Instead she turned to Calla, "That was not how I had intended to inform you of the developments, but I assure you that no one is better to look after our little Terra than Ryen. I realize that it is not what we had originally talked about, visiting and such. I hope that it will not be an extremely long stay, but only time will tell. She will communicate with you frequently," then with a pointed look at Cash, "but she will not tell you where they are."

Cash met her steely glare, but was lost, "Who is Terra?"

Luca answered with a sigh, "A lot has happened in the last few days. This was why I wanted you to come today. Lilia had her dedication to the Goddess a few days before you and Ryen came for dinner. As you know, Ryen was not there and neither of you knew. That's why Calla told you she was at a slumber party. We planned to tell you during dinner. Lady Celeste had suggested that she stay at the compound for a few days. When she had her dedication Lilia chose Terra as her witch name. Ryen was selected as her sponsor, her guide and teacher for the next year."

There was more conversation, but Cash was oblivious to all of that. Just days ago in Barcelona he had thought about Ryen helping Lilia with witchcraft, but this was not how he had planned it. It had only been a handful of months since he had laid eyes on the beautiful woman who would turn out to be his soulmate. Life before that day in Paris was like night and day compared to his life now. Life B.R.- before Ryen, was simple, not many surprises other than what type of girl would be quenching his thirsts that night. Life as a bachelor: clubs, sex, blood. Since then there had been surprise after surprise, complication after complication, moments of pure happiness and moments of anguish and despair. He had discovered emotions he wasn't aware he was capable of experiencing. This was one of those dire moments, but if his niece was with Ryen then she wasn't lost to him forever.

Kora drew him from his thoughts, "Young man, I'd like a word with you in private before I go." She looked at Luca and communicated something silently.

"You may use my wife's office. It's right around the corner." Luca directed Kora down the hall and raised his eyebrows to Cash impatiently. Still not fully roused from his inner dialogue Cash got up from his chair slowly. Kora hadn't been glaring at him for a while, but he was hesitant to be alone with her.

After Cash crossed through the doorway, Luca smiled sheepishly and closed the door. Kora had already taken a seat on a plush wingback chair, and she motioned for Cash to join her in its twin. Once he was seated she addressed him in a hushed and serious tone, "The conversation we are about to have never happened. Once we leave this room I will deny everything that I'm going to say to you."

Acknowledgements

Thank you, not only for choosing this story to read, but for finishing. I appreciate you spending time with these characters that I hold near and dear to my heart. I, too, hate to be left with unanswered questions, but hopefully you will stick around to find out what happens with my beloved characters in the future. Our couple still has quite the journey ahead of them. It was a huge leap of faith to put Ryen and Cash and their relationship on paper. They have existed for so long in the safety of my head. As a reader, the characters in stories become part of my life, and I hope that Ryen and Cash have become a part of yours.

A million thanks to all of my friends and family, especially Tara, Kathleen, Lisa, Allison, Kelsey, Mark, Kristie, and Barb, who not only provided me with helpful feedback and encouragement along the way, but with a cocoon of trust and honesty to share something so personal. An extra thanks to Lindsay who is probably the most familiar with my lack of understanding of commas ☺ and to Tasha, who pushed me out of my comfort zone and really helped me to embrace this new part of who I am- a writer. Thank you for giving me a stage to talk about my writing experience and allowing people to see a different side of me.

A very special thanks to my husband, Mark, and my little man, Augs, for allowing me time on the computer and humoring me when I was lost in thought more often than not. Neither of them knows how much focus writing requires from me, but they are patient and generous.

Thanks to my mom, who took me to K-Mart on Sundays when I was young and allowed me to pick out supernatural books that were beyond my years. Many of the life lessons I learned from her and because of her have transcribed themselves into my characters. I hope she would be proud to see me accomplish something like this.

Thank you to all of the authors who have shared their stories with me over my lifetime so far, and will continue to do so in the future. Whether I like it or not, each one has an impact on me in some way. Unfortunately I will never again care for the name Alexander. I have learned what I like as a reader by reading so many books. I hope that my story can bring the same happiness to my readers as I have gotten from the authors who have touched my soul.

About the Author

Kristine Plum lives in Cedar Rapids, Iowa, with her husband, son, and canine children. Spanish teacher by day; Author/Supermom/Super-Wife/Essential Oil Wellness Advocate by night. Her spare time (yeah right! What's that?) is spent watching reruns (or dvds) of Buffy the Vampire Slayer or other favorites and reading. She enjoys different genres but prefers those with a little darkness. Sharing the stories in her head has become her calling in life.

Connect with Kristine:

    Via Facebook: www.facebook.com/authorkristineplum

    Via twitter: twitter.com/lkl420   @lkl420

    Via website: www.kristineplum-author.com

91176102R00184

Made in the USA
Lexington, KY
19 June 2018